OTHER BOOKS BY MICHAEL A. STACKPOLE

THE WARRIOR TRILOGY
Warrior: En Garde
Warrior: Riposte
Warrior: Coupé

THE BLOOD OF KERENSKY TRILOGY
Lethal Heritage
Blood Legacy
Lost Destiny

Natural Selection
Assumption of Risk
Bred for War
Malicious Intent
Grave Covenant

Once a Hero*
Talion: Revenant*

A Hero Born
An Enemy Reborn

Dementia

THE FIDDLEBACK TRILOGY
A Gathering Evil
Evil Ascending
Evil Triumphant

THE X-WING SERIES
Rogue Squadron*
Wedge's Gamble*
The Krytos Trap*
The Bacta War*
Isard's Revenge*

*Published by Bantam Books

STAR WARS

I, JEDI

Michael A. Stackpole

BANTAM BOOKS
NEW YORK TORONTO LONDON SYDNEY AUCKLAND

STAR WARS®: I, JEDI

A Bantam Spectra Book

PUBLISHING HISTORY

Bantam Spectra hardcover edition published May 1998
Bantam Spectra mass market edition / June 1999

ISBN 0-553-57873-1

Published simultaneously in the United States and Canada

PRINTED IN THE UNITED STATES OF AMERICA

OPM   10 9 8 7 6 5

DEDICATION

This book is dedicated to my parents,
Jim and Janet K. Stackpole.
Without your support, help, and
encouragement, this and all my
other novels would just be something
I'd like to do someday.

ACKNOWLEDGMENTS

The author would like to thank the following people for their help in this project:

Janna Silverstein and Ricia Mainhardt for getting the ball rolling, Tom Dupree for naming and championing this monster and Pat LoBrutto for shepherding it home.

Sue Rostoni, Lucy Autrey Wilson and Allan Kausch for trusting me to play with such a core part of the *Star Wars* universe.

Peet Janes of Dark Horse Comics for his continued championing of Leonia Tavira, which led to her appearance here.

Kevin J. Anderson for having provided the background for half this book and A. C. Crispin and Kristine Kathryn Rusch for working tidbits of story back and forth with me.

Very special thanks to Timothy Zahn who graciously vetted all the pages that featured his characters, offered suggestions that made parts of this novel better, and who worked tirelessly to meld his two new *Star Wars* novels with this book. Working with Tim on this made the project more fun than I could have imagined.

To the Star Ladies for being a receptive audience, Kali Hale for sharp insights, Tish Pahl for quick lightsaber research and to the other Yellow Dogs—I feel your pain.

To Jennifer Roberson who, as always, caught this tale in bits and pieces and especially to Liz Danforth, who made the manic month in which this book was written endurable for me. I can't thank you enough for being there (when you're not in Spain).

STAR WARS

I, JEDI

ONE

✳

None of us liked waiting in ambush, primarily because we couldn't be wholly certain we weren't the ones being set up for a hot-vape. The Invids—the pirate crews working with the ex–Imperial Star Destroyer *Invidious*—had so far eluded the best efforts of the New Republic to engage them. They seemed to know where we would be, when we would get there, and in what force, then planned their raids appropriately. As a result we spent a lot of time doing battle-damage assessments on their efforts, and they really pushed to give us plenty of BDA work.

Rogue Squadron had gone to ground to wait on several of the larger asteroids in the K'vath system. This location put us in close proximity to K'vath 5's primary moon, Alakatha. We powered down our engines and had our sensors in passive mode only to avoid detection by the folks we wanted to trap. According to our mission briefing, New Republic Intelligence had gotten a tip they considered reliable that at least part of Leonia Tavira's pirate fleet would be hitting a luxury liner coming out of the resort coast on Alakatha's northern continent. Mirax and I had actually honeymooned there three years ago, before Thrawn turned the New Republic inside-out, so I had fond memories of the place and could well remember the wealth dripping in jewels and precious metals from the throats and hands of the New Republic's elite.

I glanced at my X-wing's chronometer. "The *Glitterstar* is still on schedule?"

Whistler, nestled behind my cockpit, hooted with just a hint of derision in his voice.

"Yes, I know I told you to let me know if there was a change and, no, I didn't think it had slipped your circuits." I forced my gloved hands open, then rotated my wrists to get rid of some of the tension. "I'm just anxious."

He blatted a quick comment at me.

"Hey, just because patience is a virtue, that doesn't make impatience a vice." I sighed and turned the latter half of it into a piece of a Jedi breathing exercise Luke Skywalker had urged upon me when trying to recruit me as a Jedi. Breathing in through my nose to a count of four, I held the breath for a seven count, then exhaled in eight beats. With each breath I let more tension flow out of me. I sought the clarity of mind I'd need for the coming battle—if the Invids materialized—but it eluded me with the ease the Invids had shown in escaping the New Republic.

Things kept seeming to happen fast. Mirax and I married fast, and while I did not at all regret having done so, events conspired to make our married life extremely difficult. Grand Admiral Thrawn and his antics ruined our first anniversary, and rescuing Jan Dodonna and the others who had once been imprisoned with me on the *Lusankya* had called me away during the second. And then the reborn Emperor's assault on Coruscant dropped a Star Destroyer on what had been our home. Neither of us were there at the time, which was standard operating procedure far too often.

In fact, the only benefit of being assigned to go after the Invids was that their leader, ex-Moff Leonia Tavira, seemed to have a taste for a life of leisure. When her *Invidious* vanished between raids, we usually had a week of down time before having to worry about another attack. Mirax and I put this free time to good use, rebuilding our home and our relationship, but with that came some consequences that I saw as incredibly disruptive—on the scale of *Thrawn* disruptive.

Mirax decided she wanted children.

I have nothing against kids—as long as they go home with their parents at the end of the day. Expressing this opinion in those terms to Mirax was not the smartest thing I had ever done and, in fact, proved to be one of the more painful ones. The hurt and pain in her eyes haunted me for a long time. Deep down, I knew there would be no dissuading her, and I wasn't even sure, in the end, I wanted to.

I did try, however, and employed most of the standard arguments to do so. The "this is an unsettled time in the galaxy" ploy lost out to the fact that our parents had faced a similar choice and we'd turned out pretty well. The "uncertainty of my job" argument wilted beneath the logic of my life insurance and then withered away when Mirax gave me a glimpse at the accounts files—the *real* ones—for her import/export business. She pointed out that she could easily support the three or four of us and I'd not have to work a single second, outside of caring for the children. And, she noted, that carrying a child for nine full months meant she would already have 3.11 years of forty-hour weeks of child-care logged and that I would owe her.

Over and above all that, she said I'd make a great father. She noted that my father had done a great job with me. Having learned from him the skills of being a father, she just knew I'd be wonderful with kids. In using that argument, she turned the love and respect I had for my father around on me. She made it seem as if I was dishonoring his memory by not bringing children into the world. It was a most persuasive argument, as she knew it would be, and hammered me pretty hard.

In retrospect, I should have given up at the start and saved the two of us a great deal of grief. She makes her living—a *very good* living, it turns out—convincing all sorts of folks that junk no one else wants is absolutely vital to them. While she engaged me in logical discussions—focusing my defenses on that avenue of attack—she slipped past my guard on a purely emotional level. Little comments about what kind of child our genetic lottery would produce got me investing brainsweat in solving that puzzle. That went straight to the detective training in me—the training that wouldn't let me drop a case until I had an answer.

Which, in this case, meant a child.

She also managed to flick on the HoloNet monitors when some event featuring news about Leia Organa Solo's three-year-old twins was being shown. The children were frighteningly cute and their very existence had been blamed for a baby-binge in the New Republic. I knew Mirax was not so shallow as to be wanting a child out of envy or to be trendy, but she did note that she was Leia's age, and that it was a good time to have a child or two.

And that cuteness factor really can get under your skin. The New Republic media avoided showing the twins drooling and dripping the way children do, and they really maximized the appealing things about the toddlers. It got so that when I did remember dreams, they were of me cradling a sleeping child in my arms. Oddly enough, I stopped thinking of those dreams as nightmares pretty quickly and did my best to preserve them in my mind.

Realizing I was lost, I began to bargain for time. Mirax flat refused to accept fixed time dates, mainly because I was thinking in *years*, so I made things conditional. I told her once the Invids were taken care of, we'd make a final decision. She accepted my decision a bit better than I expected, which started preying on me, and making me feel guilty. I would have thought that was a tactic she'd decided to use, but she thought guilt was a hammer and she's definitely a vibroblade fan.

I exhaled slowly again. "Whistler, remind me when we get home, Mirax and I need to make a decision on this baby thing, now, not later. Tavira's not going to dictate my life."

Whistler's happy high staccato sailed down into a low warning tone.

I glanced at my primary monitor. The *Glitterstar* had lifted from Alakatha and another ship had appeared in-system. Whistler identified it as a modified bulk cruiser known as the *Booty Full*. Unlike the liner's sleek design, the cruiser was studded with warty protrusions that quickly detached themselves and began to run in on the liner.

I keyed my comm. "Rogue Lead, three flight has contact. One cruiser and eighteen uglies heading in on the *Glitterstar*."

Tycho's voice came back cool and calm. "I copy, Nine. Engage the fighters with two flight. One has the cruiser."

I flicked over to three flight's tactical channel. "Light them up, Rogues, we have the fighters."

I started the engines, then shunted power to the repulsorlift coils. The X-wing rose like a ghost from a grave and came about to point its nose toward the liner. As Ooryl's X-wing pulled up on my left and my other two pilots, Vurrulf and Ghufran, arrived on the right, I punched the throttle full forward and launched myself into the fight.

A smile blossomed on my face. Any sapient creature making a claim to sanity would find hurtling along in a fragile craft of metal and ferro-ceramics to be stupid or suicidal. Pushing that same craft into battle merely compounded the situation, and I knew it. By the same token, very few experiences in life can compare to flying in combat—or engaging any enemy in a fight—because doing that is the one point where civilization demands us to harness our animal nature and employ it against a most dangerous prey. Without being physically and mentally and even mechanically at my best, I would die and my friends might even die with me.

But I had no intention of letting that happen.

With a flick of my thumb I switched from lasers over to proton torpedoes and allowed for single fire. I selected an initial target and eased the crosshairs on my heads-up display onto its outline. Whistler beeped steadily as he worked for a target lock, then the box surrounding the fighter went red and his tone became a constant.

I hit the trigger and launched my first proton torpedo. It streaked away hot and pinkish-white, trailed by others lancing out from my flight. While employing proton torpedoes against fighters is seen as overkill by some pilots, within Rogue Squadron using such a tactic was always seen as an expedient way of lowering the odds against us—odds that were usually longer than a Hutt and decidedly more ugly.

The Invids used a form of custom-designed fighter called a Tri-fighter. It started with the ball cockpit and ion engine assembly of Seinar System's basic TIE fighter—a commodity which, after hydrogen and stupidity, was the most plentiful in the galaxy—and married it to a trio of angular blades set 120 degrees apart. The bottom two served as landing gear, while the third came up over the top of the cockpit. The fighter still had the TIE's twin lasers mounted beneath the cockpit, while the third tine sprouted an ion cannon. The ships also had some basic shields, which explained why they were more successful than your basic eyeball, and side viewports cut into the hull gave the pilot more visibility. Because the trio of tines looked as if they were grasping at the cockpit, we'd nicknamed the design "clutch."

The shields and extra visibility didn't help the clutch I'd targeted. The proton torpedo jammed itself right up the left engine's exhaust port and actually punched out through the cockpit before detonating. The fighter flew into the roiling, golden ball of fire and just vanished. Three more clutches exploded nearby, then another three exploded off to starboard, where two flight was coming in.

"Pick targets carefully, three flight. Ooryl, we're on the pair to port."

"Ten copies, Nine."

I kicked my X-wing up on the port stabilizer foils and hauled back on the stick. Chopping power to the engine, I tightened the circle, then rolled out to the right as the pirates started a long serpentine turn. I switched over from missiles to dual lasers and immediately got a yellow box around the lead fighter. I goosed the throttle back to full to close range and keyed my comm. "I'm on the leader."

Ooryl gave me a double-click on his comm to let me know he'd gotten the message. Nudging the stick just a bit right, the targeting box went green and I hit the firing button. Two red bolts hit the target. The first fried the shields. The clutch trailed sparks from the shield generator like a comet trailing ice. The second bolt pierced the cockpit and though it hit kind of high, it hit hard, too. Sparks shot from the hole and the clutch began a slow spiral down toward Alakatha.

Ooryl rolled to port as the other clutch broke. I brought my X-wing around in behind him as he lined his shot up. The Gand's first two shots blasted past the shields and burned furrows in the ship's hull. The next two drilled the engines, jetting the disintegrating ship forward on a golden gout of flame. The flame abruptly died, leaving the Tri-fighter to tumble through space out toward the asteroid belt.

Up through the cockpit canopy I could see the green and white streaky ball of Alakatha and the *Glitterstar* rising up from it. Off to starboard the *Booty Full* seemed to crouch in the void like a malignant insect. The turbolasers along its spine and in a belly turret fired out, trying to track one flight's X-wings, but the shots were no real danger to the fighters. Colonel Celchu, Hobbie, Janson and Gavin Darklighter were old hands at pulling the teeth of raiders like these. As long as we kept the clutches busy, the *Booty Full* had no chance.

The X-wing's first slashing attack came from Tycho and Hobbie. They rolled through and each drove a proton torpedo into the aft shields. Coming from the other direction, Gavin and Wes Janson strafed the ship with laser fire. Gavin's second burst melted the belly turret clean away while Janson's shots nibbled away at the ship's aft vector jets. The *Booty Full* was done, though I had no doubts it would take a couple more passes before the crew realized that and surrendered.

I followed Ooryl up and around the back toward the fight. It had fairly well degenerated into a chase-and-kill run. The loss of seven ships before they even saw their enemies had clearly shocked the pirates and, more importantly, brought their numbers down close to ours. While clutches were more agile than X-wings—not by much, but by enough to make fighting them difficult—they couldn't outrun us or outgun us. Lacking the discipline of a trained military unit like Rogue Squadron, when panic set in, they fell apart and made our job that much easier.

Ooryl settled in on one and hit it with a full quad burst from his lasers. The clutch exploded, but boiling in through the explosion came another clutch making a head-to-head pass at Ooryl. The clutch got off a shot with the ion cannon that sent a lightning storm skittering over Ooryl's shields, but they died before the ion blast did. The motivator blew on his R5 unit and Whistler reported his engines were out.

"Ooryl, go for a restart." I didn't know if he still had comm or not, but I offered that bit of advice and fired a dual burst at the clutch. Hastily aimed, the shot missed low, but did cause the clutch to veer off. Rolling out to the right, I headed in after him. "This is Nine on one. Someone watch my back."

Vurrulf, the Klatooinan in three flight, barked a harsh, "I copy, on it," so I felt a bit safer in pursuing the clutch. One of the worst things a pilot can do is to get so locked in on a target that he misses what else is happening. When situational awareness focuses down on one target, the hunter becomes hunted and never knows what hits him. It's a rookie mistake and while I'm no rookie, I'm not immune to it.

The clutch's pilot was good and clearly had no desire to die, but Whistler wasn't reporting that he'd powered down his weapons, so he was just as clearly willing to fight. I tried to settle in on him, but he modulated his throttle and used his ship's agility to keep breaking before I could get a lock. I snapped a couple of shots off at him, but they missed wide or high. Try as I might, I was having trouble keeping up with his shifts and cuts.

I pulled back on the throttle and let him gain some distance. His juking antics continued, but with range the movements that had ripped him out of my sights in close barely broke the edges of my targeting box. I hit the firing button and sent two paired bursts at him. One pair lanced through the aft shield and mangled one of the landing tines. The other two energy darts clipped the thrust vector vents on the port side, limiting his maneuverability.

Whistler displayed a comm frequency being used by the clutch and I punched it up on my comm unit. "This is Captain Corran Horn of the New Republic Armed Forces. I will accept your surrender."

A woman answered me. "Don't you know, Invids never surrender?"

"Not true of the *Booty Full.*"

"Riizolo is a fool, but he doesn't have a capital warrant out on his head. I do." She laughed. "I have nothing to live for, except my honor. One pass, Horn, you and me."

"You'll die." A single pass would negate the clutch's agility advantage. She had to know that.

"But perhaps not alone." Her ship stopped jinking

and headed out on a long loop. "Allow me this honor." The clutch turned and began its run at me.

I wanted to do as she asked, and would have, except for one thing: the Invids had proved over and over again that they had no honor.

I switched to proton torpedoes, got a quick tone-lock from Whistler and pulled the trigger. The missile shot from my X-wing and sprinted straight for her ship. As good as she was, the clutch pilot knew there was no dodging it. She fired with both lasers, but they missed. Then, at the last moment, she shot an ion blast that hit the missile. Blue lightning played over it, burning out every circuit that allowed the torpedo to track and close on her ship.

I'm fairly certain, just for a second, she thought she had won.

The problem with a projectile is that even if its sophisticated circuitry fails, it still has a lot of kinetic energy built up. Even if it never senses the proximity of its target and detonates, that much mass moving that fast treats a clutch cockpit much the way a needle treats a bubble. The torpedo drove the ion engines out the back of the clutch, where they exploded. The fighter's hollow remains slowly spun off through space and would eventually burn through the atmosphere and give resort guests a thrill.

Whistler made my threat screen all green indicating no more active hostiles in the area. Three flight reported in and Ooryl was back up and running. His forward shield had collapsed and refused to come back up, but otherwise he was fine. Vurrulf and Ghufran reported no trouble with their X-wings. As it turned out only Reme Pollar in two flight had been hit hard enough to be forced extra-vehicular, but she reported she would be fine until the Skipray blast boat from the *Glitterstar* picked her up.

I switched the comm over to the command channel. "All green here, Rogue Leader."

"I copy, Nine. Looks like this wasn't the trap we feared it would be."

"No, sir, it doesn't."

"Have your people prepare to rejoin the fleet."

"As ordered, Colonel."

I relayed the order to my people, but before we could reach my designated rendezvous point, the fleet made a microjump in from the edge of the system. A Mon Calamari Cruiser and two *Victory*-class Star Destroyers formed a triangle in the space above Alakatha. We'd come to the system aboard *Home One* and used microjumps to get in as close as we did. Because the information about the *Booty Full* had been unusual, we expected it might be an ambush, so the fleet had waited to see if the Invids would pounce on the Rogues.

If they had, we would have gotten a chance to finish them once and for all.

I keyed my comm. "Colonel, if we were expecting the pirates to jump us, and they did not, was this mission a success?"

"Good question, Nine. This is one of those missions where only Intelligence will be able to tell us how we did." Tycho hesitated for a moment. "Then again, we lost only machines, not people. It's a victory anytime that happens."

Two

✳

The K'vath system was far enough from Coruscant to be trendy and desirable for seclusion—though the price of a mug of lum there would have been enough to discourage most folks from enjoying their holiday. Mirax and I never would have gone there three years ago, but Wedge Antilles had recommended it, and someone in management had been convinced that our participation in the liberation of Coruscant made Mirax and me just the sort of *glam* couple to attract the notice of the New Republic's fashionable elite. As a result we didn't pay for anything while we were there, and stopping the *Booty Full* over Alakatha helped me feel a bit better about having enjoyed the world's hospitality.

The *Glimmerstar* requested an escort all the way to Coruscant, which *Home One* agreed to supply. This meant our return trip would be at the leisurely pace dictated by the liner instead of the faster speed of which the Mon Calamari Cruiser was capable. The Rogues could have taken our X-wings home, but the trip would have locked us in the cockpit for a full twenty-four hours, which I looked forward to with the same enthusiasm I had for discussing old times with Mirax's father. It would have been nice if the *Glimmerstar* had allowed us to spend the extra day of travel time on the liner, but their gratitude extended only as far as letting us study the ship's beautiful lines from afar.

We had duties enough to keep us busy anyway, and despite the oppressive humidity, the Mon Cal Cruiser's accommodations were not that bad. After landing my X-wing and getting Whistler set up for recharging, I caught a quick meal in the galley, then joined the rest of the squadron in a briefing room for our debriefing. We all rode Reme for going EV, but we were glad to have her back and enjoyed her descriptions of the *Glimmer-star*'s blast boat. After that I grabbed some rack time, slept for eight hours, worked out a bit and headed for the galley for some breakfast.

Ooryl raised a three-fingered hand and waved me over to the table he occupied all by himself. I smiled and nodded to him, then grabbed some breakfast cakes and an artificial nerfmilk protein beverage. I almost balked at it, because consuming anything that doesn't sit well on the stomach can be a mistake when eating with a Gand, but I was very thirsty.

I dropped into the chair opposite Ooryl and did my best not to glance down into the bowl from which he was feeding. "Anything interesting happen while I've been down?"

Ooryl's mouth parts moved apart in his approximation of a smile and his compound eyes glittered brightly. His grey-green flesh was of a hue slightly darker than the sauce on the tentacles he was fishing out of the bowl, and contrasted sharply with the bright orange of his flight suit. Knobby bits of his exoskeleton poked at odd angles from within the fabric, as if his flesh were having an allergic reaction to the color.

"Nothing Ooryl considers out of the ordinary."

I frowned. The Gands had a tradition of speaking of themselves in the third person and not using the pronoun "I" because they thought it was the height of arrogance to do so. Only those Gands who had committed acts so great that all Gands would know of them were allowed to speak of themselves as "I." The whole of Rogue Squadron had even gone to Gand and been part of Ooryl's *janwuine-jika*, the ceremony that conferred that right upon him. For him to have reverted to third person meant something was bothering him.

"What is the matter?" I narrowed my green eyes and stared into his black faceted orbs. "You can't be embarrassed about getting shot by that Invid."

Ooryl slowly and deliberately shook his head. "Ooryl is ashamed that he has not been able to help you with your problem."

"*My* problem?"

"You have been distracted, Corran." Ooryl perched his hands on the tabletop like two armored spiders. "You and Mirax desire offspring. If Ooryl was on Gand, Ooryl could help solve this problem."

I stuffed a crumb from one of the cakes into my mouth, chewed quickly and swallowed. "Back up here. How do you know about the child thing?"

The Gand remained rock-still for a moment, then lowered his head. "Qrygg was told by Mirax that you and she would have children, therefore Qrygg had to do Qrygg's best to make certain you were not killed in combat."

I gave him a hard stare. "Mirax talked to you about our discussion on children?"

"Mirax wished to know if you had spoken with Qrygg about the discussion. When Qrygg said you had not, she asked Qrygg to encourage the discussion if you did." Ooryl's head came back up. "You should not have been ashamed to speak to Ooryl of it. Ooryl would have been worthy of your trust."

I gave Ooryl the biggest smile I could muster. I over-exaggerated it because he wasn't so good at reading subtlety. "Ooryl, if I was talking to anybody about our wanting kids, it would have been you. I trust you with my life every day and have never had any cause to regret it." I saw his mouth parts open, aping my smile and I realized right then and there I'd been fairly stupid in keeping the whole discussion to myself. "And I really should have spoken with you about it. Your advice has always been welcomed and wise. I just *didn't think*, which is a bad habit I had hoped to abandon."

"If Ooryl was truly wise, Ooryl would have advised you to abandon it."

"You have, in very many ways." I sighed slowly. "And, as Mirax told you, we have been talking about having kids. She went to you to learn what I was thinking. I'm sure any help you offered her was appreciated."

"Ooryl would like to think so. You will recall that during Ooryl's *janwuine-jika*, Ooryl was also initiated into the ways of being a *Findsman*. On Gand, the Findsman performs many useful tasks. He locates lost slaves, reads the mists for omens and hunts criminals. There is one more duty he performs for people like you and Mirax. He can wander into the mists and find the child they desire. These mistborn children are a gift and raised by the people as their own. I would be honored to do this for you, my friend."

I smiled. "Thanks, but I think I can handle the child production part on my own."

Ooryl's mandibles sprang open. "Then you *are* capable. . . ."

"Yes, very much so." I raised my chin. "*Very* much so. No problems here."

A membrane nictitated up over Ooryl's eyes for a moment. "Then why would you not have a child already?"

"Huh?"

"This is the purpose of life, is it not? To create life is the greatest act a living creature can commit."

The solemnity and truth in his words hit me hard. "That's true, but . . ."

"Is this a time Ooryl should remind you that you are trying to abandon being thoughtless?"

I snapped my jaw shut and narrowed my eyes. "If having kids is so important, why don't you have any?"

Ooryl shrugged. It wasn't a motion natural to him and his exoskeleton clicked in protest. "I am *janwuine*. It is not for me to choose a wife, but for Gand to choose one for me. At that time I shall proudly commit genetic fusion."

"The idea loses something in translation there." I drank a bit of the milk and used another piece of cake to get rid of the thick chalky taste. "The fact is I mean to settle this thing with Mirax once we get back to Coruscant."

"Good. With the stories you have told of your father, any child you will have will be well cared for."

I arched an eyebrow at him. "And how do you know I'll agree to have children?"

"I have spoken with Mirax. That is enough."

I sat back and laughed lightly. "I never really had a chance, did I?"

"No, Corran, but that really means you will have every chance." Ooryl slurped in a tentacle, then wiped verdant gravy from his cheek. "We have all helped create and strengthen the New Republic. Creating the generation to which it will be passed is one more duty we owe posterity.''

Ooryl's words stuck with me through the rest of the trip and worked on me like a virus. By the time I loaded myself into my X-wing and began to descend to our hangar facility, I was looking forward to heading home with Mirax and start working on a child then and there. And while that sort of an enthusiastic greeting when either one of us returned from journeys was not at all uncommon, this time it would be more than a wordless way of saying ''I missed you.''

It would mean parts of us would never be separated again.

That thought struck me as so right and good, even flying over the debris fields littering Coruscant could only *slightly* tarnish my mood. Vast swathes of destruction had been carved across the urban landscape. Ships never meant for entry into atmosphere had crashed down, glowing white from the heat, trailing thick clouds of black smoke, to slam into the cityscape. They gouged great furrows through neighborhoods and blasted huge craters out of the buildings. Hundreds of millions, perhaps even billions of people had died in the factional fighting that followed Thrawn's assault on the New Republic; and we were nowhere near recovered from it.

Looking at the shattered buildings and twisted wreckage, I found it difficult to conjure up my memories of Coruscant from before, back when it was still Imperial Center. I could remember vast rivers of light making the nightside glow with life, but here only dull grey predominated. Bright lights had once given Coruscant an artificial life and without them the urban planet seemed dead.

I knew it wasn't really that bad. Despite the vast surface destruction and tremendous loss of life, people did continue living. The catastrophic damage *did* bring out the worst in some people, but it brought out the *best* in even more. Mirax and I had planned to live in her *Pulsar Skate* when our home had been destroyed by one of the crashing ships, but friends wouldn't let us. Iella Wessiri, my old partner from the Corellian Security Force, managed to convince her boss at New Republic Intelligence that we should be given the run of a safehouse they maintained, so we ended up with a place even closer to Rogue Squadron Headquarters than before.

Ours was hardly the most remarkable of tales. Supplies that had been hoarded for years during times of political instability suddenly poured forth. People took refugees into their homes, which seems hardly unexpected, but a lot of the hosts were old Imperial families and the refugees were from the various non-human species in the galaxy. The battering Coruscant had taken at the hands of Imperial warlords had broken down the last walls of resistance. Suffering formed a common bond that began to erode xenophobia on both sides.

With the rest of the squadron I made my approach and landed in our hangar bay. I turned the X-wing over to a tech, changed into civilian clothes and caught a hoverbus south to the Manarai mountains. A mother and child in a seat up the way from me caught my eye. I watched the woman smile as the infant reached out unsteadily and grasped at her nose. She tilted her face up slightly, kissing the hand, then lowered her face until she was nose to nose with her baby. She whispered something and rubbed her nose against the child's, then pulled back accompanied by the baby's laughter.

The infant's delighted laugh still echoed in my ears as the bus broke from the darkened canyons and started flying across a ruined landscape of duracrete chunks strewn like a dewback's scales on a stable floor. The burned-out hulks of airspeeders lay twisted and half-melted all over the place. Scraps of cloth that had once clothed victims flapped and fluttered from various points in the stone piles. Bright bits of color, that could have been anything from toys to the shards of a holodisk player, littered the landscape.

Despite the utter destruction, the child's laugh overwhelmed it all. The laugh was innocent and light, it mocked the ruin surrounding us. People could create and destroy, but, the laugh seemed to suggest, anyone who thought destruction was more powerful than creation was a fool. Within the first ten years of that child's life, the scars from the battling on Coruscant would be erased. And even if they were not, that child could, in twenty or thirty years, be the person who saw to their erasure. Life truly was the antidote to destruction.

I smiled. *Mirax has been right all along, and Ooryl, too. If we live for the present and in the present, we short-change the future. Living for the future is necessary if we are to have any sort of future at all. Yes, Mirax, we'll have a child. Make that children. We'll make our contribution to the future.*

I winked at the woman with the child as I got off at my stop. I threaded my way through the buildings and over the catwalks that led to my home. I almost stopped at a store to buy a decent wine to celebrate the resolution of our problem, but decided instead to whisk Mirax off somewhere for a quiet, romantic meal. I didn't know where we'd go exactly, but with the construction droids roaming over the planet, I knew there were dozens of restaurants that had been created in the week I'd been gone. Finding a place to eat wouldn't be much of a problem.

I hit the door and punched the code into the lockplate. The door slid open and a wave of warm air cascaded down over me. I stepped into the apartment's darkened interior, letting the door close behind me. The warm air surrounded me like a thick blanket and for a moment I almost gave in to panic because it seemed suffocating and dense.

My high spirits began to die down. The air had become warm because Mirax had shut off the apartment's environmental comfort unit. We both did that when we were going to be gone for an extended period of time. It was possible she was only going to be gone during the day, but a quick glance at the food prep station told me that wasn't the case. All the dishes had been washed and put away; and the small basket of fruit she kept around wasn't in sight. That meant she'd tossed it in the conservator so it wouldn't spoil while she was gone.

I continued my way on into the apartment. I ducked my head into the darkened bedroom on the left, but saw no signs of life there. The dining area, which abutted the food prep station on the right, was likewise devoid of life. The main table had a couple days' worth of dust on it and the datacard that had been set near my place likely held all the messages that had come in for me up to the time Mirax left.

In the living room area off to the left I saw a light blinking on the holotable. I smiled. *Good girl, you didn't leave without giving me a message.* I shucked my jacket and tossed it on a nerf-hide chair, then crouched down and hit the button below the light.

Standing forty-five centimeters tall and as beautiful as ever, Mirax smiled at me. Even in miniature, her black hair shined lustrously and fire filled her brown eyes. She wore the black boots and dark blue jumpsuit in which I'd first seen her, and had a blue nerf-hide jacket slung over her shoulder. A small canvas satchel rested at her feet.

"Corran, I'd hoped to be here when you got back, but I've got a run I can't turn down. I'll tell you all about it when I get back. You should only be lonely for about a day. If my plans change, I'll let you know." She bent to pick up her satchel, then smiled at me again as she straightened up. "I love you. Don't forget it and don't doubt it. Ever. I'll be back soon, love."

Her image dissolved into static, then the holopad shut itself off. I reached out to run the message again, but hesitated. I'd come home to dozens of such messages during our time together, as had she, and never before had I wanted to play one again. *Why do I want to now?*

It struck me that I might be feeling a bit cheated and a bit vulnerable. I'd spent the better part of my time away from her thinking about children and had finally come around to her point of view, and she was gone! I'd made one of the most important and momentous decisions of my life and she was just off flitting about the galaxy as if my decision was no big thing. To have it treated so casually stung a bit and I wanted to hear her say again that she loved me.

As much as I knew my analysis of my emotions was true, I also knew my emotions were not at the core of my problem. I hit the button and listened to her message again, then nodded. She said I'd be lonely for only a day or so, and that if she had a change of plans, she would let me know. The fact was, however, that *I* had been a full day late because of our escorting the *Glitterstar* here to Coruscant, so she should have been here. I'd had no message from her about a delay here or at Squadron HQ, and that surprised me.

Others might have taken the phrase "about a day" and have seen it as a fairly loose measure of time, but to Mirax it was painfully exact. She made her living delivering items of value to various clients, on time and intact. If she had meant twelve standard hours, she'd have said so. If she'd meant twenty-five hours, she'd not have rounded them down to a day, she would have given me her best estimate, to the hour or minute.

As damning and worrisome as that might seem, I knew better than to panic. Any message could have been delayed or misrouted. She could have even stopped off to see her father on the *Errant Venture* and his communication system could be down again.

A shiver ran down my spine, but I shrugged it off. "Your good news will just have to wait, I guess." Still feeling a little achy and tired from the run home, I stripped my clothes off, hit the refresher station, cleaned myself up, then dropped into bed. I left the bedroom door open in the hopes that I'd awaken when Mirax returned.

Scant chance of that. I dropped into a deep sleep, dark and black, like the deepest shadows on Coruscant. I realized I was drifting off and tried to seek out the dream about the child, hoping my decision would paint more details onto him, but it eluded me. Consciousness evaporated in a pool of nothingness and I fell into a dreamless sleep.

Corran.

I stirred at the sound of my name but couldn't recognize the voice.

CORRAN!

Mirax's shriek ripped me to wakefulness. I sat bolt upright in bed and reached out for her. The image of her face faded from before my eyes as my hands encountered only cold sheets where she should have been. I felt about for her, seeking the warmth that her body should have deposited there, but I found none of it. For all of a heartbeat my brain chastened me with a flash of Mirax's message, then something more horrible slammed into me. Bile surged up into my throat, choking me.

In one blindingly terrible moment, I knew Mirax was gone!

THREE

✴

I stumbled out of bed on the far side and barked my shin on a low table set there. I kicked out angrily at it. *Who would have put that there?* I knew I wouldn't have put it there because even a gentle bump would have toppled it and scattered the datacards stacked there as easily as my kick had.

I looked around the room and in the half-light I saw all manner of things that were wrong about the place. The holographs on the walls were pleasant enough, and were even of scenes from Corellia, but were of locations I'd not known on my homeworld. *Who built this parody of my home?*

My feet caught in the sheets I'd tossed off and I crashed to my hands and knees. The pain in my shin found an ally in my knees and hands, and just for a moment shocked me into a clarity of mind. The holographs and the table and the datacards, all these little pieces of the apartment that were not mine, they were things Mirax had placed here. *Mirax, my wife.*

I looked up at everything she'd brought in to make our apartment feel like a home. Somehow she had found replacements for many of the things we had lost when our previous home had been destroyed. Intellectually, as

I looked around the room, I could catalog her contributions to the decor, and could even remember the when and where of her finding the items. I looked at the closet and could see her clothes hanging there. I found it easy to recall when she had purchased this gown, or where she had gotten that jacket.

But I could not recall anything about her connections to those items. In looking at the clothes I couldn't remember which gown was her favorite. I couldn't remember which jacket she considered slimming, or which blouse and slacks she considered appropriate for business, and which outfit she wore when we were out to have fun.

I studied a holograph of Vreni Island on Corellia. It showed a small island covered with trees, floating in a stormy sea as a thunderstorm approached. Shifting my view slightly I injected lightning into the picture, a massive triple fork that sent countless tendrils crawling across the waves. The image was fantastic and the holograph was a work of art, but I could not recall why Mirax had wanted it. I didn't know if she had known the holographer or if she had spent time on the island, or if she had purchased it as an investment.

Mirax is gone, and I am losing details of her life.

I got up and ran to the living room. The red light still blinked on the holopad. I punched it with the urgency of a pilot ejecting from a stricken fighter. Her image appeared once again and I smiled, but as she spoke, my smile died. The countless nuances I'd read into how she looked at me, and what she said, how she inflected her voice and shifted her balance, were gone. I could have been looking at some commercial broadcast of a beautiful woman selling anything from lum to a trip to the Alakatha resorts.

I hit another button and switched the holopad over into communications mode. I keyed in a call to Squadron Headquarters. The head and shoulders of a black droid materialized, all but lost in the darkness except for the glow of golden eyes in his clamshell head. "You have reached Rogue Squadron Headquarters. This is Emtrey. It is good to see you, Captain Horn."

"You, too, Emtrey." I raked fingers back through my short brown hair. "I'm going to ask you a question and I want a straight answer—and the question is going to sound strange."

"I understand the parameters of your request."

"Good." I hesitated for a moment. "It is approximately 1:30 in the morning, Coordinated Galactic Time, right?"

"1:31:27, to be exact, sir."

I nodded. Normally I found Emtrey's slavish adherence to reality annoying, but right now it was a lifeline to sanity. "And I'm Corran Horn, right?"

The droid's head jerked back. "Yes, sir. A moment please. . . . Your voiceprint checks to within 99.4953 percent of accuracy, the variation being accounted for by travel stress and degree of rest."

"Okay, good, Emtrey, very good." I licked my lips. "Here's the big one."

The droid's image leaned forward toward me. "I am ready, sir."

"I'm married to Mirax Terrik, right?"

Emtrey's eyes flared. "Oh, yes, sir. You will recall that I attended the ceremony Commander Antilles conducted on the *Lusankya,* and again attended the ceremony you had here on Coruscant. I believe Whistler made a holographic record of the first ceremony, and I know there were multiple holographs of the second one.''

My jaw dropped. I *knew* there were holographs of the ceremonies, but I had forgotten them. Our original copies had been destroyed when our home had been leveled, but Mirax had obtained new copies from her father. I wanted to turn to the cabinet where we stored them and play one immediately, but I hesitated. I couldn't risk finding them as emotionally empty as I had the replay of Mirax's message.

''Are you all right, Captain Horn?''

I frowned, then nodded slowly. ''I don't know, Emtrey. Is the colonel available?''

Emtrey's eyes flickered for a moment. ''The colonel is in his office. He has a meeting scheduled thirty standard minutes from now.''

''Ask him to cancel it or postpone it, please. I have to talk to him.'' I stared intently at Emtrey as if I could reach into his robotic brain and communicate my urgency. ''Mirax is gone, I mean really *gone*, and I have to find her. I'll be there in a half hour. Horn out.''

I arrived at headquarters a little later than expected because of gross indecision on my part concerning clothes. I went to toss almost anything on, but I saw too many shirts and pants and jackets that Mirax had bought for me and, rather often, transported from all over the galaxy. Try as I might, I couldn't remember what she had said about any of them. I couldn't remember her smiles or laughter as she dressed me up, or what she'd said as she later worked me back out of the clothes. Each shirt hung there like a ghost of a memory, all two dimensional and lifeless.

I'd finally shrugged something on—a hideous matching of patterns and colors, as it turned out, but I *had* dressed in the dark. I had a haunted look on my face so people on the hoverbus shied away from me. I would have taken our airspeeder and doubtlessly salvaged some of the time I'd lost dressing, but even as messed up as I was, I knew I had no place piloting anything through Imperial City even if the traffic was light.

Emtrey made no attempt to stop me in the antechamber to Tycho's office. I shot in past him, then snapped to attention and gave Tycho as crisp a salute as I could manage. "Thank you for seeing me, sir."

Standing at his desk, with a big transparisteel viewport framing a view of the Imperial Palace behind him, Tycho looked every bit the recruiting hologram image of a pilot. Steel-spined straight, wasp-waisted, with his light brown hair cut short and just beginning to show some white at the temples, he returned my salute sharply. Sympathy softened his blue eyes. "Emtrey told me about your problem, though he didn't give me much detail."

"I didn't have much to give him. I'm sorry."

Tycho shook his head and pointed me to a chair in front of his desk. "Not your fault, I think." He glanced back at the doorway. "That's why I asked General Cracken to join us."

I turned back and saw Airen Cracken enter the office. Though an older man, he had not thickened around the middle with age. White predominated in his hair, but tinges of the red hair he'd passed on to his son Pash still lingered around the sides and back. His eyes were green, like mine, but more of a sea-green, which did not make them lack for intensity. He waited for both of us to salute, which we did, and he returned it sharply.

Tycho waited for General Cracken to take the other chair and sit before he sat himself. "General Cracken was my appointment anyway, and one I could not postpone."

"No, sir," I said, as I sat. I had first met General Cracken on Coruscant, when I showed up at Tycho's treason and murder trial. My arrival seemed to surprise the general, but that was the first and last time I'd seen him taken unawares by anything. He'd asked me to help him negotiate with Booster Terrik for possession of an Imperial Star Destroyer, and I had failed in that mission rather dismally. The infrequent times we had met since then had been more satisfactory, but his presence here did nothing to put me at ease.

Cracken smiled carefully. "I wanted to discuss with Colonel Celchu the intelligence we obtained from Phan Riizolo, the *Booty Full*'s captain. From him, really, we learned very little that will help us deal with the *Invidious* and solving the mystery of its location."

I frowned. "I'd really rather talk about my wife. . . ."

"I know, but this is germane, believe me, Captain Horn."

He leaned forward and plugged a cable from the datapad he carried into the holoprojector pad on the corner of Tycho's desk. An image of an Imperial Star Destroyer hovered there as if in orbit around the crystalline model of Alderaan centered on the near edge of the desk. "This is the *Invidious*, represented in old Imperial holo-images because we have no current ones of any reliable quality. At the time of the Emperor's death, it was part of a task force commanded by High Admiral Teradoc and served as part of the fleet with which he secured his holdings as the Empire crumbled. That was a good seven years ago. Then, approximately six years ago, Leonia Tavira appears to have obtained it.''

Cracken hit a key on his datapad and the image shifted to that of a very young woman in an Imperial Naval uniform, with the rank insignia of an admiral. I'd seen enough of those rank badges on self-styled warlords to make me imagine the Empire had given them away as party favors at the Emperor's funeral, but I'd never seen them on someone so young. Her black hair had been cut to the line of her jaw, emphasizing her youth, but an ancient hunger played through her violet eyes.

I looked at Cracken. ''She's a child.''

''Was.'' Cracken sat back in his chair. ''We think she was sixteen standard years old when she began an affair with the Moff on Eiattu 4, the homeworld of a former pilot in Rogue Squadron.''

Tycho smiled. ''Plourr. We didn't know she was part of the world's ruling family until they came looking for her to come back and guide them.''

I concentrated for a moment. ''She was before my time, before the squadron was re-formed and Coruscant was taken. Didn't realize who she was when I met her on Corellia, back when I was still with CorSec.''

''Her reports on that incident spoke highly of you nonetheless, Captain Horn.'' Cracken pressed his hands together. ''Leonia proved to be ambitious, and after the apparently accidental death of the Moff's wife, he married Leonia. Then he suffered a stroke that left him speechless and paralyzed. Because of an allergy to bacta, the road back to health was not easy for him, but he worked hard in physical rehab. He regained use of his hands, a goal he had, it seems, because he then turned a blaster on himself and committed suicide. Leonia assumed his title and duties and ruled Eiattu 4 until Plourr and the Rogues forced her to flee. This she did, with a considerable portion of the planet's wealth."

I felt a chill run down my spine. Over the years I had heard countless stories of people willing to sacrifice others for their own greed. With CorSec I had even investigated a couple of these mourning-murderers, but they were nothing in comparison to Leonia Tavira. "Is there any question that she did away with her husband and his first wife?"

Cracken shook his head. "Not in my mind, but there is no evidence to prove she did. From Eiattu there is no trace of her—she escaped in a shuttle—until she had another run-in with Rogue Squadron. This time she was in command of a small band of pirates that proved somewhat less tractable than the Invids. She fled from that confrontation and hooked up with Teradoc. She obtained the *Invidious* from him by means unknown and vanished except for the occasional supply raid. She became more bold during Thrawn's campaign, and first appeared with the Invids during the Emperor's return. She was a minor concern then, but she learned very well how to manage her pirates."

An image of the *Booty Full* replaced her holograph. "What she has done is forged a loose coalition of freebooters and marauders into a fleet that looks to her for planning and coordination. She provides them times and places for rendezvous, then plots courses, downloads battleplans and uses the *Invidious'* firepower to suppress planetary defenses. Her allies then loot and pillage to their hearts' content, transferring half of what they take to her. She then vanishes and they return to their boltholes, waiting for her next call."

I frowned. "Why haven't we gone after her fleet? Tracking them can't be that difficult."

"It isn't. We know, for a fact, that many of them spend their time at Nal Hutta, or lairing up in various and sundry smugglers' hide-outs throughout the galaxy." Cracken's eyes narrowed. "Without Tavira and the *Invidious*, her fleet would fall apart and mopping them up would be simple. With her ship intact, we can't begin to prey on the fleet unless we devote sufficient forces to be able to repel an ambush. You were at K'vath. We had a Mon Cal Cruiser and two Star Destroyers there to take down a bulk cruiser and eighteen Tri-fighters."

Tycho leaned forward and rested his elbows on his desk. "The fact is, though, sir, that we were not ambushed at K'vath."

"I know, and that is one of the more troubling aspects of this whole affair." Cracken sighed and I felt a wave of fatigue wash out with his breath. "The source that tipped us to the *Booty Full*'s raid appears to be one tied to Tavira. Riizolo says he wanted to go out on his own, so he severed ties with Tavira. He says he had been holding out on her anyway, which is why he was able to buy his own clutches. He even sliced the plans for the taking of the *Glitterstar* from her computer. Because we escorted the liner back to Coruscant, he believes he just got unlucky in the timing of the raid, since we were obviously there to escort the ship, not go after him."

I shook my head. "He'd not be the first criminal to refuse to believe he was set up."

"He still is stupid enough to think what little information he was able to give us will save him from prison." Cracken hit another key on the datapad. "About the most useful thing he did give us is this updated image of Leonia Tavira."

Gone was the prim vixen from the previous image. Though still very young, Leonia had become sharper and far more beautiful. Her violet eyes had a piercing quality that belied the gentle smile on her face. Her hair had grown out somewhat and was raggedly cut, but held back with a red bandanna of the same hue as the scarlet panels on her black jacket. She wore blaster pistols on either hip, and the gunbelts that encircled her waist emphasized her slender, petite physique. Her black leggings clung to her like synthetic flesh, while armored boots encased her legs from the knees down.

I shook my head. "Looks like life gave her some Iceheart lessons."

Cracken snorted a laugh. "I hate to think what Tavira would have become if Ysanne Isard had taken her on as an apprentice. Or even Grand Admiral Thrawn, for that matter. She appears to learn from her experiences very quickly and very well, which is part of the reason we have trouble locating her. As we suspected before, and as Riizolo confirmed, she initiates contact, not the other way around. None of the Invid pirates know where she hides her ship or when she will show up. Only those individuals recruited to crew on the *Invidious* learn those secrets, but that avenue of access is one-way only. Once you are invited to the *Invidious*, you do not leave it."

Tycho studied Tavira's image, then glanced at Cracken. "I seem to recall a number of other operations launched against her that proved fruitless. Do you suspect she has sources of information that tip her to our plans?"

"I certainly would like to think so, Colonel, because that means we could trap her if we could locate her source and feed him bad data." Cracken opened his hands. "So far all efforts in that area have come up empty. In fact, I have had Iella Wessiri coordinating our efforts to locate any spies working for Tavira, and the both of you know how thorough she can be.''

I smiled. Iella had been my partner in CorSec and had been the chief prosecution investigator in Tycho's treason trial. ''If she can't find a spy, there isn't a spy.''

''A conclusion I am forced, reluctantly, to accept.'' Cracken shook his head. ''Somehow Tavira seems to know when we have prepared for one of her raids and calls it off. We've been able to figure out no pattern of behavior that would tip her off, so we have had to rely on more and more unorthodox methods for trying to locate her.''

He turned to face me and ice crystallized in my guts. ''Part of those efforts involve Mirax.''

I slumped back in my chair, suddenly feeling as old as the galaxy itself. ''I know, somehow, that she is not dead, but I cannot feel her otherwise. What do you know, General?''

''I know very little, and some of that I cannot tell you.''

Tycho frowned. ''This is his wife, General, and she's missing.''

''I know that, Colonel, and I know where she might be.'' Cracken held his hands up to forestall comment by either one of us. He needn't have done it for me because I felt as if all my bones were turning to liquid and the very act of breathing was almost more than I could manage.

''Mirax came to me to ask what she could do to help bring an end to the Invid raids. It turns out that a client of hers, a collector of antiquities, had lost some valuable items when an Invid raid hit a vacation home he maintained. He wanted the items back and was interested in having Mirax make some inquiries. She came to me offering her services, noting that such a cover story might allow her to go where my people could not. I explained to her that the Invids could prove very dangerous, but she was willing to accept that danger—though she *did* travel alone, not wanting to subject co-pilots to such risk. She said that the sooner the Invids were broken up, the less she would worry about their possibly killing Rogues, and that she and you could get back to your lives."

Somehow I balled my hands into fists and fought to stop the tears threatening to leak from my eyes. *If I had not set the destruction of the Invids as a condition for our decision about having a child, she never would have taken this risk. I should have seen that, I should have known what she would do. She never was one to stand around idle when a goal eluded her grasp.*

Was she? With that question, with my realization that I couldn't remember enough about her to answer it, the tears came. I wanted to apologize, but the lump in my throat choked off my words. My mouth gaped open in a silent scream, then I hammered my right fist down against the arm of my chair and snapped my mouth shut. I sniffed, swiped at tears, then sat back upright.

"Please, forgive me," I croaked.

"Nothing to forgive, Corran." Tycho gave me a brave smile. "You're taking this a lot better than I would if I had the equivalent news about Winter."

Cracken reached out and patted me on the knee. "But for your sense of Mirax's being gone, I would not be overly alarmed, Captain Horn. She is overdue for reporting in, but not by so much time that I see a need to assume the worst."

"I'm not assuming, sir." I opened my fists and stared down at my empty hands. "She's gone. Not dead, just *gone*! I was sleeping and heard her scream my name, and then she was gone."

Cracken's head came up. "You think this is more than a nightmare?"

"It was no nightmare."

"Then part of your Jedi heritage?"

I stopped and thought hard. Did I maintain some sort of unconscious, untrained connection with Mirax through the Force? I didn't know if that was possible.

"I don't know, General, I just know she is gone. I can't feel her anymore." I looked toward Tycho. "Tell me you can feel Winter's presence, please."

Tycho smiled quickly. "I think I know what you mean, Corran, and I do feel her presence when we're together, but it is not a constant thing. She's off nursemaiding Anakin Solo and I have no idea where she is or how she is doing. Knowing her, I assume all is well. I can't tell you, however, that I have the same bond with her that you share with Mirax."

"Thanks for your honesty." I turned back to Cracken. "Tell me where she last was."

The general shook his head. "I cannot."

"You must."

"I can't and won't, Captain Horn." Cracken's face closed. "Think about it for a minute. I have agents in place who are very vulnerable. . . ."

"It's Mirax's vulnerability I'm worrying about here."

"I know that, man, don't think I don't." An edge crept into Cracken's voice and sliced through my anger. "She's in the same position you were when we inserted you and the Rogues here, into Coruscant. If I give you that information and you head out after her, you might just cause those who are dealing with her to think they have been set up. You have to trust her and trust that she will do the right thing.''

''And if that isn't enough?'' I found my hands had become fists again, so I forced them open once more. ''You may not want to give me the information, General, but you can be ordered to do so.''

''Only by the New Republic's ruling council.''

I gave him as hard a stare as I could muster. ''I'm willing to petition them to get me that information. What I've done for the New Republic may have aged a bit, and nothing is as tiresome as yesterday's hero, but I'll burn whatever political capital I have to save Mirax.''

Cracken frowned at me. ''But we don't even know she needs saving yet.''

''*You* don't know, General. *I* do.'' I stood and offered both men a salute. ''I respect you both very much, and I do not mean to be insubordinate, but my wife is in trouble and I *will* help her. I'd like your help, but absent that, don't try to stop me.''

Four

✳

I knew General Cracken's reasons for refusing to give me the information I wanted were good and sound, and I would have resisted my request the same as he had, were I in his position. That sort of cold logic melts away, however, in the face of the sort of anger and pain I was feeling. If I had just made a decision and not tried to delay things, Mirax wouldn't be missing. I'd abrogated my responsibility *once* and I damned well wasn't going to fail her a second time.

My threat to petition the New Republic's ruling council wasn't an idle one, but Cracken knew he had little to fear from it. In theory, any citizen of the New Republic could communicate with a senator and, if their case warranted it, might even get an audience with the Council. In my case I could go more directly to Doman Beruss, the Corellian Councilor, and seek an audience that way. I was fairly certain the Council would let me speak to it, but that still put me far from getting what I needed from General Cracken.

Even before going to the Council, I needed to enlist support of various members so I had a chance of getting my request approved. In reality I knew it would be fairly easy for my request to be dismissed in the name of security, but if a couple of Council members backed me, I might win the day anyway.

To enlist that sort of support, however, I needed to ask friends for favors. My first stop in that quest—at least my first stop after returning home and changing into my service uniform—was the office of General Wedge Antilles. I did not call ahead and Wedge's executive assistant, prim and cold though she was, seemed to accept my dropping in as a matter of course.

The nature of Wedge's office revealed a lot about the man I had come to know and trust over the years. The whole of the wall behind his desk had been formed of transparisteel, providing the illusion that he worked on a balcony. It gave him a great view of Coruscant and, more importantly, a lot of sky. The desk he had been given was big enough to land an X-wing on, and Wedge kept it clear enough so he *could* land an X-wing there. Off to the left side of the room Wedge had a couch, a low table, and some battered chairs that would have looked more at home in some squadron debriefing lounge.

"I hope I'm not disturbing you, General."

Wedge gave me a big smile that pulsed some warmth back into me. "Corran, it's good to see you. Been too long."

I gave him a salute, then shook his hand. "It has, General, far too long."

He frowned and waved me to a couch off away from his desk. He came around from behind the desk and took a chair facing me, leaving the low table between us. I noticed it matched the one I'd tripped over in my bedroom and my shin throbbed sympathetically. A scattering of datacards from military historical reviews and architectural publications littered the table.

Wedge regarded me carefully as he sat. "You needn't be so formal, Corran."

"Sorry, Wedge." I forced a smile onto my face. "In the squadron we understood command moving you into fleet ops while the reborn Emperor threatened the New Republic, and even during the last four months you've been flying around pulling debris out of low orbits so it wouldn't crash down and kill more folks here. Then when you took this ground assignment instead of coming back, well, some of us wondered if you hadn't gotten used to the sound of General Antilles."

He smiled in that easy, open way he had about him, with his brown eyes bright. "Nothing I'd like better than to be back with the squadron, but, you know, I've spent the last eleven years of my life blowing things apart. When I returned to Coruscant and I saw all that had been destroyed here, and all the folks left homeless—like you and Mirax—I don't know, something in me wanted a change."

Wedge leaned forward in his chair and one lock of brown hair swung down onto his forehead. He picked up one of the architectural journal datacards. "Way back when, when I lived on the Gus Treta station with my parents, I used to dream about having a home on the ground and building incredible buildings. The Rebellion and all intervened and I'd pretty much forgotten that dream, but flying over the destruction here rekindled it. I don't know if I'll stick with it, but for now it's something I want to do."

Part of me wanted to protest and convince him to rejoin the squadron, but he just sounded so *happy* that I couldn't begrudge him his change of jobs. "You know we'll be happy to have you with us again."

"Thanks." Wedge nodded and sat back in his chair. "So, what brings you here? Just visiting?"

I swallowed hard. "Not exactly. I need a favor. A *big* favor."

His reply came a bit more gravely than before. "What is it, Corran?"

"Mirax is missing and I need to find her. General Cracken knows where she was last reported to be—she was doing a job for him at the time—and he won't tell me where that was."

Wedge frowned. "He doesn't want you running off and jeopardizing her life and his operation."

"I know, but she's in trouble and I need to help her. I want to know if you would be willing to speak to Councilor Organa Solo and see if she would help me petition the Council to order Cracken to give me that information." I tried to make my request sound reasonable, but even as I heard the words, I knew it was insane. Even if Wedge helped, the Council could never give me what I wanted. I was way out of bounds and I knew it, but I had no other choice.

Before Wedge could answer, a bright-eyed man swung in through the office doorway. He was looking back at Wedge's assistant and said, "It will just take a second, and then I'll be out again." He looked over at Wedge with a rakehell grin as wide as a Hutt and full of trouble on his face. "Wedge, want to make a run with me to Kessel?"

"Kessel? That's the last place I'd think you'd want to go." Wedge blinked away his surprise. "Thanks for the invitation, Han, but I've got duties here."

"What duties? Construction droids run themselves. You can head out with me and check on folks you left there, like that Fliry Vorru." Han Solo looked past

Wedge and acknowledged me with a quick nod. "Sorry to interrupt."

Wedge looked from him back to me, then smiled. "Have you two not met?"

I shook my head. "I know General Solo by reputation, certainly."

Han Solo's smile remained in place. "No longer a general, just a civilian, thanks."

Wedge smiled slyly. "I don't think that's the whole of the reputation he means, Han. This is Corran Horn. He used to be with CorSec."

Han extended a hand to me. "Then I know you by reputation, too. And your father."

"My father?"

Corellia's most notorious smuggler nodded. "He was on my trail once. Had to take an appointment to the Imperial Naval Academy to escape him."

Han Solo had a hint of smugness in his voice that I'd long associated with smugglers and criminals boasting of their narrow escapes, and I wanted to hate him for it. I knew he'd trafficked in spice for a Hutt and that, too, was cause for me to think him the dregs of the universe. Even the fact that Corellians were often seen as flashy scofflaws in the rest of the galaxy, largely because of the fame of his exploits, was more than enough to have earned him my enmity forever.

But there was something in his eyes and the firmness of his grip that hinted at the honorable spirit at his core. It would have been easy to deride him as nothing more than a mercenary who had found his fortune in Princess Leia, but that denied the sheer pain he'd suffered and the effort he'd put into fighting against the Empire. Something in the man struggled against taking the easy way out, against abandoning friends and abandoning hopeless causes. Perhaps it was a will to succeed or a fear of failure, both or even more, but it caused me to realize that a catalog of his crimes and deeds could not sum this man up.

"I am pleased to meet you, sir."

"You were CorSec, I'm supposed to call you *sir*." He shrugged. "But formality has never been my strong suit."

Wedge waved Han to a chair, but the man remained standing. "Corran was just asking me to speak to your wife on a very important matter. Do you remember Booster Terrik?"

Han's face brightened. "Booster? Hard to forget him. He was a legend among smugglers before Corellia cooled into a ball. Didn't your father send Booster to Kessel?"

I nodded. "Five years."

Han winced. "That's a *long* time in the mines."

Wedge nodded. "Corran married Booster's daughter, Mirax."

"Really! Someone who finally has in-laws that are as interesting as mine." Han looked at me. "What did you want Wedge to speak to Leia about?"

"Mirax is missing. I want to go after her, but Airen Cracken won't tell me where she was when she vanished." I shrugged. "I was hoping the Council could order him to give me that information."

"Leia might be able to convince them to do that, but I'd not be betting a lot on it, kid." The smuggler's brown eyes hardened. "As sympathetic as Leia might be to your cause, the fact is that your request would be pretty low on the New Republic's list of priorities. And, if you think about it the way you would have thought about it when with CorSec, there's no way you'd have turned that sort of information over to the spouse of an undercover officer.''

I glanced down at the floor. "I know."

"However," he said, letting a lighter tone bleed into his words, "New Republic Intelligence isn't the only place you can get information about Mirax. She still flying the *Pulsar Skate*?"

My head came up. "Yes, sir."

"Before I head out for Kessel—Leia has me working as a liaison to the inmates since I've been in the area before—I'll put out some feelers and see if the *Skate* has been spotted in any of the usual places. Might pop up a lead for you." Han's eyes narrowed in my direction. "But that's only if you get over this sir thing."

I smiled in spite of myself. "Thank you, Han. And I'm Corran, despite having been in CorSec."

Han smiled. "The galaxy is a big place, so your search won't be easy, but I don't expect that matters much to you."

"It doesn't."

"May the Force be with you, then." He glanced at Wedge. "You certain you don't want to come along to Kessel?"

"Next time, Han, but not right now." Wedge gave him a smile. "The last time I was there—Rogue Squadron was there—Moruth Doole didn't really take a fancy to me. Do yourself a favor and don't mention me to him."

"I copy. When I get back, I'll let you know if I've learned anything, Corran." The pirate tossed us both an easy salute. "Good flying to both of you."

Wedge and I stared after him as he spun and disappeared through the doorway. I laughed. "He has something of a presence, doesn't he?"

Wedge nodded. "Kind of hard to forget."

"Explains the bounties on his head." I felt my smile slowly receding. "Wedge, one thing, I, ah, don't know if you're planning to see Iella now that you're dirtdown, but if you do, don't ask her about Mirax. She's working for Cracken still, and might have information, but I don't want her to get into trouble giving it to me."

"I'll bear that in mind." Wedge frowned slightly. "I really should link up with her, shouldn't I?"

I smiled. "You two seemed to get along famously. I pretty much thought you'd have gotten fairly serious by this time."

"I would have, too." He shrugged uneasily. "I had intended to start dating her before her husband showed up, then after his death and Thyferra and Wraith Squadron and Thrawn . . ."

"I know, a lot of things have happened to make things tough. Can't beat a homeworld girl, though, for having someone who can share the universe with you."

"You and Mirax are certainly proving that." Wedge looked away a little wistfully. "I really should call her and give things another chance. Maybe once I get this reconstruction going well I can take the time."

"As Han said, it's a pretty big galaxy, but I don't think you'll find anyone in it better for you than she is." I forced an awkward laugh. "Big galaxy and I'm having to look for my wife, while the perfect match for you is so close. Life is never easy, is it?"

"No, that's true." Wedge's eyes brightened and a smile began to blossom on his face. "However, we might have an edge in helping you solve your problem."

"What do you mean?"

"Luke's here, on Coruscant. You should talk to him." Wedge nodded solemnly. "Finding Mirax may be akin to finding a quark in a mole of deuterium, but if that's your task, having a Jedi help you do it is not a bad way to go at all."

FIVE

✳

Despite the early hour, Wedge made a call to Luke Skywalker, and we were invited to his chambers in the Imperial Palace. Wedge obtained an airspeeder and flew us over. He wove an aggressive course through the tall towers and thick ribbons of traffic choking the airways of the palace district. Jacking the speeder up on its left side, he slid us between two heavily laden lifttrucks, then came around in a big arc that brought us in for an approach at one of the palace's many landing bays.

I glanced over at him and the look of pure pleasure on his face. "You may not believe it, but you're missing the squadron a whole bunch."

He winked at me. "I'm missing flying, certainly, but dealing with you fighter jocks and your egos was wearing thin."

"Yeah, that's all space-dust and plasma balls. Now you deal with politicians and their egos." I laughed aloud. "You just moved up to really hard targets."

Wedge frowned for a second. "More truth to that than I want to think about, my friend."

We both fell silent as the Imperial Palace came into view. An upwelling of towers and massive edifices, it appeared to be the ultimate monument to power. Even so, the various parts had been sculpted with such exquisite attention to detail that taken in isolation, portions of it appeared positively delicate. What looked like thin membranes and gossamer tracery from far off became far more solid upon approach, but proximity revealed yet more levels of detail, complete with winking lights and bright colors splashed about. *Complex* seemed to be the only word that could fully encompass the palace.

The New Republic government had tried to abandon the name Imperial Palace, and various campaigns to call it things like Republic House or simply the Capitol had been launched down through the years. None of them succeeded because none of them seemed appropriate. It was as if the building had grown up to fill every nuance suggested by the title Imperial Palace and to call it anything less just felt wrong.

Wedge gave the proper codes for us to land at the palace, then led me off through a maze of corridors to the Jedi Master's home. I would have been utterly lost in the tangle of hallways, and only had a vague sense of our moving across the tower and up, but never really knew how far we had gone. Part of this was because the ornate designs and vibrant colors used to decorate this palace tower almost overwhelmed me. The use of Imperial Scarlet predominated, with gold, silver, blue and green accenting various features. Just when the clash of color would become too much, we'd walk past an alcove or a wall panel that housed artwork from one of the myriad planets in the galaxy. I found the alcoves to be a sanctuary of sorts and greatly anticipated them, moving from one to the next as I might move from system to system on a long flight.

What struck me as odd about my reaction was that this was not my first trip to the Imperial Palace. I couldn't be certain I'd not been in this very tower before, but the fact was that quite a bit of the palace was garishly decorated. Part of me speculated that the reason for the violent use of color and ornamentation was because when the Emperor lived here, he so sucked life out of everyone, that if something was not made brutally and abundantly clear to them, they would not notice it.

The palace had not changed since my previous visits, but I had always come here before with my wife. Mirax's appreciation for art, her knowledge of the various pieces, their styles, likely origins and even market value, had provided me with a context in which to place everything. I focused upon those things that interested her and built upon a foundation my mother had given me on our visits to the museums on Corellia. Through Mirax I had been able to filter out all the irritating things, but without her the colors assaulted me.

Master Skywalker's chambers saved me. The door opened before we got to it and Wedge did not hesitate in plunging into the dimly lit room. The low lights quelled the riot of color. While the chambers still had the Imperial styling, there was no excess of furnishing to clog them with angles, plush fabrics and dangling fringes. The shelves that had been built into the walls of every chamber were all but devoid of datacard boxes and curios. Aside from a few mementos—a gaffi stick, his X-wing helmet and a couple of items I remembered from the Emperor's Jedi mausoleum—the shelves remained bare.

The Jedi's chambers reminded me of the very spare condition of the safehouse in which Mirax and I had come to live. The freedom from distractions made the rooms feel peaceful. Time seemed to slow here and for the first moment since I'd discovered Mirax was gone, I didn't feel as if a sandstorm was scourging my brain.

Luke looked over at us from the small kitchenette and gave us a smile. "Wedge, good to see you again. And you as well, Captain Horn. Can I offer you something to drink?"

"Caf, if you have it." Wedge hid a yawn with the back of his right hand. "You keep it dark enough in here for me to drop off right now."

"Caf it shall be, then." The Jedi Master looked at me and I felt electricity run through his blue-eyed gaze. When we had met before I had felt power in him, but now, after his experiences with the Emperor Reborn, his power had been redoubled. Physically he looked a bit haggard and worn, with the flesh around his eyes having tightened and wrinkles appearing at their corners. I knew we were the same age chronologically, but in experience he far surpassed me.

"And for you, Captain? I keep some of that Gizer Pale Blue ale here for Han. I'm having hot chocolate."

I thought for a moment, then shook my head. "Too early to start drinking, and I'm not sure I'd want to stop. And I certainly don't need to be more awake."

"Your agitation is easy to sense." Luke gestured toward the simple chairs and low table opposite the food prep station. "Why don't you explain what the problem is."

The soothing calmness of his voice helped quell the riot of emotions in me as I took a seat. Wedge sat at my right hand and Luke across from him. I leaned forward in my seat, resting my elbows on my knees. I took in a deep breath, held it for a moment and slowly exhaled.

"My wife, Mirax, is missing. She was off on a mission for General Cracken, a mission to see if she could discover the location of the *Invidious* so we could put an end to Leonia Tavira's raids.'' I hesitated, chewing my lower lip for a second. ''She'd not have gone except for the fact that I said once the Invids were dealt with, we could make a decision about having kids. If I hadn't put that condition on making the decision, she wouldn't have gone to Cracken and wouldn't have been taken away.''

Luke reached out and laid a hand on my left arm. ''Take a moment. Calm yourself. You are building on a foundation that is not sound.''

I frowned. ''What do you mean?''

''You are taking responsibility for Mirax's actions— responsibility that is not yours to take.'' Luke kept his voice low and even, forcing me to focus so I could hear his words. ''She may have gone to Cracken to help end the Invid raids for a whole host of reasons. Clearly she wanted to help you and Rogue Squadron deal with them quickly. You think what she did was dictated by your postponement of a decision. She was probably more interested in keeping you and your friends alive.''

Wedge nodded. ''You have to admit, Corran, that what Luke's just described is exactly the sort of thing she would do.''

I shut my eyes for a moment, then nodded slowly. ''Good point. You're right, but that doesn't mean part of her disappearance is not my fault.''

Luke's hand tightened on my forearm. ''Your sense of guilt is natural, but you can't let it paralyze you. I am curious, though, about one thing. You say she has been 'taken away.' How do you know that?''

''I don't know, I just know. I was sleeping, waiting for her to come back home, when I heard her call my name. Then I heard her scream it, then there was nothing.'' I opened my eyes and locked gazes with the Jedi

Master. "I could feel she was gone—not *dead*, just cut off from me. And then I began to forget details of her and our life. I could look around the room and identify things that she had brought to the house or that she had owned or used, but I got no emotional details. It feels as if she is dissolving from my memory."

Luke straightened up and sipped his chocolate. His eyes grew distant for a moment and his face became a dark mask. "Very curious."

"What is?"

"Having the memories fade." He looked at me again with an intensity in his eyes. "I'd like to try something, if you don't mind."

I glanced at Wedge, who gave me a reassuring nod. "Fine. What do you want me to do?"

Luke smiled easily. "Just open your mind to me. I want to probe you. You'll feel something—a little pressure. It might even tickle."

"Okay."

He drew in a deep breath and as he exhaled I felt a wave of peace wash out over me. I did my best to relax as the Jedi's eyes half-closed. I felt something in my mind, something gentle yet firm, like a reassuring pat on the back, press against my consciousness. It grew more intense and shifted from point to point—if something as ethereal as a mind can be said to have points. I felt different angles of attack and an increase in pressure that verged on painful, then it evaporated and Luke sat back.

I looked at him expectantly. "What?"

He grinned boyishly. "Very interesting. Were you trying to resist me?"

I shook my head. "Not at all. Was there a problem?"

"A bit. I could pull off some surface impressions, but you were locked up pretty tightly." He frowned for a moment. "Let me try it a different way. Wedge, I want you to start talking. What about doesn't really matter. Something simple. Maybe a joke. Corran, focus on Wedge's voice and what you feel about him. I'll do the same thing, which ought to bring our thoughts on roughly parallel courses. That might provide me an opening."

I shrugged. "Worth a shot, I guess."

We both looked at Wedge. "I'm not very good with jokes."

Luke nodded. "The sound of your voice is the focus here, not making us laugh."

"Okay. So there was this Bothan who walked into a tapcaf with a gornt under his arm. . . ."

I closed my eyes and listened to the sound of Wedge's voice. I thought back on all the times I had heard it, and all the advice and congratulations he'd given me, all the danger we'd shared, and the good times as well. I marveled at how we'd managed to scrape through impossible situations, winning against odds longer than even a Corellian would have bet on. I thought about the people we'd helped, the lives we'd saved, and even the shared pain of comrades lost in our battles along the way.

The whole of that time I only caught a hint of Luke's probing. This time instead of coming in directly, he allowed his exploration to begin flowing along in the same direction as my thoughts. The current of his sensing melded with me and whatever mental defenses I had in place failed to fully recognize this other presence in my mind. Luke's inquiry slipped past them, still bumping along my memories of Wedge, then, when he hit upon a memory in which both Wedge and Mirax appeared, he veered off sharply and I felt as if a transparisteel fang had been driven deep into my brain.

I must have blacked out for a second because the next thing I saw was Wedge standing over me. I blinked away tears and found myself staring up at the ceiling, with my chair having toppled over onto its back. I clutched at the arms so hard my hands hurt. My legs had wrapped themselves around the chair's legs so tightly I heard the fiberplast creak and snap. I felt a burning in my lungs and realized I needed to remind myself to breathe.

Wedge dropped to a knee beside me. "Are you okay, Corran? Luke, how are you doing?"

"A bit better than he is, I suspect." Luke appeared on the other side of me and pressed his left hand to my shoulder. I felt something flow from him into me and my quaking limbs slackened. "Easy now, Corran. I know that was a shock. I'm sorry."

I slowly snaked my left hand over to wipe my mouth and came away with a bit of blood from a bit lip. Pain still echoed within my brain and the hollowness in the pit of my stomach made me happy I'd not drunk anything. I coughed and forced a weak smile. "Not what you were planning?"

"Not at all."

Luke and Wedge disentangled my limbs from the chair and helped me to my feet. With a gesture the Jedi Master got another chair beneath me and I sat again. I had to fight to keep from slipping slack-spined to the floor, but I managed it. "Sorry for breaking your chair."

"Not a problem."

Wedge frowned. "So what happened? I didn't think the joke was that bad."

Luke laughed politely and even I had to smile. "No, Wedge, it wasn't. Even Corran will agree with that. What happened was that I managed to work my way in past his defenses and used a memory of you and Mirax together to make my connection to her. In doing so I poked Corran in a vast, open psychic wound.''

I shivered. ''And somehow I threw you back out of my mind.''

''Yes, you did, and quite strongly.'' Luke righted his own chair and sat down again. ''I think I have a clue about your losing emotional details concerning Mirax.''

''Tell me.''

''You've got flashburns. The trauma of hearing her shout for you and then having her gone pretty much burned out your emotions where she is concerned. Your mind is closing off access to certain points to prevent taking another shock like that.'' Luke shrugged lightly. ''Your defenses are quite strong and right now it's like swelling after a trauma. You're shut down emotionally and very tough to reach.''

Some strength had returned to my limbs, so I pulled myself into an upright sitting position. ''It's not permanent, is it?''

''I don't think so.'' Luke sipped at his drink. ''The mind can be pretty hardy.''

I waited for him to swallow another mouthful of chocolate, then asked, ''So, will you help me find her?''

''I would like to, very much. First we need to figure out why she is missing.''

Wedge frowned over the lip of his caf mug. ''She's missing because she went out to learn about the Invids.''

''That's the root cause, yes, but why her? And why wasn't she killed outright?'' Luke pressed his hands together. ''There have been points where I have felt friends being in danger over great distances, but the most powerful time was when Han and Leia and Chewbacca were on Bespin and being tortured by Darth Vader. He wanted me to come to him, so he could win me over to the dark side.''

''But he knew you had been trained as a Jedi by then. He knew you would be receptive to that sort of bait.'' I poked a thumb against my own breastbone. ''Almost no one outside the squadron knows my Jedi connections, and I haven't been trained. In fact, there's very little to link me to the Jedi at all.''

Luke nodded. ''Then what is there to link Mirax to them?''

My heart stopped for a second. ''Sithspawn, she has my Jedi Credit. I gave it to her when we were engaged. She wears it as a good luck charm when she travels.''

The Jedi Master's face darkened. ''That could be it. From what I learned of the Corellian Jedi traditions, when a Knight became a Master, he had memorial coins struck. They were given to family, friends, his Master and students. It could be that someone saw the medallion, assumed a link there and took action.''

''But why?'' It didn't make sense to me. ''You said Vader tortured your friends to lure you into a trap. I can't find Mirax, so how can I fall into a trap?''

Wedge shook his head. ''Might just be a warning, Corran, warning you off from doing something.''

''Sure, but what?''

Luke held a hand up. ''We don't know. Speculating now could be a waste of breath. My using the Bespin example might have set us off on the wrong trail. It could be nothing more than someone kidnapping Mirax because they recognized her and think they can ransom her, since both of you are known as part of the Rebellion. The warning you got may have come before any ransom demands and the kidnappers might not know you have been warned.''

My eyes narrowed. "Good, then we're a step ahead of them. With your help, we can find Mirax and take care of this situation before it becomes more dire."

"Agreed, but there is a problem."

"What's that?"

Luke sighed. "I don't have your connection to Mirax. The abruptness with which your link to her was broken makes me wonder if she's in stasis. I'll have to ask Leia what she felt when Han was sealed in carbonite—I know it hurt her terribly. What you felt, I bet, was a lot of what she felt."

I hugged my arms around myself. The thought of Mirax being frozen in carbonite, or stuffed into a hibernation tube, filled me with dread. "You're saying that you have no way of finding her."

"No, not right now, not over this distance."

My heart sank. "So she's lost."

"I didn't say that." Luke set his mug down on the table and stared into my eyes. "I think you *can* find her. I think you are strong enough in the Force to pick her out, even if she is in hibernation. Her thoughts may have been slowed to the point where they barely register, but through the Force you can find them. They will lead you to her."

"But I need to find her *now*!"

"No," he insisted calmly, "you need to find her. What you need to do *now* is learn how to find her."

Luke stood, circled behind his chair and leaned heavily on the back of it. "I've been thinking a lot on what has happened recently and I know there is no way Leia and I and her children, as they grow to maturity, can shoulder all the responsibilities that we're called upon to deal with now. Down through the thousand generations that the Jedi maintained peace in the galaxy, there were lots of Jedi; hundreds certainly, thousands probably. The Emperor's best efforts to destroy the Jedi were not wholly successful and there are Force-sensitive people still out there. Just like you, Corran, and me and Mara Jade. We need to create more Jedi to share the burden.

"I know I asked you before to join me and train with me. You refused for what were good and valuable reasons. Events since then have not let me push to reestablish the order, but now is the time. In a couple of days I plan to ask the senate to. let me establish a Jedi academy. Just a basic search through databases has turned up a number of viable candidates. If I can get a dozen I think I will have enough to start. I'd like you to be one of them."

"How can I think of training to be a Jedi when my wife is gone?"

Wedge frowned at me. "Think for a second, Corran. *If* her abduction was meant to send you a message—a message only a Jedi could understand—then whoever has her is tough enough that they think they can take on a Jedi and survive. If you don't train to be a Jedi, what do you think are the chances of your being able to rescue her?"

Luke nodded. "Wedge is right. And, if you got the message because of your sensitivity to the Force and the kidnappers know nothing about it, Jedi training will make you that much more able to deal with them and save her."

Their logic was unassailable, but I still felt uneasy about committing myself to a course of training while Mirax languished in stasis. "I don't know."

The Jedi Master slowly smiled. "I would have expected no other honest answer. Two things for you to consider, Corran. The first is this: when Vader tortured my friends, it was to lure me to him *and* to disrupt my training. I made the most serious mistake of my career leaving my master at that point. It cost me my hand, nearly cost me my life and, as events went from there, could have seriously hurt the Rebellion. You have a chance, being faced with a similar challenge, to avoid the mistake I made. I hope you will take it.''

I could feel the sincerity rolling off him. ''What's the other thing?''

''The Corellian Jedi tradition is a strong one. In the annals of the Jedi, many Corellian Jedi are noted for their devotion to service. They tended not to range far from Corellia—that system had more than enough for them to do—but their wisdom and courage made quite an impact. You are heir to that tradition and I think weaving it back into the new Jedi traditions will be very important. What you do in joining the academy will not only let you rescue Mirax, but will help others come to their full potential in the Force.''

''I hear what you are saying, Master Skywalker, but there are other problems.'' I shrugged. ''I'm not you or Han Solo, but I'm not unknown in the New Republic. If Mirax's kidnappers hear I'm at your academy and being trained as a Jedi, her life would be forfeit.''

Wedge pointed at me. ''If nothing else, his status as a hero of the Rebellion would probably distract other students.''

''Very true, but that's not too difficult a problem to handle.'' Luke smiled easily. ''Dye your hair, grow a beard, you'll look different. In your time with CorSec you performed undercover operations.''

''Sure, but I wasn't known as Corran Horn during those assignments, either.''

''No, you changed your name.'' Luke nodded solemnly. "In researching the Corellian Jedi I saw a name—probably an ancestor of yours. You may even have been named for him. He was Keiran Halcyon. You can use his name. It is close enough to your own for you to respond to it, yet far enough away to give you the cover you need."

Keiran Halcyon. The name rolled around in my brain and seemed to soothe the last lingering bits of pain from Luke's probe. "That might work. I have to think about it."

Luke reached out and patted me on the shoulder. "It is a big decision. Go home. Definitely think about it. Think about reclaiming the heritage the Empire tried to deny to you. This is yet another chance for you to defeat that evil and prepare yourself to battle new evils. If you truly want the galaxy to be safe for the children you and Mirax will have, learning to become a Jedi is the best possible course you can take."

Six

✳

Wedge ran me home and offered to stay and talk things over with me, but I let him go. "I appreciate the offer, Wedge, but you've got more important things to do than to listen to me argue this from all sides."

Wedge pressed his lips together in a grim grin. "Nothing I have to do is more important than my friends. Mirax is as close as I've ever come to having a little sister, and I definitely think of her as family. You're a good friend. As much as it bothers you to be able to do nothing at the moment, at least you have some options. I'm even more blind here than you are; but I'll be ready to help no matter what decision you make."

I shook his outstretched hand. "Thanks. Believe me, you'll be hearing from me."

"I'm counting on it."

I held a hand up. "One thing, please. Don't say anything to Booster."

Wedge frowned. "But he's her father. He should be told."

"Yeah, but if Cracken was afraid I'd be a nerf in an antiquities bazaar, just imagine what Booster will do." I shook my head. "The *Errant Venture* might not be in the greatest shape, but having an Imperial Star Destroyer show up and threaten a world probably won't be the best way to get Mirax back.''

''You have a point there.'' Wedge smiled. ''I won't lie to him, but I won't go out of my way to say anything to him until or unless I have some good news.''

''Thanks. See you later, Wedge.'' I walked down the steps from the complex's common landing area and over to the apartment. The door slid open when I punched in the code. I was two steps inside before I noticed there were more lights on than when I'd left. Without a blaster or my grandfather's lightsaber, I was defenseless against whoever had broken in. I was about to turn and head back out again, when a familiar hooting sounded from the living room.

''Yes, Whistler, it's me.''

The little green R2 unit rolled over, swiveled his head so his visual monitors could take in the hallway, then turned around and disappeared again. I walked down to the living area and found a variety of bags and containers of food piled on the holopad's table. The droid's pincer arm extended from its cylindrical body and elevated a can of nerf and gumes to the top of a shaky stack.

''Whistler, despite what Mirax told you months ago about my dietary habits when she's gone, I really can feed myself.'' I dropped to my knees on the floor beside him and caught the can he dropped in my lap. ''Yes, I'm certain this would be good, but I'm just not hungry right now.''

A whistle started low and spiked high.

''Why?'' I snorted. ''I don't know how much of this you can understand, Whistler.'' I ignored his derisive reply and pushed on, organizing my thoughts as I went. ''Since you're here, I know you pulled the *Skate*'s port logs and saw Mirax was gone. Fact is, she's really *gone*. Someone has taken her and Jedi Master Skywalker thinks she's being held in stasis somewhere. Why, none of us have any clue.''

Whistler's mournful tone raised a lump in my throat. He tweetled and hooted a bunch of things after that, but I couldn't figure out what he meant. I reached out and patted him gently on the dome. His pincer gently tugged on the sleeve of my jacket.

''I've just come from talking with Wedge and with Luke Skywalker. They both think my learning to train as a Jedi is the key to finding Mirax, but I think that will take too long. Part of me knows they are right, but another part doesn't think Mirax can afford the time. I keep trying to think about what I should do, or what my father would do, but I have so many questions that need answering that I'm lost.''

Whistler toddled forward and toppled one of the stack of cans he had created. His dataprobe came out and sank itself into the dataport on the holopad. In an instant the image of my father, standing slightly taller than Mirax had, appeared frozen on the holopad. Whistler hooted insistently at me, but I couldn't understand him.

''Slow down, slow down. What are you getting at?''

My father's image faded, replaced by the glowing words, ''All you have to do is ask.''

I was about to ask for a further explanation of that line, but the words struck a resonance inside me and I recognized them fairly quickly. Back before we had liberated Thyferra, before Thrawn and freeing the *Lusankya* prisoners, Whistler had informed me that my father had encrypted and loaded into him a holograph talking about my heritage. Whistler had said the message was recorded back before I joined CorSec. He'd been instructed to play it for me whenever I asked and could provide the encryption key.

I resisted listening to the message back then because I feared it would make me make choices that I didn't want to make. If my father had urged me to become a Jedi, to seek out a Master and to train, I knew I would have. At the time that would have meant leaving the squadron and leaving Mirax and abandoning the former *Lusankya* prisoners. I couldn't do that, so I set aside the idea of hearing what my father had to say.

After that, with Thrawn and everything else, I never got the chance to explore what my father had left for me. Mirax told me the message itself was not the last gift my father had given me. The last gift was the trust he showed in allowing me to choose when and if I listened to his message. I cherished that gift and while I knew I should listen to the message, by putting off the decision I made that final gift last longer.

Even as that thought bubbled into my brain, I realized that listening to the message would not destroy my father's gift. His trust had been implicit in every aspect of our lives. My father had died in my arms and I had been powerless to prevent his death. Because of this I had allowed myself to imagine that in his last seconds of life he wondered where I was. He wondered why I had not been there to help him. I had to hope, for the sake of my sanity, that he knew I would have given my own life to save his. Somehow I did think that; I even *knew* it.

I smiled. "He recorded that message long before he died. It was never meant to be a legacy, but a failsafe. If something happened to him, I would not be left without information he thought I needed to know. And I need to remember that he never would have put me into a position to make a choice against my own best interests. I trust him in that, but by not listening to the message I've failed to act on that trust.''

I nodded to Whistler. ''Please, play the message for me. Decryption code is Nejaa Halcyon.''

My father's image reappeared and my throat tightened. He'd always been taller than me and, with me kneeling on the floor, I once again had to look up at him. His black hair had been closely cropped, his hazel eyes had golden highlights that sparkled. He wore that easy smile I'd see so often. I'd probably been sixteen years old when he recorded the message—he still had his powerful build and only a hint of the thickening he would fight until the end of his life.

His voice came through clear and strong. ''I am making this recording for you, Corran, because there are things you should know. Being in CorSec can be dangerous and I don't want anything to happen to me that would prevent you from learning about our family. I hope and trust right now that we're sitting together watching this, laughing at how young I looked when I recorded it. If not, I want you to know I love you and have always been very proud of you.''

Whistler stopped the message as I closed my eyes against tears. The shock of Mirax's disappearance might have numbed me from feeling anything about her, but the pain of my father's death came roaring back to fill the void inside of me. I realized I was kneeling now the way I'd knelt in the cantina where he died, cradling his head in my lap. It was almost as if I could feel his blood soaking into my clothes again. The frustration I felt over Mirax compounded itself with the frustration I'd felt with my father's death and I almost walked away.

But neither of them would.

I sniffed and wiped my nose on my sleeve, then

opened my eyes and nodded to Whistler. "Thanks, my friend."

The message continued with my father smiling broadly. "This will sound like a wild tale, but it is all true. Your grandfather, Rostek Horn, is really your step-grandfather. As you know he partnered with a Jedi before the Clone Wars, and that Jedi died serving away from Corellia, right after the Clone Wars. That Jedi, Nejaa Halcyon, was my father. He served as my Master before he went away. I was all of ten years old when he died, and Rostek Horn saw to it that my mother and I wanted for nothing. My mother and Rostek fell in love and married, and Rostek adopted me. More importantly, when the Empire began to hunt down Jedi and their families, he managed to destroy records and fabricate new ones that insulated us from the Empire's wrath.

"I know this is quite a secret to keep from you, but the deception was necessary. I know you, Corran, and know you would have been very proud of your heritage. You would have told others of it, sharing it with them, and that would have been your destruction. Lord Vader and the others hunting Jedi have been relentless. I have seen the results of their handiwork. Keeping you ignorant is keeping you safe. It's a terrible bargain to make, but the only one that can be made."

My father's face screwed up in that expression he wore when things were not going exactly the way he wanted. "The Halcyon family is well known among the Corellian Jedi. We were well respected and many were the tributes to Nejaa Halcyon upon his death. You can find no record of them now, of course. What the Empire did not destroy, Rostek *did* destroy or hid away—he won't even tell me where the records are, but I cannot believe he would have allowed all traces of his friend to perish. The Halcyons were strong in the Force but not flashy or given to public displays of power. A word here, an act there, allowing people to choose between good or evil at their own speed and peril was more our way.

"And so, here, with this message, I give you a choice. I will be proud of you and love you no matter what you choose. The fact that you say you want to join CorSec has filled me and your grandfather with more pride than you can imagine. There is no greater honor you could show us than to follow in our footsteps. I do want you to know, though, that my choice bridges two paths. While Rostek and my father worked together, CorSec and Jedi, I have used what I learned from my father to work within CorSec. In this way I serve both the Halcyon and Horn traditions."

My father's image opened his hands. "If you have the chance, if you feel the need, I hope you will also make yourself open to both traditions. It is not that being a Jedi is better than serving in CorSec—not at all. But there are so few who are able to become Jedi that to turn away from that path is a tragedy. I have been forced away from it. It is my hope that you will not also be barred from it and, if possible, that I will be able to instruct you the way my father instructed me."

My father smiled and pride burned in his eyes. "There you have it, my son. Now you know more of who you are and what you have the potential to become. The only limits on you are the limits you will place on yourself. I know that whatever you will decide, it will be the right thing. You're that good, Corran, and that special. I will know great joy if you bring the Halcyons back into the Jedi Order, but even that will be nothing compared to the joy I know in having you as my son and knowing you are happy and well.''

The message stopped and Whistler offered to play it again, but I shook my head. "He wants me to train. He knows it is the right thing for me to do.'' I thought for a moment. "And I guess I know it, too. I always saw my service in CorSec as the utmost I could do to prevent the innocent from coming to harm from evil. That's what it was then, just as flying with Rogue Squadron became later. Now, the utmost I can do is to become a Jedi, like Luke Skywalker and my father's father. To do anything less is to be unworthy of the trust they all place in me.''

I slowly stood. "To do anything less means I fail in my responsibilities to Mirax. I'm not going to let that happen.''

I walked down the hallway and into my bedroom. I slid back a false panel in my nightstand and withdrew the slender silver cylinder that had been Nejaa Halcyon's lightsaber. My right thumb punched the black button on it, allowing the silver-white blade to hiss to life. It hummed as I turned toward Whistler and wove the blade through the air.

"Luke Skywalker is looking for students, and I need a teacher.'' I smiled as Whistler trumpeted triumphantly. "Keiran Halcyon is born.''

SEVEN

✳

I emerged from the apartment's refresher, finished toweling off my hair as I walked toward the living room, and smiled at Iella as she came into view. "There, what do you think?"

She narrowed her brown eyes at me, then nodded. "Not a hint of green."

"Good." I hung the white towel around my neck, holding on to each end of it. "It's going to take a while to get used to seeing my reflection with my hair this close to white."

She tucked a lock of golden-brown hair behind her left ear. "It makes you look older. The moustache and goatee change the outline of your chin just enough that I almost didn't recognize you when you called earlier."

"You don't think the green had anything to do with that?" I snorted. "I didn't think dyeing my hair would be that complicated."

"Corran, you're supposed to read the instructions on the box."

"I did."

"And *then* you're supposed to follow them." She gave me a look of mock disgust. "Once you've ingested the metabolizing agent, you have to be very specific about how long you leave the color targeting gel on. If you get the timing wrong, you have problems.''

I plucked at the hair on my chest. ''Yeah, but I was trying to do my whole body here. Slathering that stuff on takes time.''

''Which is why you take it in stages, not try to do it all at once.'' She began to laugh and I blushed. ''You went from emerald to pale green at your toes. Your beard *did* match your eyes, though.''

''But it would have been unending trouble to accessorize.'' I gave her a snooty glare, then smiled. ''At least I won't need to repeat this ordeal for a year or so.''

''True, that's usually how long it takes for the metabolizer to leave the follicles, but be careful. Weird foods can affect the chemistry there.'' She stretched. ''Speaking of which, where are you going to take me for this lunch you promised?''

I shrugged. ''You pick. Fact is that I've not been thinking much about food over the past couple of weeks.''

Iella frowned at me. ''You know, I'm still a bit angry with you. I thought we were friends, but your wife goes missing and you don't call me or tell me about it?''

I closed my eyes and nodded. ''I know I should have.''

''You're damned right you should have.'' Her voice softened and I felt her hand caress my bare arm. ''You were there for me when I lost Diric. I don't think I could have gotten through it without you. I owe you a lot and even if I didn't, I'd want to help with this sort of thing.''

I opened my eyes and gave her a brave smile, but swiped at a tear with my towel. ''I wanted to talk to you, but you're working for New Republic Intelligence and I didn't want to place you in a position where you'd feel a conflict between your job and our friendship. No, wait. I know you and respect you and your professionalism. I know you would have and will do what is right and in the best interest for everyone. I also know that isn't exactly what I want. I didn't want you thinking you'd failed me because you couldn't say anything.''

Iella nodded, then gave me that indulgent grin I remembered from our years partnering in CorSec. ''Your squadron briefings about the Invids probably have told you just about everything I know *of fact* about the Invids.''

I arched a newly blond eyebrow. ''But there are rumors?''

''Vague, insubstantial rumors.'' She pursed her lips for a moment. ''On some of the early raids, when Leonia Tavira deigned to travel dirtdown and tour the ruins her people left behind, survivors have reported seeing armored figures accompanying her. Never more than one, and everyone has described them as having a Vaderish air about them; but both male and female figures have been described. With Riizolo's report to add into the mix, we think we have at least four distinct individuals.''

I scratched at the back of my neck. ''When you say 'Vaderish,' are we just talking masks, cloaks and heavy breathing, or are they doing the virtual-garrote thing or other Force power displays?''

''Nothing more solid than image, though Riizolo insists they were special. I don't know to trust his reports, though. I think he's telling us a lot of what we want to hear so we'll find him a hole to hide in.'' Iella shrugged. ''From everything we know about Tavira, it would be just like her to cultivate a Vader image for her henchmen, making her appear to them as the Emperor was to

Vader. All reports seem to agree that she may be smart, but she's also decidedly vain.''

I nodded. ''Interesting information. Thanks. So, where do you want to eat?''

She slapped a hand playfully against my belly. ''We should find a place to fatten you up. You've lost weight.''

''I've been in training. It's been almost two weeks since I decided to join the Jedi academy and took my leave from the squadron.'' I tossed my towel on a chair, not really caring that the cleaning droid would notify Whistler and he'd scold me for it. ''You remember how the Corellian Security Force academy training went, and I got through that when I was a kid. Physical training at dawn, long runs, classes, more runs, exercises, standing watch. We're going to have all that and more in the Jedi academy.''

Iella smiled. ''You will be the elite of the elite. Think you're up to it?''

''I hope so. I'm Master Skywalker's age and probably in as good physical shape as he is, but I'll bet he's going to be bringing in a bunch of kids. I'll really have to push myself. Gotta do it, though, because Mirax is counting on me.''

''You'll do fine, Corran. Or should I call you Keiran?''

''Corran will do.''

''Okay. How do you feel about eating Ithorian?''

I wrinkled my nose. ''Food's good, but I want something with a bit more animal protein.''

''There's a new Twi'lek place that opened up a couple of sectors down and away from here.''

''Car'ulorn's *Kavsrach*?''

She nodded. "I think that's the place. I heard they do something special with mynock."

"If I'm eating mynock, it will have to be very special." I winked at her. "Nawara said the food was good there, so it looks like that's a go. Let me pull on some real clothes and we're out of here."

While I changed Iella consulted the Imperial City directory and discovered the restaurant was actually closer than either one of us thought it was. We decided to walk there and slipped into the easy gait we'd used when walking patrol duty together back on Corellia. A lot of years seemed to melt away as she pointed out the things she knew I'd find amusing and I did the same for her.

I elbowed her gently in the ribs. "You ever figure we'd end up on Coruscant back when we were partners?"

Her eyes narrowed for a moment, then she shrugged. "Maybe on vacation, though I can think of hundreds of worlds where I'd rather go. Diric always wanted to come here, to see the hub of the galaxy. Back then I thought of it as too urban."

"And now?"

"Once you get here you find out that it's not all one big city, but it has neighborhoods and little city-states. It's not just one big uniform block of grey." She shot me a sly grin. "I'd still like to head out to some place like Alakatha."

I stopped abruptly as two small Rodian children went racing past me, and leaned heavily on Iella for support. "You might ask General Cracken to send you there to check out how Riizolo picked his target."

"Thought of that, but I'd have to haul that piece of

pirate Huttpuss along with me, so I don't think it's an assignment I want."

I smiled. "Talk to Wedge. He could use a vacation."

"There's an idea." Iella slipped ahead of me as the walkway we were on became more crowded. She slipped past a knot of Whiphids, then pointed at a small ball of lurid red light a couple of levels down. "That's the place."

We hurried on over and down. Car'ulorn's *Kavsrach* had quite a crowd in it already, and most of them Twi'leks. We took this as a good sign, even though we found it somewhat unsettling as we were led on a twisting path to a small table back near the kitchen. Because Twi'leks use the twitches and shakes of their braintails— more properly, *lekku*—the way humans use their hands to emphasize things they say, the whole room was alive with serpentine writhings.

I looked over at Iella through the holographic projection of the menu. "Remind me, I don't want anything with noodles."

She laughed and pointed to an item three down from the top. "Mynock Coronet City. A spicy combination of marinated mynock strips with *vweilu* nuts and Ithorian *chale*, in a lum sauce."

"Sounds good, but the roast gornt sounds better to me." I smiled at her. "Reminds me of a joke I heard from Wedge the other day."

"Not the Bothan and a gornt in a cantina?"

"You've heard it? You talked to Wedge?"

"There are about a billion Bothan and gornt jokes, Corran, and I've probably heard them all. Tend to be rather popular in Intel." Iella glanced down at the table. "But, no, I've not spoken to Wedge."

Our server came and took our order. She told us we'd

made good choices, but the quick shiver running down one of her lekku suggested to me she'd rather drink rancor spit than have the roast gornt. I refused to let that intimidate me. "And a little extra of the gravy on that, please."

As she whirled away, I fixed Iella with a stare. "What's going on between you two? You both seem to like each other and get along well."

Iella frowned and picked at a thumbnail, which I recognized as a sign of her not being certain how to answer me. "I wish I knew. We definitely hit it off and he was very understanding when Diric returned and very supportive after Diric died. You know what our duties have been like, so there hasn't been that much time to get together. And now he has new responsibilities that take up even more of his time."

"Yeah, but you could convince him to make time."

"I'd like to think so. I don't know." She sat back and shrugged. "You remember back when Inspector Sassich made CorSec chief? She was all of forty at the time, a great accomplishment."

I thought back. "She ditched her husband, bought that *chirq* red ZRX-29 airspeeder and started taking personal training lessons from those twins about half her age. I remember that."

"You just wish you were one of the twins."

"No, at that point I just wished I could borrow the airspeeder." I laughed. "I seem to recall my mother had a few choice things to say about her."

Iella frowned. "Your mother actually said something critical of someone?"

"I didn't say that. As I recall my mother commented that the Incom ZX-26 would have been a more practical vehicle." I shrugged. "That's about as critical as she got. She always thought gossip was in such poor taste. However, your point about Wedge is what?''

''I think he's in that same sort of transitional phase of his life. For better than a decade he's been responsible for the life-and-death decisions that have cost a lot of people their lives. That's not saying someone else wouldn't have caused more people to die by making worse decisions—that's pretty much a given—but he's been going like that since before you joined CorSec. He's, what, two years older than you? That means he's had a lot of pressure since a time when you were still a kid. Given the death of his parents and his trying to make a living shipping . . .''

''And his time spent with Booster Terrik . . .''

''. . . right, he's never had a chance to cut loose and be himself. I think that's what he's doing and I'm not certain he wants that many reminders of his previous life around right now.''

Her analysis of Wedge's situation seemed to hit pretty well dead on, but she'd always been a good judge of character. ''So that means you're just going to back off?''

She nodded, then smiled at our server as the Twi'lek female placed our meals in front of us. ''That smells wonderful. Thank you.''

I glanced down at a bowl filled with gravy. A lump floated to the surface and a couple of bubbles thinned from brown to khaki, then burst. ''And the thing is, I'm pretty sure this will be lots better than the academy food.''

The server gave me an ''I told you so'' twitch of a lek and wandered off.

Iella popped a forkful of her mynock into her mouth, closed her eyes and sighed. ''This is really very good.''

The aroma of her meal wafted over my way, starting my mouth watering. To curb that behavior, I poked my fork at a lump of what I hoped was gornt, but it just sank away out of sight. "I'm so happy for you, Iella." A growl from my stomach underscored my sarcastic remark.

She leaned forward and whispered conspiratorially to me. "It's your own fault. Twi'leks consider gornt to be tourist food. You might as well walk into a cantina and order nerfmilk."

"Hey, I'd order it straight up."

She laughed and I realized I was going to miss that sound. "If I didn't feel I had to go to the academy, if I didn't feel my father wanted me to go, I don't think I would."

"Yes, you would, Corran." She shook her head at me. "Once you heard about the academy you would have been going—even *if* Mirax wasn't missing."

"What do you mean?" I manfully speared a chunk of gornt and tucked it into my cheek. "How can you say that?"

"I was your partner, remember? You're very competitive, which can be cute and endearing at times, as long as someone stays out of your way. You want to know why you were the first person ever to escape from Isard's *Lusankya* prison? Because there was no way you were going to let her beat you."

"What's that got to do with the academy?"

"You've always wanted to be the best, and becoming a Jedi Knight will be that for you. Look at yourself. You're already beginning training before you begin training. You've figured out that Master Skywalker will be bringing in folks who are younger than you are, and you're already figuring out how to be better than they are.''

I chewed on the gornt and thought. And chewed some more. Actually I was finding acknowledging the truth in Iella's words about as tough as the gornt I was chewing, and swallowing either would hurt. Despite the impending discomfort, I knew she was right. I swallowed the gornt, then coughed lightly and nodded to her.

She reached out and tapped a finger against my forehead. ''The one thing you haven't figured out yet is that the person you're really in competition with is yourself. Luke Skywalker will be a tough taskmaster. Of that I have no doubt. And I know Wedge was, but they weren't as hard on you as you'll be on yourself. I know you well enough to know you won't back off, so I just hope you remember that when you feel all that pressure on you, the majority is coming from right inside your thinkbox.''

I thumped a fist against my breastbone to help the gornt go down. ''You know, you could have told me this a long time ago.''

''I did. Several times. You weren't much into listening back then.''

I glanced down. ''Back when my father died.''

''Right.'' Her voice softened. ''You can learn a lot from Luke Skywalker. It may be part of being a Jedi, but he seems to work a lot from his heart, following his feelings. You work primarily in your brain. Thinking all the time is definitely you, Corran, and was very useful back in CorSec, but I think you'll need to open up more with this training.''

I nodded slowly. ''You're probably right. I guess we'll see how long it takes for old habits to die.''

Iella rolled her eyes. ''That means you'll be a Jedi, what, about the time the sun goes nova?''

"I get your point."

"Good." She gave me a wink. "Want to try some of this mynock?"

I looked back up and shook my head. "Nope. I laid in my course, now I'll fly it. This gornt isn't bad once you get past the tasting, chewing and choking part."

"Yeah, tell me that in half an hour."

That prospect began to sour my stomach. I sighed. "Look, Iella, I appreciate what you've just said, and just knowing you were here and would have helped me out with Mirax's disappearance, that was enough to help me keep going. I want you to know that."

Her brown eyes studied my face for a moment. "I believe you."

"And I want you to know I really do value your help. With the dye and with those rumors." I forced my fork into a smaller piece of gornt. "I have a question that you can probably answer more easily than anyone else."

"Go ahead."

"I've talked to everyone about my decision except for my grandfather. What are the chances, do you think, of my being able to slip onto Corellia, seeing him, and getting back out?"

She thought for a moment, then set her fork down. "I don't think anyone in the Diktat's regime is watching Rostek, so seeing him wouldn't be a problem. You still *do* have the murder warrants out for your arrest, however. Kirtan Loor's legacy could still cause you trouble if you were to be identified and apprehended. As for getting in and out, the current government really isn't much better than any other Corellian regime at keeping smugglers out. With what you know about the system, you could manage to get in. The real problem is that with the relationship between the Corellian government and the

New Republic being something less than a happy one, I wouldn't want to get caught on Corellia if I were you."

"I see. I get the impression that the last hologram I sent my grandfather was chopped to bits before he got it. Even reading between the lines of what little of his return message got back to me, I know he didn't track a lot of what I said to him." The new piece of gornt I started working on kind of forestalled further speech, so I just shrugged.

"If you want, Corran, I'll see about finding you a secure communications route in to Rostek. Shouldn't tax our resources that much. That way you won't make a run and risk getting caught before you have a chance to train."

I nodded, then chanced a swallow. "I appreciate it."

"I don't mind keeping you out of trouble. That's what friends do for friends."

"Thanks." I smiled up at our server as she asked if everything was to our liking. "Oh yes, quite."

Both her lekku shuddered. "And you would like a confection to finish the meal?"

I smiled, then winked at Iella. "We would. And my friend will order for us. That's what friends do for friends."

EIGHT

✳

With Ooryl in the co-pilot's seat beside me, I flicked on the *Lambda*-class shuttle's descent warning indicators, then angled the ship into the atmosphere of Yavin 4's jungle moon. We were coming in on the night side of the moon—its rotation had it facing away from the star at the center of the system—but it faced the day side of the gas giant around which it orbited. This meant we had a fair amount of reflected orange light by which to make our approach.

I looked over at the Gand and smiled. "I appreciate your letting me drive this thing down."

Ooryl's mouth parts opened. "I understand you will not be flying while you are here."

"Yeah, Whistler is not happy about being left behind on Coruscant, but Master Skywalker wants to minimize the distractions here. It makes sense, and I'll be far too busy to be taking flights. And Whistler should have plenty to do reviewing all reports on the Invids and pulling a criminal activities analysis for me."

"I will see to it that Whistler is taken care of."

"Thanks." The controls bucked a bit beneath my hands as we hit some turbulence coming down through the atmosphere. The jungle moon had fairly humid air which, if the documents I'd read were accurate, remained fairly stable except in the transition from day to night and vice versa, when cooling and warming took effect. I maintained control as we dropped down through a thin canopy of clouds.

Luke Skywalker appeared between us and pointed dead ahead. "There it is. Bring us down on this side."

"As ordered." I glanced over at him. "You want to strap in, sir?"

"As smooth a ride as you're giving us?" He patted my shoulder. "I will if it will make you feel better."

"No reason to have more variables in play than I really need." I cut the throttle back and began to boost the power on the repulsorlift coils. "Stand by to retract wings on my mark, and lower landing gear."

Ooryl leaned forward, his fingers poised to flip the appropriate switches. "As ordered."

I watched the altimeter slowly scroll down and pulled the shuttle's nose up in a slightly better glide path. The jungle's thick foliage looked like mottled carpeting, with the occasional giant tree spiking upward. Further on the Great Temple, a squared off, pyramidal stone structure, loomed like an alien creature amid the greenery. I'd seen images of that structure for years—first in Imperial newsholos and later in every history of the victorious Rebellion ever made. It had looked impressive in the holograms, but never real and certainly not this majestic.

"Mark." As Ooryl snapped the wing switches in the up position, I throttled back to ten percent of power and boosted the engine feed to the repulsorlift coils. The shuttle flew on easily and just missed clipping some trees as we came down in the clearing on the east side of the Temple. There, at the base, I saw a long, low opening of sufficient height that I could have tucked the shuttle on inside, but a landing zone had been laid out well clear of that area.

And back away from it had gathered the two dozen New Republic engineers that had been present preparing the Great Temple for its new role as the home of the Jedi academy. Ooryl would take them home, leaving Master Skywalker, two other recruits and me behind. Nine more recruits would be following us, making the first class at the academy an even dozen.

I set the shuttle down without so much as a bump and shot Ooryl a wink. "Haven't lost my touch, but I'm going to miss flying."

"I am Findsman. I will help you find your skill again, Keiran." Ooryl turned his chair and bowed his head toward Luke. "Provided Master Skywalker would not object to Qrygg's doing so."

The Jedi Master gave Ooryl a broad smile. "You are welcome to hone his old skills as I hone his new ones."

"Ooryl is honored."

"Good, don't want to lose my flight certification." I flipped a switch and lowered the boarding ramp. Warm, moist air immediately jetted up into the shuttle. I hit my restraining strap release and stood. "Thanks, Ooryl. I'll see you next time you come through."

"Ooryl will be proud to have a Jedi Knight as a friend."

"And wingman."

"And wingman."

The Gand settled into the pilot's seat as I followed Luke back into the passenger compartment. Luke Skywalker was slightly taller than I was, but we had similar builds. The other two passengers towered over each of us. Brakiss stood a good fifteen centimeters taller than me, and Kam Solusar another ten centimeters above that. Brakiss had the slender build and sharp features of an aristocrat. If it weren't for the haunted look in his blue eyes, and the way they sunk back a bit in his skull, I would have taken him for some planetary noble out for a lark in taking on the training.

Kam Solusar was really Brakiss' antithesis, despite sharing his blond coloration. Kam's hair had been cut short and a bit raggedly. The strong blocky nature of his features was enhanced by the stubble on his cheeks and chin. His powerfully athletic build marked him as the physically strongest of us, and the seams on his face and leathery quality of flesh on his hands clued me in to both his age and the hardships he'd lived through.

The fact that he already wore a lightsaber also meant there was more to him than was easily apparent. I'd brought my grandfather's lightsaber with me, but I'd packed it in the small satchel loaded in the cargo bay. I didn't feel inclined to wear it yet, despite Master Skywalker's insistence that I had every right to do so. Until I had more training it was little more than a tool and I felt it deserved to be more.

We grabbed our bags from the pile of supplies the engineers had unloaded, then Luke led us away to the area where the engineers had awaited our arrival. I waved to Ooryl as the boarding ramp retracted and the shuttle took off again. Ooryl piloted the shuttle out in a grand circle around the Great Temple, then shot off around to the moon's day side, vanishing from sight as if swallowed by the forests.

Luke let his black cloak slip back from his shoulders as he opened his arms. "Welcome to Yavin 4. This will be your new home. I wanted the three of you to be the first students here because all three of you have a greater understanding of what we will be doing here. Your foundation means you will progress more quickly, therefore I may ask you to perform extra duties, like helping other students.''

He nodded toward Kam. ''Kam's father, Ranik Solusar, was a great Jedi Master. Kam studied under him, became a Jedi Knight, then was co-opted by the Empire. He became one of the Emperor's dark-side warriors, but has rejected the dark side.''

Muscles bunched at the corners of Kam's jaws. ''Master Skywalker was able to touch the foundation my father had laid down in me. I now serve him.''

Luke pointed a hand toward the other man. ''Brakiss here was discovered by the Empire to be Force-sensitive. They trained him to use his abilities, using him largely as a spy. They held the threat of destroying his family over his head to make him comply with their wishes. He is here to learn how to use his abilities for the benefit of other living creatures.''

Brakiss gave us a weak smile but offered no comment.

Luke shifted his attention to me. ''Keiran Halcyon's grandfather was a Jedi who died in the Clone Wars. Keiran's family has a strong Jedi tradition and he is here to reclaim it. As you have seen, he is also a skilled pilot and has had training that I think will be useful as we go along.''

Kam offered me his hand, so I shook it, and Brakiss and I exchanged nods.

Master Skywalker started walking toward the Grand Temple. ''There are five levels to the structure here—six if you want to count the observation level at the top. The lowest level, the one beneath the ground floor, was something the Rebellion put in for storage and servicing of our fighters. The main floor houses the flight operations area, as well as some living quarters. The two levels above that were used by the Rebellion as the base command center and the combat operations center. These levels are most of what we will use, but they only have some basic computer, training and library facilities. Their value comes to us from student housing and what will serve us for a meal hall. The highest level here is the Grand Chamber, which I had left alone.''

He smiled carefully. "I thought I would allow you to choose your own quarters and get some rest. We can continue orientation tomorrow.''

I raised a hand. "I have a few questions, if you don't mind.''

"Certainly.''

"Are we going to be using Coordinated Galactic Time here or are we going to just work with Yavin's normal day? The moon's rotation is slightly faster than that of Coruscant, so keeping on the galactic scale will put us out of sync with the planet.''

The Jedi Master hesitated for a moment, his blue eyes reflecting the sky's orange highlights. "With your training, time will very much become subjective. I will teach you Jedi refreshing techniques, so your need for sleep will change. Worrying about time might create pressure on the students. I don't want that.''

I frowned. "But if we don't have a coordinated sense of time here, how will we know when our watches begin or end?''

Luke regarded me quizzically. "Why would we need to stand watch?''

I wanted to answer that if someone like Thrawn wanted to show up with an Imperial fleet to raze the planet, warning would be a good thing. Of course, all the warning in the world about a fleet coming to attack would be useless since we didn't have any ships here to let us evacuate. There was, then, absolutely no practical reason to have folks stand watch, so I fell back on the reasons given for such things at the CorSec Academy.

"Standing watch provides us with a sense of responsibility and fosters trust between the students, since we are looking out for each other."

Luke nodded. "This is good, but here I want you to come to trust the Force. You will find, as your understanding and skill grow, that the Force will provide us all the warning we need if there is a threat. We will know it and have ample time to react to it."

Which seems to describe how the Invids avoid all the traps we set for them. A chill breeze seemed to cut at my spine. *Is it possible for someone sufficiently versed in the Force to hide his presence from detection?*

"I stand corrected, Master." I bowed my head toward him. "Then will we just get up at dawn to begin physical training?"

He opened his hands. "You may do whatever you feel necessary to make yourself feel at ease and receptive to the Force."

"So there will be no organized physical training?"

Kam laughed gruffly. "You sound disappointed, Keiran."

"Not really, just confused."

Luke smiled. "You will find your training demanding enough, I think, and quite exhausting."

I pointed toward Kam's lightsaber. "We will, at least, have combat training, correct?"

"Yes, you will be trained in the ways of the lightsaber."

"Not the question I asked."

Luke's head came up. "You had better explain, then."

I pressed my fingertips together. "The lightsaber, as all of us know, is a very powerful and lethal weapon. My father once said to me that no one ever regretted hitting a target with a stunbolt as opposed to a lethal shot from a blaster. Basic combat training could help us avoid having to use a lightsaber where a less dangerous method might work. Training in that area means we will have more options available to us."

The Jedi Master narrowed his eyes. "These would be defensive techniques?"

"They are combat techniques, which can be employed offensively or defensively, just like a lightsaber." I shrugged. "It's just an idea."

Kam nodded. "Such training would lay the foundation for any lightsaber training we do later."

"Okay, Kam and Keiran, you will come up with a plan for that type of training. We will discuss it further when you have something." Luke regarded me with the hint of a smile on his lips. "Anything else?"

"No, Master."

"If you think of something, let me know." He waved us on toward the Temple. "Now find yourselves quarters."

The trio of us left him behind and did not speak as we approached the Great Temple. Having lived on Coruscant, I had seen much more massive buildings, but little there had the antiquity and sense of stability that I found in the Temple. It did not strike me as odd that a building which had been old millennia before the Empire came into existence had sheltered a movement that overthrew that Empire. I could easily imagine the dignity of this building being offended by the city world that had been

Imperial Center and doing what it could to contribute to the Empire's destruction.

Why the Empire had not flattened the place after the Rebellion abandoned it was a puzzle I figured could never be solved.

Generators and lights left behind by the engineers brightened the large hangar area. Aside from stockpiled supplies, the room stood empty, but echoes of the urgency the Rebels had felt the day they flew off to destroy the Death Star still reached me. The fear, the panic, and the giddy confidence in their cause still permeated the walls. For the first time in all the time I'd been associated with Rogue Squadron, I could feel what Wedge and Biggs and Luke had felt when they faced the Death Star. Their emotions set off resonances inside me, bringing up memories of the last mission to Blackmoon and the final assault against Isard's forces at Thyferra.

For the first time I actually felt the connection the new Rogues had to the heroes who had gone before.

I'm not certain at which point I veered off from Kam and Brakiss, but it was before they headed to the upper levels. I found myself alone on the ground level and in a small chamber built into the structure of the Temple itself. The engineers had set it up with a pair of cots and some lockers for gear, with blankets and sheets piled at the foot of the bed. I tossed my satchel on the bed and smiled. I couldn't place why the room felt familiar or right, but it did.

"I thought I might find you here."

I turned and saw Luke standing in the doorway. "Am I not supposed to be here?"

Luke held his hands up. "This room is perfect for you, believe me. It's certainly better for you than any of those in the upper levels." He gestured easily and one of the lockers slid silently fifty centimeters to the left. "Look down there, at the block three up from the floor.

I walked over and crouched down. Mildew and some lichen had grown over that block, creeping up from the ground, but I easily managed to brush it away. Sunk into the stone were letters and I smiled as I read aloud. "The Empire or Us—there is no compromise. Biggs Darklighter, Wedge Antilles, Jek Porkins."

A boyish grin tugged at the corner of Luke's mouth. "Back then the three of them bunked in here—I came late and had the room up above. We met here and swapped stories before we headed out—we were too excited to sleep. We all thought we would survive, despite the odds. I think their inscription was a hedge against death for them. If they didn't survive, if the whole Rebellion died, at least there would be a record of their names."

"But your success has guaranteed everyone knows those names, and yours as well. What you did here changed the course of life for billions."

Luke lowered his hands and his cloak enfolded him in shadow. "What we will do *here*, now, will change the lives of billions."

I straightened up and turned back toward him. "I want to apologize for my questions. You're a Jedi Master and I'm here to learn. I did not mean to show you any disrespect."

"No offense taken. Your questions were valid, but you based them on a life lived without the touch of the Force." His grin broadened somewhat. "My Master, Yoda, thought me impatient and impossible to train. You fare much better in that regard. You do tend, by nature, to think too much and to be suspicious. This could be a problem. Suspicion raises walls, allows fear to grow. That can interfere with your ability to use the Force."

I nodded. "Then, at the risk of making you worried about me even more, I need to ask you another question."

"Please."

"You mentioned that both Kam and Brakiss have experiences connected with the dark side. You didn't bring the three of us in together with the intent of having me watch over them, did you?"

Luke adamantly shook his head. "Not at all." His eyes hooded themselves in shadow, yet pinpoints of light seemed to sparkle at their centers. "During the time of the Emperor's return, I, too, went over to the dark side. I did so for a variety of reasons, some of which seemed to make sense at the time, and many of which still cause me difficulty. What I experienced then has given me an understanding of the dark side which is vital to fight it. More importantly, the love of my sister and my friends drew me back. It redeemed me. Even the most foul victim of the dark side can be redeemed. By turning their backs on evil, Brakiss and Kam have already begun their journey into the light. I want to help them complete that journey.

"Don't be so suspicious. Don't think, *feel*. Your task is not to watch over them, but to learn from them." Luke's voice began to harden and his words thundered through me. "You will find, at some point, that the dark side will speak to you. It is seductive, offering you everything with little effort on your part. Learn from the lessons the others have endured, so their strength can become *your* strength when you face this test."

I nodded slowly. "I understand."

The Jedi Master's face brightened. "Good. Sleep well, Keiran Halcyon. What you will face in the future might not seem as difficult as destroying a Death Star, but I assure you that it is easily just as important."

NINE

✳

Within a week the rest of the Jedi candidates had reached the academy, filling the Great Temple with the life and color and laughter I guessed it had not known since the celebration following the Death Star's destruction. Still, that celebration had to be tinged with sadness at the loss of so many comrades, whereas we were looking forward to the future and that made us much happier.

Master Skywalker allowed each of us to approach our training on an individual basis. While there were group exercises and organized teaching sessions, we all had a fair amount of latitude in what we did. I missed the sense of camaraderie I'd established with other trainees at the CorSec Academy; but we all knew here that we were pioneers and vital to the future of the New Republic. That put a significant amount of pressure on us to succeed, and a harder, tougher training program could easily have ended up pitting us against each other.

And some of that happened naturally anyway. Because I took to heart Luke's suggestion that he wanted each of us to be comfortable with ourselves and our efforts, I would get up at dawn and go for runs along trails within the rainforests. Being up that early I got a chance to see what I dubbed Prisma storms. When the moon traveled behind the gas giant and spent time in its shadow, the nights would get very cold. Water crystals would form in the upper atmosphere and as the moon came out from behind the gas giant, the sunlight would be shattered by millions of prisms. The light danced and sparked through the atmosphere, crackling along like varicolored lightning. The first time I saw it I thought a fleet had showed up in orbit and had started fighting with another fleet. I quickly saw it was nothing to worry about and learned to look forward to seeing it.

I shared the news of it with the others, of course, and some of them dragged themselves out of warm bunks to watch the storm's brilliant display. They stood there looking skyward while I stretched out and prepared for my run. As I started off and turned to toss a quick wave to them, I noticed that one of them was more intent on watching me than the storm.

Gantoris.

I think I knew that personality conflicts would be inevitable, but with our unity of purpose I was hoping they would be trivial. A tall, broad-faced man who wore his long black hair woven into a braid, Gantoris had been something of a head man in his community. His abilities in the Force helped his people survive and he had all the earmarks of being a leader. He carried himself as one and had a healthy ego. He was not used to being second to anyone in anything, and I think he decided I did all the extra training I did to curry favor with Master Skywalker.

In truth, I was doing the extra physical training because I was just stubborn. I had decided before I arrived here that I needed to get into shape to be able to do well, and if I didn't continue, I'd have to acknowledge that I'd been in error. Gantoris was not the only person present with a healthy ego, and mine wasn't inclined to take any shots by having me admit I was wrong.

I did my best to ignore the hard glance Gantoris had shot me and just tried to enjoy the run. The rainforest and humidity made doing just that very difficult. Despite small herds of runyips coursing their way along these paths often enough to leave a crowd of hoofprints, the local vegetation seemed determined to reclaim the paths. If it wasn't knobby tree roots trying to trip me, the woody, skeletal roots of nebula orchids clawed at my face. The orchids were eye-catching in another sense— I'd never seen flowers that had such swirls of color in them. Part of me wondered what other patterns someone like Ooryl, who could see in the ultraviolet range, would discover in their blossoms.

The humidity dragged at me the most and my clothes would become soaked with sweat within the first kilometer and a half. My run took me out and around past the Temple of the Blueleaf Cluster. With such a name you would expect it to be surrounded with the blueleaf shrubs that tended to encroach on most other clearings, but this was not true. The name came from the leaf patterns carved onto the surface and around the doors of this smaller temple. I'd not yet been inside, but Master Skywalker had mentioned it contained a blue crystal that pulsed with power. He said he had no clue as to its origin or purpose, leaving me a mystery to solve in my spare time—if we ever had any.

The main hazard in running through the forest came from some of the creatures living there. Running into a swarm of piranha-beetles would put an end to my career as a Jedi fairly quickly. The blue bugs could strip flesh off bone faster than Jawas took to dismantle an airspeeder. Fortunately the beetles tended to move through the upper reaches of the forests, and most creatures cleared out of their path with a maximum of hooting, hollering and other useful warning sounds.

Woolamanders with their blue and gold fur moved in packs through the forest and seemed to take great delight showering passing targets with leaves, sticks, fruit and anything else that comes easily to paw, like the occasional tree-tick. I learned not to like woolamanders pretty early on, and found myself cheering silently for the prowling stintarils stalking through the trees like an army on a search and destroy mission. The rodents had enough teeth and powerful enough jaws to take healthy bites out of the bigger woolamanders. While I didn't want a host of stintarils to move into the Great Temple, I was happy to see them flocking in the direction of any woolamander pack that decided to harass me.

The thing I enjoyed most about the runs was that it gave me something to do that was distinctly mine and for me. That sounds selfish, but Luke had begun to stress that each of us would find that we had talents in certain areas of the Force—talents that no one else might share, in fact. Their discovery would be just a small part of our self-discovery and growth as a Jedi. The runs gave me something to bridge my past life with my new one, and they also provided me a chance to think about what I was learning and where I wanted to direct my efforts in the future.

Running was good for me, no matter what Gantoris or anyone else thought of my efforts.

Kam and I had come up with a plan for teaching some basic combat skills to the other recruits, and Master Skywalker approved our plans with a few slight modifi-

cations. We took the others through the standard procedures, walking them through drills at slow speeds, then
working along faster and faster until their reflexes sharpened and responses to attacks came automatically. Into
this whole mix Luke injected the Force, asking us to feel
our opponents through the Force and monitor what was
happening to them.

In the walk-throughs I had a great deal of trouble
doing what he asked. I remember squaring off with
Tionne, the slender, silver-haired woman who was more
scholar and singer than she ever would be a warrior.
Still, her enthusiasm for becoming a Jedi, and her ready
laugh, made her a good student and a better comrade.
She came at me, her hands held high as if she meant to
batter me down with overhand blows. I sensed her approach and could feel subtle shifts in her balance as she
came in, but what I felt had little significance to me,
since it was very easy to turn into the direction of her
attack and use her momentum to toss her over my hip.

Which was exactly what she and I knew would happen the second the exercise began.

As Kam began to layer in lessons about fighting with
a lightsaber, sensing my opponent became more important. My ability in that area began to grow, but I didn't
trust it enough to abandon myself to it. Though we
sparred with padded wooden practice swords, I treated
each cut or slash as if it were from a true lightsaber. Very
defensive, I relied upon the basics that Kam taught and
found they stood me in good stead close to ninety percent of the time.

In that other ten percent, Gantoris inflicted some
nasty bruises on me.

Kam's instruction can't be faulted at all in this regard
because he taught us well the three rings of defense. The

outermost ring consisted of four guard positions: upper right, upper left, lower right and lower left. The lightsaber's hilt would end up wide of the body, with the tip coming back toward the middle to pick up the grand sweeping blows that are very powerful, but also take longer to deliver.

The middle ring also involved four guard positions: high, low, left and right. Whereas in the outer ring the blade tended to be held at a diagonal, in the middle ring up and down were parallel to the ground at head and knee height, while left and right were perpendicular to it. The idea with the middle ring was to pick up quicker blows and stop them before they could intersect with the body. Luke also noted that the middle ring was effective against picking off blaster bolts.

The inner ring involved parries instead of blocks and was proof against lunging attacks. For this third line of defense, the lightsaber was kept in close, with the hilt covering the navel. By angling the blade's tip and picking up attacks on the lower third of the blade, attacks could be shunted aside, and a riposte to the opponent's chest or stomach became a very real possibility. The inner ring was the last line of defense, dangerous to be defending from, and dangerous to be attacking from.

That afternoon saw me pitted against Gantoris in a basic sparring match. Because he was taller than me, he had something of a power and reach advantage. My only salvation would be quickness *and* the years I'd spent involved in rough and tumble battles as a CorSec officer. It also helped that, because of my CorSec experience, I knew I could beat someone as big as he was; whereas I doubted Gantoris ever had found himself in a real fight with someone like me.

We bowed to each other as we entered the circle de-

scribed by our panting and sweating comrades. I turned
to my right and saluted Master Skywalker, and then to
my left and saluted Kam. Kam raised his right hand, then
lowered it quickly and shouted, ''Begin.''

Expecting a charge, I took a step back. Gantoris' eyes
blazed with triumph as if this concession of a meter's
worth of territory was somehow a great victory. He gave
me a cold smile, then slowly began to pace forward,
much like a stintaril stalking a tree-tick. He kept his feet
shoulder width apart as he came in, and his knees bent,
but I knew the attack wasn't going to be coming until he
rose on the balls of his feet and set himself to strike.

My sense that he was going to do just that came nanoseconds before I saw him gather himself for the attack. I
almost lost the impression in the violence of his attack,
but I'd begun to react to the Force-sense before the attack came in. My blade rose up to the upper right guard
while I slipped to the left. I picked up his attack and
knocked it aside so quickly that I surprised myself. Because I had moved out of the line of his attack and was
already drifting past his left flank, with a flip of my
wrists I could have brought the wooden blade down and
across his stomach, but I didn't. Instead, trying to cling
to the warning I'd been given, I danced past him and set
myself for a new attack.

Another one came hard and fast. Gantoris' blade
came up, around and down in a crowning blow that
would have split me from skull to navel. I snapped my
blade up into the high guard, bracing myself to pick up
the blow, but it never landed. Proving himself far quicker
than I expected, Gantoris whipped the wooden practice
sword around in his left hand and slapped it across my
right shin.

Despite the padding on the blade, the blow hurt a

great deal. As pain jolted its way up my leg, I tried to remember some of the Jedi techniques for shunting aside pain that we'd been taught, but being in the middle of a fight wasn't the most conducive circumstance for meditative arts. As I reeled away, Gantoris slashed at me again, catching me across the back of my thighs, making me yelp aloud.

My face burned with shame. Here I was, someone who was helping instruct the others in self-defense, and Gantoris was slashing at me with impunity. He had me hurt and I was all turned around and vulnerable. My self-image imploded as I read the shock and horror and comical smiles on my friends' faces. In their minds I was victim and clown, and those two images succeeded in grinding the image I'd held of myself as Keiran Halcyon, Jedi Hero, into little tiny bits.

Then I got the very clear impression that the next blow would land on my right ear and do all it could to drive it into my brain. Without conscious thought, I dove forward on my belly, then scissored my legs and rolled over onto my back. My legs tangled themselves up with Gantoris' legs and twisted the larger man to the ground. I brought my own stick around and smacked him across the buttocks, then kicked his legs free of mine.

Gantoris got up, his eyes narrowed, while I just sat on the ground and drew my knees up to my chin. I resisted the urge to rub my shin and forced myself to think past the pain about what had just happened. At that moment when I had been the most vulnerable, when I had been beaten, I had known what he was going to do and I had been able to react to it.

What surprised me was that my access to the Force had come at a point when I had been forced to abandon the image I had been trying to present to the others.

Once I got past pretense and had just been what I was, the Force flowed more freely. It was as if the role I had created for myself had inhibited the flow, whereas abandoning the role brought me closer to it.

Perhaps it is not for me to sculpt the Force's flow to my purposes, but for me to be sculpted into that which more easily works with the Force.

Gantoris pointed his practice sword at me. "Let us go again."

I tossed my wooden blade aside. "I'm ready. Come on."

"Take up your blade, Keiran."

I shook my head. "Whenever you want, I'm here."

Gantoris looked over at the Jedi Master. "Tell him to defend himself, Master Skywalker."

Luke's blue-eyed gaze flicked between Gantoris and me, and then back again. "It appears he is content with his defensive posture, Gantoris."

The taller man pulled his chin up. "It is dishonorable for me to strike someone who is defenseless."

Luke smiled. "Then, if you will not strike, he has won. Won without striking a blow. That is a lesson for you to learn, Gantoris."

"Yes, Master."

Luke gestured to my sword and it floated back over to me. "That, however, is not the lesson Keiran needs to learn. If you will, Keiran, defend yourself."

I plucked the sword out of the air and stood. I started to smile and offer a challenge to Gantoris, but I realized that would just be helping rebuild the illusion that choked off my access to the Force. I set myself and offered Gantoris a quick salute. "Whenever you want to start."

He approached cautiously, but as I watched him, bits

and pieces of my visual perspective shifted. I saw a second and third image of him arise, with each of them moving to the right or the left, with arms coming up or around and only when his true form rose up to match it would I know where his attack was coming from. I realized the images I was seeing were a sense of his thought processes, a reflection of strategies weighed and rejected. When he made his choice, I'd already seen it and could sidestep it with ease.

Over the next ten minutes we continued to spar. My reading of his intention was far from foolproof, and I had the bruises to prove it. I did notice a pattern: after four or five successful evasions I would become confident and even cocky, which is when the sense would fail me and I'd pay an agonizing price for my arrogance. By keeping myself calm and focused, by letting my senses project themselves beyond my mortal shell, I could *feel* Gantoris as well as see and hear and smell him. In the end I evaded him for a full minute with only the breeze from his blade hitting me.

His chest heaving and sweat staining his khaki robes, Gantoris leaned heavily forward on his sword. "This dodging and evading works well against sticks, but it will not protect you against a lightsaber."

Feeling similarly drained, I sat down on the grasses. "I don't expect to face many foes wielding lightsabers."

Gantoris' eyes sharpened. "But someday that will happen. When it does, beware."

Luke entered the circle and dropped to one knee between the two of us. "When that day comes, your progress in the Force will mean you'll have other, better tools to use in defense. Remember, today you are in your infancy in the Force. The lessons learned here are but the beginning."

TEN

✳

If we were in our infancy in the Force, I was not proving myself to be a boy genius. The warnings I had been able to use, the dim sense of others grew slightly, then plateaued. If I was concentrating or if I wasn't thinking at all, I might notice someone approaching the doorway of my room. This definitely was an improvement over the split-second warnings I sometimes got when flying or back with CorSec, but not the sort of practical application of an ability that would allow me to find Mirax. Measured against that goal, my progress seemed far too little, far too late.

That's not to say I found the training disappointing. I didn't, not at all. In fact, I found in it a great deal about myself that surprised me. I didn't notice new talents or new sides of myself, but I recovered things I had long forgotten.

Master Skywalker took all of us through a series of exercises he said he'd learned from his teachers, Obi-Wan Kenobi and Yoda. The exercises were typically little things that seemed, on the surface, to be child's play. Trying some of them seemed silly, but Tionne and Kirana Ti—the green-eyed witch from Dathomir—and even the hermit gas-prospector from Bespin, Streen, all approached these things with an open wonder and humor that made being silly a lot easier for me.

Master Skywalker stood before us, having arranged us in a semicircle on the grassy clearing near the Great Temple. "This is an exercise in two parts that will build on what we learned a week ago. What I showed you then was a simple technique for shunting aside pain. Its use is obvious. That same skill also allows you to shut off sensory input. Why would you want to do that? Brakiss?"

The blond man gave Luke a smirk. "Your roommate might snore, so you could cut off your hearing to sleep."

The Jedi Master smiled. "Very good. I recall using it for that a couple of times myself. Another reason?"

Kirana Ti raised a hand. "Since we rely heavily on visual senses, a visual illusion might blind us to what is truly going on. Being able to cut down or cut out our vision would allow us to determine what is truly happening."

Gantoris frowned. "But that would leave you blind."

Kam disagreed. "You would rely upon your ability to sense things through the Force to make up for the lack. Without the visual confusion, this sense should come much more clearly."

Luke raised a hand and nodded. "Good points, all. The key here is learning to control perceptions. First you need to make certain that the data coming in is correct. Filtering out distractions, or sharpening a sense to gather more information, will let you do that. We will work on that in this exercise. The second thing we will deal with, later, is determining the truth or falsehood of what you perceive."

I scratched at the back of my neck. "Truth and falsehood seem pretty straightforward to me."

"On the surface they are fairly clear, but truth can

depend upon a certain point of view. As Obi-Wan Kenobi said to me, 'Many of the truths we cling to depend greatly on our own point of view.' " Luke smiled indulgently at me. "You would like an example to show this?"

I nodded. "I work better with duracrete than I do vapor."

"Good." Luke's blue eyes narrowed until they became chips of ice in shadowed wells. "You all know of Darth Vader as the most vile creature that ever lived. He became a symbol of the Emperor's evil. He personified evil in the minds of many, including all of you."

Luke's voice dropped to a harsh whisper, forcing us to strain to hear him. "But I tell you this, he was *good.*"

My jaw dropped open in complete disbelief. "That's some point of view."

The Jedi Master nodded. "Please understand this: there was, inside Darth Vader, the core of the man he had once been. Though wrapped in layers of evil, this man still existed. In Vader's final moments, he won out. He rejected the evil that had become his life. He rejected his master, the Emperor, and killed him."

Brakiss' head came up. "I thought *you* killed the Emperor?"

Luke shook his head. "I caused the Emperor to be destroyed by reaching out to the good in Darth Vader and making him change his heart. I was just the instrument of change that allowed Darth Vader to redeem himself."

I dimly recalled Luke having said that he had been turned back from the dark side by the love of his sister and friends. "You must have made a powerful appeal to him."

"I did. Love is a powerful tool to employ against the

dark side. My sister's love saved me.'' Luke hesitated for a moment. ''And the love of a son for his father is what saved Darth Vader.''

I would like to claim that I instantly tracked the full import of what Luke said because I had been trained as a detective to analyze confessions and figure out what people were truly saying. The fact is, however, that with his words came beams of pride and compassion and just a hint of fear that played over me like an ion blast. My flesh puckered and I suppressed a shudder when the realization that Luke Skywalker was Darth Vader's son finally exploded in my brain.

I nodded again. ''Quite a perspective there.'' Knowing how much I revered my father and his memory, I could have nothing but sympathy for Luke. I had been lucky enough to know my father, to have him guide me. Even as we worked our way through these simple exercises, I recall watching my father do some of them when I was a child. As any child will, I imitated him, and he instructed me, telling me it was our private game, and that I should reveal it to no one. He taught me nothing that, in a display of youthful enthusiasm, could have revealed my Jedi proclivities to any of the Emperor's Jedi-hunters. Even so, they formed a foundation for my current training without which I would have been utterly useless.

I had a million questions I wanted to ask him about when and where he learned about his father. I wanted to know everything to fill in the background of the familiar ''orphaned hero from a desert world'' biography we'd all heard countless times about him. The Vader revelation suddenly added depth to what we had been told. At the moment of his greatest victory, he lost the goal he sought. He redeemed his father and lost him at the same time. At least in my case, though I lost my father, I had all the good things about him to remember and cherish.

Luke looked down at the ground, almost penitent. "I have told you this to provide Keiran his example, and to lower a barrier between us. I want you to know that no decision is final. If you are to avoid the lures of the dark side, you must be constantly vigilant. If you fall to the dark side, you can be brought back. I have been re-deemed. I have been a redeemer. Now I wish to guide you so that you will never have to fall. You have the last of my secrets now. I trust you with it and look forward to when you will trust me with whatever secrets trouble you."

His head came up and his face brightened, shattering the dull mood that had settled over us. "Brooding over this will waste the day, so I want to return to the exercise. You will choose a partner and each of you will bare a forearm. You will close your eyes and use what you have been taught to block feeling to that forearm. Then each of you will take a small stone and grasp it between the thumb and forefinger of the non-numbed arm. Using your remaining senses—and concentrating on the other person's senses through the Force—you are to bring that stone as close as possible to touching the other person's flesh as you can. Once you sense the touch of the stone through the Force, gently reach up and tap your partner's arm. The goal is to come as close as possible to touching without actually doing so, and to react only when a touch is sensed, but not felt."

I partnered up with Tionne and knelt knee to knee with her. We both drew our sleeves back from our left forearms and presented them, wrists upward, to the other. Fairly easily we located small pebbles with our free hands and held them poised above the other's forearm. Giving her a brave smile, I closed my eyes and shut off the feeling to my left forearm. Then I tried to sense Tionne's presence.

To say that I stretched out with my senses is really an exaggeration. I wanted to produce a field effect, allowing my senses to spread out and encompass Tionne, but I found the effort as difficult and painful as trying to will my flesh to split so my muscles could expand outward. I took in a deep breath and let it out slowly, focusing on it to regain my concentration.

I wondered what to do for a moment, then realized I was really trying to spread myself too thin. First of all, I needed to be able to sense Tionne's arms, not her whole body and presence. Narrowing the task before me made it far more manageable, and I immediately felt a burst of self-confidence pump more energy into me. Then, following along the same lines of thought, I realized I didn't need to sense to the micron where her hand or arm was, since both were fairly large. I shifted my thinking around to a new paradigm in which I saw the hairs on my arm exuding little Force tendrils that wove themselves into a glowing mesh. When I felt a contact, I made the mesh even more fine beneath it, and added depth to it, so as her pebble approached my skin I watched it penetrating layers of my screen.

A smile blossomed on my face. The difference between contact and non-contact was just a layer, a layer defined as a micron, but a layer that was easy to perceive when I was able to focus. As her stone touched my skin and the last layer parted beneath it, I poked a finger up and tapped her elbow. That brought a little gasp from her and I smiled a bit more.

Then I shifted my concentration to my right hand. I projected similar tendrils from my fingers, forming them into a capsule that surrounded my stone. I shaped it using what I could feel of it with my fingers. The resolution at the point of my fleshy contact with it became very fine, but remained indistinct where I imagined the point of stone to be. Regardless, I lowered the stone toward her arm, and began to inject color into my sensory capsule. At the point of contact with her skin I made the capsule turn green. As the stone got closer and closer to her flesh, the color shifted to yellow. Then the final layer flashed red and I halted my movement without touching her.

Then she tapped me on the elbow.

I jerked back and my sensory capsule vanished for a moment. I reestablished it and redefined the shape of the rock. Again I made an approach and stopped before what I thought was contact, but it wasn't until the sixth time that I had managed to define the rock's shape with enough precision that I stopped before I touched her.

We continued the exercise and quick laughs and triumphant cries soon echoed from the pairs. We became almost playful in what we were doing, teasing each other. As it became more of a game, I found it easier to project my screen and push it out further. Part of me wanted to try to use it to read the contours of Tionne's face, to see when she was smiling and to see her brow knitted in concentration, but I held back.

My unwillingness to gain a greater sense of Tionne surprised me because I found myself reacting to her as if she were a danger. She certainly was beautiful and decidedly attractive, though her coloration set her outside what I'd previously seen as my ''type.'' Her physical beauty was less a danger, it occurred to me, than her very open and friendly way of dealing with everyone. If, at this stage, it was possible to identify someone who would form the heart of the group, I would have picked her. As such, if she knew who I was and my reasons for being at the academy, she would have offered me comfort.

Comfort I would relish.

Comfort that would cost me.

I wasn't worried about being seduced by her—my assumption was that Tionne had no interest in me, and I had no interest in anyone besides my wife. What worried me was accepting the sympathy she would offer. I had, since the time of my father's death, held myself closed to all but a very few good friends. With Mirax I had opened myself even more and while I could be very open with friends, joking with them and accepting their jibes; vulnerability still scared me.

In part it came with the jobs I'd had. In CorSec the last thing you want to let a criminal see is that he can get to you and can hurt you emotionally. To combat that you tend to deaden your feelings and deal with the people you meet professionally as "them." *They* are not part of your family or your organization. *They* are not as real and therefore what *they* think and say can't get to you. It is a dehumanization of people that allows for detachment; a detachment you need if you are going to survive while dealing with grand tragedies and cruelties.

Even in Rogue Squadron I fell prey to this distancing. When friends died, it hurt a lot, so I held myself back from becoming engaged with the new pilots. I didn't really even realize I was doing that until Wedge called me on it one day. He sort of smiled and told me he'd caught himself doing the same thing, but that by overcoming that natural tendency, he found he could reach out to pilots, help make them better, so he wouldn't lose them.

The sense of Tionne as a danger set itself up as another wall around my heart. I suspected it would interfere with my accessing and feeling the Force much as my inflated self-conception had previously. The fear of vulnerability was really just another aspect of my core personality. To reach my full potential as a Jedi I knew I would have to work around it or blast past it, but I didn't feel ready to decide on how I wanted to do that yet.

The sound of Luke's voice brought me out of my introspection. "Without opening your eyes or shifting away from your partner, I want you to place your pebble in the palm of your partner's hand. I want you then to reach out, to find that pebble, and use the Force to make it move. This is a big step. Up to now you have used the Force in a passive sense, to enhance your perceptions. Now you will apply the Force more directly and use its energy to make the stone move. If you can lift it clear of your partner's palm, so much the better."

I felt Tionne's stone land in my hand. "This will be fantastic, Keiran. Stories of Jedi levitating all sorts of things abound."

"I'm certain." I dropped my stone in her hand and immediately lost all sense of it. This boded ill for me. I reached down and just touched it with a finger, hoping to kindle echoes of my tactile sense of it.

Nothing.

"You touched it with your finger, Keiran."

"I know. Sorry."

I drew in a deep breath and let it out slowly. I gathered my thoughts and reconstructed my sensory screen. I projected it out and down toward her palm and mapped her hand. I could feel her flesh and how the Force flowed through her. Between us I could feel a resonance and I could even detect a dead spot in the middle of it. The stone, it had to be the stone. I smiled and bent my will to shifting the stone.

Nothing.

It did not help at all that at this moment her stone danced in my palm as if a groundquake was shaking the planet. Her sharp giggle—half shriek, half laugh—let me know that she'd sensed the rock's movement. I felt pure joy wash out from her and couldn't help but smile, even though my rock lay as still as the Great Temple's foundation stones.

I tried to push and make it move again, but got nothing.

I opened my eyes and looked up at Master Skywalker. "I think nothing's happening."

He smiled. "Don't think, *feel* it. It will happen."

I shrugged. "I'm not even moving the dust on this rock."

"You don't believe, which is why you fail." Luke opened his arms to take in the other students. As I looked around I saw that the short hops Tionne's stone had taken were insignificant compared to what others had accomplished. Worst of all, Gantoris had a halo of pebbles whirling at different speeds around his head. "You see, size matters not, numbers matter not. If you believe, you open the way for the Force to come through you."

I shook my head. "I believe, but apparently not well enough."

Gantoris' eyes opened and he stared at me past Streen's head. "You believe in failure, Keiran, which is why you fail. It is a never-ending cycle."

Luke gestured toward Gantoris and the stones he'd had orbiting his head flew up into the air. They wove themselves through an intricate pattern almost too fast for the eye to follow. It would have been all but impossible to watch, but Luke struck one stone off another, creating sparks at this point and that. Then, like a swarm of piranha-beetles on the hunt, the stones flew off and vanished into the rainforest.

"There is only one cycle that is without end, Gantoris. That cycle is life and life is what creates the Force. Success comes with feeling, understanding and controlling the Force." He smiled. "The pace may be different, but the progression is the same for all of you. Setbacks are expected. Success and failure will always be part of your training."

"Not for me." Gantoris shook his head adamantly. "I do not choose to fail."

Gantoris' declaration sent a chill down my spine. I'd heard that tone many times before, though the words had been different. "You'll never take me alive, CorSec," was how it always came out, and disaster almost always followed it. Here, at the Jedi academy, where we were learning to manipulate the energy that bound the universe together, I didn't even want to think about what sort of tragedy Gantoris' comment could spawn.

Eleven

That evening, after dinner, I found myself thinking about what Luke had said. The idea that I had to first feel the Force before I could employ it made me reevaluate what I had learned so far. Luke had also said that prior to what we tried earlier we had only been using the Force passively, to enhance our senses. This made me wonder if I had been tapping the reservoir of Force energy that my body produced. It occurred to me that each living creature generated enough of the Force to keep them aware of and in touch with the world, but to push beyond that required an expanded flow of energy.

It required tapping into the Force itself. Luke said that I had to believe, but that meant letting go of doubts. This brought me back to the realization that my doubts were part and parcel of who I was, and unless or until I could push beyond them, I would be blocked from access to the Force. I felt as if I had to sacrifice myself to be able to feel the Force and use it, and yet I did not want to do that.

Still, my little chamber reeked of sacrifice. The names sunk in the stone made it crystal clear. Porkins and Biggs had died at Yavin, sacrificing all they were and could ever be. Wedge's life had been sacrificed to the

Rebellion; his dreams deferred, his access to a life others would consider normal denied. And if I included Luke in the group, he was left with a mission to recreate an order of peacekeepers that his father had destroyed, to be able to rebuild a galaxy his father had helped take apart.

Suddenly my room became cloying and close. Here three men had vowed to put an end to the Empire or to die. Knowing less about their probable futures than I did about mine, having lived less of a life than I have lived, they made their choice; and a similar choice was asked of me. And my choice was easier, since all I needed to let go of were my preconceptions and prejudices, not my flesh and blood and brains and life.

I have to stop thinking and feel. I have to let go. I sighed aloud. *Maybe Iella was right, maybe Coruscant's sun will go nova before I can do that.*

I fled my room and quickly found myself in the turbolift to the rooftop. Our moon was slipping behind the gas giant and had turned its face away from it, so we were entering Truenight, not just Twilight night. I expected it to be cold and got a good chill blast of air when the lift door opened. I reveled in the way the breeze sucked warmth from me and hoped my thoughts could be as cold as my flesh.

I knew my fear of change was silly. Intellectually I could see my transition as that of an insect moving from one life stage to another. The creature was the same, had the same genetic code, but moved into a phase that gave it greater abilities. In my case the greater abilities would bring with them greater responsibilities. I didn't think I was afraid of them, but in the questioning mood I was in, I wasn't sure of anything about myself.

I began a slow circuit around the Temple's squared-off top and saw a figure sitting on the northeast corner. I tried to reach my senses out to see who it was, but they never got very far. He turned to face me, letting the wind tease his fluffy beard, then turned back to look out over the forest and at the black blanket of sky in which billions of stars nested.

I approached him, but hung back several paces to give him space. "I didn't think anyone else would be up here, Streen."

The old man shrugged. "I am so used to being alone that I can only stand so much in the way of company."

"I'll leave you, then."

"No, no need." Though shadows hid his face as he turned toward me again, I felt an intensity radiating out from his invisible eyes. "You hold yourself in tightly enough that your presence is not painful."

"Thanks, I think."

"Forgive me. My personal relation skills are not what they should be." He smiled as the undulating cry of hunting stintarils seemed to mock him. "For years my only companions were Bespin rawwks—large black scavengers with leathery wings. They have a rudimentary intelligence. Never taught one a useful trick, but they would come when I had food to feed them."

I smiled and sat down on the cold stone. "I've had friends I couldn't say as much about."

"Gas prospecting on Bespin was lonely work, but I didn't mind." The old man tapped his head with a finger. "Kept hearing voices in my head, feeling people's moods. Only by getting away could I shut them out. Now Master Luke's training is helping me do that consciously. Don't miss it. Puts mystery back into life."

I shot him a bemused smile. "Mystery?"

"Yeah. Like you, for example."

"Me?"

"You're very closed, but bits leak out. Pride's hot enough to melt durasteel." Streen shrugged. "And pain. Sense of judgment cuts like a lightsaber."

"Really." My expression sharpened. Streen could easily be taken for a doddering old fool, but he clearly was perceptive. Dismissing him would be doing him a disservice. "What do you mean?"

Streen chuckled. "You don't like Gantoris."

"Doesn't take Jedi skills to figure that out."

"No, guess it doesn't. He doesn't like you much, either." Streen sat back, leaning on his elbows and forearms. "Remember that exercise today?"

"With Gantoris putting rocks in orbit?"

"The same. You shouldn't be discouraged. When Master Luke and Gantoris came to Bespin to find me, they gave me a practical demonstration of how the Force can be used. Gantoris learned to *push* with his mind to make something move a ways away."

My head came up. "I see." Gantoris already knew how to use the Force to manipulate matter, which is why he excelled at the exercise. Luke didn't call him on it, on this advantage, when Gantoris started in on me. He could have had a thousand reasons for not doing that, not the least of which could have been to let Gantoris' words fuel my competitive sense. I didn't know if that was Luke's goal, or if what had happened would accomplish that goal, but knowing Gantoris wasn't above taking advantage of an opportunity was another datapoint I willingly logged.

Regardless, even that information didn't bring me any closer to feeling the Force.

"Can I ask you a question, Streen?"

"You just did, but I'll give you another."

"Thanks." I leaned forward, resting my elbows on my knees. "What does the Force feel like to you?"

"It feels like ten kilos of life in a five-kilo box." His voice gained in strength and lightened in tone. "I can only feel a trickle now, like dust motes floating in a sunbeam, one by one, just moving through me, but it's just so right there's no describing it. It tickles a bit, feels like a first kiss, or the jolt you feel when the flux in sabacc just makes your hand better than what you were already betting."

I wanted to quip that I'd had dates like that, but the pure wonderment in his voice would have made the joke sound bitter. "Wow."

"What's it feel like for you?"

I shook my head. "Don't know. I'm not feeling it. I think the Force in me is strong enough to let me do little things, but I've not felt what you describe. Nothing even close."

"You will."

"I hope so."

"You will." Streen's voice sank back to its lower tone. "Let me ask you a question."

"Fair trade."

"Master Skywalker's talked a lot to us about the dark side and how it's selfish and evil and cruel."

"Right."

"Okay, now you remember them rawwks I mentioned, how I never could teach one a trick? Well there was this one time there was one that seemed to be smarter than the others. Just a bit, not a whole lot, but a bit. And I thought he had real promise, so I tried to teach him to unfurl one wing, then the other and hop up and down in time with a tune I was whistling. I just wanted to see him dance a little, just a little."

The loneliness in Streen's voice started to squeeze my heart. "I'm with you."

"Now I thought, maybe, somehow, I didn't know how, that if I could just convince him to do it once and reward him, he'd do it more. I was getting real frustrated and even angry. And I guess I used the Force to make him do the dance to the music. Just once. And I didn't hurt him and I gave him food and all." Streen's voice died amid a cacophony of stintaril howls. "Was I using the dark side? Was I doing evil?"

"I'm not sure that's a question I can answer."

"Give it a try."

I nodded and sighed heavily, watching my breath congeal into a cloud of white vapor. "In an absolute sense, based on what Master Skywalker has told us, yes, you might have brushed up against the dark side. In a very real sense, though, what you did was selfish, but so minor, that on a scale of one to destroying Alderaan, it doesn't even rate a decimal point."

The older man's nodding silhouette eclipsed stars. "And where would you rate your fabrications about your past?"

"What?"

"I've been told you're from a Corellian Jedi family and that you fought with the Rebellion."

"That's all true."

"But that pride in you, that's the sort of pride built up from having done something. The story being told about you doesn't back it well."

"I can see that. I guess it's all a matter of perspective." I climbed back to my feet again. "Fact is, what we were before probably isn't that important. I could tell you all sorts of things about myself. Some you might believe. Some you won't believe. Ultimately, though, not a one of them will help us become Jedi Knights. I'm proud of what I have done, but I'll be more proud to be a Jedi.''

Streen laughed a bit. "So you're not lying, you're just not telling the whole truth because it won't mean much right now.''

"I guess that's about it, yes.''

"I can live with that.'' Streen hauled himself up to his feet and pointed to the turbolift. "Well, we might as well show the others we're smart enough to head in when it gets cold.''

"Wouldn't do to have Jedi Knights seen as that stupid, would it?'' I asked as I fell in step with him.

"Nope, wouldn't do at all.''

Over the next several days we rotated through a series of exercises that underscored my inability to feel the Force. Other students had difficulties with various aspects of what I came to call *pushing*. Whether I was supposed to send something away, bring it near, raise it, lower it, move it at a distance or up close, I proved hideously inept at it. Whereas Luke used the aphorism "Size matters not,'' to encourage others to forget their doubts; with me it became praise for even the least little twitch of a rock.

The fact was, however, that I couldn't make a ripple in a cup of water. And while my ability to sense foes and what they were planning to do got better, I still didn't feel the Force entering me from outside. My progression in defensive areas came from opening up more of the Force within me, but that opening seemed to come as part of my instinctual desire for self-preservation.

And I was blocked by my internal desire for preservation of self.

Something had to give, and I thought I saw a way to make it give. Luke had arranged us in a circle around a huge boulder buried halfway into the ground. He nodded toward it. "You have all been told repeatedly that size does not matter. This is true. However, this does not mean all tasks will be simple. This rock, for all we know, is really just the top of a long plinth. We don't know how big it is. Moving it may not only take a titanic effort, but a sustained effort. With the Force flowing through you, you will be able to move it. If the Force is not flowing, the task will not be completed."

He looked at each and everyone of us openly. "Who would be first to try?"

Gantoris took a step forward. "Master, I would."

"Master, if you please" I bowed my head toward him. "I would be the first to *do*."

Gantoris sneered in my direction. "You? You will *do* nothing."

Luke looked at me. "Do you think you are ready?"

I shrugged. "I believe I *must* do this. Perhaps in focusing on small things I have closed myself down to the Force. To feel it I must open myself to something more grand." I looked around the circle, making eye contact with everyone. "I must move this rock, therefore I *will* move it. This I believe."

I was counting heavily on the internal pressures of not wanting to fail. I accepted that failure was possible, and was willing to live with the consequences of failure, which meant my attempt would not be frenzied or full of the negative emotions that heralded the dark side. I would just put my honest best effort forward. I would do all the things I had been taught to do, and I would succeed.

The Jedi Master nodded. "It is yours to do, then."

Closing my eyes, I set myself and drew in a deep breath. Exhaling it slowly I let my senses expand and touch Tionne and Streen on either side of me. Then my consciousness leaped, link by link until I knew where everyone was in the circle. From there I began to work inward, and as I did so I began to feel the first faint tingles of energy. It felt almost like an ion bolt hitting close by. It made the hair on my arms stand up.

I didn't push, I didn't race after it, but spread myself out to let it come to me. As I made myself receptive, as I caught more of the Force the way a solar sail catches sunlight, my sense of the world became more complete. The blackness before my eyes did not lighten or brighten, but I found structures there and things. Spots that moved were insects. Lines that crawled beneath the dirt were worms. I traced bushes and grasses from leaftip to root. If it was alive I could feel it, and what I felt outside I could also feel inside.

The way Luke had molded his thoughts to mine to probe me about Mirax's absence came back to me in a rush. I looked at the currents of Force inside of me and the currents swirling about outside. Little by little, slowly modifying a thought here, calming a doubt there, setting aside fear and encouraging hope, I changed how the Force flowed within me. I let it erode from the inside out all the walls isolating me from the universal torrent of Force energy.

With the first breach in my defenses the Force slammed into me like high pressure fluid jetting through a pinpoint gap in a pipe. It filled me up in an instant and I imagined it leaking from my eyes, nose and mouth. I wanted to shout and dance with joy because it was everything Streen had described. It was what I felt when Mirax first said she loved me. It was the scent of the perfume my mother wore, and the warm laugh my father used to have when he was proud of me. It was the hearty slap on the back from Wedge after a mission and even a touch of Whistler's triumphant serenades. It was everything that was good and right and positive and alive; and it was waiting for me to bend it to my will.

Newly empowered, I reached out for the stone. In a heartbeat I plumbed its depths. I knew its size and mass, I knew its contours and its weaknesses. I knew I could shape the Force into a hammer and shatter it, but that was not the task at hand. My task was to move it, to rip it from the ground, to raise it up so all could see what I had done.

I poured the Force into my effort. At first I felt resistance, but I expected that. The stone had been firmly stuck in the ground for years. I tugged at it and could see it rocking back and forth. Small pebbles cascaded off it, bouncing down into the grasses at its base. I worried it like a loose tooth, then I prepared to pull it.

I gritted my teeth against the effort. I felt the stone shift. Before my mind's eye I saw it quiver and shake. Slowly, slowly at first it began to move upward. A micron here, a millimeter there, then a centimeter, then two. And four and six and twenty. Rich brown loam fell from it as the lower half of the stone began to rise above the surface. Faster it moved now, slowed only by the occasional clumsy bump against the side of the hole it had inhabited. My control was not yet fine, but I knew it would get better, so I pushed on, working on lifting it higher.

The stone came fully clear of the ground, but that was

not enough for me. I could feel the Force pulsing into me, full and insistent. I channeled it back out through my mind and made the rock's ascent smooth. I lifted it and lifted it up so high that when I opened my eyes, I knew I would be able to see beneath it and find Master Luke across the circle from me. I would lift it so high, in fact, that not even Gantoris could deny what I had done.

Finally I had success. The stone hung in the air better than two meters above the ground. I held it there and redoubled my effort to quell the list in it. I wanted it as firmly embedded in the Force and air as it had been in the ground. When it stopped moving, I smiled and opened my eyes.

The rock remained in the ground.

I stared at it and tried to remember if I had heard it crash back down into the ground. I couldn't remember such a sound, nor could I remember feeling the shockwave that would have resulted from a crash landing. I glanced up at where the rock should have been, then back down. I couldn't believe it had not moved because I knew I had felt the Force, and I knew the rock had flown.

Then I noticed that all the others, every single one of them, were looking at the spot in the air where I had seen the rock floating. Tionne and Streen wore open expressions of wonderment. Kam wore the smirk with which he rewarded good efforts. Gantoris looked as if he'd seen a ghost and the others just looked amazed.

Across from me Luke shook his head, then passed a hand over his eyes. He glanced back at the spot in the air where the rock should have been, then his gaze flicked toward where it really lay. He looked around at the other students, then gently passed a hand through the air, causing them to blink and rub their eyes.

Gantoris looked at the rock and then accusingly at me. "What did you do?"

"What Keiran did, was feel the Force." The Jedi Master nodded to me, then advanced and rested a hand on Gantoris' shoulder. "He opened the pathway to his future. What he did or did not do here should not concern you. Instead, be happy knowing yet another of you is past the first hurdle on the road to becoming a Jedi Knight."

TWELVE

✳

The next morning I found Master Skywalker waiting for me in my chamber after I finished my run. Dripping with sweat, my chest heaving with exertion, I bowed to him, then remained hunched over, with my hands resting on my knees. "It is an honor, Master."

Cloaked in black, he nodded to me. "You can tap into the Force to revitalize yourself, you know."

I slowly straightened up and smiled. "I know, but I choose not to. The fatigue and little aches and pains feel good. They remind me I'm human and mortal, and I think that is a good thing right now."

"Certainly not a bad one." His right hand came out from beneath his cloak. Hovering above his outstretched palm I saw a milky jade crystal block. It rotated slowly there in the air and glowed with an internal light that gave Luke's flesh a nasty green cast to it. "You remember what this is?"

"A Jedi Holocron. It contains histories and wisdom and information about the Jedi, collected down through the years." I twisted my torso left and right to stretch some of the muscles in my back. "Tionne has been using it to research Jedi history. She said the gatekeeper is an alien Jedi named Bodo Baas."

"Exactly right." Luke cupped his hands and touched the floating cube with his fingertips.

The crystal flared white for a moment, then the hologram of a hunched insectoid creature with a bulbous carapace congealed above it like a green ghost. The creature oriented itself toward Luke. "Greetings, Jedi," it intoned, "I am Bodo Baas, the gatekeeper of the Holocron. Do you have a question for me?"

Luke looked through the hologram at me. "A model of Bodo Baas' cognitive network functions as a search, recovery and storage allocation program. There is quite a bit of information stored here. I spent some time researching last evening to see if what you did the other day has been done before."

"Has it?"

The Jedi Master smiled. "It has. In fact, one of the first manifestations of Jedi skill showed to me by Obi-Wan Kenobi was very similar. Gatekeeper, explain the power classified as Alter Mind to Keiran Halcyon."

The gatekeeper turned toward me. Its black compound eyes fixed me with a stare. "Jedi skills in the Force are rooted in three areas. Control is internal. It is the Jedi's ability to recognize the Force in himself and to use it to his benefit. Sense involves the next step, in which the Jedi recognizes the Force in the universe outside herself. Here she feels the Force and is able to draw upon it for information about the world around her. Through it she is connected to the rest of the universe. Alter is the third and most difficult area to master, for it involves the student's ability to modify the Force and redistribute its energies. Through these skills, the Jedi can influence the universe, making changes as needed to accomplish its goals.

"The power known as Alter Mind bridges all these

skill areas. Through it a Jedi can project her perception of reality into the mind of another, or an illusion or conclusion that she needs the other to hold as true. This is a most magnificent and useful power, but it is also one fraught with danger. Bending the will of another for a benign purpose can be noble and good. The dark side lurks nearby in this power, so it should be used with caution."

I blinked my eyes. "Well, that's very interesting."

Luke nodded. "When confronted by a stormtrooper looking for droids back on Tatooine, Obi-Wan used this power to convince a stormtrooper that our droids were not the ones he was looking for."

"I remember having a stormtrooper searching for me during my escape from *Lusankya*. I was doing all I could to make myself unseen and he didn't see me."

The Jedi Master's eyes narrowed for a moment. "You think you unconsciously tapped this power before you began training?"

"I guess so. Is that bad?"

"No, actually, it is good. It explains some things." Luke nodded toward Bodo Baas' image. "As the gatekeeper indicated, it's a very powerful Force ability. Some individuals show a certain aptitude for areas of Jedi power—they have an inborn talent for it. It could be your talent falls into this area."

"Could be. It's good I have aptitude in something, because I am useless when it comes to telekinesis. Then again, I'm not certain how adept I am at influencing minds. I remember trying to influence a stormtrooper on Thyferra with disastrous results."

"Just because you have a talent for it doesn't mean you will always succeed." Luke grinned somewhat sheepishly. "When I visited Jabba the Hutt's den I managed to use it on his Twi'lek aide to get myself an audience. My attempt to use it on Jabba failed right after that. The Hutt may have been stronger-willed, and a Hutt's thought patterns are a bit further from human than those of a Twi'lek. Success was not guaranteed for me, either.''

I nodded. ''I should also take the caution about the dark side to heart as well.''

''Yes, definitely.'' Luke released the Holocron and the gatekeeper evaporated. ''The dark side is seductive for those who want too much too fast. I was concerned at how easily you managed to make us all see what you wanted us to see, which is why I consulted the Holocron about your ability. I think you should be very careful about how you employ it. I would like you to team up with another student and try to alter the perception of color or simple things that don't matter, to test your limits. Of course, I want you only to work with that student's permission and full knowledge.''

''Got it.'' I smiled. ''However, the temptation to make Gantoris think he's already dressed when he isn't does exist.''

Luke laughed lightly for a moment, then withdrew the Holocron from sight. ''You still think like a pilot— maybe this room wasn't a good idea after all. Please don't do that to Gantoris. Jedi powers are not for playing pranks. Later on testing yourselves against each other will hone your skills, but we have to work together at it. Your rivalry with Gantoris concerns me.''

I held my hands up. ''Master, I don't consider Gantoris a rival. I don't particularly like him. He reminds me of a pilot I knew when I first joined Rogue Squadron. Bror Jace and I didn't get along at first, but we grew to understand each other. We never became good friends, but we managed to work together and managed to liberate his homeworld from Isard.''

The Jedi Master lowered his head for a moment. ''Gantoris has had a lot of hardships in his life. He managed to keep the people of Eol Sha alive in a very difficult place. We have moved his colony to Dantooine and relieved him of his responsibility for them. Despite that he pushes himself and holds himself to the strict level of discipline that kept him alive on Eol Sha. Here he sees you pushing yourself harder than he does, and your work pays off with surprising successes. He cannot beat you physically. While you failed to raise the rock, you exhibited a power for which he has no aptitude and can't understand.''

''You're saying he is having trouble enjoying the freedom he now has because it's new to him. All the measures for his conduct he would have used before have no value here, so he has seized upon me as a scale against which to measure himself?'' I shook my head. ''He's worse off than I would have thought.''

''Maybe you can do things to help him.''

I felt a cold draft seep in through my sweaty tunic. ''I can try.''

''You should *do*.''

''If he lets me. I will *do* what I can, but if he is not receptive, my efforts won't work.''

''I appreciate what you will do.'' The Jedi Master nodded beyond me toward the communal refresher station. ''Go get cleaned up and get some food. It will be a busy day for everyone. If things work the way I intend, more will learn what you have learned and we can move into the next stage of development for Jedi Knights.''

•   •   •

In the several days that followed our conversation, a variety of things became readily apparent to me. The first was that my ability to feel the Force followed a simple pattern: when the pressure was on, I could touch it and use it. When just practicing I found it elusive. I did manage to make nebula orchid blossoms change colors for Kirana Ti, and let Tionne see what she would look like if she changed her hair color, but even those simple efforts tired me.

Master Skywalker found this problem more alarming than I did. I think I was able to put it into perspective because of my training for CorSec. All recruits were taught how to handle a variety of blasters. We had it drilled into us over and over again that the only time we should draw a blaster and point it at someone was if we fully intended to use it, or were willing to use it. We were told that to use methods that escalated the tension in a situation was a bad thing, which meant my default mode was to hold back. Only when I *had* to succeed would I cut loose.

That being said, I was able to access the Force more than I had before. Luke was right: tapping into the Force could refresh me after a long run. It could sharpen me up when I was feeling drowsy. It could convince my body that I really didn't need to eat yet and could dull the aches and pains of life. The most faint trickle of Force energy was enough to accomplish these simple things and, not needing the vast power I had previously, I didn't draw on it.

I know Master Skywalker wanted all of us to feel comfortable in the Force and to progress at our own rates in finding out how we would use the Force, but I wanted a bit more discipline in our training. We had no baseline against which to measure ourselves—in many ways

Gantoris' problem was one we all shared. Progress was difficult to determine, and with a more organized approach we could have tried to duplicate previous efforts and learned how to actually do them again.

I don't think it helped that Luke had trained with two teachers and under extreme conditions. He presented us with the lessons Yoda and Obi-Wan had taught, but they weren't always directly on point for what we needed at the moment. Tionne helped a lot, offering other examples from the Holocron, but there were times when Luke had difficulty getting his message across.

One night, in the deepest of Truenight, Master Skywalker summoned us all without a word. Wearing only a hooded cloak, I joined the rest of my comrades and padded along silently in their wake. Far ahead of me, leading the way with a dim glowlamp, Master Skywalker conducted us through the Great Temple and down a tunnel I had never previously noticed. The dusty stones leached warmth from my feet and the tiny wisps of cool air that sliced in through the gap in my cloak tightened my flesh.

Down and down we walked, deep into the bowels of the moon. The steps were worn, but not slick, and somehow I got the impression that this pathway predated even the Temple itself. Eventually our descent ended, and I sensed Tionne's closeness a second before I bumped into her. Past her shoulder I could see the circle of light playing up against what appeared to be a solid stone wall, but a hint of steam and a whiff of sulfur suggested something more lay beyond it.

Luke praised Gantoris and Kam for voicing their suspicions that the trail had not ended, then he worked some sort of switch that slid a panel of stone aside. The resulting hole swallowed the light from his lamp. Our line began to move again and as the trail curved to the left, the scent of sulfur grew. With it came a feeling of humidity and heat. Condensation slicked the stones on the pathway.

I came into the underground grotto last of all and found a place with my back to the tunnel, facing Luke across the circle. His glowlamp played over the surface of a bubbling mineral spring. Steam coursed over the water and washed up to tease us with warm caresses. The random staccato of bursting bubbles filled the silence, and the acrid air began to burn in the back of my throat. Beneath the glowlamp's light, the water appeared to be an inviting blue, which contrasted easily with the white mineral crusts on the visible rocks and edges of the pool.

"This is our destination," Luke intoned solemnly. He snapped off the glowlamp, plunging us into darkness. A couple of the students gasped, but I'd sort of expected him to do that. Whatever he intended for us in this place, something mechanical like the glowlamp seemed unlikely to be part of it.

After a time distant starlight poured through a crevasse in the stone ceiling above us, allowing us to perceive shapes and the wavering rippled reflections of stars in the pool's bubble-wracked mirror. The algae in the pool gave off a dim glow itself, outlining the edge of the pool, but doing nothing to dispel the black murk of its depths.

Luke's voice filled the grotto. "This is an exercise to help you concentrate and attune yourself to the Force. The water is a perfect temperature: you will float, you will drift, you will reach out and touch the rest of the universe." As the last of his words echoed through the cave, the water rippled outward from where he had been standing, indicating he had somehow silently slipped into the water.

Without waiting for more of an invitation, I shed my robe and eased myself into the pool. The water at first seemed scaldingly hot, but I knew that was only because I had been cold once I stripped out of my robe. I sank myself gingerly up to my waist, then released the pool's edge and sank beneath the surface. The water washed the last of the cold from my hair and goatee while bubbles marched up through the hair on my chest.

I broke the surface again and shook my head to clear water from my eyes. The pool eased aches and pains easily, with the heat pouring in through my flesh to warm muscle and bone. I stretched my arms out and brought my legs up, doing my best to relax so I could float there. Tipping my head back, I looked up at the stars and idly wondered how many of them I had visited in my lifetime.

I heard the occasional splash and whispered apology as one apprentice floated into another. With the warmth of the water and the way it held us up, it was very easy to forget our physical bodies. I recall Luke remarking that Yoda had told him we are all luminous creatures, not crude conglomerations of flesh and bone. Here in the grotto pool, warm and isolated in the dark, forgetting our physical selves became more easy than ever before.

And absent contact with our physical selves, we are left feeling the Force within us.

Luke's voice again broke the silence. "There is no emotion, there is peace. There is no ignorance, there is knowledge. There is no passion, there is serenity. There is no death, there is the Force." He spoke the words of the Jedi Code with such power and solemnity, I found myself whispering them along with him. My voice joined that of the other students, until our declarations filled the grotto, binding us together.

Master Skywalker urged us to use the water and the warmth to free us so we could *feel*, really feel, the Force. I lay back and could hear the echoes of my heartbeat pounding in my ears. I concentrated on it, knowing it as a sign of life. I let my heartbeat meld with the rhythms of the Force and felt the sizzle of the Force soaking into me.

I heard Luke saying more, but the words lost their meaning in what I was seeing through the Force. Instead of hearing every syllable, stringing them together, then translating sounds into concepts, through the Force I saw his intent create eddies and currents. He herded our attention to the stars above us, then redirected us back down and into the pool.

I rolled over and floated vertically, staring down into the pool. The sky's reflection sank beneath the rippling surface, then took on depth. The sliver of sky expanded as if the rocks above us had become transparisteel. As Luke asked, "Can you see it?" the pool was gone and I found myself floating in the limitless depths of space.

With my mind I reached out and grafted my thoughts to those of the Jedi Master. I clung to his energy as he soared us through various solar systems. Nebulae gave birth to stars as we flew past, and suns went nova, consuming whole planetary systems. Worlds flashed past, some which I recognized, others I did not. We visited systems where Imperial warlords battled each other for supremacy, and planets where refugees sought new lives.

On our journey I caught a flicker of something I recognized. I wanted to linger for a second while I identified the feather-light brush of consciousness against mine. The second it took me to make contact proved too long because even as I knew I felt Mirax's presence, Luke had torn me away from her. I spun around, trying to find her again, but I could not.

In her place I sensed malevolence and danger. At first it came from where I had felt Mirax, then it sank deep into the moon and focused itself beneath us. I knew what I had felt had been one danger, and what I was feeling now was part of a warning from Master Skywalker about another. He'd felt another menace, one closer and more immediate.

Somewhere, deep inside the moon's crust, searingly hot gasses had been released and were jetting their way upward. They would bubble up and into the pool through the same cracks that allowed the water to fill the basin. In a heartbeat or three the water would be flooded with hot gasses, roasting us alive.

I fought panic and would not have made it but for two things. Above the splashing of others striking for the side of the pool, Master Skywalker's voice rose. "A Jedi feels no heat or cold. A Jedi can extinguish pain. Strengthen yourselves with the Force." The calm strength in his words banished my fear and allowed me to concentrate.

The second thing was a choked gasp from Tionne. She had lunged for the side of the pool but her slender fingers had failed to hang on. She sank abruptly and came back up, sputtering. She coughed hard and noisily sucked in air, then realized she would never get clear. In the lichen's light reflected by her pearly eyes, I saw that she knew she would die.

I refused to let her die. The frustration, pain and sorrow that had tortured me when my father died in my arms, became transformed into a determination that Tionne would not die here. I knew I had it within me, using the Force, to prevent her death. I opened myself to the Force, adamant that I would do whatever I needed to do—even dying—to save her.

The Force flooded into me as the superheated gasses hit the pool. I felt the heat hit my feet first and expected the Force to channel it around me. Instead the heat poured up through me. The Force insulated me from its destructive potential, then seemed to digest it into energy I could use. Without thinking I gestured toward Tionne with my cupped right hand and raised it.

As if riding a repulsorlift couch, the silver-haired apprentice rose from the water and drifted to the side. I set her down as gently as I could. She dropped to one knee and coughed again, with her silvery hair flowing down like a curtain between us.

I turned about to see if there was anyone else who needed help, but the roiling surface of the water had reverted to a more placid state and everyone else appeared to be fine. I sensed no pain, just surprise and gratitude and confidence. A smile blossomed on my face as I realized that I, too, had survived a lethal challenge by using the Force.

"Enough for tonight." I heard the splash as Luke pulled himself up out of the pool. "Think about what you have learned."

Once again, I found that when it was necessary I was able to use the Force. Lifting Tionne clear of danger surprised me, causing me to assume that the energy I had absorbed needed to be expended in some way. I had used it to power telekinesis—something I had shown no talent for in the past. It was nice to know that with an energy boost I could do telekinesis, but without one it would still be hopeless. That didn't matter, though. Tionne was safe and I was plenty pleased with that.

I swam to the side of the pool and pulled myself from the water. The cooler air immediately raked cold claws over me, puckering my flesh. I looked around for my robe, then found it drifting through the air toward me. I pulled it on and nodded my thanks to Luke.

The Jedi Master watched me cautiously, his blue eyes intense even in the dim light. "Do you know what you did here?"

"As nearly as I can tell, the Force allowed me to serve as a conduit for the heat."

"Very good. There is another Jedi power that manifests with the absorption and dissipation of energy. My father had skill in it. He could absorb or deflect a blaster bolt without harm." Luke's voice became colder. "He even managed telekinetic tricks with the energy he pulled in."

"I don't like the sound of that, Master." I opened my hands toward him. "I just knew Tionne would die if I did nothing. Lifting her from the water seemed the most direct method for saving her. I did not think, I just acted."

"I know, and that's very good. The Force is more heart than brain. I did not mean what I said to sound like criticism." His voice softened a bit. "It is just that doing anything with haste can lead to impatience, and that invites the dark side. You would be better off to let the power bleed back away into the galaxy through the Force. If you are going to employ it the way you did, avoid haste so you avoid problems."

"Yes, Master."

Luke approached and slapped me on the shoulder.

"You did well, Gantoris did well and saved Dorsk 81 in the process, and the others also survived this unexpected challenge. This is a good sign for our future."

"I'm sure you are right, Master," I found myself saying, but the chill creeping into my feet as we climbed back toward the Temple left me wondering if another disaster lurked to rip us apart.

Thirteen

✳

The next morning I woke all muzzy and, as a result, didn't realize I was starting out on my run later than usual. About halfway through the run, at the point in my circuit furthest from the Great Temple, I realized what time it was. While Luke still allowed flexibility in training times, in the mornings he usually appreciated our getting an early start. I tried to pick up my pace, but I knew I'd arrive back at the Temple well after everyone else had assembled to start working.

I wanted to kick myself for being so stupid. The previous evening had been an impressive victory in the battle to open ourselves up to the Force. While the emergency had opened me broadly to the Force, I'd been feeling it before that. I knew I could make great progress and had been looking forward to the morning's exercises to see if I could capitalize on what I had learned the night before.

The reason I'd awakened rather dull was because I'd not gotten much sleep at all. Master Skywalker had mentioned that dreams rarely disturbed a Jedi's sleep. I don't know why, but I'd never dreamed much. When I did dream I tended toward nightmares that ruined my sleep.

Nightmares had kept my sleep uneven and fragmentary. I kept drifting back to the place where I had felt Mirax's presence. I tried to freeze the stars in place so I could figure out where I was supposed to be, but one by one they winked out. They left me alone and in the dark. When I tried to look at my hands, I saw through my flesh as rot ate away at the bones, then I fell into nothingness, forever to exist in the knowledge that when Mirax needed me, I had failed her.

Pretty much my definition of a nightmare.

Nearing the Great Temple on my return, I heard something that made me push myself and increase my speed. The hum-hiss of a lightsaber and the spit-crack of it slicing through something is unforgettable once heard. I couldn't imagine Luke and Kam would have begun to teach anyone how to fight with lightsabers without me there. I realized in an instant that such a thought was unworthy and arrogant, but since I had the only other lightsaber on Yavin, including me made sense to me.

I entered the clearing just as Luke drove Gantoris back into a purple-boled Massassi tree. *Where did Gantoris get a lightsaber?* With the black-haired apprentice's braid whiplashing through the air, he fell, scattering purple bits of tree bark. His knees resting on a thick root, and his elbows keeping his back off the ground, he stared up at Luke as the Jedi Master approached. Gantoris' white-violet blade still pointed up toward Luke, but from where he was there was no way the apprentice could strike at the Master.

Then Gantoris did something that extended the blade, doubling its length. He slashed at Luke, but the Jedi Master moved faster than I ever thought possible. The sleeve of Luke's grey flightsuit smoked from where the lightsaber's blade had caressed it, but Gantoris had done no real harm. Luke set himself, imposing his green blade between himself and his student, bracing for another attack.

Gantoris had rolled to his feet while Luke retreated and advanced confidently. The length of the blade on his lightsaber gave him an advantage and he clearly meant to use it. He waded in toward Luke, crashing down blow after blow with a ferocity I'd only ever seen in a glitbiter gripped by spice paranoia. Though Luke picked off each blow with ease, never letting Gantoris make him defend in the Inner Ring, the apprentice kept coming. His intensity and singlemindedness kept Luke falling back to the point where the Jedi Master's only escape was to leap away and levitate himself onto a branch of a Massassi tree.

I watched, stunned, as Gantoris waited for Luke to descend again. All the other students had pressed back away from the clearing. They lurked in the edges of the forest, waiting, uncertain what to do. Like me, Kam had no lightsaber with him. As he glanced over at me, I knew we both weighed the chances of our being able to race to the Temple, getting our lightsabers and managing to return in time to make a difference.

And if Gantoris can kill a Jedi Master, what chance would I have of stopping him?

Luke asked Gantoris a question, but the hum of lightsabers stole both it and Gantoris' shouted reply. Then the apprentice slashed at the Massassi tree with his lightsaber, shearing all the way through it. Stintarils in the highest branches shrieked as they leaped away. The scent of spicy sap reached me about the same time as the tree slowly toppled into the rainforest with a crackling and snap of bushes and saplings caught beneath it.

Master Skywalker floated to the ground unharmed and again set himself to receive Gantoris' attacks. Gantoris shortened his blade and came on. Luke gave ground, blocking the attacks in closer to him than before. He gave the impression that he was tiring, weakening. I guessed it was a ploy to draw Gantoris on, but the apprentice was not thinking clearly enough to see that. He pressed forward, slashing his way through leafy ferns and chopping apart nebula orchids.

Suddenly Luke went down and I couldn't see him. Gantoris rushed forward, his spitting blade shredding the jungle. I started to sprint toward them, cursing the fact that I couldn't lift Gantoris up the way I had Tionne only hours before. I tried to think of what image I could project into Gantoris' mind to deflect him and distract him, but I never got the chance.

Gantoris' purple blade came down in an overhand strike that burned its way through the underbrush. I heard a startled squeal, then an orange furred runyip broke from the brush, darting into the clearing right behind Gantoris. As he turned to face this new threat, his lightsaber flew up out of his hands and the blade died.

Luke plucked the lightsaber from the air, then extinguished his own blade. The two of them stood there, facing each other. Sweat streamed down their faces and their breath came ragged, yet neither one wanted to show any sign of weakness. In the absence of the lightsaber hissing, the fading sounds of the runyip's squeals and the normal sound of the rainforest fought for supremacy.

Then Luke did something that stunned me. He flipped Gantoris' lightsaber around and extended it to him hilt first. Gantoris accepted it timidly, clutching it in both hands. He studied it, turning it over and around as if seeing it for the first time, then he looked back at Luke.

The Jedi Master nodded. "Good exercise, Gantoris,

but you must learn to control your anger. It could be your undoing.''

I dropped to my knees in utter astonishment. I watched Gantoris turn away and retreat into the rainforest. The other apprentices seemed as surprised at what had happened as I was. They whispered together in little knots as Luke emerged from the undergrowth, clipped his lightsaber to his belt, and pulled his cloak back on.

He looked around calmly and even gave us the hint of a smile. ''Perhaps, after last evening, we started too early today. We will reconvene this afternoon.'' In his words I felt a gentle urging to go back to my room, but I resisted it. The others did not and melted away unseen into the rainforest.

Luke glanced back at me, a half-smile on his face. ''I thought you would still be here. You did not see the beginning?''

I shook my head. ''The ending was more than enough. What are you going to do?''

''Do? This is done already.''

My jaw dropped open. ''Unless I missed something, one of your apprentices found or somehow constructed a lightsaber and just tried to kill you with it. You don't see this as cause for alarm?''

''How can it surprise you that Gantoris has found a way to fashion a lightsaber? You and Kam already possess one. We've talked about Gantoris' competition with you.''

I held my hands up. ''That may be an issue, but not the core one as I see it.''

Luke's eyes narrowed. ''So your vision here is paramount.''

I hesitated and felt my stomach collapse in on itself.

"No, Master Skywalker, it is not. I mean no disrespect."
I sighed. "I just want to understand. Gantoris has gotten
into something he shouldn't have. You have to discipline
him."

"He's going to be a Jedi Knight. I cannot treat him
like a child." Luke shook his head. "To do that would
stunt his development. He's very good and one of the
best students here. He just needs guidance."

"Then give it to him." My hands convulsed into fists,
then I forced them open again. "You're assuming that he
will see the error of his ways and never do this again. He
attacked you! He's already shown he's not scanning
right and wrong correctly. He can't begin to figure out
where the line between them runs if you don't find a way
to punish him when he crosses that line."

The Master shook his head slowly. "I can tell you
that Gantoris already regrets what he has done here.
Stretch out with your feelings. You'll feel it, too. He is
teaching himself where the line is and how to stay on the
light side of it."

I did as I was bidden and did sense both remorse and
confusion from Gantoris. "You are right, Master. I know
you believe in redemption. What you say about Gantoris
is true. I guess I don't see why he should not be punished for having done something wrong."

"You're not supposed to see it, Keiran, you're supposed to *feel* it." Luke rubbed a hand against his forehead. "Retribution leads to the dark side."

I sighed. "I know. I would argue that a little punishment now could prevent a disaster later, but I don't think
that will get me anywhere."

"You see, Keiran, you grow in wisdom as well as the
Force."

I didn't want to laugh, but his comment was funny.

Still, coming from someone my age, it also rankled a bit. Luke obviously deserved the title Jedi Master, but part of me wished we weren't the group on which he first practiced being a teacher. He clearly had his ideas about how we should learn, and we *were* all making progress. *Some faster than others.*

Even so, I wasn't used to his methods. I flashed on Iella's heart and mind split and knew it was a key to my problem. "I shall think further on my ignorance, Master, that I may see how much wisdom I yet need to learn. If you would permit it, though, I want to ask you a question."

"Please."

I scratched at the back of my neck. "What did you ask Gantoris and what did he shout at you before he cut down the tree?"

"I asked how he had learned what he needed to know to make a lightsaber." Luke shifted his shoulders stiffly. "He replied that I was not the only teacher of the Jedi way."

"Not a very good answer. Do you think he would have gotten the knowledge from the Holocron?"

"I can't see how. The Holocron detects a student's ability and holds back things they are not prepared to know." He smiled carefully. "It works so well, in fact, that I do not know if there are things there that I have yet to learn."

"If not from Bodo Baas, then from whom did he learn?" I frowned. "I couldn't teach it to him. I don't think Kam would and you, I take it, have not. Who did?"

Luke remained very still for a moment, then slowly shook his head. "I don't know."

"But it would have to be a Jedi, or someone with the

knowledge of the Jedi ways and, presumably, considerable power in the Force.''

''I think so, yes.''

''And yet, last night, when we were all so open to the Force that we were able to catalog stars, we didn't feel the presence of such an individual right here?''

Luke's eyes became sapphire slits. ''No.''

I shivered, and it wasn't because I was soaked in sweat. ''Does that worry you as much as it does me?''

''More, I think, Keiran.'' Luke's cloak rippled with a shudder. ''Much more.''

FOURTEEN

✳

Running down the hallway toward Gantoris' room I caught a whiff of the poisonously sweet scent I'd smelled a couple of times before during my days with CorSec. I didn't want to look inside the room because I knew what I would see. The knot of students at the doorway shielded me from the sight, but did nothing to block the scent.

I heard Master Skywalker say, ''Beware the dark side,'' then a greasy thread of smoke twisted through the apprentices, driving them apart. Several turned away and stumbled down the corridor with hands over their mouths. Streen and Kam Solusar hung on either side of the doorway, ashen-faced and staring inside. I slipped between them, raising the neck of my tunic to cover my nose. They turned away, leaving me alone with Luke and what was left of Gantoris.

Gantoris' body lay near the far wall of his small stone chamber—at least I assumed it was Gantoris because it did not much look like him. He had been burned to death. Carbonized flesh had crumbled to ash at some points, revealing blackened bone. The heat had contracted his muscles, arching his spine and pulling his head back. His mouth remained open in a wordless scream. Smoke still rose from the charred remnants of his Jedi robes, and his lightsaber had rolled over to rest against the wall itself.

Luke Skywalker stood over him, staring down at his blackened remains.

"What happened here? Did he attack you again?"

Luke turned to look at me with haunted, red-rimmed eyes and I could tell this wasn't the first time he'd seen a body in this condition. "Do you think I did this?" The pain in his voice knifed right through me.

"I wasn't accusing you. I just want to know what happened." I crouched by the body. "Occupational hazard. Who found him?"

"Dorsk 81 came for me, so I suppose he did. The others gathered after we got here."

I nodded. "I'll want to talk to them."

Luke blinked away some of the shock in his eyes. "You are going to investigate this situation?"

My head came up. "Shouldn't I?"

The Jedi Master hesitated for a moment, then nodded. "Yes, of course you should. We need to know what happened here."

"Right." I pointed toward the body and circled my finger around the general area. "I can give you some basics right now. The lack of a consistent pattern of charring, as well as the absence of a chemical scent, suggests no accelerant was used. In other words, no one poured something flammable over him and turned him into a torch."

Luke winced at that description. "I see."

"Take a look at the fingers and ears."

"Badly burned."

"Right, but they're not gone. Bodies lit on fire tend to have those little bits burn off quickly. And the fact that he's still got clothes on him, albeit badly charred. . . ." I let my voice trail off because the conclusion I was being led toward ran counter to my previous experience. "It almost seems as if he was burned from the inside out. That would require an incredible amount of energy: a lightning strike or lots of microwaves, and we don't have either here."

"Yes, but he had such energy." Luke's voice dropped to a whisper. "His anger."

"You think he was consumed by his anger?"

"I do. I think he used it to unleash dark-side forces he could not control. Had you not been able to shunt aside the energies you absorbed last evening in the grotto, you, too, might have been burned up by them."

I reached a hand out toward the lightsaber, but could feel no heat from it, nor see any signs that it had been damaged by the fire. "I'd like to get a full laboratory work-up on the lightsaber. Fingerprints, tissue residue matches, the works, both inside and out."

Luke shook his head. "You will find that only Gantoris and I have touched that lightsaber."

"How do you know?"

"I *know*." Luke raised his hands. "If you open yourself to this room, you can feel the residue of Gantoris' last moments. There is much pain and much anger, as well as doubt and outrage. The pain is physical, of course, and mental. It feels as if he was tortured before he died."

I stood again. Gantoris' body lay between us like a wall. "Who would have done that to him?"

Luke shook his head. "None of you. Shock and surprise and horror radiates off everyone else very openly. They were not involved."

"And me?"

"Some surprise, certainly, but also a determination to solve this puzzle." Luke regarded me through half-lidded eyes. "If you were to kill him, you would have goaded him into a duel or used an illusion to make him have a fatal accident. You wouldn't have been this clumsy or left this sort of evidence, you would have been subtle."

"Thanks, I think." I folded my arms across my chest. "So if we didn't do it, who did?"

"I don't know." Luke's face darkened. "Gantoris did have premonitions of disaster, however. Even when I first met him, he wondered if I were the 'dark man' who would bring him to ruin. He said 'If I go with you, I am lost.' At the time I thought he was just afraid of what would happen to his people if he left them. Then, last evening, as he was leaving the grotto he told me that I was *not* the dark man."

I chewed my lower lip for a moment. "So Gantoris positively identified his dark man. You told me that Gantoris also mentioned to you that you were not the *only* teacher of the Jedi way. I don't think it's a stretch to think this dark man might be the other instructor. The fact that you can't feel this other individual here is not a good sign."

"He cannot remain hidden forever."

"I don't think he intends to."

"What do you mean?"

I glanced down at Gantoris' body. "You said that if I wanted to kill Gantoris, I'd have been subtle. This death is anything but subtle. We have someone dead by means that are impossible, and he was killed right here in the heart of the academy. You can see by that one diagonal cut on the wall there that Gantoris apparently tried to strike at his attacker, but that did no good.

"In my time with CorSec I helped track a sociopathic killer or two. Leaving a body out in the open like this was a taunt. It was the killer saying that he's smarter than we are, more powerful and more cunning. Gantoris tried to kill him with a lightsaber and failed. That means the rest of us have little chance of hurting him. He is challenging us and challenging you. He obviously won one of your students over to the dark side, then left him here like a discarded plaything to show his contempt for you."

Luke hugged his arms around himself. "I think he may have been even more direct."

I shook my head. "I'm not tracking here."

"Tonight I had a nightmare. I stood with my father on top of this temple, but it was back when the Massassi people still lived. It must have been millennia ago. My father tried to explain to me how it was Obi-Wan's fault that he had been corrupted by his studies of Sith material. What he told me seemed to make sense for the most part, but then he invited me to follow him down that path, which I knew my father never would do. I accused him of not being my father. The image then shifted into that of a shadow that swallowed everything. At that point Artoo awakened me, so I don't know what else would have happened."

"He became a shadow?" I shivered. "Gantoris' dark man?"

"Obi-Wan suggested there was no such thing as coincidence. I would have to suppose that all this is related." Luke's expression hardened. "I have to decide very carefully how to proceed from here."

"If you will, let me suggest two things."

"Go ahead."

"First, this dark man apparently managed to convince

Gantoris that he could offer him things you could not or would not. Gantoris' knowledge of and control of the Force was insufficient to allow him to avoid such seductive ideas. I think you need to use the Holocron as a way to instill in us a sense of history and purpose for what we're doing, so we have even more incentive to help rebuild the Jedi.''

''And avoid the easy solutions offered by the dark side.''

''Exactly.''

The Jedi Master thought for a moment, then nodded. ''And the other thing?''

''In this dream you said you saw the Massassi and the pyramids the way they were millennia ago. I think we might want to do some investigating to see what we can learn about Yavin 4 and the Temples. The Holocron might well be able to give us information. If we can put a face and name to this dark man, or figure out what he's after here, we'll have a better chance of stopping him.''

''Both plans seem to make sense.'' Luke smiled at me grimly. ''I shall work on the first. Tionne is spending a lot of time pulling legends from the Holocron, so she can help me. With your background as an investigator, you should handle the gathering of information about our dark man.''

''I'll build a profile on him. If we can figure out what he wants and how he thinks, we have him.''

''Good.'' Luke glanced back down at Gantoris' body, then up at me. ''If the New Republic is to thrive, we can't allow the Jedi to be destroyed.''

There was no returning to sleep that night, so I made my way to the small library where we studied the Jedi

Holocron. I really didn't feel up to beginning any investigation at the moment, but playing around with the Holocron and learning how it worked seemed to be something I could handle. The greenish glow making its way out into the corridor told me someone else was using the device, and my curiosity carried me right into the room.

There, bathed in the green glow from Bodo Baas, sat Tionne. She looked long and lean and lovely, with the greenish tint the light gave her hair looking far better on her than it ever did on me. She would have been unarguably gorgeous, except that her hands covered her face and her shoulders shook with sobs.

Bodo Baas' image reached a clawed limb toward her. "For a Jedi, there is no emotion, there is only peace."

Tionne looked up, her face wet with tears. "It was more horrible than you could imagine."

The Jedi simulacrum bobbed its head. "But are the tears for your fallen comrade, or for you?"

"What?" Shock rode through her voice. She swiped at her tears and pointed a finger at the hologram, then caught sight of me in the corner of her eye. My presence cut off whatever she would have said to him. Instead of replying, she bowed her head toward me and shivered. "How could anyone do that to Gantoris?"

I nodded toward Bodo Baas, then knelt by Tionne's side. I gathered her into my arms and held her, letting her tears stain my emerald tunic. She clung to me fiercely at first, burying her head against my neck. I stroked her hair and resisted the impulse to kiss the crown of her head.

"Take it easy, Tionne. What happened to Gantoris was hideous, but it's not going to happen to anyone else."

Bodo Baas' inhuman gaze caught and held my own. "You speak of certainties, Jedi, where there are many unknowns."

I quoted back a piece of the Jedi Code. "There is no ignorance, there is knowledge."

"Yes," the gatekeeper hissed. "Do you have a question for me?"

"One moment." I eased my hands down onto Tionne's shoulders and pulled back away from her a bit. "Can you help me with the Holocron? You know more about it than I do."

She sniffed and wiped tears away with delicately long fingers. "How can you be so calm after what you have seen?"

For just a second I wasn't holding her in my arms, but holding my father's lifeless body. "The past prepares us for the present. I hate to say it, but I've seen other bodies that were just as horrible. What I saw in Gantoris' room was awful. It scares me, too, but I'm doing my best to keep things under control."

Tionne sniffed again and sat back against the cold stone wall of the small room. She folded her arms across her chest and stared forward at the base of the pedestal on which the Holocron rested. "You must think me weak."

"Not at all."

"Don't lie. You had to rescue me last night, and now you find me here, like this." She looked at me accusingly. "How you keep your contempt for me hidden I don't know."

"You can believe it's hidden, or you can believe it doesn't exist." I forced myself to remain calm. "The second choice is right."

She reached out to me and I took her hand in mine.

Tionne closed her eyes and I could feel her consciousness drifting toward me. The touch of her mind was but a faint whisper of what I'd felt from Luke, yet she managed to infuse herself into my surface thoughts. I consciously left them open to her, and beneath them hardened the layer that was Keiran Halcyon. Even though I tried to keep her away from plunging deeper, she managed to twist down through my thoughts about her and stabbed deep into my heart.

She jerked back sharply, breaking our contact, and stared at me with wild wide eyes. "You've been hurt, very hurt."

I shrugged. "I've survived."

"But there is so much of you that is hidden." She blinked at me. "Master Skywalker has told us his father was Darth Vader. What secrets could you have that would be more dangerous than that to share?"

"Not more dangerous, just boring. They would distract you and training here is hard enough without distractions."

Tionne smiled and it felt good to see animation return to her face. "They might distract others, but not me. I plan to sing of the exploits of the Jedi, so I need to know about Keiran Halcyon."

Before I could deny I was worth knowing about, Bodo Baas spoke. "Keiran Halcyon was a famed Corellian Jedi. He successfully put an end to the Selonian *Afarathu* sect and its marauding within the Corellian system." As he spoke, the Holocron presented an image of a man built more solidly than I was, but who wore the same sort of moustache and goatee I had chosen to grow. His long, dark hair had been gathered back into a loose tail and the lightsaber he held had a silver blade.

A smile unconsciously rose to my lips. Luke said

Keiran Halcyon was the name of one of my ancestors. The *Afarathu* problem had taken place four centuries back and had all but been forgotten until Imperial officials used the spectre of it to incite xenophobia among the human populations in the Corellian system. Fortunately for the Selonians, they had not been warlike for so long, few of us saw them as a true threat.

Tionne's eyes sparkled with absolute delight. "Is that your secret? Are you this Keiran Halcyon come back to us?"

"I don't think even carbonite freezing would have preserved me that long." I laughed gently. "I was named for him. I have a lot to live up to."

"Well, we can learn all about him, if you want. I can even compose a ballad about him."

I winced. "Might put some of the others off, though I would love to learn more about him. Actually, what I had hoped to study through the Holocron was any information it had about this world and the Massassi. Will you help me with that?"

"Gladly." Her hair shimmered with green highlights as she nodded. "It would be my pleasure and will be a way to repay you for saving me in the grotto."

"You don't need to repay me for that." Extending my right hand, I gave her left shoulder a squeeze. "And I want you to know I don't think you are weak. Your nature is to be far more emotionally open and receptive than I am. This is why you have clearer access to the Force than I do. It may make it difficult for you to concentrate sometimes, but it is easier to learn to concentrate than it is to learn to open up."

"I would hate to think you are right, Keiran, because I would hate to think you could not open up your emotions." Her friendly smile warmed me. "You have friends here with whom you can be open. You can trust us as we trust you."

"I know." I gave her a brave smile, but I also knew I could not share my true identity with her or anyone else. Luke Skywalker, in suggesting I adopt another name, was right to think I might be a distraction to the others. He also had another purpose—one rooted in his understanding of fighter pilots and Corellians. By having me be someone else, he made it unnecessary for me to be the legend I had become. As much as I had seen my self-conception insulating me from the Force, Luke had seen it even more and had taken steps to solve the problem before I even realized I had it.

I nodded to Tionne. "Believe me, when I can open up, you'll be the first to know. If there is to be a ballad of *this* Keiran Halcyon, I want you to compose and sing it."

"Gladly, Keiran." She lifted her head toward Bodo Baas. "Now let's see what we can find out about this world and our predecessors here. This planet has as many secrets as you do, if not more, and I have the feeling puzzling them out will provide a basis for a very important ballad."

FIFTEEN

✳

The tragedy of Gantoris' death did bring the remaining apprentices together. No one did so much as whisper anything bad about Gantoris, but we all tried to be nicer and more supportive of each other. Any victory for one—size mattered not—became a victory for all. We became not so much a team as a union of equals, united in our quests to become Jedi Knights.

As part of my investigation, I suggested that Jedi Knights needed to be very observant. Toward this end I organized scouting missions throughout the surrounding area. We started with data collected by a Rebel scout, a Sullustan named Dr'uun Unnh, back when he surveyed the moon as the Rebels prepared to use it as their head-quarters. Using his information, we surveyed the immediate area, taking detailed notes on the flora, fauna, natural outcroppings of stone and various Massassi-made structures.

Right from the start Luke made a decision not to tell the other students about the dark man or his dream. I agreed with the decision primarily because panic would only help a creature of the dark side. To fight panic, Luke had us practice calming and concentration techniques, and worked on having us feel the Force more fully. He took great pains to praise us for our successes. In providing us such feedback, we all felt we were making great progress, even though our actual gains were hard to measure.

My progress in certain areas almost seemed negative. While others were able to levitate rocks while standing on their hands, or braid branches of Massassi trees together through the Force, I had no strength and no endurance when it came to telekinesis. Unfortunately for me this inability also manifested itself in my failure to levitate myself or make the sort of prodigious leap that carried Luke clear of Gantoris' blade in their duel.

Worse yet, Tionne discovered that this lack seemed to be a hallmark of the Halcyon line. As a result we were known for stubbornly standing our ground in various dangerous situations. A couple of times this had resulted in a rally of the forces on our side, driving the enemy back and defeating them. Most of the time, however, it meant a Halcyon bravely volunteered to act as the rear guard and valiantly trade his life for those of his comrades.

Tionne thought this idea made for great ballad material.

Knowing that some very powerful individual with a taste for apprentices was out there, I found the stories of my family tradition a little more ominous.

But, in keeping with Halcyon tradition, I didn't let that stop me in my search for whoever had killed Gantoris. After a hard morning of trying to move pebbles the length of my shadow, and succeeding only as noon approached, I grabbed some field rations and water, then prepared to head out on a survey of the Blueleaf Temple. Unnh's survey notes reported some weird anomalies there—weird enough that General Jan Dodonna had ordered the Temple sealed and placed off limits to all personnel.

I had intended on going alone, but Kam Solusar and Brakiss joined me at the last moment. "It's probably still sealed up tight, guys. Could be very boring."

Kam smiled and pointed to the lightsaber clipped to my belt. "I have the distinct feeling you are planning to reopen the Temple."

"Not really what I had in mind, but if circumstances demanded." I shrugged easily. "C'mon, let's go."

I started us off at a fairly good clip, then slowed my pace a bit as Brakiss struggled to keep up. Being as tall as he was, the orchid roots were giving him trouble. Kam, though middle-aged, was in better shape than Brakiss, but he, too, seemed to prefer a more leisurely pace.

We crossed the river separating the Great Temple from the Blueleaf Temple by walking along the trunk of a Massassi tree that had been uprooted by the river. The river itself was actually shallow enough at a nearby ford that I usually just splashed my way across when running, but Brakiss didn't really look like he wanted to get his feet wet. Kam and I kidded him, asking him if he wanted us to use our lightsabers to cut him some steps and level off the bumpy parts of the tree, but he just blushed and told us to walk on.

The Great Temple dwarfed the Blueleaf Temple, but the latter building had a great deal of elegance to its construction. It rose only half as high as the Great Temple, but proportionally had a bigger footprint. A lot of brush and scrub shrubs had grown up around it, but not enough to stop us from getting to it.

Brakiss led the way around to the eastern side of the structure. "The Sullustan's survey said the main entrance faced east so the orange light from the gas giant could fill the lower chamber in the evening.''

We reached the entrance and could see where the Rebels had indeed sealed the doorway with large stone blocks. Clearly they had intended no one ever be able to get into it again. And just as clearly, the Imperial survey team that had studied Yavin 4 after the Rebels abandoned it was just as determined to get in. They'd melted a hole straight through the plug to do so.

Kam ignited his lightsaber and swept some cobwebs from the hole. ''The webs aren't as thick as might be expected. Gantoris may have been in here and the spiders just busy since.''

I unhooked a glowrod from my belt and handed it to him. ''Assuming you want to go first.''

''Sure.'' Kam snapped it on, then ducked his head and worked his way in. Being smaller and somewhat thinner, I slipped sideways through the hole pretty easily after him. Brakiss brought up the rear and joined us, brushing dust from his robe's shoulders.

The green light from Kam's lightsaber and the glowrod's golden beam didn't penetrate very far. We found ourselves on a landing with stairs before us going down. Stretching out to fill the foundation of the Temple was one huge chamber with little alcoves built into the walls. We could only dimly see the ones closest to our position, but they looked smaller and slightly more cramped than the rooms we had in the Great Temple.

To either side of us, stairs doubled back up to the next level. I took the glowrod from Kam and played the light over the stairs going down and the two sets heading up. ''Dust looks fairly undisturbed. If Gantoris came in here, he was floating himself along, and I don't think he was quite that good.''

"Maybe this landing is just as far as he got." Brakiss shrugged his shoulders. "Maybe he didn't dare go any further."

"I don't believe that." Kam pointed with his light-saber toward the stairs going up. "Shall we?"

Brakiss smiled. "This is what we came for, after all."

Kam led the way. Our footfalls echoed dryly through the Temple and my flesh began to crawl as we ascended. From having read Unnh's survey report, we knew what to expect, and the anticipation had me a little scared. Knowing there was evil afoot and heading toward the reason General Dodonna had ordered the place sealed, I felt we were courting disaster.

Proving I was a true Halcyon, however, I had no intention of retreating.

The stairs came out onto another landing that served as a foyer for the Temple's Grand Audience Chamber. The sharply sloped outer walls came together high above the chamber floor to form the ceiling. Three towers set equidistant down the chamber's midline came to a point well below the roof's apex, yet somehow seemed to be holding the roof aloft nonetheless. The conical tower nearest us and its companion at the far end of the chamber were covered in rings of odd runes and sigils that I couldn't identify, much less read. Window-slits in the west wall let sunlight paint golden bars down the length of the floor, providing a warm glow for the room.

As warm as that glow was, however, it did little to dispel the chill I felt coming from the Temple's main and most disturbing feature.

The third tower—also a tall, narrow cone—had been shaped entirely out of a blue crystal. I would have almost called it sapphire, because it did glow with its own internal light, but the light did not shift as we moved closer.

Instead it seemed more to flow as if it were a liquid bubbling up and around inside the crystal, swirling in some great cycle.

"The Sullustan said the stone feels oily, and you can feel the tingle of energy pulsing off it." Brakiss rubbed his hands together. "Care to confirm the veracity of that report?"

I shivered. "Not me. Not yet."

Kam extinguished the blade on his lightsaber and clipped it back to his belt. "I'll take a pass. You probably ought not to touch it either."

Brakiss frowned. "You're no fun."

"Touching that thing will not be fun." I walked closer to it, being careful not to step into the circular pit surrounding it. The nearer I drew to it, the colder I felt. The energy pulsing out of it was not palpably evil, but I could sense a host of negative emotions like despair and anger. Worse yet, as I stared into the translucent stone's depths, I saw ghostly images drifting past. Some seemed utterly unfamiliar: gangling creatures with clawed hands and feet. Others were more familiar, often human, with their faces destroyed by damage or just contorted in agony. Even so, I thought I recognized some of them. A few comrades who had fallen along the way, more enemies I had slain.

Then Gantoris' face appeared and stared at me with dead eyes.

I jerked back and pointed. "Do you see it? Do you see Gantoris?"

Kam's head snapped around to look at me, his eyes slowly focusing. "I didn't see him. I saw . . . others."

The hint of a smile played over Brakiss' face as he turned toward us. "I really didn't see much of anything."

I glanced back at the stone and Gantoris' image had vanished. "I could have sworn I saw him."

Brakiss shrugged. "Trick of the light." His voice came weightlessly, scourging me with a hint of scorn.

I fixed him with an emerald stare. "You still want to touch it?"

He shook his head. "No, that's okay."

Kam wore a grim expression. "I don't know what this thing is or why it is, but I do know I'm not comfortable here." He jerked a thumb at the lightbars on the floor. "And the way the sunlight moved between when we started looking and now, we were staring into that thing for a good fifteen minutes."

I shook my head. "Not possible."

"Very possible. Very odd." Kam frowned heavily. "I'm all for leaving."

Brakiss agreed. "No sign Gantoris was ever here."

"Right. Let's go, then."

It wouldn't really do to suggest that three grown men, Jedi apprentices all and two of them armed with lightsabers, fled from an uninhabited temple. I prefer to think of it as our having moved quickly to upset the plans of anyone preparing to ambush us. The fact that we didn't know of anyone else being on the world save our friends still didn't preclude that possibility and I thought our caution quite admirable.

As we retreated from it, Brakiss took one long look back at the Blueleaf Temple. "It's rather amazing, I think, that creatures lacking in sophisticated technology could build such a monument and have it stand the test of time. Unnh's commentary suggests these ruins were all millennia old."

"The Old Republic was well established by that time." I held a branch back, opening the way to the trail that had brought us to the temple. "For all we know they could have used lasers to quarry the rock and carve it, then slid it into place with repulsorlift technology."

"Moreover," Kam offered, "they could have used the Force. As massive as those blocks are, do you think it would be impossible for Master Skywalker to move them?"

"Impossible for him to move them, no, not at all." I heard doubt in Brakiss' voice. "I don't know that I believe Master Skywalker could create a temple like that, however."

I laughed. "Have you forgotten, 'size matters not?' "

"I haven't forgotten it at all, but that's not my point." Brakiss snapped a dead branch from a Massassi sapling and broke himself off a forty-centimeter length of it. "Master Skywalker might have the power, but he's a farm boy from some desiccated, silicon ball. He would be incapable of creating such a work of vision and elegance."

As Brakiss spoke he waved the stick through the air. Kam and I exchanged secret smiles behind his back, then Kam cleared his voice. "So you don't think Master Skywalker could learn to create something like that?"

"Certainly he could, but it would take him forever."

"I see." I narrowed my eyes. "And the crystal cone, could he create one of those?"

Brakiss' shoulders twitched through a shrug. "I don't know, but I would love to try. I think that crystal was incredible. I'd hesitate to call it a work of art because it was unsettling." He turned around, his eyes ablaze. "Imagine having the power to be able to create such a thing."

"Wouldn't want it." Kam shook his head. "I didn't like the crystal at all."

"Yes, but imagine the power to make something like it, something you would like. Using the Force to create a work that would endure for so long." Brakiss laughed aloud and spun as if dancing to some music neither Kam nor I could hear. "It would be fantastic."

I gave him a hard cold look, but he didn't notice. "The lure of that sort of power can be seductive, but it's not easy to come by."

"Unless you resort to the dark side." Kam hunched his shoulders forward. "I know what it is like, and as exhilarating as it can be, it leaves you hollow. Better to work for the true Force than settle for its shadow."

"Yes, but think of what you can do with that power." Brakiss thrust his stick up toward the sky. "A Jedi Master with enough power could have reached up from here and have torn the heart out of the Death Star. Wouldn't have mattered if he was using the dark side, he would have done a good thing."

I reached out and grabbed the back of Brakiss' neck. "Wait just one minute. What you're saying is that the ends justify the means for attaining them, and that's just plain wrong. It's as wrong as anything because it allows you to rationalize away any behavior as good. Sure, let's murder this criminal because we know he's killed folks in the past, or probably will kill them in the future. Or let's destroy this planet because we know, someday, it will slam into that planet. So what if folks on the planet we destroy die—they would have died anyway, and with our way the folks on the other world are saved."

Brakiss spun and nearly slashed my face with his stick. Fortunately for me I'd had forewarning about the arc of his arm and ducked beneath it. A momentary mask of anger slipped over his face, but it almost immediately dissolved into shock and remorse. "Keiran, I'm sorry."

"It's okay, Brakiss. No blood, no report."

Kam came around and draped an arm rather heavily over Brakiss' shoulders. "What Keiran's telling you is right, kid. People start telling themselves they're amassing power for this goal or that, and they convince themselves that it's a good thing. Then when they get enough they find circumstances have changed. They find they need more power or they need to wield this power in ways they didn't expect before. An opponent who won't listen to reason becomes a bug to be squashed instead of a friend who just needs to be convinced. Power comes to poison those who hoard it. They assume others want their power, will resort to any means to get it, and that frees folks up to retaliate in any way they can."

I nodded. "And there's no good that comes from evil. Your example of someone using dark-side power to destroy the Death Star is fine until you ask why he would do that. Is it for his own good, and that of his people? If so, how will he deal with the next threat to them? If he hears of another Death Star and knows someone like the Caamasi are building it, does he destroy them?"

Kam frowned. "Bad example. Everyone knows the Caamasi were committed pacifists."

"I know, Kam, but someone could rationalize them as evil and go after them." I opened my hands. "Face it, someone *did* go after them and nearly wiped out the whole lot of them. I even heard there was a big Caamasi refugee group on Alderaan when it was destroyed. If someone could have seen the Caamasi as a threat, they could have seen anyone as a threat. A child. Anyone."

Brakiss furrowed his brows. "I hear what you are saying and I want to believe you. Part of me says, though, that you can't argue an absolute case that no good can come from wielding dark-side powers. There has to be a time when that could happen.''

"That's theory, Brakiss, but we've got to deal with the practical realities of manipulating the Force." I shook my head. "I don't want to entertain the idea that I could remain uncorrupted by dealing with evil for what I see as a good purpose. That's setting the first foot on a very steep and slippery slope. Maybe, with the help of Master Skywalker, it would be possible to get back to the top, but someone will pay a fearful price during my descent, and I don't want to inflict that on anyone. Neither should you.''

Sixteen

✳

A quick blast from the transport's landing jets lifted debris on a searing wind that made some of the other apprentices duck back or raise their hands to shield their faces. I pulled the heat in and immediately used that energy to impose a tiny Force shield before me. It split the wind and saved me the annoyance of having to blink grit from my eyes and spit dirt from my mouth.

The boxy transport touched down as gently as a feather, but I expected no less from the pilot at the helm. As it settled on its landing struts and the passenger compartment gangway slowly lowered, the apprentices moved in behind Master Skywalker. Kam directed all of them but me to the opening cargo hatch. I walked over by Luke and smiled as Wedge descended from the ship's interior.

Luke waved a greeting at Wedge and the blue-skinned woman following in his wake. The bright-eyed young man coming third down the gangway won a smile from Luke. "Welcome, Kyp Durron."

The wiry youth returned Luke's smile. "I'm ready, Master Skywalker. Teach me the Jedi ways."

"It will be my pleasure." Luke waved him toward the line of folks hauling supplies from the transport's cargo hold. "We will start by unloading the ship. Keiran, if you will see to General Antilles' and Qwi Xux's comfort."

"As you wish, Master." I smiled at Wedge and waved him toward the Great Temple. "You will find our accommodations are a bit less primitive than they were when last you dropped off supplies. This way, please."

Wedge nodded solemnly. "It appears you have made much progress."

Qwi Xux fell into step with Wedge. "Wedge, could you tell me, please, when we will meet this friend of yours that you were anxious to see again?"

Wedge looked about to see we were out of earshot of the others, then his smile broadened warmly. "You have, Doctor Xux. Qwi Xux, meet Corran Horn."

The alien woman frowned. "But Master Skywalker called him Keiran."

Wedge nodded. "He is here under an alias for a variety of reasons. Corran, this is Qwi Xux."

I turned in mid-stride and bowed my head to her. The friendly tone in Wedge's voice when he introduced her made me wonder if I shouldn't offer her my hand, but I felt reluctant to do so. As brilliant as she was beautiful, she had been a key researcher in the Maw installation—the Imperial think-tank that had created the Death Stars, the World Devastators that had ravaged Mon Calamari and the starfighter-sized, invincible Sun Crusher that Kyp Durron had just sunk into the depths of Yavin for safe-keeping. What little gossip we got out here suggested that she had been an unwilling dupe of the Imperials, someone only interested in pure research. That might well have been true, but I had to wonder how someone so bright could fail to notice all the projects she worked on had hideous names and could be so incredibly lethal.

"Welcome to Yavin 4." I pointed toward the sky. "The first Death Star died up there before it could destroy this place."

A hint of pain passed through Wedge's eyes as I spoke, but Qwi just turned to look up toward where I had pointed. "Most of the debris would have fallen into the gas giant, I would suspect, but some must have impacted here." She looked at me with open cerulean eyes. "Have you found such debris?"

I shook my head. "Haven't been looking. There was an Imperial survey team or two here after the Rebellion abandoned the planet, so I would assume they collected what they could for analysis."

"Pity."

"Right." I led the two of them into the Great Temple and took the turbolift to the second level. "Here we have refresher stations and rooms for you, if you wish to catch up on sleep. I can also get you food."

The doctor smiled. "I would like a quick nap, if that is acceptable."

Wedge nodded. "I'll check in with you in an hour, how's that?"

She nodded. "Good. Nice to meet you, Cor . . . er, Keiran."

"Sleep well, Doctor Xux." I pointed her to the room I'd prepared for her earlier, then steered Wedge toward the room I'd prepped for him.

Inside Wedge appropriated a chair and sat, tilting it back so it rested against the wall and his feet dangled above the floor. "You don't like her, do you?"

I caught just a hint of pique in Wedge's voice. "Don't know her well enough to form an opinion, but her playthings have made quite an impression. Maybe because you helped destroy two of them you have a different perspective on her, but I'd not consider myself a big fan of her work."

"She really didn't know what she was getting into, what they were doing with her research."

"Are you sure? The code names should have told her what was going on. She should have at least asked herself what would happen *if*, by mistake, these things were used on inhabited planets. We have life-sign sensors. How tough would it have been to put a life-sensor interlock on the Death Star so it couldn't kill Alderaan?" I found anger creeping into my voice and raised both of my hands. "I shouldn't have said that, sorry."

Wedge glanced down at his hands. "Don't be. Nothing I haven't asked myself a million times since I started acting as her bodyguard. When she's around, when I speak with her, she's just so bright and innocent—the antithesis of the Death Star and the World Devastators and the Sun Crusher. I think she thought the Sun Crusher would be used to eliminate beta stars from binary systems to provide system stability or to clear uninhabited systems from navigational routes."

My eyes narrowed. "Oh, no. You *like* her."

Wedge's head came up. "What?"

I whirled the room's other chair around and dropped into it, letting my chest press against its back. "You're supposed to be her bodyguard and you're falling for her."

"You'd like her if you'd spend more time around her."

"Don't do it, Wedge, don't do it."

He glanced over at me, letting a sloppy grin tug at one

corner of his mouth. "Why not? Wouldn't this be a final reconciliation of the Rebels and the Imperials?"

"Wedge, I'm speaking from experience." I sagged forward against the chair-back. "When I was with Cor-Sec I had several assignments where I was to see to the personal safety of someone important. In fact, I once had to deal with your sister on a visit to Corellia. Didn't know she was your sister at the time, however."

"If you're going to tell me you fell for my sister while guarding her, I don't want to hear it."

"Nope, not her. It was the daughter of the shipping magnate who owned Tinta Lines. She was the target of a kidnapper. Of course, when I was guarding someone, we found a hole and crawled in, didn't gallivant around the galaxy."

"Moving target is harder to hit."

"Good point." I smiled. "Anyway, Siolle Tinta and I got along famously once we discovered we shared similar opinions about art. In close quarters, we reinforced each other's ideas and it quickly became us against the world. On the outside, Iella nailed the kidnapper, so we only spent three days together, but if you'd asked me at the end of that time if it was love and lasers for life, I would have told you all systems were go."

"What happened?"

"While we had one thing in common, we had all sorts of things that weren't. I was with CorSec, which meant I couldn't take off and hit a spa on Selonia, or travel to Imperial Center for the opening of an art exhibit in the Galactic Museum. The gulf between us proved insurmountable. We parted friends, but we both knew that what we'd had while together was a supernova that was collapsing in on itself. We might have generated a lot of heat and light, but eventually the black hole would have torn us apart.''

Wedge nodded, but stared past me. ''You'll allow me to plot my own course through this?''

''I can't stop you.''

''But I thought you Jedi could easily influence weak minds.''

I laughed lightly along with him. ''*This* Jedi knows better than to think of your mind as weak, and I've no desire to go mucking about without good reason. You're a big boy. If it works, great. If it doesn't, you've got friends. I imagine my wife would give you an earful on this.''

''Yeah, and Mirax can be a mite more persuasive than you can.'' He tipped his chair forward onto all four feet. ''No word yet from Han and any of his contacts about Mirax. Sorry.''

I sighed heavily. ''I didn't expect he would have much to say, given that he's been on Kessel recently. Booster's not been talking to you?''

''I've been hard to find, but I've had no messages.''

''Best to let sleeping Hutts snore.'' I felt anger gathering, but I dissipated it with a quick calming breath. ''You'll let me know if you *do* hear anything, right?''

''As soon as I do get word, you'll know.'' Wedge smiled solemnly. ''It's the least I can do for a friend.''

Wedge and Xux left in the evening and I felt sorry to see them go. The one truly difficult aspect of the Jedi academy for me was isolation from news of the outside world. Han Solo's adventure on Kessel and the theft of the Sun Crusher had been presented to us as asides— sidebars to lessons Master Skywalker taught us. More information came out now that Kyp Durron was with us as a student, but even that was tantalizingly spare.

Even more spare was any word on the Invids.

Kyp's presence seemed to put a spark back into Master Skywalker—the spark that had been diminished since Gantoris' death. Kyp proved almost immediately to be the greatest of the apprentices gathered here. With only a minimum of training, he blasted on past all of us in terms of what he could do. Supporting himself on one hand only, he could balance rocks and fallen tree boles with ease. Given my lack of ability in that area, I found his skills somewhat intimidating.

Master Skywalker found Kyp's abilities all but mesmerizing and devoted a lot of time to directing his studies. I guess that made sense in a variety of ways. I suspected that Luke saw a lot of himself in Kyp. They both came from brutal worlds—Tatooine and Kessel respectively. Kyp had received initial instruction from the fallen Jedi female Vima-Da-Boda much as Obi-Wan had taught Luke. Kyp had also proved adept at piloting a ship and had saved Han Solo's life—a positive endorsement, to be sure. Lastly, Kyp's power dwarfed that of Gantoris, making him the perfect candidate to eclipse the memory of the academy's first failure.

Of course, no one stated that directly, nor did we think of Gantoris in that way. Gantoris' remains had been interred in the midst of a beautiful grove, and Master Skywalker himself had driven a grey plinth into the ground to mark the spot. We knew it was the sort of paradisiacal place Gantoris would have wanted for himself and his people. Several of us noted that we wouldn't mind being buried there when we fell, but none of us hoped that would be soon. Still, the spectre of Gantoris' failure haunted us all to a greater or lesser extent.

Luke turned much of the instruction of the other apprentices over to Kam Solusar, and Kam did a good job. As a taskmaster he was fair but firm, and everyone progressed steadily under his guidance. Luke made good use of Tionne's research to instill us with a sense of community and continuity. We began to think of the Imperium as Jedi Twilight, and we were the dawning of a new day of a new era.

Luke did allow Kam to start training me in lightsaber combat. I used my grandfather's lightsaber and relished its cool, smooth weight in my hand. I could feel the antiquity in the weapon and almost feel Nejaa Halcyon's hands pressed there with mine. I think that sensation broke the final wall for me, allowing me to accept my position in the grand tradition of the Jedi. If I could feel my grandfather's essence in the weapon he had wielded, then I felt the weight of his responsibilities on me as well.

We began with remote training. I had a nodding acquaintance with the little floating balls that could sting you with a quick needle of blazing energy. At the CorSec Academy remotes played a part in blaster training. A blaster set on stun could knock a remote out, so trainees used them as targets. In my time at the academy I became very good orienting on movement and nailing a remote with a blue bolt.

"The object of the exercise here, Keiran, is not to kill the remote, but to defend yourself from its shots." Kam let one of the small balls hover over his outstretched palm. "Use your lightsaber to block the stingshots. Once you can do this with one remote, we'll work with more. And once you can defend yourself against a handful, we will work on redirecting the bolts at various targets."

I gave Kam a smile. "It's a goal."

Kam released the remote and I ignited my lightsaber. The silvery blade splashed cold light over the interior of what had been the Rebel hangar in the Great Temple. We chose to work inside instead of out because the Temple's walls would stop the remote's bolts. While they wouldn't do more than wound my vanity, a stray shot could stun a woolamander and probably kill a stintaril. Since I was as much of a danger to myself with the lightsaber as anything else, doing everything possible to avoid collateral damage was a good idea.

The remote hissed and puffed as it floated through the air. It spun, then spat out a quick ruby dart that lanced into my thigh. I cursed and hopped back, but the remote came in, pressing the attack. I set myself and willed away the pain, then worked on picking up the remote and its next blast.

While the remote, being lifeless, did not have a direct connection to the Force, it existed within the universe bound together by the Force. I made myself *disfocus* my attention on it directly and instead gain an impression of where it fit within the immediate area. I opened myself to the Force, allowing it to seep in and extend my sensory perception. Then, there, I saw the remote moving through the Force, leaving little oscillations in it like a moth moving through smoke. By spotting the disturbances it created, I was able to pick it up and track it.

Likewise, within it, the transference of energy created even smaller vibrations within the Force. I sensed the microtremors of energy gathering to fire a stinger. I pinpointed where that reservoir of energy existed and began to bring my lightsaber up and around. As the stinger diode spat scarlet fire, I swept my lightsaber in an arc that picked off the dart heading for my stomach. A nanosecond later I caught hints of another bolt, but missed blocking it.

The dart pinned my left foot to the floor. I yelped—and Kam's laughter did not help ease the pain—and danced back. My retreat bumped me into a pillar I'd not expected to be there, rebounding me back toward the remote. It fired again, but the lunge I took at it got enough blade in front of me to deflect the bolt back off over my right shoulder.

And right past Kam's right ear.

He arched an eyebrow at me and hit a button on his remote controller, powering the unit down. "Did you manage that on purpose?"

I dropped to one knee and rubbed my foot. "I'd love to claim credit, but I'm not the Force genius that Kyp is."

"That's readily apparent." Kam came over and plucked the remote from the air. "Think back for a second. You didn't know where the pillar was. Had you extended your senses enough to know where I was?"

I frowned and tried to recall. "Nope. I think my sensory range was about two meters, and you were outside it. So was the pillar until I jumped back."

"And when you were hurt you probably pulled the sphere in even tighter." He opened a panel on the remote and twisted a small dial. "I'm going to move it out to four meters. You need to be able to push your sphere out larger and larger, and track the things inside it. If you don't know where you are and what you're doing, you're in deep trouble."

"Got it. Pilots refer to it as 'situational awareness.' If you can't track your own people and the enemy in a vape-brawl, you end up doing a burn-in on some world."

"That's it exactly. My father used to refer to it as a sphere of responsibility. He used to tell me that as Jedi our sphere of responsibility was as big as the galaxy, and the best Jedi could understand and sort out whole star systems. I'd not actually felt that until the other night, in the grotto."

I nodded. "I copy. As a pilot I tended to be pretty good in the situational awareness area, but using the Force is like trying to learn to see after having been blind for most of my life."

"Not easy, but you can do it." Kam slapped me on the shoulder. "And don't let Kyp's progress bother you."

"Bother me?" I gave him an annoyed stare. "Kyp's progress doesn't bother me. It really has no effect on me."

"Really." Kam's eyes narrowed and sank back into shadows. "You're not a bit envious of the attention he is getting from Master Skywalker?"

I hesitated for a moment and let the question roam around in my brain. I shook my head. "I know I'm competitive, and I would have thought you'd be right, but I don't see Kyp as someone I'm competing with. I've been second best before. That's a role I can accept. I make it my mission to make sure the front runner can't relax, but I'm more concerned with doing *my* best than I am with beating someone else's best."

Kam's expression lightened considerably. "That shows a fair amount of maturity."

"Kinda scary, isn't it?"

"Not in a Jedi Knight." Kam tossed the remote into the air and it withdrew to a range of four meters. "Go again, Keiran Halcyon. Concentrate. Show me your best."

Seventeen

Of course, my best was nothing compared to Kyp Dur-ron's best. Kyp's growth in the Force was nothing shy of incredible. In just over a week he surpassed anything the rest of us were doing by light-years. Master Skywalker didn't know what to do with him, he was so good. Kyp gave us hope that reestablishing the Jedi Order *could* be and *would* be done.

I tried to get to know Kyp, but he kept himself aloof and apart from me. He made other friends among us. Dorsk 81, the yellow-fleshed clone from Khomm, had been closer to Gantoris than most, and Kyp's friendship filled a void in his life. They spent a fair amount of time together, heading off into the surrounding jungle as a survey team all by themselves.

Kyp had grown up in the spice mines of Kessel and was very strong in the Force. Growing up in prison made him hold himself very close, and he didn't take to prying into his life. My attempts to open him up just drove him away from me, so I backed off. I didn't want to do any-thing that would make getting to know him impossible later.

And it wasn't as if I didn't have other things to do.

Gantoris had been dead for over two weeks, and I was

really no closer to finding out who or what had killed him than when the smoke was still curling up off his body. I still felt we had a sociopathic killer on Yavin 4, but no one had found any clues of someone lurking here. We had Gantoris' body, but his killer had vanished without a trace.

The Holocron was not much more help in solving the murder, but it did give us some planetary history to work from. Yavin 4, it turned out, had been the seat of power of a formidable Dark Lord of the Sith, a fallen Jedi known as Exar Kun. He had been seduced to the dark side when he studied the ways of the Sith and incorporated their magics into his manipulation of the Force. He had come to Yavin 4 and had enslaved the Massassi people. He used them to create all the temples on the world to help focus his power. Only when the Jedi of the Old Republic came after him in what became known as the Sith War was he defeated and his evil expunged from the galaxy for all time.

Luke's admonition about the dark side when he saw Gantoris' body made me wonder if, somehow, Gantoris had managed to dig up, decipher and study some Sith artifacts or manuals. Somewhere he had learned to make a lightsaber. I didn't want to think one of the Emperor's Dark Jedi had managed to slip onto Yavin 4 and was tutoring students. Figuring that Gantoris had gotten himself in trouble was a more pleasant alternative theory.

Unfortunately for my peace of mind, the idea of Gantoris' body being a taunt and a challenge fit all too well patterns I had seen before. My father had always told me to follow my gut. He'd really been encouraging my reliance in the Force, so I started with the assumption that an active intelligence had instructed Gantoris and then killed him.

The problem with that assumption remained the same as it had always been: if such a person existed, Master Skywalker should have detected him. A droid doing the teaching would explain why we didn't detect him in the network of life on Yavin 4. A droid might even have the knowledge to teach Gantoris, but since it could not manipulate the Force, the lessons learned would be relatively useless.

Off the other edge of the scale we had the possibility of someone so powerful in the Force that he could remain undetected even by a Master. Gantoris' "dark man" and the person in Master Luke's nightmare could fit that profile. Putting Exar Kun at the top of the list of suspects was easy. He'd certainly not have balked at roasting Gantoris alive, but he'd been dead for four thousand years. Master Luke had alluded to the idea that he had seen and spoken with Obi-Wan Kenobi after the Jedi Master had been killed, but within a decade after his death, Obi-Wan had gone away forever. A Dark Lord of the Sith might have more staying power than that, but four millennia?

In addition to working with Tionne to uncover more data about the Jedi, I got to spend more time with Kam learning how to use a lightsaber. We managed to expand my sphere of responsibility up to sixteen meters for fine control, which meant I could pretty much own a city block. If I focused in one direction I was good up to two hundred fifty meters for fine control on picking off blaster bolts, or line of sight for sensing presence. In one experiment, I implanted a vision of dinner being served in Dorsk 81's mind, summoning him and Kyp back from one of their hikes though they were still half a kilometer away.

I tried to get into Kyp's mind on that occasion, but I

didn't know him well enough to break through. That confirmed one of my theories about who I could and could not influence. The better I knew someone, the more receptive they seemed to be to my projections. If they were hostile or unknown to me and/or the image was terribly complex, I had a lot of trouble making them see anything.

After a particularly grueling day I ended up lounging around with the rest of the students in the early evening. We'd spent half the day listening to one of the auxiliary Holocron gatekeepers spin stories of court intrigues in the Old Republic—intrigues that must have been fascinating when you knew who he was talking about, but the gatekeeper's stunning inability to characterize anyone meant that I lost track of what was going on almost immediately. After that another gatekeeper told the story of how Yoda had become a Jedi. That story was actually pretty good and undoubtedly saved my life because a minute more of the Old Republic stories and I'd have slipped into a coma. After that I went out on a ten-kilometer run just to convince myself I was, in fact, alive.

The academy personnel had all gathered in one of the larger seminar rooms on the second level to listen to Tionne's latest ballad. I knew she had drawn it from material we had researched together, but she promised it was not a Halcyon ballad, so I was willing to come listen. Actually, I'd have come listen even if she were singing about Old Republic court intrigues because when her voice filled a room, there was no question about it: you were very much alive.

She accompanied herself on a unique instrument that had two resonating boxes mounted on a shaft. Strings ran over the boxes, allowing her to pluck or strum them. The arrangement almost made the instrument sound like two separate instruments, and her skill with it brought it close to being orchestral. Most of her ballads, like the new one, the ballad of Nomi Sunrider, had a stately lyrical theme running beneath them. Occasionally Tionne would also break into a slightly more raucous tune that usually got me to hum along.

Nomi Sunrider's ballad came from the era of Exar Kun and the Sith War. She was a woman whose husband had been slain, so she took his place in a Jedi training cadre. She went on to become an acclaimed Jedi who played a key role in the Sith War. Singing about her might have been considered sacrilege in the Great Temple of Yavin 4, but I didn't think anyone would protest the fact after four thousand years.

I was wrong.

Halfway through the song, Kyp got up from the floor, his face contorted with disgust. "I wish you wouldn't perpetuate that ridiculous story. Nomi Sunrider was a victim. She fought in the Sith War without ever knowing what the battles were about. She listened blindly to her Jedi Masters, who were afraid because Exar Kun had discovered a way for the Jedi to expand their power."

Tionne set her instrument down, surprised and a little hurt. She asked Kyp why he hadn't helped her reconstruct that legend if he had special information like that. Luke asked him where he'd learned what he'd just said, but that question had already answered itself in my gut: Exar Kun. I'd been there with Tionne as we listened to Bodo Baas talk about the Sith War. Kyp's take on it was decidedly pro–Exar Kun and, as nearly as we had been able to discover, there were no minority opinions on the subject available from the Holocron.

I came out of my reverie as Kyp's blazing gaze

brushed past my own. ". . . they wouldn't all have been slaughtered. The Jedi would never have fallen, and we wouldn't be *here*, taught by someone who doesn't know any more than we do."

Luke again asked Kyp where he had learned his history. The young man hesitated for a moment, then mumbled something about having used the Holocron. I shot Tionne a glance and she frowned. Between the lessons we'd all learned from it and the work she was doing with it, unless Kyp was an insomniac, he really didn't have time to study it.

Before I could call him on that lie, Master Skywalker's R2 unit rolled into the room and whistled at him. I caught a bit of the code for "incoming," and stretched out with my senses. Even before Luke announced to us that we had a visitor, I caught a sense of a powerful Force presence descending toward the moon. By the time we left the Great Temple, a Z-95 Headhunter was setting down on the landing grid.

The pilot emerged wearing a silvery, form-fitting flightsuit. She removed her helmet and shook out red-gold hair. Even in the twilight, I noticed the green of her eyes—lighter and more striking than mine. She looked quite beautiful, though the smile she gave Master Skywalker seemed to rest uncomfortably on her lips.

"Mara Jade," Luke greeted her.

I missed her reply as the uneasiness I felt over Kyp suddenly became compounded. Iella had told me about this Mara Jade. She had been groomed by the Emperor to be an agent who was adept in use of the Force. Her very existence had been unknown to all but a handful of Imperials, and she would have remained hidden save for her role in defeating Grand Admiral Thrawn. Details on that were all very sketchy, but I'd been left with the impression that she was very competent, very lethal and not that positively disposed toward Jedi.

Despite that, she pulled from a pouch at her side a Jedi cloak. Luke smiled as he turned and presented her to us. "This is Mara Jade. She has come here to learn the ways of the Jedi."

Everyone applauded her—even Kyp, though he remained sullen. Luke apparently noticed that as easily as I did because he waved me over. "Keiran, will you please see to Mara's billeting? I have something to which I want to attend, if you don't mind, Mara."

She gave him a quick nod, then turned and regarded me up and down. "Have we met before?"

I knew we had not, but I still found something disturbingly familiar about her. "No, I don't think so."

"Odd, I usually don't forget a face."

"And I think I would remember you." I waved her toward the Great Temple. "We have a variety of rooms ready. Master Skywalker's chambers are on the third level. Likewise some of the students. Most visitors are housed on the second level."

I felt tendrils of the Force snake out from her and probe the fringes of my mind. "But that's not where you live."

I concentrated for a nanosecond and shut her out of my mind. "No. I was attracted to the old pilot billets on the ground floor."

Mara Jade smiled and I found it all too predatory for me. "Then I'll look there first for a place to stay. If you don't mind."

"Mine is not to mind, but to obey the wishes of my Master."

She clapped her hands mockingly. "Oh, very good. Spoken like an obsequious Imperial courtier."

I gave her a quick smile as we entered the Great Temple. "Glad to make you feel at home."

That remark brought her head up. "The Empire's dead."

"But not all loyalties to it."

She stopped in the middle of the hangar floor and I noticed her spacesuit had shifted to darker, flatter colors to blend in with the surroundings. "You said we'd not met, but you clearly have a problem with me. Shall we settle it now?" The narrowed stare she gave me was pure fire and won a smile from me.

I was just about to rise to her challenge and let her have a catalog of hideous things the Empire had done, beginning with the death of the Jedi Knights and working on up to Gantoris' murder, when sense kicked back in. Here I was, standing in the middle of the place from which a desperate strike at the Empire had been launched. It had succeeded. I had been part of subsequent attacks against the Empire, attacks that brought it to its knees and took away its capital world: Coruscant. I had helped destroy the Empire that had been her home, and there was no reason why she shouldn't long for things from her past as much as I did.

I drew in a deep breath, held it, then slowly exhaled it. "Please, forgive my being rude. It is very easy, when things are not going as planned, to trace the fault back to the Empire. You are not the Empire. To accuse you of loyalties or sympathies is unfair and probably stupid. Not the first time I've been either, but I try not to do both with people I've just met."

I extended my hand to her. "I am Corran Horn." My true name almost caught in my throat, but offering it to her came as a sign of trust. Luke clearly trusted her and my gut told me I should do the same.

Mara Jade shook my hand and looked me over again. "I've heard of you. I apologize for the probe. I knew you were familiar, but the name 'Keiran' didn't fit. I didn't know why. Since I sensed no deception from Luke—Master Skywalker—I wondered if he knew you were here under a lie."

"He suggested it." I smiled. "In many ways I think he thinks of me as Keiran Halcyon. Seems Keiran Halcyon was an ancestor of mine and a Jedi of some note in the Corellian system."

"I see."

The smile on her face slowly died and I sensed her closing toward me. I didn't know why and was fairly certain I could have tried to probe her for eons without getting so much as a sign of life from her. Part of me wanted to once again become very suspicious, but I kept that side of myself at bay. I had decided to trust her, so I trusted her. That might have seemed stupid, but it *felt* very right.

"Master Skywalker felt I should attend the academy under this alias so I wouldn't distract the students."

"And there were other reasons you didn't want to attract attention?"

"Why would you ask that?"

"Your father-in-law is Booster Terrik." Mara Jade let the barest shadow of a smile tug at the corners of her mouth. "That's reason enough for anyone to go into hiding. I don't seem to recall having heard anything of Mirax for six weeks or so. You've been here, what, a month?"

"And you wonder if I murdered her and have come here to hide?"

"No." Mara's words came cold and solemn. "I wondered if someone else murdered her and you're here learning how to find them."

Her hitting so close to the mark sent a jolt through me. "How is it that you know how long ago anyone heard about my wife?"

She shrugged easily as we passed into the back corridor leading to the old pilots' quarters. "She's very good at what she does, you know. As a smuggler, she's easily in the ninety-fifth percentile in finding exotic goods and finding buyers for them. Talon Karrde still talks about the Sith lanvarok she enabled him to unload. When someone like her drops out for more than a couple of weeks, either they're up to something big, or they're dead."

I flicked on the glowlamps in a small room. "This room belonged to a female Rebel pilot. She died before the Death Star battle."

Mara took a quick look around the room, then nodded. "It'll suit me. So, what happened to Mirax?"

"She's alive, but that's all I know." I leaned against the door jamb. "Master Skywalker and Wedge think she was kidnapped for reasons unknown. They think someone has her in hibernation. She's out there, somewhere, waiting."

The fire-haired woman folded her arms across her chest. "And you're here learning what you can so you can find her."

"Find her and save her."

Mara nodded. "Lucky woman."

"I hope so." I let my voice descend into a growl. "If she's not, if I arrive too late; her captors are going to find all the luck in the galaxy won't do them any good."

EIGHTEEN

I think Master Skywalker planned on or hoped for something a bit festive in the way of a meal for our guest. This meant I got tagged with kitchen duty. While I didn't really have any formal training in the culinary arts—and the Holocron had not revealed any Jedi power oriented toward making food taste good—I *had* been raised on Corellia and had seen a fair amount of the galaxy. Luke reasoned that I knew more about interesting food than a Bespin hermit or Dorsk 81—especially because the clone's digestive system was so specialized he could only eat processed food wafers.

Ugh.

Luckily for me, I'd learned all I needed to know about cooking from the chef on Siolle Tinta's private yacht. During a party with which I had become bored I met Chid—like all great artists, he asserted he only needed one name—and we chatted about the self-important guests on the cruise. We also drank, and after a lot of chatting and even more drinking, Chid confided in me the keys of great culinary success.

"First, make portions small. If they want more, they think it was good. Two, give the dish an exotic name and make it sound like there are secret spices in there. Snobs will spend much time trying to see if their palate is sophisticated enough to detect one part per million of Ithorian saffron and they won't dare pass judgment on the food for fear someone will think them a boor. Three, serve things that are supposed to be cooked *raw*, and serve hot things *cold*. Makes them think it's special. Four—most important—tell them you created it special for them. Only a Gamorrean would protest such an honor.''

The academy's supplies weren't really long on spices—calling them survival rations would actually be stretching a point—but mashing up ration bars, mixing them with fruit compotes and baking them into long slender loaves that I sliced on a bias made for an interesting breadlike food. Dried meat became something of a stew with enough boiling, and tossing the dried veggies into the meat broth allowed them to soak up some flavor. And since we'd all gotten to realizing that the grain gruel the New Republic sent probably wouldn't kill us, I concentrated on spicing it, and garnished a big plate of it with a couple blueleaf sprigs that made the yellowish mound of grain look special for the occasion. I also included the obligatory salad of local greens, but only because Master Skywalker seemed to enjoy it.

I'd just finished serving everything and was returning from the kitchen after shutting down the stove, when Kyp stormed out of the dining room and clipped me with a shoulder.

"Hey, Kyp, what's the problem?"

The younger man said nothing and continued to stalk down the corridor. I ran after him and caught up with him after a couple of steps. I dropped my left hand on his left shoulder. "Kyp, answer me."

Kyp whirled beneath my hand, his dark eyes blazing. I

felt something solid hit my chest, but I'd already begun to move to my right. The Force blow he aimed at me glanced off the left side of my chest, yet was strong enough to bounce me off the corridor wall. I caught myself against the rough stones, but not before I'd slid halfway to the floor.

"*You* are not my master." Kyp shifted from pointing at me to pointing back toward the dining room. "*He* is not my master. What good is it being a Jedi if we do not act?"

"What good is it if we are Jedi that don't act responsibly?" I hauled myself upright. "Remember, Kyp, 'no-good Jedi' kicked Exar Kun's butt."

Kyp struck at me again through the Force, but I expected it this time. I relaxed and let the Force energy flow over and through me. I absorbed enough of it to let me create a shield that split the attack. The fact that I didn't end up being ground back against the wall surprised him.

"You're good, Kyp, but you're not great." I held my hands up in a nonthreatening gesture. "You're involved with someone who lost a long time ago. Don't compound his error."

"And who will stop me?"

I hesitated because Kyp's words seemed to echo within themselves. It took me a second or two to figure out that the echo wasn't a purely auditory phenomenon. I was hearing Kyp's voice through my ears, but the undertones were coming to me through the Force. We were not alone, which meant Kyp's mentor had come to aid his apprentice.

"I will, if you make it necessary."

An ancient sneer of contempt twisted Kyp's features. "Puny Jedi, you are of no concern to me."

Even though I braced myself for another attack, it did no good. Kyp's previous Force blows were like light breezes compared with a full-out gale. I slammed back into the wall with a teeth-rattling impact. As my body absorbed Force energy and fed it back out, the shield I'd created grew in size. More importantly, my surprise and survival instinct opened me up to the Force and allowed it to flow into the shield. Even so, Kyp's attack jammed the shield back against the wall and I watched stone crumble beneath its rim.

The safe area I had began to shrink, and my chest became tight as it compressed my ribs. I looked Kyp straight in the eyes and tried to shoot into his brain the image of the mask of hate he wore, but the world around me went black before I could tell if I'd had any success at all.

I awakened probably less than a minute after that, judging by how much of the grain gruel had been consumed in my absence. I hung in the doorway to the dining room, my ribs a bit sore. Streen got up from his place and helped me to a chair while Tionne poured me a glass of water.

I drank it, wishing it was full of Corellian whiskey.

Luke's blue eyes became slits. "What happened to you?"

"Kyp didn't like the menu." I winced as a twinge ran through my ribs. "We had a discussion in the hallway. You didn't feel anything?"

Heads all around the table shook and I felt cold dread begin to congeal in my stomach. If Exar Kun could mask the attack on me in such a way that Luke could not feel it barely fifteen meters away, then he could have slain

Gantoris and could still wreak more havoc here with impunity. We were up against something more powerful than I'd ever cared to imagine existing.

I stood. "Master Skywalker, I would have a word with you, alone."

The other apprentices started to get up, but Luke waved them back down into their seats. "We will be but a moment. The kitchen?"

I nodded and followed him. Once alone in the kitchen, Luke turned on me. "You should not have attempted to interfere with Kyp."

I blinked with surprise. "I wasn't trying to interfere. He was upset. I just asked what was happening."

"But you did something to provoke an attack, didn't you?"

I rubbed a hand along my jaw and leaned back against the conservator. "It's an old interrogation technique. I drew a conclusion from what I saw earlier this evening and tried it out. I told him Exar Kun had gotten his butt kicked by the Jedi, and that Kun was wrong. I got a reaction, a very strong one."

"Kyp is strong in the Force." Luke folded his arms over his chest. "He has a certain sympathy for Exar Kun. The reaction was not to be unexpected."

"I could buy into that, but I felt another presence. Not strongly, but it was there and it helped Kyp's next attack pack a wallop."

"And you think that was Exar Kun?"

I thought for a moment before answering. "Either it is Exar Kun or someone calling himself Exar Kun because Kyp reacted to that name. Could be it's someone just trying to wrap himself up in Kun's legend, just the way he presented himself to you as your father. Regardless, he's powerful. Kind of what I would expect from a Dark Lord of the Sith.''

Luke shook his head. "You're making a mistake jumping to the conclusion that we're dealing with Exar Kun. We don't know what happened to him in the end.''

"Look, I've been with Tionne as she's pulled as much information as we can from the Holocron about Kun. He was running the culture here and a massive Jedi strike wiped it out. Certain conclusions seem logical from there." I shrugged. "I think planning for the worst case scenario can't hurt.''

"There might be gatekeepers in the Holocron that have data about Exar Kun that neither you nor Tionne can access. I will have to conduct my own investigation in that area.''

I caught a note of hesitancy in his voice. "You're not thinking that just because you were able to redeem the last Dark Lord of the Sith that Exar Kun might have had a change of heart, are you?''

Luke's face became impassive. "That can't be ruled out.''

"Wait a minute, you can't be serious." I watched him carefully. "Look, if Exar Kun was never redeemed, if no other Dark Lord of the Sith ever saw the error of his ways and came back to the light side, that means nothing concerning your father. You're letting yourself think that if you'd been good enough, if you'd done everything right, your father could have, *would have* survived. You're thinking that you didn't work hard enough to redeem him because, if you had, he'd still be here. And you're thinking that if another Dark Lord had been redeemed, then you could compare what you did to what happened to him and learn if you really did do all you could do.''

"No, no way." Luke shook his head adamantly. "You have it all wrong."

"Could be, Master Skywalker, but . . ." I swallowed hard. "Look, I know exactly how this game is played because I did the same thing when *my* father died. Neither one of us can be certain that we did all we could to save them, but all the second guessing in the galaxy won't give us a second chance at saving them. The only thing we can do is accept responsibility and live with the consequences."

Luke's expression remained impassive, but even that told a story. Just for a moment I got to see him as the human being he was. Raised by relatives on Tatooine, always wondering about his parents, never learning how to properly deal with a mother or father. He had to constantly wonder why his life wasn't "normal," not realizing that *everyone* asks themselves that question. And then, when he discovered who his father was, it turned out that his father was the trusted henchman of the galaxy's most hated individual. His father had not only killed people, but he had been the betrayer of the most noble tradition in the galaxy. He determined he would save his father and did, just in time to lose him forever.

I walked over and rested my hands on his shoulders. "You did all you could do. You know that. Here, with this academy, you are helping erase the legacy your father left behind. What you are doing is good and vital, but you can't let your need for reassurance blind you to what's going on here, right now. Kyp is out of control and under the influence of someone that is steeped in the dark side. You have to talk to him and straighten him out."

I felt a wave of peace flow down over Luke. "You've now reasoned your way to a conclusion I made before your confrontation with him. Kyp is still in a state of turmoil. I think he would see intervention right now as a confrontation, don't you?''

I nodded. "Let him sort his head out himself? He's a smart kid, it could definitely work. If I can be of any help . . .''

"Just don't provoke him.''

I shook my head. "I'm sorry for interfering, Master Skywalker. I'll gladly leave him alone. With his ally he's out of my weight class anyway.'' I smiled carefully. "I don't pick fights where I know I'll get pounded.''

Luke returned my smile. "Unless there is a good reason.''

"Right, and I can't think of one that will be good enough to deal with Kyp any time soon.''

In retrospect, there were billions of reasons to confront Kyp and risk getting my head handed to me. Luke was the Jedi Master and he asked me to step away, so I did because I agreed with his plans. Even now I wish I'd tried to do something, but all the scenarios I worked out in my head turned out just as bloody as the real thing did.

Short of murdering Kyp, I could have changed nothing.

And by murdering him, I would have irrevocably changed myself for the worst.

I returned to a meal that we completed in relative silence. What comments were offered were light, often of pleasant remembrances of childhood days. I noticed that Master Skywalker and Mara Jade remained quiet during those exchanges, as did Brakiss and I. The food itself was actually pretty good, though no one seemed to notice. And no matter how small the portions, no one seemed to finish what they had taken.

After cleaning up I retreated to my room, and heard Mara eventually go to hers. I was having trouble getting to sleep and almost strolled over to talk with her, but the way she'd politely shut me out earlier gave me a clue that I would just be courting rejection. I clearly didn't need that, so I remained in my room, mentally reviewing and rehearsing the various moves I'd learned in using the lightsaber.

At some point the shrill bleating of an R2 unit penetrated my meditations. It took me a second to realize it wasn't Whistler. I grabbed my lightsaber and went running out of the Great Temple, trailing two silhouettes that had to be Master Skywalker and Mara Jade. As I came out into the cool night air, I saw Mara Jade's Z-95 Headhunter streaking away into the starry sky.

"He stole *my* ship!" Anger poured off Mara Jade in waves. "We've got to go after him."

Luke shook his head. "We cannot."

"What do you mean?"

I cleared my voice. "We don't have any ships here."

Mara's jaw dropped. "No ships. No X-wings? You two without X-wings?"

"This is a school for Jedi, not pilots." Luke's face closed up as the other apprentices began to filter out of the Great Temple. "Kyp is gone. I don't know if he will be back or not. I hope so."

"Me, too." Mara slowly ground a fist in the palm of her opposite hand. "Steal my ship, will he?"

Luke fixed her with a hard stare. "Mara, please, calm yourself. You're not helping the situation. I've got to deal with my apprentices and explain this to them. After I see to them . . ."

The anger pulsating out from Mara lessened, but I had the feeling she'd just shielded its output. "Go, Luke. I understand."

Master Skywalker walked back toward the Great Temple and never gave me a glance. I watched him go, but felt no inclination to follow. I didn't know what he was going to tell everyone else, but I was fairly certain I already knew more than he would share with them. Being there and questioning his motives and thinking would have been as disruptive as Mara's anger, so I remained behind.

She glared at me. "You can go, too."

I shook my head. "Kind of a chilly night. Basking in the heat of your anger seems like a good choice."

"And if I don't want you here?"

"Easy now, Mara. Your ship was stolen, that's all." I kept a light tone in my voice. "It's not like the sun went supernova."

"It might as well have."

I frowned. "Am I missing something? That was just a Z-95 Headhunter, right?"

"Right. It was nothing." She scowled and then let it melt with a sigh. "It was everything."

"I'm not tracking."

"Of course not, you've never had to track." Mara graced me with a disgusted look. "You were incredibly lucky, you know that? Your family was part of CorSec so your life was all mapped out for you. You went as far as you could there, then joined Rogue Squadron and strung victories together there. And then you find out that you're really from a Jedi family and you end up here training to be what you've been destined to be since birth. It must've all just come very easy to you."

"It wasn't very easy at all."

"But at least you had a course plotted out for you. You had family supporting you in your decisions." She shook her head. "In a galaxy coming apart at the fusion joints, you were able to cruise along smoothly. You're even here, studying to become a Jedi while your wife has been taken away from you. You're so sure that what you're doing is right that you can set aside the anxiety and concentrate here, and you can do that because this is just one more trial in the life of a hero."

I started to protest what she was saying, but faint echoes of it rang true. They meant little to me, however, because of the chill cutting at my spine as I reversed her words and applied them to what little I knew about her. "You thought you were on the same sort of hero path, doing what you had to do to make a difference in the Empire. Then, bang, it's all gone. Everything you worked for and with vanishes, cutting you off, leaving you adrift."

"You've made your point."

"Sorry." I glanced away from her and off toward the jungle. "You're smart enough and skilled enough to take care of yourself, but you've no longer got the benchmarks you used to use to measure your performance."

"Right, and everything has been swapped black for white in the galaxy." She turned to look off in the same direction as me, but jerked a thumb back toward the Great Temple. "I came here for instruction and to learn where I fit into the new order of things. . . ."

"And the ship was your escape valve. If you didn't like things, you could take off."

I felt a hint of resentment from her. "I'm not one to quit a project I start."

"Didn't say you were. It's just you might find that

what you get here isn't actually what you want or need.'' I turned to face her. ''You're not wholly wrong about my life, but you're not right about it, either. When my parents died, I was left without knowing how to calibrate my moral compass. I found others who stepped in and helped me, but the search for that sort of support is one that goes on forever. You'll continue to do it. I'll continue to do it. Even Master Skywalker will do it.''

''Is that so?''

''It is.'' I found my hands had knotted into fists so I willfully opened them. ''You and I are lucky in that we've got someone like Master Skywalker around to help us figure out where we are and where we're going.''

Her voice hardened. ''But you don't think he's handling this Kyp Durron thing correctly.''

''He's not doing it the way I would, but that doesn't mean I think Luke's heart isn't in the right place. It is. He knows where he wants to go and where he wants to take the Jedi. I'm just not sure he's navigating as smooth a course as he would like for the journey.''

Her head nodded, but she said nothing for a bit. I remained quiet, listening to the hunting cries of stintarils split the night. For all the turmoil of the earlier evening, once Kyp had left, things seemed to settle down. I let the evening's growing peace slowly seep into me.

''I don't like losing my freedom like this.''

''I understand, but it really isn't a critical loss. New supply ship is due in a week, and it took Kyp at least that long to get as good as he is.'' I gave her a quick smile. ''Allow yourself the chance to see if what Master Skywalker offers really is what you need.''

''It's as good a plan as any.''

''Considering there's no alternative.''

Mara Jade let a little laugh slip out. "You're destroying this image I had of you as a dumb fighter jock."

"Serves you right. You've been listening to things Booster Terrik has to say about me."

"True enough." She turned and started walking back to the Grand Temple. "I understand you get up early and run in the morning."

"With the dawn."

"Mind company?"

"You'd go running with me?" I trotted over and fell into step with her. "I generally take a pretty nasty course."

"You set it, I'll run it."

"Good enough," I smiled. "Welcome to the Jedi academy, Mara Jade. I hope you'll enjoy your stay."

NINETEEN

✳

Enjoy her stay she did, at least as measured by the purely pleasurable expressions she wore when showing me up on our runs, or holding off one more remote than I possibly could at lightsaber practice. She might have been little accustomed to smiling, but she had a triumphant smirk down perfectly, and I got to study it enough to be able to etch it into stone from memory.

This fact was made all that more damning because we actually saw very little of each other. In the mornings we would run together, then Luke would concentrate on working with Mara much as he had with Kyp. That left Kam instructing the rest of us. After lunch we would listen to more Jedi lore from the Holocron, then Mara and I would practice with the lightsaber. While I was not her equal with the shimmering blade, we would have been closely enough matched to seriously hurt each other, so Kam just pitted us against remotes.

Kyp's disappearance left the apprentices a bit uneasy. The arrival of a new apprentice, the Mon Calamari Ambassador, Cilghal, both brought relief from the dismal mood that had fallen over the students and linked us back to the rest of the galaxy. She told of Admiral Daala's assault on Mon Calamari and the loss of one of her Star Destroyers, which was good news. The fact that pro-Imperial forces still existed out there also reinforced our resolve to become Jedi Knights, since the need for our presence was very clear.

Early one afternoon I sat in the common room, listening to Tionne practice her ballads and Mara Jade interrogating Cilghal for details about the Imperial assault on Mon Calamari, when Artoo rolled over and tugged on the shoulder of my robe with his pincer. He tootled briefly at me, then spun around and headed back out of the room. I followed him and, not surprisingly, he led me to Luke's chambers.

Inside the door I caught the acrid scent of melted electronics. A blackened puddle of melted plasteel on the room's table was the source of the stink. It still smoked and some of it appeared to still be liquid. I looked over toward where Luke sat on his bunk, his brows knotted with concentration.

"What happened?"

Luke glanced at the little droid. "Artoo, close the door." He waited until the droid had complied with his wishes before continuing. "You remember I said I'd check the Holocron for more information on Exar Kun?"

"I do."

"There was. Vodo-Siosk Baas was modeled on the Jedi that trained Exar Kun. I used him as a vector for my inquiries about what happened to Kun." Luke fell silent for a moment. "Baas went to Coruscant, to speak to his disciple, to get him to return to the way of the Jedi. Kun killed him in the Senate Chamber."

I drew in a deep breath through my nose. "That's not good news."

"No, it isn't. When I asked what happened

then . . ." He pointed mutely at the melted device. "In the resulting fire and bright light I thought I saw the shadow of the dark man and heard his laughter."

I stared at the black mess again and felt my mouth go dry. "*That* is the Holocron?"

"I think *was* is the correct verb tense."

I ran a hand back through my hair. "I think my brain hurts. And the shadow you saw, could it have been a trick of the light?"

The Jedi Master shrugged uneasily. "Could have been."

I passed my hand above the melted Holocron and caught some residual heat. "Is Exar Kun our guy?"

Luke shook his head. "I don't know. Four thousand years is a long time. I'd rather think someone being trained by the Empire, someone being used like Mara, discovered Exar Kun's studies and has fashioned himself into a new Dark Lord of the Sith."

"Don't have to go far for a candidate." My nostrils flared. "I think Kyp will do."

"Don't think that's not crossed my mind. He was so powerful and eager, but that just fed his impatience." Luke looked up at me. "You said the other day I was afraid I'd failed my father. Maybe that's true. I know I've failed Kyp."

"No, Kyp failed you." I leaned back on the table. "Kyp agreed to undergo serious training, but didn't know what he was getting into. He'd been a mine slave all his life. You showed him how powerful he was. He was learning how to make his own decisions and suddenly, grand new vistas opened up for him. It's all but impossible for people like me or Kam or Mara to deal with such power, but Kyp . . . ?"

Luke's expression darkened. "You're not making things better here."

"I'm sorry. You're the Jedi Master and you know what you're doing, but I think you need to refocus on those students still here." I sighed loudly. "Kyp may be gone forever, or he may come back. We don't know. What we do know is that your original mission, the reason you created the academy, is still valid. The Jedi Knights need to return to the galaxy and you're the only hope to make that happen."

The Jedi Master remained silent for a moment, then nodded just once. "The Order *is* what we need. That has to be my focus."

"Agreed." I gave him a hopeful look. "I also think we need to decide what we're going to do about Exar Kun."

"Right." Luke hunched forward, resting his elbows on his knees. His cloak slid down around his shoulders and flanks, making him look smaller than I'd ever seen him before. "Evidence we've got points to Exar Kun or a disciple of his pretending to be. I've searched this temple and have found tiny traces of evil. Not enough for Exar Kun."

I toyed with my goatee for a moment. "I thought I heard someone—Bodo Baas, perhaps—say the temples here had all been raised as a focus for Exar Kun's power. Maybe this temple isn't the focus of it, but just linked to it. If the link was forged of Sith magic, Exar Kun might be able to block back-tracing. Another of the temples here, then, would be the centerpoint of his power."

Luke nodded, then sat back. "Good idea. That temple could also be where Gantoris and Kyp obtained instruction. If we only knew where it was."

I smiled. "I think we can find out."

"How?"

"Survey logs. Everyone has been out surveying the local sights."

"Yes, but that was *after* Gantoris died." Luke's eyes narrowed. "And Kyp would have falsified his logs to hide where he had been."

"True, but he was out all the time with Dorsk 81, who wouldn't have any reason to falsify *his* survey reports." I smiled slowly. "If you ask for everyone to turn in their survey logs and tell them you will be conducting an exercise about observation, I can go over them and sort out the likely spots our Kun-clone is hiding out."

"Okay, we'll do that." Luke stood and came over to stare at the ruined Holocron. "By destroying the Holocron, our enemy may have done more to hurt us than he knows."

"In his fondest dreams." I gave him an easy grin. "What we've learned of Jedi history is good. We're certain we're heirs to that tradition. Now you need to use what you know to transform us into the people who will further that legend."

Feeling Mara Jade's back pressed against mine, I had to smile. "Kam isn't making this easy, is he?"

Her blue lightsaber hummed then spat as it batted away a remote's fiery dart. "Easy isn't for Jedi, is it?"

"Nope." I extended my senses as far as I could, taking in most of the darkened hangar space. Kam had closed the door and turned off all the lights, leaving our lightsabers to provide the only illumination. Eight remotes floated out through the darkness, dancing through a complex weave of paths that allowed one to eclipse another. If we did not concentrate enough to project our senses into the hollows behind the remotes or the pillars, we left ourselves pitifully vulnerable.

Kam had also turned the exercise into one of teamwork because half the remotes were meant for me to deal with and half for Mara, yet they could target either one of us. For every dart from one of ours that would hit home, we lost a point—points we earned by blocking shots. I was actually less worried about losing in score to Mara than having her at my back with a lightsaber when my remotes peppered her rump with stingers I should have blocked.

Out there, in the darkness, I felt a shift of energy. With my lightsaber on my right, I swept it out parallel to the floor, picking off a low shot coming in at my right knee. At my midline I snapped the blade vertical, then waggled it right and left, intercepting two more bolts sizzling through the dark. Then, releasing with my right hand, I dropped to my left knee and slashed out, deflecting a dart coming in from my flank.

I cranked my left wrist around, relishing the lightsaber's tenor hum and getting my right hand back on the hilt. While I'd learned enough to be fairly good with the blade in one hand, my left was still my off hand and didn't possess all the fine control I wanted. The blade itself could be wielded effortlessly, but that made it deceptively dangerous. Twirling it in my hands would have been as easy as twirling a stylus through my fingers, but dropping the lightsaber, or having it wobble in the direction of face or knee, would have hurt. A lot.

I felt a shot coming in from directly above me. My initial reaction was to raise the blade and stab it back behind my head, but Mara was standing there. Given no choice, I leaped up as high as I could and thrust the lightsaber above my head. The silvery blade took the dart on the point, infusing my blade with a red sheen for a moment. I laughed triumphantly, then saw Mara's cerulean blade whirl through a complete circle, passing beneath me, as it picked off three darts vectoring in at odd angles.

I landed and crouched again, then pivoted left and blocked another shot a second before Mara's blade came around and struck mine. Light flared where our blades intersected, then I threw myself backward and rolled off to the right, letting the strength of her cut provide the energy for my roll. Coming around and up I one-handed the blade with my right hand, flicking two more remote darts off into the darkness, then I took one straight in the stomach.

I shunted the pain away immediately and stepped back. I saw Mara spin away from a trio of darts, one of which hit her in her right shoulder. Her blade moved a fraction too slow after that, allowing two more to lance through her right hip. Her spin, which had started voluntarily, continued without her consent, dropping her to the hangar floor. Her blade came up and warded off another shot, then a dart hit her in the small of the back, collapsing her legs as she tried to get back up.

I saw her lying there on her belly, her legs tangled, her hair a veil that picked up argent highlights from my lightsaber. At the same time I felt three remotes moving around, closing in for the kill. Two were coming in toward her feet and one near her head. Her lightsaber had winked out and lay there, next to her left hand, now useless in her defense.

I was left one choice that was no real choice at all.

I dove toward her, slicing my lightsaber through the air near her legs with my right hand. The argent blade blocked the two darts meant to further cripple her. I couldn't help letting a smile get started when that happened because I knew it would not last long.

Two centimeters in front of her face, my left hand snatched the third bolt from the air. Searing pain shot up my arm, but I pulled the energy into me and turned it around to help calm furious nerves. My smile continued to grow as that transformation took place and my spirit soared because of my success.

Unfortunately, a soaring spirit does little for a falling body. I hit the floor rather hard, landing solidly on my chest. I bounced back up a bit, with my toes hitting just before my knees. I tried to twist around and land on my left hip so I could keep my blade in the air and active, but all I really managed to do was start myself rolling, which resulted in my wrapping myself around a pillar. My lightsaber whirled out of my grasp and spun to a stop about ten meters away.

Its silvery glow illuminated the remotes closing in on me.

I sighed. "I have a bad feeling about this."

The remotes did not shoot.

I rolled over and flopped on my back. In the distance, between my upraised knees, I could see Mara Jade on her side, dragging herself along in my direction. Sweat had pasted strands of her hair to her face and gave her skin an icy blue gleam in her reignited lightsaber's backlight. The flesh around her eyes tightened as she moved her legs, but she gave no other indication that she felt any discomfort.

Kam's voice echoed through the chamber. "That's enough for now. You did pretty well."

I laughed. "If that's true, why do I feel so bad?"

"It's because, Keiran, you didn't do well *enough*."

"Thanks for the clarification, Kam." I dropped my

knees and laid my head back down on the cold stone floor. I ran a hand through my goatee, brushing away the sweat that had collected in it, then felt the sting of sweat leaking into my eyes. I let my head loll to the left and smiled as Mara inched her way into view. "Hurt much?"

"A Jedi doesn't know pain."

"Right. Me, too." I looked over at where my lightsaber still lay. I extended a hand in that direction and tried to call the blade to me, but all I got was a little twitching of the hilt. "These are the times I could really use better telekinesis skills."

"You're just being lazy. Just walk over and get it."

"Okay. In a minute."

Mara laughed lightly, then sighed. "Thanks for the save."

"No problem. You'd do the same for me."

Her voice drained of all lighter tones. "Would I?"

I had to think for a second. "You would. The universe you knew growing up may have changed, but your core values of duty and loyalty haven't. Not that I think you'd ever feel yourself that beholden to someone else, but you'd extend that sort of courtesy to someone you see as a friend, right?"

Silence answered me.

I rolled myself up on my left flank and rested my head on my left hand. "We are friends, right?"

Her eyes narrowed, then her lightsaber went out again, sinking her into shadow. "I don't know if I really know what it means to have a friend in the same sense you think of it. I do think I trust you."

"I'll take that."

"Is that why you sacrificed your hand to protect my face, because you think of me as a friend?"

"In part, yes. A very big part." I nibbled my lower lip for a moment, then continued. "I also did it because I knew I could and, therefore, it was my duty to do so. Even back when I entered CorSec, I knew there were things that I'd be called upon to do, dangerous things, that I would do because others could not. My role in society was to take action and responsibility for those who could not. I think, deep down, that's the essence of being a Jedi. A Jedi places himself where he can defend the greatest number of people from the greatest evil."

"Even if it costs him his life?"

I exhaled slowly. "You never want to think about that, but it's part of the job. I remember a couple of times in my life, with Rogue Squadron and before, when I knew it was my duty to get a job done. I felt pretty certain I would die in those attempts and nearly did on Talasea. Fact was, though, that I had friends who would die if I didn't do anything and somehow my life didn't seem to matter all that much in the equation."

Mara snorted. "The Emperor would have considered you a sentimental fool who deserved to die."

"I'll remember that next time I dance on his grave." I levered myself up into a sitting position and crossed my legs beneath me. "There are just times the sacrifice feels right. It did then, it did today. Just a judgment you'll have to make for yourself when the time comes, I guess."

"Not an easy decision to make. . . ."

"Nope." I stood and offered her a hand. She took it and I steadied her as she got back onto her feet. "But then, as you said, easy isn't for a Jedi, is it?"

TWENTY

Master Skywalker tossed his cloak to Kam and brought the hilt of his lightsaber to hand. "Thank you, Kam. If you would see to the others for a while."

"As you wish, Master Skywalker."

The Jedi Master looked up at me as I slipped my lightsaber into my right hand. "We don't have to do this, Keiran."

I gave him a wry grin. "I think we do, Master. And I think you have a question you want to ask."

Luke nodded slowly. "Is our duel a prelude to your leaving, too?"

The pure pain in his voice sank into me and pinned my heart against my spine. Luke was watching his dream of the Jedi academy collapse around him. Gantoris had been roasted alive with his own hatred and anger. Kyp, his most promising student, had fallen under the sway of an ancient evil and had vanished. Mara Jade, one of the Emperor's trusted practitioners of the Force, had come to the academy for instruction, but inside a week had chosen to leave again and even that morning had been whisked away by Han Solo and Lando Calrissian aboard the *Millennium Falcon*.

For having been open for only a little more than a

month, the failure rate for promising students was staggering. I could have taken Luke's question as a confirmation of my abilities, but I felt it really marked how battered he felt at the moment. I could understand that because I was feeling a little betrayed by Mara's departure as well.

I saw her that morning when I'd arrived to get her for our run. "Ready to go?"

"Yeah," she replied, "but not running." She stood in her room in the color-shifting flightsuit in which she had arrived. Her bed had been made up and the Jedi robe she'd worn had been folded neatly and placed at the foot of the bed beside her heavy satchel. "Thought another candidate might find a use for the robe."

I leaned against the door jamb, using my body to bar the way out. "I thought you told me you weren't a quitter."

A little fire blazed in her eyes, but she brought it under control with an ease that surprised me. "I'm not. I've learned a lot here, but what I needed to learn isn't exactly what you need, or what others here need to learn."

"Want to run that by me again, with the help files enabled this time?"

She relaxed just ever so slightly, shifting her weight to her back foot. "When the Empire trained me, I learned a lot of the things all of you are learning. I practiced them and perfected them. You and I have trained together with lightsabers. Do you think I picked all that up in an afternoon or two of quick study?"

I shrugged. "Well, with Kam and me as examples, it's possible."

"Cute, Corran, but you know it's not true."

"Okay, score one for Mara Jade."

The flesh around her eyes tightened. "My Imperial training directed me toward using dark-side techniques for tapping the Force. I let emotions fuel what I did. I came here thinking Luke would show me new things I could do, new abilities to learn, but what he did instead was show me how to employ the light side. I'm still doing the same things, but I have a new fuel source."

"One that runs a bit leaner, isn't as easily accessible. . . ."

"Right, but one that won't burn the engine out." She graced me with an open, green-eyed gaze that surprised me with its vulnerability. "The other day, when you were talking about the willingness to sacrifice yourself for others, you mentioned friends and those who could not take responsibility for themselves. I started thinking about the Smugglers' Alliance. I've got a lot of things to think about."

I nodded slowly. "And your little sojourn here was prompted, in part, by being uncomfortable with that responsibility."

"And here I thought all CorSec agents were not that bright."

"We have our moments."

"Up to now I've been responsible for myself. I've been able to make decisions, but I've been comfortable with them on a tactical level. With Karrde putting me in charge of the alliance, I need to think more strategically. He's counting on me to do the right thing. More pressure. I can handle it—I refuse to fail him—but . . ."

"But you aren't sure you're comfortable doing it." I smiled. "I understand. This is why I am content to be a pilot in Rogue Squadron, not someone leading my own group of fighter pilots. I don't want to get so spread out that I can't make a difference when I need to."

Mara's gaze sharpened. "I bet the smugglers working your sector of the Corellian system didn't like you at all."

"Can't understand why. Should I have had my sting operations catered or something?" I shook my head. "They traded in rare commodities and I traded them the rarest of all for their wares: time."

"Yeah, on Kessel. Time goes a long way there."

"And I didn't even charge extra for it." I straightened up and offered her my hand. "I'm sorry to see you go. I thought between us we could really kick some life into this place and help Luke move the students on to the next level of development. I hesitate to say it, but it's been fun working with you."

Mara gave me one of her carefully hoarded smiles. "For something that started off with our arguing and my ship getting stolen, the experience hasn't been as bad as I would have thought. Thanks for your help. If there is anything I can do for you . . ."

"Actually there is." I gave her a weak smile. "With your contacts in the smuggling community, maybe you will hear something about Mirax. I'd appreciate hearing anything. I'd owe you."

"How about a swap?" She hitched for a second, then glanced down at the floor. "Watch out for Luke for me, will you?"

"Sure, gladly." I frowned. "Anything specific? I know he won't like your leaving. . . ."

"That, certainly." Her voice shrank a bit. "His involvement with the dark side. I know it functions as a spur to drive him on to teach his students, but I don't think he knows how much he was hurt by it. The experience had to be unbelievably traumatic and he's still healing. I don't fear a relapse, but maybe, I don't know."

"He might try to do too much, too fast?"

"That would be like him."

I nodded and wanted to kick myself for not having seen it sooner. For Luke, for anyone, the journey to the dark side and back would have been like being shot multiple times at point-blank range. Bacta therapy might heal the physical wounds, but the memories and nightmares resulting would take time to work out. While the Jedi calming techniques might get rid of the resulting anxiety, they just treated the symptoms without curing the underlying problems. Only time could heal them; time and the love and support of friends.

"I'll watch him for you. Take care of yourself, okay?"

"Will do."

"And if any of your smuggler pals manage to have some spare food—*good* food they need to offload somewhere, you know where we could use it."

Mara shouldered her satchel and slipped past me. "You've got it, CorSec. See you a couple parsecs down the line."

After Luke saw her off, he took us listlessly through the morning's exercises. He clearly was trying to do his best with us, but his heart wasn't in it. I recognized in him the same sort of behavior Iella had reported in me after my father's death. He was thinking too hard about what had happened and allowing himself to dwell in the past while the rest of the universe was sliding on into the future.

In my case, Iella and Gil Bastra had taken me to one of the seediest cantinas on Treasure Ship Row. The place called the *Fel Swoop* was packed with a rough crowd of swoop-riders and speeder bike jockeys. After a *lot* of Corellian whiskey, they got me singing a little song about the lack of brains and intestinal fortitude of speeder bike enthusiasts. My singing voice, even at the best of times, would cause a riot in a receptive audience, and the resulting brawl kind of tore the place apart. Fact was, though, that the aches and pains and scars that resulted brought me back into the real world and anchored me there.

Unfortunately for me, we didn't have any cantina to hit, nor did we have any whiskey to drink. I felt a little physical activity would still be good for Luke and help ground him again, so I challenged him to a duel. Kam explained that there were things I needed to learn from a living foe and that he, Kam, did not have the control necessary to spar with me. It would be up to Luke to make sure I didn't hit him and he didn't hit me, causing him to concentrate.

I lit my lightsaber, letting its snap-hiss fill the hangar. "Fair question to ask, if I'm leaving or not. You've got ample reason to ask it. No, I'm not going anywhere unless, of course, this fight goes badly for one or the other of us."

Luke's green blade sprang to life. "Let me see what you have learned."

I closed with him and arced a cut in toward his left shoulder. He came up and blocked it high left, picking it up in the outer ring of defense. I came down and around in a sweeping blow at his left leg, but he brought his lightsaber down and batted mine aside easily. The spark of light exploding from the contact of the two blades washed shadows across Luke's disinterested expression.

About what I expected. Shifting my lightsaber to my right hand, I closed quickly and snapped the blade down in an overhand cut. I picked up my speed on the cut, forcing Luke to block me in the middle ring. Continuing my forward movement, I pushed in with my right hand, then slid the lightsaber's hilt down. I hammered his breastbone with the lightsaber's hilt, then hooked my right leg behind Luke's right leg and dumped him to the ground.

I backed off as his blade's green light illuminated the surprise on his face. I let an edge drift into my voice. "If you aren't going to respect me, at least respect what Kam has taught me."

Luke slowly climbed back to his feet, but did so with his lightsaber always remaining between the two of us. I kept my blade angled across my body, with my hands held near my right hip and the blade's tip hovering near my left shoulder. I stamp-feinted with my right foot, as if I were beginning a charge, and Luke withdrew a half-step.

He's got to focus. I waited for him to set himself, then I came in on a circular approach that worked me toward his left. I slashed twice, crosswise, forehand and back, to keep him away from me, then drove straight toward him. I lunged with the blade. Luke's green lightsaber came around in a circular parry that carried my blade wide to my right.

His triumphant laugh died abruptly as my right foot kicked him in the gut. While he'd parried, I'd recovered from my lunge and kicked out straight into his midsection. He doubled over and fell back a couple of steps, his left hand rubbing his belly, but I gave him no chance to recover. I came on hard and fast, whipping my silver blade through an infinity loop, lashing out high and low.

Luke looked up at me and his eyes hardened.

Which is when I ran into a Force wall that bounced me back a couple of feet and set me on my heels. I tasted blood on my lips, but knew it was really coming from my nose, which hurt. I didn't think it was broken, but bumping it up against anything solid is seldom a pleasant experience.

I wiped it off on the sleeve of my green tunic, but in the half-light both it and the blood looked black. "Nice trick."

A feral grin twisted Luke's mouth. He came forward, wordlessly, moving with a fluidity I'd not seen in him before. He aimed a slash at me that would have bisected me from right shoulder to left hip. I caught a momentary flash of surprise from him because he'd expected me to block it high right, but I let it come through the outer and middle rings of defense. With a quick parry, I slid it wide of my right shoulder, then I stepped forward and slammed my right shoulder into Luke's chin.

That stood him up, clicking his teeth sharply together. I drove a weak jab with my left hand into his ribs, then ducked a slash that should have trimmed my hair at roughly the level of my earlobes. Dropping into a crouch, I whipped my left leg out and scythed it through his legs, bashing his ankles together and again dropping him onto his back.

I whirled away and stood, looking down at him. "I would have thought you'd be better than this."

Luke slowly got up and wiped a trickle of blood from his split lip away with his left hand. "Never had much rough and tumble growing up. My friends and I were more involved in racing than fighting."

"Then maybe you should be a Jedi Racer, not a Knight."

"You don't understand." Luke spat out some bloody saliva. "There are things in play here, forces shifting."

"Maybe I could understand, if you'd talk about it." I lowered my blade. "You're the Jedi Master but that doesn't mean you should shoulder *all* the responsibility. You know that already: you've been letting Tionne learn and share history. Kam's been handling some of the instruction and you've had me working on the dark man problem—and I think I have Exar Kun's temple pegged from Dorsk 81's survey logs, by the way. Figured I'd check it later this afternoon.''

''No.'' Luke shook his head adamantly. ''You're not to go there alone. I don't want any of the students going there.''

''So you go and I'll back you up.''

He hesitated, then shook his head. ''Can't, not now.''

''Why not?''

Luke closed his eyes and sighed. ''Do you recall how I told you of knowing my friends were in trouble on Bespin?''

''Yes. You said that was a vision of the future.'' I narrowed my eyes. ''You said Darth Vader allowed you to sense it to lure you into a trap.''

''I have had other visions, other feelings.'' Pain tightened Luke's expression. ''There is disaster in the offing. It remained a bit more distant when Mara was here, but now I feel it is much closer.''

''Do something about it.''

''What?'' Luke's question came almost as a plea. ''I have this oppressive sense of doom approaching. It touches on everyone and everything. All the things I think about doing don't seem to make it go away.''

I swiped at more blood from my nose with my left hand. ''Slow down for a moment. Do you know if this doom, this future, is locked in holo, or is it morphable?''

''The future is always morphable, but nothing I think to do will change it.''

''Two things you're overlooking here, Master

Skywalker. First, thinking is closer to trying than doing, if you catch my drift. Changing the future has got to require action, not just planning for action. While a Jedi acts in defense and not out of aggression, that doesn't mean aggressively putting a defense into place is bad.''

Luke nodded slowly. ''And the second thing?''

''Maybe you're not the one who has to act. Maybe it's me or Kam or all of us together.'' I sighed. ''You're teaching us how to use the Force, you're opening us up to new powers, and you've established that we are heirs to a Jedi tradition full of responsibility. Fact is, though, that you've not *given us* any responsibility. Defeating this disaster you feel coming, getting rid of Exar Kun or whoever the dark man is might just require *all* of us finally accepting our responsibilities as Jedi.

''Right now you're accepting every scrap of responsibility here. You're getting buried under the weight of what you see as a string of failures. Mara Jade didn't leave here because you failed her, she left because you succeeded. She learned what she needed to learn— which might not have been what you thought she needed to learn. She left because she didn't want to fail others to whom *she* felt responsible.''

He opened his eyes. ''You think I've been treating all of you like children.''

''Closer to the mark than you want to know.''

''I haven't meant to, but you *are* children within the Force.''

''That's fine, Master Skywalker, and true; but we're also a disparate group of adults. Kyp was what, our youngest, and he was the age you were when you started your training? He was the age I was when I went into the CorSec Academy. We're pretty well formed at that point, personality-wise. Those who have come here to learn from you have already made a decision to explore a new life. You need to let us do that. You need to challenge us, and challenges aren't just the size of rocks or the range of a vision one can project. Those challenges test our skills, not our characters, and the failures here have been failures of character.''

''But you are not ready for such challenges.''

''Not if you're going to make them marrow-blasting challenges, no.'' I pointed at his right hand. ''Did you learn a lot from your failure at Bespin?''

Luke's fingers flexed. ''Yes.''

''Then let us fail a bit and learn how to deal with it. As we used to say in CorSec, there are two types of speeder bike riders: those who have fallen off, and those who are going to fall off. Jedi will fail, and if they don't learn how to deal with failure, if they don't have the spine to recover from it, you'll lose them.''

Luke's lightsaber died. ''I have to think about what you've said.''

''Don't just think, Master, *act*.'' I thumbed my blade off as well, letting darkness swallow us. ''If you don't act, the disaster you feel could be on a scale from which none of us can possibly recover.''

TWENTY-ONE

I awoke slowly, feeling as if I'd done my best to drain every drop of liquor from a cantina where the drinks weren't watered, the mugs weren't cleaned, the bottles weren't labeled and the first-aid kit consisted of a blaster with which you could put yourself out of your misery. Actually, I didn't even feel that good. I was pretty sure I'd not been on such a bender because I didn't find any tattoos or scars on me, and the bruises were ones I recognized from my training. The fact that the nearest cantina was a good five parsecs away, as the *Falcon* flies, coupled with the fact that I didn't have a ship, likewise contraindicated a hangover.

But, then again, I did kinda feel as if I'd walked that far.

Despite my better judgment—which was urging me just to lie down and die—I oozed out of bed and pulled on my running clothes. That helped wake me up, largely because they were still damp, cold and clammy from the short run I'd taken the night before to burn off some of my frustration with Master Skywalker. Nothing like the feel of wet fabric against the flesh in the morning to remind you that you're alive. Doesn't do much for the quality of life issues some folks find important, but I'd reached that point where I decided being alive was better than the nearest alternative.

I even managed a smile. "And if I die, I don't want to spend the rest of eternity locked in the rocks on this place. Might be good enough for Exar Kun, but not me."

My muscles felt as if they were encased in carbonite, but I managed to get them going and actually had worked up to a brisk stumble when I emerged from the Great Temple. There I moved into a *real* stumble, landing on my hands and knees, because a Z-95 Headhunter rested on the landing pad outside. I panicked for a second, thinking I might, in fact, have stolen it from near the cantina where I did all the drinking, but I calmed myself quickly. Didn't even have to use a Jedi technique to do it, either.

I knew, had I flown in the condition I was in, the only landing I could have managed was a crash. *And Mara Jade wouldn't like that happening to her Headhunter.*

The realization that I was looking at her fighter washed the last of the muzziness from my brain. Kyp had stolen that ship and if it was back, that meant he was, too. I got up and ran over to the craft, stretching out my feelings to see if I could detect his presence. I caught some faint traces of him, but they emanated mostly from the controls, which looked as if he'd reached a hand into them and just squeezed. *Mara Jade isn't going to like that one bit.*

I turned around, following a wisp of Kyp's essence to the base of the Great Temple. A path had been cleared through the rusty vines overgrowing much of the temple. The vines nearest the uncovered stairway looked pale and stunted. They had recoiled from the steps like snakes preparing to strike, and had withered considerably in the process.

I took the steps two at a time. I had no idea what I would find at the top or what I would do to confront Kyp if I found him there. I steeled myself for a confrontation, and worked to tap the Force to fortify myself for one. Even as I did that, however, I had the sinking feeling that no amount of preparation would be enough for dealing with what I would find.

As I mounted the final flight of steps, new sensations cascaded down from the top of the pyramid. I sensed the other students up there, and their emotions ran from shock and outrage to sorrow and despair. I crested the edge of the Temple and saw the Mon Calamari, Cilghal, cradling Luke's head in her lap. Streen, his eyes wide with fear, stood over her.

"Is he alive? I can't hear him."

The Mon Cal concentrated on Luke, then shook her orange and algae-green head. She reported finding a heartbeat and I could see his chest moving with shallow respiration. "But I can't find *him* inside. When I touch him with the Force, all I find is a great empty spot. . . ."

I reached out with my senses and tried to find what she could not. Pushing hard, I wove some of the external Force with my internal energy and tried to see if I could find a spark of Master Skywalker in his body. I recalled his noting that he had been taught we were luminous beings, not creatures of crude matter, but I found it hard to accept his having abandoned his body. Still, the evidence of that very thing was right there, since I could not feel him at all.

Kirana Ti pulled her robe tightly closed at her throat. "What can we do?"

Cilghal blinked her eyes. "We are all alone now."

The despair in her voice found an ally in the fear writhing into my belly. It had never seemed odd to me that Kyp had been able to slam me into a wall because he had always been more powerful than me. Even when I felt the other presence reinforcing him and got hammered by the combination of them, I never imagined that they could be more powerful than Luke Skywalker. I had even rationalized away the dark man's ability to avoid detection as his being talented in that area, just as I was talented in the area of image projection.

Had I even dreamed Luke was in danger I would have worked harder to convince him we had to act. The saliva in my mouth soured. *When we start handing out citations for failure, let me get in the front of the line.* I'd told Luke we were dealing with a sociopathic murderer, but I'd not convinced him of the gravity of that situation. He seemed to be in a position to handle it and all he wanted from me was information that would have given him a direction.

And I let him do just that. I closed my eyes for a moment and wanted to smack my head with the heel of my hand. *What had I been thinking?* I was the one who had experience with such monsters, not Luke Skywalker. I surrendered responsibility for such things to him when he was no more able to deal with it than he felt we were ready to deal with the fate of the universe. My mistake was the reverse of his, yet mine *compounded* his.

The pure arrogance and stupidity of those ideas slammed hard into me. Luke Skywalker had dealt with Darth Vader and the Emperor, even the Emperor Reborn. If they weren't monsters, monsters didn't exist. Master Skywalker was more than capable of dealing with them, which made his condition now that much more stunning and terrifying.

I looked down at his body as Cilghal straightened his limbs. I'd screwed up badly, and because of it he was lying there. If I'd done things differently, there was no guarantee he wouldn't have ended up in the same place, but things might have taken another turn, one for the better. I'd failed him, and I'd had the arrogance to suggest he was failing us.

Failure stops here and now. Muscles bunched at the corners of my jaw. "We're not alone. We have each other. We may not be Jedi, but we're not helpless either."

The Dathomiri witch looked at me and restated her question. "What can we do?"

"We can do the obvious, can't we?" I jerked a thumb back down toward the Headhunter. "Kyp was here and, if I had to guess, I'd say he was responsible for what happened to Master Skywalker. First thing we need to do is to let Coruscant know Luke has been hurt and that Kyp Durron was involved."

The Mon Calamari Ambassador looked up. "Until you have solid evidence that Kyp was here, blaming him for this is wrong."

I frowned at her. "But the Headhunter . . ."

"Could have been stolen from him and used by someone else."

"Your caution is good, Cilghal, but Kyp's being here isn't that hard a conclusion to draw." Kam walked over to the edge of the pyramid, looked down at the landing pad, then grunted. "Think Kyp is still hiding on this rock?"

Streen shook his head. "I can't hear Kyp."

"I'd like to hope that means he's dead, but I don't

believe it.'' I glanced at Kam. ''You're wondering how he got off this rock if he left the fighter behind.''

''Yes, and the only other ride in the system, unless we missed his coming with allies in the middle of the night, is the Sun Crusher.'' His hands contracted into fists. ''Kyp knew how to make it work.''

Tionne shivered. ''Could he have been powerful enough to recall it from the heart of the gas giant?''

Streen crouched down and plucked from the Temple's roof a small stone that scintillated brilliantly in the dawning sun. ''Corusca gem. The only place in the universe they are formed is in Yavin's heart. It could have been lodged in the hatch assembly and fallen off when Kyp entered the Sun Crusher.''

I groaned. ''Not the news I wanted to hear.''

Cilghal raised a hand. ''Corusca gems can be found here on Yavin, and we have no way of knowing how long that piece of one has been here. More importantly, we have no way of knowing if the Sun Crusher is still in the gas giant or not. Again, you're reaching conclusions on the most circumstantial of evidence.''

''I can see why you were a diplomat, Ambassador.'' I sighed heavily. ''Okay, look, we have to take this in steps. First thing, we get Master Skywalker down and out of the elements.''

Tionne smiled. ''We should place him in the Grand Audience Chamber.''

I winced. ''Won't that be like having him lie in state? He isn't dead.''

Her smile contracted. ''I was just thinking that he liked the chamber and the acoustics are good for singing and it was the site of a great victory celebration.''

Kam came around behind her and rested his hands on her shoulders. ''Good thinking, Tionne. There's room enough there that we can all gather around and listen to you singing. We want him to feel he's still part of our community." Kam looked past her at me and raised an eyebrow.

"Right, exactly. You're thinking a lot more quickly today than I am, Tionne." I glanced at the Mon Calamari. "Ambassador, you've got a talent for healing. Will you monitor Master Skywalker and let us know what we need to help him? Our medical supplies are limited here. . . ."

"I can see to his initial care, yes. We should certainly get a full medical team out here as fast as possible, however." Cilghal slowly blinked her eyes. "We must also notify the New Republic and Councilor Organa Solo that something has happened to her brother."

Brakiss added, "And let them know Kyp Durron has the Sun Crusher. With his hatred for remnants of the Empire, there is no telling what he will do with a weapon of that power."

I cut off Cilghal's protest of Brakiss' remarks. "At the very least we need to get a survey team out here that can check to see if the Sun Crusher is still in the gas giant or not."

Kirana Ti crouched and mopped sweat from Luke's brow with the hem of her Jedi robe. "We should also make certain Master Skywalker is never alone. He should always have an honor guard with him."

Dorsk 81 looked at her with horror on his face. "You think Master Skywalker is still in jeopardy?"

I cleared my throat. "We can't discount that possibility. Kyp may have wanted him dead and held back at the last moment, for reasons we can't begin to plot. He might return to finish the job." *Or the dark man might try.* "Having someone with Master Skywalker also makes sense on the medical front, in case there is a change.''

The Mon Calamari nodded. ''We should get him inside now. He is stable enough to move, I believe.''

''Good. I'll get on the HoloNet and speak to Coruscant to start notification going. Ambassador, I'd like you to later speak with Councilor Organa Solo. You can answer her questions about her brother better than I can, and news of what has happened here should come from someone who knows her, not a stranger.''

Brakiss peered imperiously at me. ''What about the rest of us?''

''I don't know. Do what you're able to do. Help Cilghal. Make food. Meditate.''

The slender man frowned. ''Meditate? Hardly helpful in this situation, wouldn't you say?''

Kam shook his head vehemently. ''We need to avoid panic and keep our wits about us. We should practice what we have learned so far, strengthening ourselves. If Kyp returns, if another problem arises, we need to be able to deal with it.'' His head came up. ''I'll expect everyone who isn't assigned other duties to meet for exercises as usual.''

''It's a plan.'' I gave Kam a nod. ''And a good one. Everyone clear? Good. Go to it.''

I descended to the communications center and powered up the system. Luke's R2 unit stood faithfully by to help me, but his anxiety kept him bouncing from tread to tread. His whistles took on a pinched tone, reminding me of Whistler when he really wanted to have his gears lubed.

''Go, Artoo, having you near him will make Master

Skywalker feel a lot better, I'm certain. And you can monitor lifesigns better than any of the rest of us." I smiled as the droid raced from the comm center. I wasn't certain I wanted him around while I worked anyway.

I tried first to reach Wedge, but could only leave a message in his personal holocache. Next I tried Tycho and managed to get him at Squadron Headquarters.

He gave me a big smile. "Didn't expect to be hearing from you for a while. How is the training going?"

I shook my head and his smile atrophied. "We just took a big hit. Luke Skywalker is down."

"Down?"

"Hurt, but we don't know how badly. We can only guess what happened and it's not good. Luke's stable right now, and we hope he'll recover, but we're going to need a full medical team out here as fast as possible."

Tycho glanced out of the holograph's frame, then nodded. "I've got a shuttle fueling and preflighting right now. I'll alert a med team and fly it out myself."

"Good. I also have a list of other things I want you to bring."

"Whatever you need."

"Could be tough to get." I paused for a moment. "I need enough nergon 14 charges to level something like the Great Temple here."

Tycho sat back and blinked away some surprise. "Are things that drastic?"

"Could be. I hope what I think might be happening isn't actually going on here, but if it is, I might need to take down a temple to act as a circuit breaker." I lowered my voice. "I need the crates mislabeled, too. I don't know that I can trust everyone here. . . ."

"So you can't really trust anyone but yourself."

"That's pretty much it."

Tycho looked at me, then slowly nodded. "I trust you know what you're doing."

"I think so." I ran my hands back through my hair. "Last thing, I need you to put me through to General Cracken. It is vital I speak to him."

"Okay, I'll do that now." Tycho gave me a quick grin. "See you in the better part of thirty hours."

"Thanks, Colonel."

The Rogue Squadron crest hung in air above the comm unit's holoprojection pad. It brought an unconscious smile to my face. I remembered when Gavin Darklighter had designed it, surrounding the Rebel crest with twelve X-wings streaking outward. For almost five years that insignia had helped define who I was. Now it helped remind me of where I came from, and another proud tradition that I was weaving into my new life.

Cracken's face replaced it. "Colonel Celchu suggested you had something urgent for me."

I nodded. "You remember that Sun Crusher you *thought* you'd taken care of by dumping it in the Yavin gas giant?"

"I don't like the sound of that question, Captain."

"Then you're really going to hate the reason I'm asking it." I set my face into an impassive mask. "Some time past midnight local time, person or persons unknown arrived on Yavin 4. They confronted Master Skywalker, defeated him, and departed again. They left behind a Z-95 Headhunter with the controls destroyed. Kyp Durron, one of the few, if only, people who knows how to pilot that Sun Crusher, was last seen in possession of the Headhunter in question. I don't have tissue samples and fingerprints to prove he was in it when it arrived here yet, but, trust me, he was." I felt a little twinge of guilt at violating Cilghal's caution, but soft-soaping facts wasn't going to help New Republic Intelligence deal with the situation.

Cracken's face sagged and his mouth slowly opened. "You have no idea where he went, who he was with?"

"None you'd believe." I let a grim note play through my voice. "Given things Kyp said before he left earlier, his ire seems directed at the Empire. If I had to guess, I'd say he'd be hunting whoever the latest self-styled warlord is, or maybe going after the remnants of Thrawn's fleet. When he finds a target, you'll know."

"An eighteen-year-old kid who grew up in a prison mine in control of a weapon that can destroy star systems." Cracken scratched at a spot on his forehead. "At least when we were dealing with Imperials we had a chance of predicting their behavior, but a kid who's angry with the galaxy?"

"Not one of the better days for the New Republic, I agree."

"You said Luke Skywalker was defeated. What's his status?"

"He's hurt and in a coma. No telling when or if he will come out of it."

Cracken nodded wearily. "So we're on our own for this one."

"Right. Ambassador Cilghal will be communicating with Councilor Organa Solo when we have more information on Master Skywalker's status. Colonel Celchu is going to run a medical team and some supplies out here inside a day from now." I shrugged. "I'll keep you informed as I am able."

"Thank you."

I hesitated for a second, then looked at him. "Might seem kind of trivial given what I've just told you, but any word about Mirax?"

"Not trivial at all, Captain. I admire your restraint in asking." The general gave me an open stare. "No word, no leads that are panning out. No ransom demands. We're still looking and have hope."

"I'm sure you are, and I share your hope. Thank you, sir." I tossed him a quick salute. "Yavin 4 out."

TWENTY-TWO

Frustration largely characterized the week between Master Skywalker's fall and the arrival of his sister and her family. When Ambassador Cilghal had told her what had happened, Leia Organa Solo had wanted to travel to Yavin 4 immediately, but the demands of her office were not such that they could be so easily dismissed. Ambassador Cilghal suggested she could wait until the medical team had arrived and made its evaluation, and promised to keep her informed of any changes.

This direct link with Luke's sister made Ambassador Cilghal, our newest student, the de facto leader of the academy, at least from the New Republic's point of view. Kam Solusar still oversaw our instruction, but he didn't push to expand what we knew, just perfect it. I understood his reluctance to teach us more in Luke's absence, but this meant Kam was inclined to be conservative in what he allowed to go on at the academy. He kept us all close to the Great Temple and even asked me to curtail my runs. I flat refused to do that, but found myself a circuit that always kept me relatively close to home.

Frustration set in, because with Cilghal and Kam in charge I really had no standing where I wanted it. When the survey team came to see if the Sun Crusher was still in the heart of Yavin, they roundly ignored me. Some shave-tailed lieutenant told me that all information was on a need-to-know basis, and he'd decide when or if I needed to know. Had he any idea who I really was, he'd have been answering "Yes, sir," and "No, sir" and not daring to breathe unless I gave him leave to do so, but as a Jedi wannabe, I was just seen as "part of the problem."

Of course, it would have been child's-play to meddle with his mind and make him think I was *not* present in the comm center when he filed his report with General Cracken, but I was fairly certain such a capricious use of my abilities would have left me dabbling in the dark side. While I did want to know what he had to report, I didn't want to put myself in harm's way learning it. Still, I did consider myself as having a need to know, so I convinced Luke's R2 unit to pull the report from the comm center computer.

I could have saved myself and Artoo the trouble if I remembered the first lesson about junior officers: if they know something neat, they can't wait to share it. If they know nothing, they use ranks and regs to cover their ignorance. This Lieutenant Morrs was about as ignorant as a Hutt is ugly. Because of storms raging in the gas giant's heart, he couldn't be certain if the Sun Crusher was there, had been destroyed or had been taken away. His survey results were labeled inconclusive and seemed to have put the New Republic somewhat at ease concerning the Sun Crusher.

While I would have liked to have taken heart in the idea that the Sun Crusher might not have gone anywhere, another development, or lack of one actually, had me worried. Since Luke's defeat, there had been no sign of the dark man. This scared me a great deal because his lack of activity was somewhat uncharacteristic and made me think we were just on the cusp of the disaster Master Skywalker had foreseen.

I still thought of the dark man as a sociopath, and nothing I'd learned about Exar Kun suggested he didn't fit that mold perfectly. Sociopathic murderers tend to cycle—they commit their crimes on a schedule that makes sense for them. As their crimes become more and more horrific, the cycle tends to speed up until whatever little control they had over themselves erodes and they get sloppy enough to get captured. The havoc they wreak in that time is nothing short of devastating and brutally cruel.

Gantoris was on Yavin just over two weeks before his death, which could be seen as a cap to one cycle. Kyp arrived a week or so later and was here just over a week before he stole the Headhunter. Inside a week he came back and dropped Luke like a hot rock. By rights the dark man should have been back preying on us within days after Luke's defeat, but he wasn't, and this frightened me.

There were ample explanations for why he wasn't causing us trouble. The first is that he wanted to give us time to despair over Luke's condition. That would leave us more vulnerable to him. The second reason, and one that chilled me to the marrow, was that he was devoting his energies to controlling Kyp Durron and the Sun Crusher. If it was Exar Kun who had influenced Kyp, I didn't know what target he'd pick for the Sun Crusher, but I'd hate to be on a world he decided to pay back after four thousand years.

The only vaguely positive explanation for Exar Kun's dormancy that I could come up with was that his effort to draw the Sun Crusher from Yavin and to down Luke had tired him out. I had no way to determine how powerful Exar Kun could be, but it struck me as possible that he'd expended a lot of energy to defeat a Jedi Master. There was no telling how long it would take for him to recover, but with each passing day the apprentices grew in strength as well.

In blackest night, any light is welcome.

Tycho brought the medical team and my special supplies as quickly as possible. He told me the shuttle he had brought had a fully operational proton torpedo launching system and offered to take me on a strafing run of any Temple I wanted to destroy, but I held back. Proton torpedoes probably would have been the most effective way to deal with Exar Kun's stronghold, but I still recalled how adamant Luke had been that neither I nor any of the other students travel there. If we weren't strong enough to deal with the problem, I didn't want to put Tycho in jeopardy.

"I'll leave you the coordinates, Colonel." I tossed him a salute as he boarded the shuttle to leave. "If things go very badly, talk Admiral Ackbar into a planetary bombardment that will raze it."

"I copy." He returned my salute. "May the Force be with you."

The medical team he'd brought went over Luke from top to bottom, inside and out. His systems seemed to be functioning just fine, but there was no one in residence inside him. The doctors and med-techs and droids all listened to us try to explain that fact to them, but they were creatures of science. While they could watch us do simple things with the Force, they sought physical and scientific explanations for what were spiritual phenomena. Trying to explain the Force to them was like trying to explain altruism to a rancor.

Their departure left us with nothing to do but wait for Leia Organa Solo's arrival. It could have come at any time, so we spent the better part of a week waiting. I've probably spent longer weeks on boring stake-outs, but nanoseconds seemed to pass in hours—and long hours at that. And, despite Kam's best efforts to keep us focused, our spirits began to ebb.

Princess Leia's arrival worked wonders for us. She looked tired and a bit haggard, but still every bit the exciting and heroic icon she had been during the Rebellion. Her twins, dark-haired and bright eyed, looked around at Yavin 4 with a mixture of wonder and trepidation. Last down the egress ramp from the *Millennium Falcon* came Han Solo. He looked to me as if he'd lost a bit of weight during his recent adventure on Kessel, but still cut a dashing and vital figure.

Ambassador Cilghal led the Solos to the Grand Audience Chamber. Sunlight filled the room with a golden glow and warmth that belied the cold and stark reality of Luke lying on a bier as if dead. The sight seemed to stagger his sister for a moment. I hung back enough that I could not hear the family's whispered remarks, but Jaina squirmed down out of her father's arms and gave her uncle a kiss. All of us hoped that gesture might work where our powers and medical science had failed, and my heart ached when the disappointed child turned away, defeated.

The enthusiasm spawned by the Solo family's arrival drained away during the rest of the day, leaving us a sullen and worn company by the time for the evening meal. Han Solo did what he could to help out by using the *Falcon's* food prep unit to create a dinner of Corellian food—fried *endwa* in an orange gravy and butterboiled *csolcir* with *vweilu*-nut slivers. While I didn't think he normally approached cooking with any more joy than I did, being the only person on the moon who was not Force-sensitive had to be rough on him. The conversations we all had were, in retrospect, very selfindulgent and, in the long run, rather trivial. Providing food was what he could do to help the situation that was beyond helping—and it kept him from having to listen to what we were saying.

I picked at the food, not really listening to the others. I catalogued their voices and relied on the recall I'd developed as a detective to let me replay things later, when I could divorce myself from the fears and defeatism some of my colleagues were voicing. It wasn't really fair to them, but I had spent a week trying to quell fears and had had enough of it.

Leia Organa Solo tolerated none of the self-pitying chatter, and ended it by slapping her hands on the stone table. "Stop this talk!" She berated us for shying from the risk involved with becoming Jedi Knights and reminded us that the New Republic was counting on us. "You must work together, discover things you don't know, fight what has to be fought. But the one thing you can't do is give up!"

I wanted to cheer, but a mouthful of *endwa* prevented me from doing so. I chewed quickly, chewed a bit more and swallowed hard. The *endwa* slowly slid down my throat—as good *endwa* will do—and eventually gave me back my voice.

Just in time for me to scream.

Luke Skywalker had told us that at the moment of

Alderaan's destruction, his master, Obi-Wan Kenobi, had said he felt "a disturbance in the Force." Anyone who could label what I felt a "disturbance" could think of Hutts as cuddly. The hollow shock one feels when told of a close friend's sudden death slammed into me at lightspeed. My conscious mind searched in vain for an identity to attach to that feeling, finding a way to contain it, but the hollowness opened into a bottomless void. Not only did I not know who had died, but I would never have a *chance* to know them, and this seemed the greatest tragedy possible.

Flashes of faces, snippets of dreams, laughter aborted and the sweet scent of a newborn's flesh undergoing a greasy transformation into roast meat all roared through me. Thousands upon thousands, millions upon millions, these images and impressions came in a whirlwind that screwed itself down into my belly. Hope melted into fear, wonder into terror, innocence into nothingness. Bright futures, all planned, proved the ultimate in morphability when a fundamental truth in these lives proved wrong. For these people there never had been a question of whether or not the sun would rise tomorrow, and yet in an instant they were proved wrong, as their sun reached out and devoured their world.

I heard Streen screaming that there were too many voices for him to handle before he slumped to the floor. I envied him in that moment for the same clarity of recall I cherished seconds before meant I watched a vast parade of dead flicker through my consciousness. A mother, acting on instinct, sheltered a child in the nanosecond before both of them were vaporized. Young lovers, lying together in the afterglow of the moment, hoping what they felt would never end, got their wish as they were torn into their constituent atoms. Criminals, triumphant in some small success, were reduced to fearful puling animals as their world evaporated.

I don't recall leaving the dining hall, but my mind was not my own as the Force carried to me the annihilation of a world far away. When clarity began to return, I found myself outside, on the top of the Great Temple. My throat burned. Trembling arms held me up above a pool of my own vomit and I would have sagged to the side, but strong hands on my shoulders steadied me.

"I didn't think the food was that bad." Han Solo set a cup of water down on the stone beside me. "Wash your mouth out."

I sloshed half the water from the container as I raised it to my lips, then rinsed my mouth and spat the foul water over the edge of the pyramid. "Thanks," I said. At least I think I said it.

Han half dragged me away from the remains of my dinner. "Leia said it was something horrible. Sun Crusher killed a system?"

I wiped my mouth on the sleeve of my tunic. "Unless you know of another superweapon sitting around that could explode a star."

A smile started to grow on his face and his dark eyes sparked for a second as a wiseass remark formed itself in his head, but he never let it out. Instead his grin melted into a more serious expression. "It has to be the Sun Crusher—that or there *is* another superweapon out there."

The fleeting image of someone who looked like Kyp surfaced in my brain. Through his eyes I saw the slender craft, I felt his joy at seeing his brother again, pain from betrayal that stretched into untold agony as his body melted. "Kyp had a brother?"

Han's eyes focused distantly. "Imps took him to the Academy at Carida."

"He's gone. So's Carida."

"I guess they won't be inviting me back for a class reunion, then." Han glanced down at me. "New Republic Intelligence will confirm that, but now I know where to start looking."

I looked hard at him. "You're going after Kyp?"

"Have to. He'll listen to me."

"You hope."

"Hmmm, your lips move but I hear my wife's voice." Han sighed. "I have a history with the kid. He's angry and he needs someone to trust. I'm it."

I nodded, then lifted my head. "Take me with you."

"Look, kid, I work best alone."

"So I've heard." I projected an image of my old self into his brain. "We've met before, Captain Solo. Wedge Antilles introduced us. I'm here incognito at Master Skywalker's suggestion."

"Horn, right." Han blinked his eyes. "You're a hot hand in an X-wing, but a Death Star couldn't take out the Sun Crusher. If I needed anyone with me, you'd be the first I'd tap."

"You're going after someone with incredible power, and I'm not just talking about that ship. I can't allow you to go alone."

Han's face clouded over. " 'Can't allow?' My ship, my rules, and don't try to pull any rank on me. I was a general with the Rebellion before you ever left Corellia. I can handle Kyp just fine. And I'm not so sure it's Kyp you're afraid of."

My eyes narrowed. "What do you mean?"

"You were CorSec. You just don't like the idea of someone like me with his hands on the Sun Crusher."

That brought me up short. I looked at him, then away at the dark jungle. *Was I allowing old prejudices to rear up and influence me?* For years I'd looked forward to getting a shot at Han Solo if he ever ventured back into the Corellian system. Even after joining the Rebellion I had severe reservations about him. In meeting him the first time I thought I had laid all that to rest.

I looked back at him. "Time once was when you'd have been right. Not now. If I actually thought that, I'd be down there stealing the *Falcon* and going after Kyp myself."

Han slowly nodded. "Look, kid, Corran; going after Kyp is the *only* thing I can do. You're a Jedi. You can be here and help Luke in ways I can't. I've got to do what I *can* do, and so do you. I'm going to leave you here so you can take care of Luke; so you can help my wife and watch my kids."

"You'd allow someone from CorSec to watch over your kids?"

"Getting soft in my old age, I know, but I understand it's possible to let old opinions die."

"Thanks." I narrowed my eyes. "What's going to happen if . . ."

"Kyp turns on me?" Han slowly shook his head. "I think I told you, your father hunted me once. I had to run to Carida to escape having a Horn on my tail. Doing what he's done, Kyp's destroyed even that haven. If it comes to that, good hunting."

TWENTY-THREE

That night, as I fell into bed and waited for sleep, I refused to review the dinner conversation, even though I had a nagging sense something of importance had been said during it. I didn't want to get anywhere close to going over again what I'd felt during Carida's death. I had once thought myself so hardened that a distant tragedy like this would tote itself up as just a statistic.

My training in the Force had changed all that. It hadn't made me any softer or weaker, but just more *aware*. I became cognizant of more of the connections between things and people. The pain of those who had died at Carida had echoes in the pain of relatives who would never see kin again, expatriates who could never go home again, people like Han Solo, whose memories of Carida would forever be tarnished because of what Kyp had done. While all of this would have been obvious to someone who sat down to think about it, it had come to me full blown through the Force. It amazed me, and also reinforced how vast my sphere of responsibility had become.

Sleep, when it finally came, was mercifully dreamless. I awoke a bit late and skipped my run, instead helping Han pre-flight the *Falcon*. He loaned me a couple of hydrospanners so I could work on Mara's Head-hunter. He then said his farewells to his family and raced off, leaving his children flanking their mother, waving fervently until the *Falcon* vanished from sight.

I spent much of the rest of the day working on the Headhunter. When Artoo was not busy with babysitting duties, he helped me out. He saved me from a mistake where I crosswired two boards in the navicomp that would have transposed coordinates, sending me off in directions I didn't want to go. By early evening I'd fixed most of the things Kyp had broken and figured I would resume where I left off the next morning. I finished the day with an evening run and a long soak in a cool stream, then dropped into bed.

I *felt* more than *heard* the children scream. I bolted from bed and ran to the turbolift, but the car was already moving upward and away from my level. I ran to the internal stairwell and started sprinting upward as fast as I could. Above me, in the Grand Audience Chamber, I could feel forces gathering, and was surprised that the person sitting with Luke had not raised an alarm. *Streen is smart enough to summon help.*

The second the old man's image popped into my mind, a piece of the dinner conversation echoed through my head. "I can't get away from him," he'd said desperately. "The dark man. A dark man, a shadow. He talked to Gantoris. He talked to Kyp. You shine the light, but the shadow always stays, whispering, talking." My chest tightened. *By all of Alderaan's ghosts, we've doomed Master Skywalker!*

A raging windstorm howled through the Grand Audience Chamber and battered me as I burst through the stairwell doorway. As I entered the room, I saw Leia leap for her brother's legs and get carried upward toward the ceiling by the cyclone. At the heart of the storm, Streen danced around in a circle, his arms spread wide, his eyes open but unseeing. He clearly meant for the storm to blow Luke and Leia out through the skylights and hurl them into the jungle, where the fall would kill them.

And without any telekinesis, I was powerless to halt the storm. Something urged me to despair over the fact, but I brushed it aside. *I'll just have to make Streen stop it himself.*

As the turbolift door opened and Kirana Ti boiled into the storm armoring Streen, I set myself and concentrated. Summoning the Force, I projected into Streen's brain a vision of the room that did not include me or Kirana or the other apprentices coming out of the lift. I also showed him that the room was empty save for himself. Those he wished to blow out of here were gone, sent off on the fate he had intended for them. I shoved into him a sense of his mission having been accomplished fully and totally and I felt an alien wave of satisfaction roll back out from him.

Then Kirana Ti battered her way past his defenses and tackled him. The wind died, allowing Luke and Leia to plunge toward the ground. Kam Solusar and Tionne rushed forward and used their telekinetic abilities to catch the siblings and lower them to the ground slowly.

Master Skywalker appeared to be unhurt. Streen slowly recovered himself and explained that in his nightmare, he thought he was fighting the dark man. He had tried to destroy him, thought he had, and then awoke to find he had actually been trying to kill Master Skywalker.

Standing up, Streen put an edge into his voice. "We must destroy the dark man before he kills all of us!"

· · ·

I retreated back down the stairs, mulling over Streen's words. I'd always known it would come down to that. While I used sociopathic murderers as mental models for Exar Kun, I hadn't located the logical flaw in my thinking. When hunting a sociopathic killer on Corellia, we could still have our blasters set on stun. We could capture him, have him treated for mental illness, have him incarcerated so he would do no more harm or even exile him to Kessel or some other hideous penal colony. We could also kill him, but only after court proceedings and judicial reviews. If we had to, if we were given no choice, we could employ deadly force against him, but few serial murderers fought to the bitter end.

Capture and rehabilitation were not options with Exar Kun. Master Skywalker might have been able to redeem his father, but I held out no such hope for the dark man. Luke had a stake in redeeming his father, and his father had a connection to him that invited redemption. Exar Kun had just spent four millennia trapped on this rock—virtually forever to think on what he had done—and if he hadn't decided to mend his ways in that time, it wasn't going to happen when one of us asked nicely.

But how does one kill a creature of the dark side? I had no clue as to the answer to that question. We would just have to find a way and then do it.

It really came as no surprise when, as I lay down in my bunk, an oily, glistening black stain seeped into the ceiling above me. It resolved itself into the shadowy image of a tall, slender, sharp-featured man. He wore archaic clothes and long hair. He knitted his long fingers together at his waist.

"Your mind-trick was quite good, Keiran Halcyon."

"High praise from a Dark Lord of the Sith." I watched him through half-lidded eyes. "Did it really fool you, Exar Kun, or were you just too trusting in using Streen's senses?''

The Dark Lord threw his head back in a silent laugh. "Fire and spirit, good. I had misjudged you because Gantoris and Kyp held you in such contempt."

"And here I thought a man should be known by his enemies."

"A truism I once lived by." The shade descended from the ceiling and stood at the foot of my bed. "I was once like you, a mere man filled with ambitions."

I sat up and snorted. "If you're the 'after' holograph, I'm not interested."

"Quite droll, Keiran, not as full of anger or fear as the others." Exar Kun's obsidian gaze bored into me. I tried to armor my mind against him the way I had with Mara Jade, but he was in and out too quickly for me to stop him. "You have more experience and more maturity. You are a riper fruit."

"But not to be plucked by you." I drew my knees up and hugged them to my chest. "You continue to misjudge me if you think there is anything I want from you."

"Oh, there is, you just don't realize it." A confident grin twisted his ebon features. He gestured casually with his right hand and a window opened in the air, hanging there in the center of my room. Within its confines I saw an Imperial Star Destroyer and I knew I was looking at the *Invidious*. It looked more worn than it had in the image General Cracken had showed me, but battle damage had far from crippled it. Swarms of Tri-fighters cruised around it on picket duty.

The image zoomed in, closing on the bridge, and exploded in through the forward view port. There stood Leonia Tavira, a bit older than Cracken's image of her, but all the more beautiful for it. She wore her black hair longer, so it fell to the swell of her breasts. Her figure had become less gangling and more rounded—while still petite, she had developed symmetrically so without other things or people around to judge scale, she appeared perfectly normal. Her violet eyes gleamed with a feral cunning that sizzled electrically through the image I was being shown.

The long-dead Sith Lord laughed lightly. "I can give you the power to destroy the Invids. Wipe them out. Or . . ." The image of Leonia brightened slightly. "I can give you the power to possess her and rule beside her. I will use the two of you as the focal point for a new Empire that I will spread throughout the galaxy."

I felt a stirring in my loins, then forced myself to laugh and shake my head. "It's been a while for me, and she's pretty, but I'm not interested."

"No, of course, you are not. You are a man of duty. Still here, on the *Invidious*, there are things you want."

The image pulled back a bit and slid over to center itself on an armored figure standing well back of Tavira. Two meters tall and apparently male, he wore a grey cloak over steel-grey armor. The armor looked as if it were made of the same plasteel used in stormtrooper armor, but had been shaped differently and layered with another material that provided texture and the grey color. The styling appeared more natural and primitive, as if designed to mimic the armored hide of some animal. This remained true of the facemask the figure wore. Serpentine styling and diagonal eye slits gave it a very viperish cast.

As soon as I saw him I knew he was the reason the *Invidious* could remain hidden. As I watched, his head came up and he stared straight out at me. His head then dipped and the image faded for a moment. Then I saw him striding forward toward Tavira. He gestured and she began shouting orders that started a flurry of activity.

Exar Kun yawned. "He is the true foe you seek. He is responsible for her successes. With my power you can defeat him, supplant him, do with her what you wish."

"I'll get there without your help at all, Exar Kun."

The shade's voice sharpened. "Perhaps, but you will *not* get *here* without it."

The image he presented me shifted and my stomach imploded. I saw Mirax lying on a bier, very much like Master Skywalker above us. A soft silver light bathed her. Her arms rested at her sides and she looked as if she were just napping. The only anomalous feature in the image was a small grey band resting on her forehead, pulsing with red and green lights. She looked very peaceful, and try as I might, I could sense no distress from her.

And nothing else.

"I can give her to you. I can tell you exactly where she is." Exar Kun shaped his face into what he thought was a compassionate expression. "You know the Force allows me to show you the past, the present, the future. This is where she is, your wife, right now. Hidden away, where you will never find her without my help."

"And what would you have me do for your help?"

"Kill Skywalker."

I smiled. "Mirax's life for his? No deal."

"You want more?" The Dark Lord laughed defiantly. "I can give you more, I *will* give you more. I will give you your wife *and* Tavira. You can have her ship and destroy her fleet. You can destroy your father-in-law's ship. You can return to Corellia and destroy those who hate you there!"

I shook my head. "No."

"No?"

"No." I sighed. "You don't get it, do you? You've already lost and you're continuing down that losing path. Haven't the last four thousand years taught you anything?"

"I know more than you could ever hope to learn in four thousand years or forty thousand years."

"That may be, but I know the one thing you don't." I rose from my bed and pointed a finger at him. "You're never going to win. You destroy those who oppose you, and what does that leave you?"

"The faithful."

"From among whom arises a rival. You have a schism."

"And I destroy the heretics."

"Yes, you do." I nodded carefully. "And again and again that cycle repeats itself and you let it go on because you've forgotten the most fundamental truth of reality: *Life* creates the Force. When Kyp destroyed Carida, he diminished your power. When you destroyed Gantoris, you diminished your power. You're a predator over-grazing your prey, but you can't stop because the dark side fills you with this aching hunger that will never be satisfied."

"Ha!" Exar Kun's laughter slashed at me, but sounded just a bit too shrill. "You cannot speak of the dark side until you have experienced it. Join me and learn that you are wrong."

"I don't think so. A Two-Onebee droid doesn't need to contract a disease to diagnose and treat it." I folded my arms across my chest and laughed at him. "I'm not fodder for your fantasies, go away."

Exar Kun lifted his head. "I came to you, now, inviting you to join me. I would have given you much. When next *you* come to *me*, and you will, I shall not be so generous.''

As he spoke the image of Mirax began to fade, but it did so in a most horrible way. I watched her lying there, aging years for every passing second. Her dark hair became grey and brittle, then fell out in clumps. Her flesh became ashen, her eyes sunken. Her body puddled out through the seams of her clothing, then they split, letting me see bare bones. A gust of wind came up, scattering them, spinning her skull around like a child's toy. Finally it came to rest, gap-toothed, staring at me with empty sockets.

I blinked the image away and found myself alone again. I sat back down on my bed and discovered I was trembling. It surprised me, so I made myself laugh. I had to push at first, but it came more easily. The warm sound filled my small room and I swore I could hear the echoes of laughter that Biggs, Wedge and Porkins had shared in here. They had laughed because they knew they had the secret of destroying the Death Star.

I laughed along with them. Exar Kun had come to me to entice me to join him. What he didn't know, what fueled my laughter even more, was that in doing so, he gave me the secret of destroying him.

I hoped for a moment alone with Leia Organa Solo to tell her what I'd discovered about Exar Kun, but between her caring for her children and the unexpected arrival of a B-wing fighter, I had no chance to speak with her. I wanted to talk to her alone because I was operating on the assumption that the dark man might have gotten to others of the students. She'd not been on Yavin long enough to fall under his sway, and I had no doubt that she'd be able to resist him. Letting everyone know that I had a way to hurt Kun was a good way to let him know that, too, and that would rob us of our weapon.

The pilot of the B-wing turned out to be a Mon Calamari named Terpfen, who blubbered out a confession about having been an agent under Imperial control who had betrayed to the Imps the location of the world Anoth, where Winter and the youngest Organa Solo child, Anakin, had been sent for safe keeping. He urged Leia to head immediately for Anoth, but she said she didn't know its coordinates. Only Winter, Master Skywalker and Admiral Ackbar did. She determined to head immediately for Mon Calamari to find Ackbar, and then off to rescue her youngest child.

While the other students took charge of the twins and helped Terpfen recover from his journey, I caught up with her in the Great Temple. "Councilor Organa Solo, I need to speak with you."

"Make it brief. I'm heading out as soon as I can get my stuff together."

I hit the button for the turbolift. "You can't go with Terpfen. He's a known traitor."

She preceded me into the lift. "I can handle myself on that count."

"Despite the assurances that Ambassador Cilghal gave you that we can protect your twins, you can't leave them here."

Her brown eyes sparked dangerously. "So, what, I load them into a fighter with a known traitor and take them off to a world where Imperial assassins are going to be trying to kill them?"

"No, but leaving them here, where a four-thousand-year-old Dark Lord of the Sith is turning apprentices into puppets isn't much of a choice, either.'' I shook my head. ''You don't know any of us. How can you trust all of us with your kids?''

''I can't trust all of you.'' She poked a finger square in my chest. ''I'm trusting *you*.''

''What?''

Her expression sharpened as the lift doors opened and she started down the hall to her room. ''When my husband left here, he said I could trust you. Not an easy man to earn trust from, my husband. That got me wondering and you'd be surprised what the president of the New Republic can learn when she's curious and has got a HoloNet connection. The fact that my brother picked you to be here counts a lot in your favor, but the rest of your record doesn't hurt at all. I think my children are safe with Corran Horn.''

''Look, since you know who I am, let me fly you to Mon Calamari. I'm a hot hand with a fighter. I can help when you get to Anoth.''

She shook her head. ''Can't do it—and that's because I *do* know who you are. I know that if you wanted to be my chauffeur, you'd not have come to me privately. You want something else, and I'm willing to bet that something else means you're going to be staying here. Let me have it.''

I nodded as she started shoving clothes into a satchel. ''First, I think the apprentices who are vulnerable to Exar Kun are those who have had some brush with the dark side in the past. Streen once asked me about something I considered minor, but it might be the vector in for Exar Kun. Can't confirm that about Gantoris or Kyp, but it would make sense since those who have fallen once can more easily be lured back to old paths of behavior.''

Leia paused for a moment. "That would put Kam at risk."

"He's pretty tough, but, yes, there's a chance." I glanced down. "Streen remains a risk. Can't pinpoint any others, though Brakiss has an Imperial background that would make him prey."

"Right. What else?"

"We have a basic problem if we're going to figure out a way to deal with Exar Kun. If we exclude everyone who is suspect, he could know something is afoot because of that fact."

"And he could use any paranoia that develops as a way into those who aren't yet tainted." She zipped up her bag. "So is there a solution to this problem, or do we evac Yavin?"

"With Kyp running around in an invincible ship? No way. We're all that can stand between him and his returning with a way to move Exar Kun off this ball."

"Evac is out. The problem still stands then." She watched a smile grow on my face. "I hate it when a Corellian smiles like that. Usually means Han's about to lose the *Falcon* to Lando in some sabacc game."

"Well, it's Exar Kun's chance to lose this time, because he overplayed his hand." My smile broadened. "Your brother identified an ability in me, one to project thoughts into others. How well I know them, the degree of contact I feel for them, determines how much I can pump through. Exar Kun came to me last night, after I helped take Streen down by projecting into him the idea that he'd succeeded at what he tried to do. Kun tried to bring me over to his side, but I resisted. He got a good read on me and tried to play me."

Leia smiled and it became easy for me to see why thousands of Rebel hearts had been broken when she married Han Solo. "And while he was playing you, you got a good read on him. You can track him, when he's active?"

"I think so. I also think these displays take a lot out of him. I think he'll be keeping a low profile, probably tapping in on Streen, to find out what we're doing."

She nodded. "And you can feed enough back through that connection to deceive him?"

I nodded. "Giving us time to find a way to deal with him."

"Good, very good." Her eyes sharpened. "I can't leave you in charge—he'd notice the change in routine and spot you as a danger."

"Right. I'll have to keep a low profile, too. I'll keep quiet unless things aren't going to work or start going really badly." I moved from the doorway as she headed out toward the turbolift. "I know I can buy us time, but not much. At the rate he recovers, Kun should be ready for something tomorrow, maybe tonight."

"I know you'll do what you can." She stopped at the turbolift and offered me her hand. "May the Force be with you."

"And you."

"I hope so." She smiled at me grimly as the turbolift doors closed. "I have a feeling we'll both need it."

TWENTY-FOUR

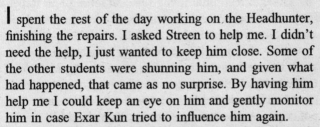

I spent the rest of the day working on the Headhunter, finishing the repairs. I asked Streen to help me. I didn't need the help, I just wanted to keep him close. Some of the other students were shunning him, and given what had happened, that came as no surprise. By having him help me I could keep an eye on him and gently monitor him in case Exar Kun tried to influence him again.

I also offered Kun the Headhunter as bait through Streen. The old gas prospector knew enough about flying a ship that he was able to hover the fighter and bring it into the hangar proper from the landing pad, but he didn't seem able to work the weapons. Mara's ship no longer had the standard weapons package it had been built with. The concussion missile launchers had been scrapped and replaced with a center-mounted ion-cannon. Each wing still sported a triple-blaster, but they were hardwired for dual-fire mode, which isn't a choice I'd have made.

I told Streen enough about the weapons to make him think he could work them, but I didn't tell him about having installed a command override code that was required to use them. If weapons were engaged without the code, the Headhunter would cut thrust to zero, click in the repulsorlift coils, and hover. The onboard computers also had the Great Temple designated as a passive flight zone: there would be no running it up to speed and slamming into the Temple. The navicomp would just take over and land the ship in the face of such an obvious pilot error.

My thinking was that Kun, still taxed from his having funneled enough power through Streen to create that cyclone, would take the chance at having Streen use the Headhunter to kill Luke. I tried to make it easy for him by giving Streen little flying tips and telling him Rebellion pilot stories, but Exar Kun never took the bait. I felt a bit disappointed in him at that, but didn't push the issue for fear of tipping him to our connection.

It wasn't until that evening, as I was trying to drop off to sleep, that I realized Kun wasn't quite as sophisticated as I had expected. Alarms triggered by Artoo, who was stationed in the Grand Audience Chamber, jolted me out of bed. I stretched out my senses and caught spiky impressions of creatures that just felt *wrong* up at the ziggurat's pinnacle.

I didn't even think about hitting the stairs or waiting for the turbolift. I sprinted to the Headhunter, punched in the ignition code and enabled the weapons. I overrode the passive flight directives and cruised out of the hangar into the orange twilight of the night. I looped and rolled the fighter and took a pass above the Temple, but all I could see was the hint of a triangular wingtip slipping through one of the skylights.

Frustration rippled through me, but I shoved it away. *Those creatures are not my problem right now. Exar Kun* is. Stretching out my senses, I discovered slender ebon threads of influence, three of them, linked to the creatures the Dark Lord had sent to kill Luke Skywalker. The creatures were mindless beasts, far easier to control than Streen, affording Kun maximum destruction with a minimal amount of energy expended.

I overshot the Temple, then killed my thrust and cut in the repulsorlift coils. This left me hovering four hundred meters above the ground. Using the Headhunter's etheric rudder, I twitched the ship around until the nose pointed off toward where I felt Kun's influence originating. I hit a button on my console, locking in that heading.

Nudging the throttle forward, I rolled to starboard and cruised back past the Great Temple by a kilometer. I killed thrust again, hovered and pointed the nose off in the direction I felt Kun's influence coming from. I logged those coordinates in the navicomp.

My comm unit beeped and an "all-clear" signal from Artoo appeared on my main screen. I smiled and felt the little link tendrils withering and retreating back to Exar Kun. I pushed my feelings, focusing them tightly, hoping to pick up a flash of anger or disappointment from him, but I got nothing of the sort. Instead I found four more of the anomalous lifeforms winging their way to the Great Temple from deep in the jungle.

I allowed myself a low laugh. The one problem with starfighter targeting systems is that they are built around a sensor package that recognizes the durasteel and other components that make up other starfighters or ships or anything else that can legitimately be classed as a target. Additional software uploads can define new targets, allowing systems to be updated as new foes and new equipment come online. And while these creatures did have metal claws, they actually had less metal content than the average civilian strolling around on Coruscant. As far as the Headhunter was concerned, they just weren't really targets.

As a Jedi, I found them to be big *fat* targets.

They flew in toward the Temple, no more able to recognize the Headhunter as a threat than it was able to recognize them. The huge creatures were easily as tall in body as a man, with a huge wingspan of ugly, fleshy wings. They had two heads, each with a low enough cranium to only be sporting a cubic centimeter of brains. They also each had a muscular tail that ended in a nasty crystalline stinger. Decidedly scary and lethal.

Unless you're a pilot in a starfighter.

My first shot crisscrossed twin blaster bolts in the thorax of the lead creature. Flesh boiled and scales melted, then the bolts burst out of its back and flew on only slightly spent. The creature's heads curled inward, looking down at the smoking hole in its chest, then the wings collapsed. The creature dropped to the ground with the speed of a droid ejected from a fighter. It impaled itself on the branches of a massive Massassi tree below.

My shot at the next beastie came fast and much sloppier—only one bolt hit. The single energy projectile did the job, however. It burned a wing off the one it hit. The creature flapped furiously with the one good wing, but to no discernible benefit. Screaming, the beast spiraled down and smashed into the Temple's stone base.

For the last two monsters I switched to the ion cannon. The initial shot from it caught the third monster in the pelvis. The blue ion bolt shattered into hundreds of little lightning tendrils. The bolt fired all of the creature's nerves at once, making the creature's limbs spasm. Its tail jerked backward and forward so violently that it stabbed itself. The creature's heads struck at its own tail, tearing great jagged hunks out of it, then its wings folded in on it and the falling beast splattered itself down the pyramid's north side.

The last beast proved more agile than the others and, freed of Kun's waning influence, wheeled through the sky and dove at the Headhunter. I got the nose up and flicked on the shields in time to intercept its attack. The beast rebounded off the forward shield, but stabbed out with one clawed foot and snagged hold of the Head-hunter's nose. Sparks shot through the cockpit as the forward shield failed, and the short circuit killed the ion cannon. The beast grabbed the nose with its other foot, durasteel screaming as it sank its talons in. It hunched forward over the fuselage, its wings wrapping the Head-hunter in an embrace, as its heads snapped at me in the cockpit.

The blasters couldn't hit it and the ion cannon wouldn't fire. I could have hovered the craft, opened the cockpit canopy and engaged the monster with my light-saber, except I'd left it back in my room. As one thrust-ing head ricocheted off the transparisteel canopy, I knew it was only a matter of time before the canopy gave way.

"Fine." I smiled. "You want to play? Let's play."

I pointed the nose up and kicked the thrusters in full.

At top speed it only took a handful of seconds to reach the edge of the atmosphere. Air pressure slammed the beast against the hull and kept it laid out there like a blanket. The friction heated up the ship's durasteel hull, causing bits and pieces of the creature's wings to fry. When it tried to rear back and unfurl its wings to get them off the hot metal, the air pressure snapped both of them and swept them in around the monster, then pitched it forward and smashed it down on the hull again.

Once outside the atmosphere, a different problem presented itself for the creature. The vacuum of space effectively cooled the hull, sucking all the heat out of it. It did the same thing for the creature, leaving the angry and fearful expressions on both of its faces frozen there for an eternity. I killed thrust as the beast cooled, letting the Headhunter drift as my nose ornament chilled rather quickly. I was quite relieved to see the beast wasn't suited to surviving in space's cold void, but then I'd not thought anything originating on Yavin 4 would be.

Finally, when I thought it had gotten cold enough, I hit the right rudder hard. While the ship's inertial damper field kept me and the Headhunter from feeling any of the effects of such a violent maneuver, the creature was not so lucky. Its body sheared off at the ankles and started a rolling tumble off toward the gas giant, while I looped the Headhunter and started back down toward the Temple.

Kam met me in the hangar as I brought the Headhunter to a stop. I popped the cockpit canopy and hopped down to the deck. Kam regarded me with cold eyes as I swung under the fighter's nose.

"There was an attack on Master Skywalker. Where were you?"

I smiled, then reached up and plucked a talon from where it had lodged in the Headhunter's nose. I tossed it to him. "Target practice."

"That's not the sort of thing you should do on your own."

I frowned at him. "It was the only thing I could do, Kam. I couldn't get up there fast enough to help inside, so I stopped Kun's reinforcements."

"You don't know it's Kun."

"I *know*."

Kam shook his head and jerked a thumb toward the audience chamber. "But we just learned that, from Luke."

"Luke's awake?"

"No, but his nephew and niece can hear him. He said Exar Kun was behind the trouble." Kam's face darkened. "We have to defeat Kun if we are to get Luke back. We're preparing a council of war right now to figure out what we're going to do."

"Council of war, good. Right now, not good." I sighed. "Kun has been defeated tonight. He's not going to be coming back right away."

"How do you know that?" Hints of betrayal and confusion arced through Kam's question.

"Trust me on this, Kam, I know it." I reached out with a hand and laid it on his shoulder, but he shrugged me off. "Look, if I was on Kun's side, I'd not have vaped four of his pets, would I? I've got my own lightsaber and I could have filleted Master Skywalker on any of my watches. You can trust me."

"But you have secrets." Kam's eyes became crescent slits. "You and Master Skywalker have not been wholly forthcoming."

"True, but there are good reasons for this, reasons Master Skywalker himself gave me. His sister, despite the dire circumstances here, chose not to violate those confidences." I looked him straight in the eye. "You have your reasons for being here, so you can shore up your personality against the weaknesses that allowed you to be seduced by the dark side. My reasons for being here are different, but no less important to me. I want Exar Kun's influence as dead as you do. Together we can accomplish this, each doing our parts. Mine are just going to be different than yours.''

Kam considered my words for a moment, then slowly nodded. ''I'll tell the others you think tonight is not a good time for planning against Kun.''

''Leave me out of it. It's only logical that working on things now will be to no one's benefit. Let's get some sleep and plan tomorrow, during the day. Kun doesn't seem to strike effectively during the day.'' I gave him a solid smile. ''We are going to win against him, you know.''

''We've got no choice.''

''Agreed.'' I slapped him on the shoulder. ''Kun's picked the wrong people to fight at the wrong time, and that's the last mistake we'll let him make.''

The council of war convened in what had once been the Rebel command post for the first strike on the Death Star. Dust shrouded the various artifacts that hadn't been hauled away by Imperial survey teams or New Republic museum curators. What remained was largely serviceable and permitted all fourteen of us to sit around comfortably. Despite there being ample room for me at the central table, I hung back and pushed my sphere of responsibility out to fill the room and monitor what was going on with my fellow apprentices.

I immediately picked up a jet-black strand connecting Streen to Kun. I was sure the old gas prospector had no idea it was there. He was still mortified at his near-murder of Master Skywalker and his dwelling on what he had almost done was what allowed Kun to maintain the link. More fortunately, Streen's emotional turmoil meant any information coursing down that line to Kun was unreliable, carrying with it dour emotional impressions.

If that were not enough to make Kun think we were hopelessly incompetent, Ambassador Cilghal's curious logic must have convinced him of it. She dismissed Dorsk 81's fear that Kun could listen in on our planning sessions by saying, "We must operate on the assumption we can still fight him. We have enough real problems to confront—there's no need to manufacture worse ones from our imagination." As a warrior, I couldn't imagine anything worse than our side remaining willfully ignorant of the possibility that our enemy knew what we were planning, but in the espionage-laden world of diplomacy, that didn't appear to be so important.

I kept careful track of what information moved through the conduit from Streen to Exar Kun and found I really needed to inject very little into it, or edit very little from it. Twelve half-trained apprentices and two toddlers planning to annihilate someone who had survived an onslaught by the combined might of the Jedi of his age sounded ridiculous on the surface of it. Tionne carefully told us how our own little council mirrored that of the Great Council of Deneba, when the Jedi united to defeat Kun. She made it sound grand and hopeful, but with only a little push I was able to make it sound hopeless.

I let Streen fill Kun with our resolve to unite and defeat him, but Kun's contempt for us came rolling back along the line like an echo. He had faced fleets of ships and all the known Jedi. He had slain his own master. His power was unrivaled. He had defeated our Master and beyond our resolve to fight, we had no operative plans and nothing with which to challenge him. We were snacks he would devour at his leisure, not morsels that might choke him.

His connection to Streen atrophied and died as various of us offered plans that wouldn't trap a stintaril.

My quiet laughter from the corner brought Cilghal's head around. "This is hardly a matter that is amusing, Keiran. If you will not contribute . . ."

I stood and narrowed my eyes. "I'll contribute. You've plotted the right course: uniting is the only way to get him. That's good."

Brakiss sniffed. "We're pleased you approve."

I ignored his comment. "What you've missed is the key. Streen, what do you call him?"

The prospector raked fingers back through his frizzy grey hair. "The Dark Man."

"Right. Master Skywalker described him to me as a shadow, and that was close to what Gantoris reported as well." I watched Kam carefully. "And that's what I saw the one time he came to recruit me."

Kam's head came up. "So, what is your point?"

"My point is that he's a creature of shadow, a creature of the dark side. What has Master Skywalker drilled into us since day one?"

Kirana Ti's eyes widened. "The antidote to the dark side is the light side."

"Right. It will have to shine so brightly no shadow can withstand it." I looked around at all of them. "That's your job. When he comes for Luke again, you give him more light than he can ever handle."

The Mon Calamari Ambassador cocked her head at me. "*Our* job? You must be with us, be part of our united force."

"Not going to happen." I leaned forward, holding myself up by posting my arms on the table. "Up to this point, Exar Kun has acted on his own schedule. He's moved when he wants to move, done what he's wanted to do. Not anymore. Tomorrow evening, as night is coming on, we'll force him to act. He won't be ready, but he'll think he can still beat us. He'll be wrong."

Tionne regarded me with her pearl eyes. "What are you going to do?"

I shook my head. "You can't know, just as I can't know exactly what you want to do. The key is that when we move," I pointed at Streen, "he'll be guarding Luke Skywalker's body."

"Streen?" Kam shook his head adamantly. "Impossible."

"Me?" Streen looked stricken.

"You, Streen. You're going to be just like the winds you summoned the other night. You're going to seem weak, but you'll be strong. You won't break, you'll hold." I smiled. "You'll all hold."

The Dathomiri witch watched me carefully. "You make it sound as if you will go after Exar Kun by yourself. You know it will be impossible to stand against him alone."

Dorsk 81 nodded. "He defeated Master Skywalker. Your mission will be impossible."

"Could be." I smiled, remembering similar assessments of missions with Rogue Squadron. "Then again, I've been to the land of the impossible before. If we all do our parts, I may even survive another little visit there."

TWENTY-FIVE

I used the Headhunter's blasters to burn back enough
jungle at the edge of the lake to provide me with a landing site, then I set the fighter down. The landing was a
touch rougher than I would have liked. Given that the
belly cargo compartment contained a dozen nergon 14
charges all ready to go, I should have focused more on
flying, but I couldn't. Using the same technique Luke
had showed Streen to shield his mind against picking up
the thoughts of others, I was keeping my presence within
the Force as undetectable as I could. I found it tiring, but
took heart from the fact that Exar Kun likewise liked to
remain hidden, and had to expend portions of his power
to do so as well.

I climbed out of the fighter and opened the cargo
compartment. I shouldered two packs with the explosives in them, gingerly shifting them about to let me
maintain good balance. All I needed was to get careless
and slip on my way to my destination. *Do that and our
war against Exar Kun will be lost before it even starts.*

I looked out across the expanse of the lake at the
small island centered in it. An obsidian pyramid with
smooth sides had been erected there, then a wedge had
been chopped out of the center of it. From the shore, the

interior angles drew my attention to a massive statue of a man. I was too far away to discern much in the way of detail, but I had no doubt I looked upon Exar Kun—if for no other reason than that someone of his ego never would have let a statue to *another* be raised on his world.

I knew this is where I would find him. The clues had been painfully easy to put together. Dorsk 81 had reported traveling in this direction, but the survey logs that Kyp Durron had prepared showed no trip here. What little information about this place that had been recorded by the Rebel scout Unnh indicated that he found it unsettling and likely a monument to some ancient lord. The fact that it had escaped the ravages of time further suggested it was a focus for Kun's power. In addition, when I'd plotted the direction from which Kun's power had flowed the other evening, the two courses crossed over this location.

And, as if I needed more proof, I really didn't feel like marching in there.

I frowned at myself. "You've survived having Booster Terrik for a father-in-law, you can survive this."

The water surrounding the island picked up orange highlights from the gas giant, but the system's dying sun still streaked it with jets of gold. I moved forward, stepping on the first of the stones set bare centimeters beneath the surface of the water. One misstep would plunge me deep into the pond's icy depths, so I moved cautiously. I watched where I placed my feet and had a moment of grudging admiration for Exar Kun. By making the pathway to his shrine so tricky and difficult, he forced all who approached him to do so with bowed heads so they could watch their feet.

Ripples spread out from my every step and lapped against the far shore, but they provided the only activity I saw over there. This pleased me because I was really in no position to deal with Kun's winged terrors. The fact that Jacen Solo, though not quite yet three years old, had managed to hold a trio of them at bay with his uncle's lightsaber did not make me think my chances would be good in dealing with them. Though I thought myself more nimble than a toddler, with thirty kilos of explosives hanging on my back like lead wings, graceful wasn't going to describe me at all.

I reached the island's shore without opposition and mounted the steps to the temple. Sith hieroglyphs had been incised into the stones, still as crisp and sharp as the day the Massassi had carved them. The Sullustan scout had translated some of them as magics to preserve the temple, and others to call down doom on defilers. Somehow the Massassi script, with hooks and barbs on each glyph, seemed more menacing than any curses they could call down.

Once inside the pyramid I worked quickly, distributing the nergon 14 charges and arming them. I tried to put them near structural points that would promote the collapse of the whole building, but with that massive sort of block construction, I couldn't be certain it would work. The detonators could either be set for a time and triggered manually, or keyed by remote through codes I could broadcast from the Headhunter's comm unit. Having seen the results produced by such charges in the past, I didn't want to be anywhere nearby when they went off.

The last charge I brought forward like a sacrificial offering. I paced quickly across the open courtyard and laid it at the base of the pedestal on which Exar Kun's colossal statue stood. I made certain to wedge the charge tightly against the base and the floor, so when it went off it would open enough of a crater to topple the statue. I measured the height of the pedestal with my eye, then glanced back toward the lake.

I smiled. "Mon Calamari tourists will get a chance to have a good look at you, once this goes."

I retreated to the center of the small courtyard, then unveiled my presence. I pushed my sphere of responsibility out, but had barely gotten it two meters before Kun appeared and swallowed my reflection in the obsidian stones of the pedestal.

"So, you have come to me to ask me to help you." Haughtiness rippled through the Force. "I warned you that I would not be generous with you this time."

I laughed at him. "I remember. That's not why I'm here."

Kun's head came up as his face contracted into a fierce scowl. "What? Why have you violated my sanctuary?"

"Just the thing I wanted to talk with you about." I stroked my goatee and began pacing back and forth before him. "I checked New Republic law. Property claims are abandoned well shy of four millennia. As a result, I've filed a claim for this place, and now it's mine. I'd love to have you stick around, but your statue is right where the wife will want the entertainment center. You understand, don't you?"

"You insolent bug!" Kun opened his shadowy arms wide. "You prattle on as if your wit can armor you against my might."

"And you think you can hurt me?" I scoffed at him. "This is your eviction notice."

"You're playing with powers more titanic than you could ever know."

"Save the threats." I yawned. "I've been going over all the stuff you've done, and I've figured out your weakness. While disembodied, you can't affect the physical world.''

Kun's expression darkened. ''No?''

I shook my head. ''No.''

''Ah, then I cannot do this.'' The wraith waved an ethereal hand and sparks shot from each of the explosive packets I'd scattered about. Blue flames flared as the detonators each melted.

Just like the Jedi Holocron!

My nose closing against the stink of melted plastic, I glanced up at Kun. ''Ooops.''

Kun flicked a finger at me, sending me whirling across the courtyard. I tried to gather the Force around me to protect myself, but the shock at my error kept me from it. I slammed into an obsidian wall and heard a bone in my right forearm crack. I clutched the limb to my chest, but Kun spun me again, smashing my flank into a low wall. Ribs crunched with that impact and I felt something inside go, as well.

Kun was enjoying himself, probably for the first time in millennia, the very thought of which made me vomit. Kun's laughter echoed through his stronghold as he pitched me around, dancing me and rolling me back and forth across the courtyard. I thought his actions were haphazard, especially when he lifted me into the air, then dashed me down, shattering my left leg, but even through the pain I had a clarity of mind. He wanted me thinking, not dead, *yet*, and that made my stomach roil again.

Eventually, like a child tiring of a toy, he let me go. I slumped to my side and involuntarily flinched as his shade came to cover me. ''Just because you never saw me affect the material world, it doesn't mean I *couldn't*. And even if it is something of an effort to do so, here, in my *stronghold*, it is a pleasure beyond your possible ken.''

I let my words hiss out between clenched teeth. "I think I'll put a wideview holoprojector right where you're standing."

"Childish jokes from a childish mind." He gestured casually and all the explosive charges I'd placed sailed out of the temple and splashed in the black lake. Glancing down at me, Kun let his voice become icy. "You could have been raised to the level of divinity by my hand. Now you will be destroyed by it."

Even before I could taunt him again, he gestured and I felt a presence behind me. I rolled over and saw Mirax standing there, her eyes full of fire. "I should have known, *CorSec*, that you would abandon me. You said you wanted *me* more than you wanted your Jedi heritage. I gave you all that I am. I want to bear your children. This is how you repay me? You leave me alone, all alone, *dying* alone; while you play games with rocks and pictures?"

The vehemence in her voice ripped straight through me. It collapsed my stomach and shoved it out through my spine. I wrapped my hands around my belly and hunched forward. "No, Mirax, no!"

The wailing calls of all the infants who had died on Carida swirled around me to accompany her voice. "Hear them, Corran. They are your sons, your daughters. They are the children you have denied to the world. You accused Exar Kun of being a fool because he destroys life, but you are more of a fool. You could have created it. With me. *If* you wanted me. *If* you truly loved me."

I hugged my broken arm to fractured ribs, folding around the pain in my middle. I knew she was nothing but an illusion Kun had conjured from my mind, but it seemed too real for me to disbelieve it. Kun was feeding back to me my own image of Mirax, and infusing it with everything I feared. Because the attack came from within, I had no emotional armor with which to shield myself. I heard in her voice exactly the words that terrified me.

I reached out to her with my left hand, lifting my face toward her. "No, Mirax, no. I *do* love you!"

"How can you love *her*?" My father's voice slashed at me from behind. "Her father hired the bounty hunter who murdered me. A murder you could have prevented. Was that it? Had she seduced you even then? Were you her creature? Did she lay warm in your arms so I could lay cold in them?"

I levered myself around into a sitting position to meet my father's accusing stare, then had to tear my eyes from him. Gone was the man I had known in life. His flesh had become ashen, his eyes holes onto a void. The only color on him came from the blood spurting from his wounds to puddle around him. I heard it splashing from him. I couldn't get the cloying scent out of my nostrils and dreaded the touch of the rivulet slowly snaking its way toward me.

"You know that's not true!"

"I only know you failed me. You left me to die."

Mirax chimed in. "As you leave me to die."

My mother's voice joined them. "He never cared if I died, either."

Laughter, low and cold, echoed from the obsidian walls. I looked up and saw the image of Lujayne Forge, one of my first friends in Rogue Squadron. The right side of her face had been burned away by blaster fire. "He let me die. He wanted to play the hero, so I paid the price."

"No!" I slammed my right fist against the courtyard stones, breaking it and grinding the bones in my arm. I latched onto the pain and used it to recapture control of my mind. Their accusations bored into me, freeing the part of me that second-guessed everything I did. I knew that piece of me well and loathed it. I could replay conversations in my mind for hours when it held sway, wishing I'd said this, wondering why I'd said that, hoping things would not be taken in the worst way, but dreading the fact that they would. When I began doubting myself, I was paralyzed. The cycle always built on itself, growing, reviewing more things, until I dissected my whole life.

And it continues until I get angry at myself and stop it.

The desire to give in to the anger and cut Exar Kun short almost overwhelmed me. That option hung there, tantalizing me. I could use my anger like a lightsaber. I could slice to ribbons these false spirits, these treacherous phantoms. I would cut down Exar Kun's army, then I would rip into him. He would be nothing before me and my anger. I would sunder him the way my explosives should have sundered his shrine.

And then I can find other targets that deserve destruction. . . . I raised my right hand triumphantly, then curled it down into a fist.

Pain jolted through me again and in its wake came outrage. I slammed my hand against the ground and screamed, then shot Exar Kun a sidelong glance. "No. My anger is not for you to use."

The Dark Lord towered above me. "Anger is a most sweet nectar. Despair will also suffice."

Another phantom congealed before me, looking and feeling and smelling and sounding more real than I was myself. The little boy, all tow-headed and grey-eyed, barely older than Jacen Solo, looked at me with his lower lip quivering. Tears formed at the corners of his eyes. He reached out with little stubby-fingered hands and took my broken hand into his.

"Who hurt you, Daddy?" His innocent gaze searched my face. "I can make it better. I can. Let me. Please . . ." His voice became a plaintive wail that faded with his image. I felt his grip, feathery and gentle, soothing and kind, fading to be replaced with pain. "Why won't you let me help?"

The lump rising in my throat strangled me. Through the boy's fading image I saw Mirax, no longer hateful, standing there. She wore a simple white gown. She rubbed her hands lovingly over her swollen belly, the look on her face one of pure, unadulterated joy. The image shifted slightly as the boy reappeared, older, yet still a child, to place his hand against his mother's rounded stomach.

Then both of their images blew apart into a million razor-edged fragments that burned through me.

"Just as well," I heard my father say, "any child of that union would have been as disappointing as you have been."

That simple remark detonated like a bomb inside me. I had forever hoped that I would win my father's approval, that he would like me for who and what I was. He was never stinting with his praise, but with his death I had been left trying to guess what he would have thought about this action or that. Even my decision to become a Jedi had been made to win his approval and to model myself on him.

Yet in his voice, I heard that I had failed. The sum and total of my life, the sum and total of the lives of any children I helped create, and whatever they would create; all of it would be worthless in his eyes. One of the anchor points for my life crumbled, eroding in uncertainty, cutting me adrift without a chance of recovering myself.

I was lost.

I was hopeless.

I was the ultimate failure.

I could take no more.

"Is that the best you've got?" The tone of the voice had enough edge to etch transparisteel and would have flensed me alive, but I knew it wasn't directed at me. Through tear-clouded eyes I looked up and saw Mara Jade sauntering into the temple. "Babies crying and ghosts whispering lies from beyond the grave? The Dark Lord of the Sith *I* knew would have been ashamed to use such tactics."

"What?" Exar Kun's voice roared, as if in volume and intensity it could batter her down. "Who dares?"

"Who *cares*, more correctly." She pointed at me. "Horn here has been worked over by the Empire's best and never broke. Isard would have had you digitized, analyzed and discarded without a second thought, and she wasn't even Force-sensitive. Darth Vader would have found you amusingly quaint, and the Emperor . . . well . . ." Mara Jade's eyes flashed mercilessly. "The Emperor *succeeded* in destroying the Jedi, so he'd see you as the very definition of failure!"

"Yes, but your vaunted Emperor is *dead*!"

I found my voice again. "Something the two of you have in common, then." I shoved myself up and balanced awkwardly on my good leg. "And something else: he didn't know when he'd lost, either. It's over!"

Kun regarded me anew and I felt his consciousness stab into my brain. It withdrew quickly, as if it had been stung by the thought I had nestled there. Kun laughed aloud. "A trap? You and your companions seek to trap *me*?"

Kun doubled his image's volume and smiled most cruelly at us. "You think your petty plans will work against me? You thought your coming here would defeat me? Never." He looked away toward the Great Temple, then back down at us. "This may have been a brave attempt on your part, but your friends have made a grave error. Their defense of Skywalker is only as strong as the weakest person defending him, and they have left him vulnerable again."

Mara looked at me, clearly alarmed. "What's he talking about?"

"Luke's hurt." I winced as pain shot through my belly. "Streen is guarding him."

Exar Kun laughed again. "Yes, Streen. *My* Streen." The Dark Lord's image began to shrink back into the obsidian of his temple. "I will finish him, then come again for you. Tremble in fear. Cower in anticipation."

His presence faded from the Temple and I tried to straighten up. I managed a half-staggered step, then went down on one knee. I guess I fell further or faster than I expected because I next found Mara kneeling next to me. "C'mon, Horn, wake up. What's this about Streen?"

I managed a weak smile. "Bait. Kun's heading into a trap. A big trap."

She weighed my words. "Any chance he can get out of it?"

"Shouldn't be able to. It really *is* over for him." I coughed once and felt pain in my chest. "Gonna have to help me out of here, because I can't make it on my own."

"I think I can handle that." She reached down,

helped haul me to my feet, then dipped a shoulder and lifted me in a rescue-carry. "Always glad to help a friend."

The sun had set by the time we got back to my Head-hunter and the other one that had brought Mara Jade on her second trip to Yavin 4. She lugged me back to shore and eased me to the ground without complaining about what a burden I'd been. She ran to her ship and got a first aid kit.

"Sorry for the rough spots out there."

"No problem. Beats swimming." I coughed lightly. "Besides, a Jedi does not know pain."

"Need to be more convincing when you say that." Mara shook her head. "Your arm fracture is dislocated. I should set it—unless you want to do it yourself."

I stared up at her. "Set my own arm? Only an idiot would set his own broken arm."

"Some would say only an idiot would go after a Dark Lord of the Sith by himself."

"Ah, that's *big* idiot, thank you." I held my arm out toward her. "Do what has to be done—which is what I was doing out here myself."

Mara crouched beside me and grasped my wrist and elbow. "He worked you over pretty solidly. What little I saw wasn't very pleasant."

The image of the boy's face surfaced in my mind again. "If I never go through that again, I'll be happy." I looked up at her. "Thanks for intervening. If you hadn't have come in then . . ."

"You'd have just broken your other hand." She shrugged her shoulders, then summoned the Force, pulled on my wrist and twisted the bone into place before I even knew what was happening. "There."

I slumped down on my back, determined not to scream. "Sithspawn! Don't ever go into medicine."

"You're welcome, Horn." Mara tucked a strand of red-gold hair behind her right ear. "I found some stuff out about Mirax, which is why I came back here. Details are on a datacard you can review while you're recovering. Anyway, when I entered the atmosphere I could feel you and Kun tangling. The Force was boiling."

"And you came anyway?"

"I owed you. We're even now."

I leaned my head back and uttered as much of a laugh as I could muster. "If that's how you repay debts, I'll catch remote bolts for you any day."

"But not today." She reached out and took my left hand. "I'll slave your ship to mine and we'll go back to the Great Temple."

"Right, see if Luke is okay."

Mara paused for a moment, then nodded. "He is, and they know you're incoming wounded."

I rolled myself forward and stood with her help. "They succeeded?"

"They did. Exar Kun is no more." Mara smiled unguardedly. "The Jedi academy, it seems, has gotten rid of a Dark Lord, and produced itself a crop of Jedi."

TWENTY-SIX

✳

Exar Kun's attacks had messed me up more than I knew. My left leg and right arm were broken, as well as my right hand. I'd cracked a half-dozen ribs and had bruises and lacerations on my liver and kidneys. My blood chemistry was all off and the Two-Onebee that looked me over thought I'd ejected from a crashing fighter and never had my parasail open.

In reality I wished I actually felt half that good.

Upon my return I got immediately dunked in the bacta tank that Tycho had shipped out with the medical team for Luke barely a week and a half earlier. I'd been in bacta tanks more than I cared to think about in my life, but this was the first time in one of the emergency ones. Most tanks are vertical tubes, but this one was a horizontal box. I got to lie there being very still because there was no place to go, and the treatment was broken up into six hour stints because the bacta had to be drained, filtered and replaced.

Luke visited me a couple of times, and I read Mara's datacard while not doing a bacta-soak, but I was pretty well out of it in the beginning. As I started to come around, Kyp Durron was returned to Yavin after Han Solo had gotten him so Luke Skywalker could judge him for his crimes. I was back in the tank when that took place and by the time I got back out, Luke, Kyp and Cilghal had departed Yavin to destroy the Sun Crusher and heal Mon Mothma of a mysterious malady. Tionne did her best to keep me company after that, and fill me in on details of the academy life, but I wasn't really fit to be around.

The physical damage Exar Kun had done to me had healed on schedule—had I had access to and used Jedi healing techniques I might have been fitter faster, but that really didn't matter. The battering my mind had taken shook me badly. I knew Kun had only plucked my fears from my mind and displayed them for me in all their ugly glory, but I still had to deal with the fact that they were *my* fears, generated by me and mine alone to conquer.

After Master Skywalker returned with Kyp from destroying the Sun Crusher, and after Kyp had healed up from his injuries, I asked to speak to Luke alone. We met in the simple room where he lived. He looked a bit weary, but buoyant nonetheless. "What is it, Keiran?"

I leaned against the doorjamb with my right shoulder, taking pressure off my left leg. "I can't stay here any longer."

Looking up from the bed where he sat, Luke stared through me for a moment. "Not you, too."

I wasn't certain what he meant by that remark. I suspected it might have had something to do with Mara Jade and her quick departure after delivering me back to the Great Temple. Tionne had said that Mara looked in on Luke while he slept, but left without speaking to him. Luke had clearly assumed that she had come to Yavin when she heard he had fallen ill, and his discovering that was not the case seemed to cause him some discomfort.

"I can't stay because there are things here that just are not working." I glanced down and added in a smaller voice. "For me, they're not working."

"Things have not been perfect by any means, but that's no reason for you to leave." Luke frowned at me. "There could be adjustments. We can fix things."

I shook my head. "I don't think you can."

"Give me an example."

I stepped into the room and found both of my hands balled into fists. "It's a lot of things. Just the way you run this place. If it weren't for the bugs, the monsters and the Dark Lords of the Sith, this place would be a holiday resort. I've had more challenges learning how to eat Twi'lek food."

Luke's jaw dropped open. "How can you say that?"

I tapped my breastbone with my right hand. "I've been through a training academy, remember? I recall having my life radically altered. A training camp breaks you down and rebuilds you into the person the organization wants you to be."

The Jedi Master's face darkened. "I don't want to be turning out Jedi clones."

"You're missing the point. Training academies don't turn out clones. They don't erase the personality of the people they're dealing with, they merely make sure that individual is prepared to handle all of the challenges their new job will thrust at them." I spread my arms wide. "While we did manage to deal with Exar Kun, we could have done things more efficiently and more effectively had we been a team before that, not becoming one because of it."

Luke closed his eyes for a second, then nodded. "I understand what you are telling me. There certainly is room for change. I can look at the CorSec Academy and see if there are things we need to adapt. You can help me do that."

"You can get New Republic Armed Forces drill instructors to do that sort of stuff." I hesitated for a moment, then glanced down at the floor. "The fact is, I can't remain here with Kyp."

"He's changed, Keiran, changed a lot."

"I don't doubt it. Murdering billions will do that to a fellow." My eyes narrowed as I looked up. "I know the New Republic turned him over to you for judgment and he passed some sort of test. . . ."

"Yes. I took him to Exar Kun's temple. . . ."

"You what?" My mouth hung open. "You took him back to that Sith stronghold?"

Luke nodded calmly. "In that domain of evil he was able to come to grips with his dark side. He has been able to lay his past behind him."

"And that's *it*?!"

"No, he further atoned by helping to destroy the Sun Crusher." Luke's face sharpened. "He almost died doing that."

I pulled a chair out from Luke's desk and dropped myself down in it. "I'm sure it was harrowing for him, but I have a hard time with someone who destroyed star systems being made a Jedi Knight and held up as an example to the people of the New Republic."

Luke stiffened. "Don't you believe he could be redeemed? Don't you believe it is possible for people to learn their lessons and refrain from evil in the future?"

"Sure. I believed that of many of the criminals I arrested with CorSec, but that doesn't mean I think they should be released from Kessel before their sentences are up."

"Compassion is a Jedi's strength."

"And how compassionate is it to the friends and relatives of Kyp's victims to see him free and exalted?"

The Jedi Master regarded me warily. "The blood of millions is on my hands, too. The crew of the Death Star. The people slain while I served the Emperor reborn."

I sat forward, resting my elbows on my knees. "The Death Star was a military installation and self-defense, pure and simple. While you served the Emperor, yes, people did die—but you sabotaged the Imperial effort, saving the lives of many more than you killed. In a time when all choices are evil, choosing the least of the evils is a virtue."

I paused for a moment. "Punishment for a crime serves a multitude of purposes. It proves there is a consequence for violating the social contract that binds us all. It serves as a deterrent to others who contemplate committing such acts. Lastly, and most important here, is that the infliction of just punishment establishes and sustains the moral authority of a group. In trying to reestablish the Jedi Knights, this is important."

Luke shook his head. "And I think it is just as important to show that evil can be forgiven, amends can be made. I think you also need to remember Kyp was under Exar Kun's control when he committed his crimes."

I shook my head. "I don't believe it. Under his *influence*, perhaps, but not under his *control*."

"How can you say that?"

"It's simple." I looked at him openly. "If Kyp had been under Exar Kun's control, you'd be dead."

"What?"

"Think about it, Master Skywalker. Kun uses Kyp to force you out of your body, then spends the next ten days trying to get someone *else* to kill you? He uses ancient monsters and poor old Streen to get the job done, when all he needed to do was have Kyp strap your body to the Sun Crusher and fly on out into space. Or, to make it simpler, though messier, Kyp just parks the Sun Crusher on your unconscious form. Why didn't that happen? Because Kyp didn't *want* to kill you. You weren't *his* enemy, only Exar Kun's enemy. Kyp wouldn't have attacked you except that you would have stopped him from taking the Sun Crusher out and killing Imps.''

"No, that's not possible.'' Luke stood and began pacing beside his bed, then glanced over at me. "I think your time with CorSec has made you too suspicious. You think too much about this stuff.''

"Oh?'' My head came up and I felt anger beginning to rise in me. "I think, sometimes, you don't think *enough,* Master Skywalker.''

That stopped him. "Really?'' His blue eyes became as icy as the tone of his voice. "Would you care to enlighten me?''

I sat back and held my hands up. "You don't want me to do this.''

Luke nodded and opened his hands toward me. "No, please.''

"You're the Jedi Master. You know better than I what you're doing.''

Luke's expression hardened. "Tell me what you think, tell me where you think I am going wrong.''

"Okay.'' Gathering my courage, I kept my face impassive and my voice even. "Obi-Wan Kenobi and Yoda both knew your father had been Anakin Skywalker, and had become Darth Vader. You and your sister were separated at birth and hidden away from him to keep you safe, correct?''

Luke nodded.

"Then how is it that you were brought to live on

Tatooine? Wasn't that Obi-Wan Kenobi's homeworld? You were allowed to live under the name Skywalker. Did they expect Vader's people would overlook such a reference? And weren't you trying to get into the Imperial Academy at Carida? Wouldn't Vader's people notice that name on your application?''

Luke focused distantly. ''Are you trying to say they were using me as bait to lure Vader into a trap where Obi-Wan could confront him?''

''I don't know, but from *a certain point of view*, that could appear to be the truth, couldn't it? Or it could be something as benign as wanting you to grow up with the Skywalker name to provide you with greater motivation to want to redeem it. And they could have had you on Tatooine so there was a logical reason why traces of Obi-Wan's presence would be detected there—where he once lived—in case your guardian's attempts to keep himself hidden failed somehow.'' I watched him carefully. ''I do think, however, your education has channeled your thinking into certain pathways, just as you suspect my training has done with mine.''

''Such as?''

''You see everything in black and white—cleanly defined absolutes. I think, whatever they had intended at first, Obi-Wan and Yoda decided they needed to shape you into a weapon they could use against Vader and the Emperor. Why didn't they tell you Vader was your father? They knew, as an orphan, you wanted to know who your father was. They didn't let you see him that way so you would not be vulnerable. When he told you who he was, he blunted their strategy, but he didn't count on your strength. You saw his admission to you as a covert cry for help, a bid for salvation. From what you've said, your mentors doubted it, as did the Emperor. You fooled them all and succeeded. Now you've turned that success into a validation of everything you were taught, even though what you were taught doesn't support the results you got."

Luke stared hard at me. "You do not think there is only light and dark? If you leave here with that thought in your mind, you will be vulnerable to the dark side. You will be seduced by it."

I shook my head slowly. "I've nothing to fear from the dark side."

Luke's voice became cold. "You're as good as lost to it, then. You know nothing of its power, its draw. You know nothing of its temptations."

I stood abruptly, tipping my chair over backward and I poked a finger toward his chest. "No, Master Skywalker, you know nothing of what I have been through in my life. I've been eyeball to eyeball with the dark side more than you will ever know. You stand back and see good and evil on a grand and cosmic scale, but I've been right down there, right at the point where light meets dark. I know that border intimately and while I've toed the terminator line, I've not strayed as much as a micron over it."

I tried to tamp down my anger, but I found it very difficult to do. "I've been called out to a domestic disturbance and walked into an apartment where the woman of the house is lying there on the floor, in a pool of blood and vomit. Her nose has been pulverized. Her eyes have been blacked and are swollen shut. Her throat has bruises that show a hand and fingers, and fading bruises cover the rest of her body. Standing over her are two teary-eyed toddlers the age of your niece and nephew. And lying there, on the couch a room away, is her glitbiting husband, his fists still raw and bloody from the beating, his clothes spattered with her blood. His snores are enough to cover her sobs. I've seen that and had every fiber of my being wanting me to give that animal the rudest wake-up he's ever had. I've wanted to beat him so badly he'd look like a rancor's chew-toy, but I didn't. I pulled back.

"I've walked into a warehouse and arrested a spicelord in his office. He opened a case and it had over a million credits in it. A million—more money than I'll ever see in my lifetime. It was mine, he said, if I'd just take it and walk away. No one would ever know." I narrowed my eyes. "But I'd know, and I didn't do it."

He started to say something, but I cut him off with a wave of my hand. "My father died in my arms, his life leaking out of him. I had no good-bye. I had no chance to tell him I loved him. I had to hold him, feeling his life fade, hoping for a response, anything to let me know I'd not failed him, and I didn't get it.

"I went out and I found the bounty hunter scum that killed my father, and I arrested him. There wasn't a person in CorSec that would have whispered in protest if I'd shot him 'resisting arrest.' I could have marched Bossk into One CorSec Plaza, right there in the lobby, and blown his head off in front of hundreds of witnesses, and they'd have all said the prisoner was escaping and a threat to others. I could have killed him, I could have avenged my father, and I didn't. And when our Imp liaison officer let Bossk go, I didn't hunt either one down."

I tapped myself on the breastbone again. "I don't know if you think that makes me weak or just stupid. Maybe by not taking revenge I can't be the kind of Jedi you want, maybe by not having wallowed in the dark side and returning you can't be certain of me. I don't know, but don't tell me I don't know the dark side, that I don't know its temptations. I've been there, *and* I've walked away."

Luke looked ashen-faced, then glanced away from me. "I don't think you are weak or stupid. I think you will make a fine Jedi Knight." He hesitated for a moment, then plunged on. "I am concerned, though, that you think I'm an incompetent idiot. You don't like how I run the academy, my choices concerning other students and my view of the way the universe works."

I shook my head slowly. "No, I just don't think those things work for me. Couple of points here. You were trained to be a Jedi Knight, and you have become a Jedi Master. I accept that and respect you for all you've been through and learned. What you've done I never could do." I softened my tone as I realized I was jumping all over him while he was at a low point. Though I had problems with the academy, he didn't deserve to be beaten up.

"Despite all that, there's no guarantee you're going to be an ace at teaching, especially the first time out. That said, you've done a fine job with the majority of the students. Even tossing Gantoris, me, Mara, Cilghal and Kyp into the mix, your first class only has three failures out of fifteen. That's only a twenty percent failure rate, and I don't think Mara was really a failure. Me, neither.

"As for what I said, that's just one opinion. As we used to say in CorSec, if one guy calls you a Hutt, ignore him. If a second calls you a Hutt, begin to wonder. If a third calls you a Hutt, buy a drool bucket and start stockpiling spice."

The Jedi Master smiled for a second. "You really are going to leave?"

"I have to." I closed my eyes for a second, then opened them again. "You told me, Tionne has told me and even the Holocron told me about how the Corellian Jedi tradition was different from other traditions. We have the Jedi credits and tended to keep more to our home system. You invited me here to bring part of that tradition with me, but I'm not truly following it unless I head out and discover more about it myself.''

Luke nodded slowly. ''I am still concerned about you and your development. There are things, in the future, challenges you will face. . . .''

''I know.'' I shrugged. ''I can only face them as I find them.''

He sighed. ''Well, you have some time to reconsider. It will take a while to get a ship out here to take you away.''

''I have Mara's Headhunter.''

Luke frowned. ''I thought the hyperdrive motivator was shot.''

''True.''

Before I could finish my explanation, Artoo rolled into Luke's room, bleating frantically.

Luke squatted in front of the droid. ''What is it, Artoo? What's the matter?''

The droid's holographic display unit glowed. Hovering in the space between us I saw the image of an Imperial Star Destroyer in orbit over the academy.

The Jedi Master groaned. ''What now?''

I patted him on the shoulder. ''I wouldn't worry too much, Master Skywalker.''

''An Imperial Star Destroyer shows up here and we shouldn't worry?''

''Nope,'' I said, letting a smile grow on my face, ''that's just my ride.''

TWENTY-SEVEN

From far enough away, the *Errant Venture* looked like an Imperial Star Destroyer. There was no mistaking that daggerish shape or the tall bridge. The ship's stark bone-white color and sheer size invoked memories of the days when the Empire's need for discipline often dispatched such ships to punish worlds that harbored Rebels. It was truly a sight to behold, and one from which I would have flown as fast as possible if I did not know what the *Errant Venture* really was.

I brought the Headhunter up and around in a loop over midships on the ImpStar. Its normal complement of weapons had been stripped down, leaving it two tractor beams, ten ion cannons and ten heavy turbolaser batteries. That amount of firepower left the ship well defended, though as I did a flyby I noticed a couple of the laser batteries were not tracking that well and at least one froze in the middle as it followed my flight.

Coming over the top, I rolled the Headhunter and chopped the throttle back. I keyed the comm unit. "This is Headhunter 079 requesting permission to board and land."

"079, this is *Errant Venture* control. Please state the nature of your business."

I rolled my eyes. ''You tell Booster Terrik that he lets me park this fighter on his ship, or he's going to be down more than just three turbolaser batteries.''

Silence reigned on the comm channel for a moment, then the controller's voice returned with a degree of weariness edging into it. ''079, you are clear to land in docking slot 1127. Make sure your weapons are powered down.''

''What?''

''That is the message, 079.''

''I copy.'' I brought the Headhunter in toward the egress bay and powered up the repulsorlift coils. I throttled back to ten percent of thrust, and slowly worked the fighter into the docking bay. Slot 1127 was back against a bulkhead and would force me to take a long walk around the bay itself to reach Booster's office. *If he knew I'd broken my leg, I'd be parking back in the garbage hold and hiking even further.*

As I closed in on my parking place, the only unusual thing I noticed was that no other ships were parked near me, and the few people on the ground were scurrying away. I ignored them—no one wanted to be caught in the backwash from engine thrust. I concentrated on setting the ship down easily, which I did—giving Booster no reason to complain about my scratching his precious deck. I quickly went through an engine lockdown and provided a security passcode for engine restart. It wouldn't stop anyone from stealing the ship, but it might slow them down.

I smiled and keyed in a message on the ignition screen. ''This Headhunter is the property of Mara Jade.'' *Anyone nuts enough to steal it now deserves what he gets.*

I popped the cockpit hatch, which is when I noticed

something rather out of the ordinary. Booster's security detail wore Imperial style uniforms, but they had light green torsos on the tunics and bright yellow sleeves, bright yellow trousers and green caps with yellow buttons. The effect was a touch unsettling, especially with such a crowd of them around ship.

Their blasters, which were nowhere near as colorful as their uniforms, were all pointed in my direction.

A Weequay whose face looked as if it were made of flaking ceramics motioned for me to come out of the Headhunter. As I stood and my lightsaber came into view, half the guards crouched while the others moved behind convenient cover. I looked around at the dozen of them and shook my head. "No trouble, no trouble."

For the first time I really wished I had skill in the area of Jedi levitation because trying to get out of a fighter that had me a good three meters off the deck while my hands were in the air was not an easy thing to do. I would have just jumped out, but my left leg still wasn't one hundred percent, and I didn't want to be limping around on the *Errant Venture*. What I ended up doing was sitting on the side of the cockpit and sliding down toward the floor, catching my weight mostly on my right leg.

The Weequay jabbed me in the back with a truncheon which, I imagined, could deliver a nasty jolt to me if he only pushed the red button near his thumb. "Boss Booster wants you."

"Good, I want to see him, too."

"Surrender lightsaber."

I turned slowly on my heels and faced him, setting myself. "Not going to happen, quark-for-brains."

He poked me with the truncheon again and hit the button. I felt the tingle of the electricity, but just absorbed it. I smiled as I did so. "Power cells are dead. Really. I don't feel a thing."

The Weequay hit the button again, but my smile did not fade. I bled the energy off into the decking, which raised the fur on the head of a passing Bothan, but none of the guards seemed to notice. The Weequay looked at the stun baton as if it had betrayed him, then pressed his free hand against the tip and hit the button.

I snatched the truncheon from the air before it could hit the floor, and looked past the Weequay's twitching form. I reversed the baton and offered the handle to another of the guards. "Clearly, it's defective. Now if you will take me to Booster . . ."

I turned back to head toward his office, when I discovered my quarry had come to me. This wouldn't have been a bad thing, but the flesh of Booster's face was as red as his artificial left eye. He grabbed big handfuls of my green flightsuit, hoisted me up off the deck and slammed me into a bulkhead.

"Where's my daughter?" His short, bristly white hair and the goatee he'd taken to wearing made him look more like me than I even wanted to think about. "What have you done with Mirax?"

I groaned, less from the impact than the sheer fury in his words. "Let me explain."

He jammed me into the wall again. "You think you're that persuasive, CorSec?"

Booster released me and I fell to the floor. He looked at his guards and shook his head. "Fyg and Kruqr, escort him to my office. *Now.*"

Another Weequay and a fairly scrawny human grabbed my arms, jerked me to my feet and Rybet-marched me off to the wardroom that Booster used as his docking bay office. It felt odd for me to be conducted to his office in the same manner I'd hauled so many prisoners along in my day. I knew that even without using any Jedi techniques I could break their grips and get rid of them. Because of the unseemliness of being hustled along that way I almost did make a break.

I didn't because I realized there was no purpose to my doing so. Yes, I might feel embarrassed at being manhandled so, but what difference did it make? Was my pride worth injuring someone? No. They were conducting me to where I wanted to go anyway. What they or anyone else thought of me was really immaterial.

I smiled. *Some of that Jedi training got through.*

Reverting to type, I studied my surroundings. The docking bay had plenty of room for ships and approached capacity. The old TIE fighter launch racks still had a few TIEs in them, but many of them were missing parts. Other smaller ships had been fitted with unusual suspension collars that allowed them to hang from the racks as well. In that way Booster was able to fit a lot more ships into his hold.

The vast majority of ships in the docking bay were freighters, though few were as big as Mirax's *Pulsar Skate* or the *Millennium Falcon.* Most ships of that size couldn't afford docking space on the *Errant Venture* anyway. The ships present were those of smugglers who dealt in rare, exotic and high priced items, or the idle rich who found slumming on the *Errant Venture* something of a thrill. Most of the ships bringing goods for trade and transshipment on the *Errant Venture* just offloaded their items into one of the supply holds and left a crewman or agent on board the *EV* to handle the transactions.

Booster's people brought me to his office, tossed me inside, then shut the hatch. I had to hit a glowpanel switch, and when I did, I shuddered. Clutter filled the room—cracked duraplast boxes leaking streaky red, viscous fluids, piles of datacards leaning precariously one against another, chairs filled with cast-off clothing and in the corner stood a deactivated 3PO droid festooned with a dozen gunbelts complete with blasters. Booster's desk dominated the room and appeared neat in comparison to the rest of it. The single layer of datacards, datapads, wires and odds and ends had been cleared back from a small cube projecting various holographs of Mirax.

I shifted stuff from the chair in front of the desk to the floor and sat, watching the ever-changing display. Though Booster would deny having a single sentimental bone in his body, his projector cube had arranged the images by chronology and subject. They flashed up every ten seconds or so. The display might follow a theme, like images of Mirax working on the *Skate,* then move along through her life, forward or back, until it shot off again on a themed tangent. It wove a web of her life—a web in which I felt fully ensnared.

In watching the display I realized the detachment I had felt before, when she vanished, had finally faded. The "flash-blindness" Luke had diagnosed had lifted, and I might have noticed it sooner, but on Yavin 4 I had so little to remind me of her. It was probably just as well that the detachment existed while I started my training because I would have gotten nowhere while distracted.

Now, though, watching her images, the full weight of her disappearance crashed in on me. I *had* felt her presence that night in the grotto, and Exar Kun had showed her to me, but I knew I could not trust what I had seen through his power. The fact that I had sensed her when Luke took us on a sojourn through the universe helped sustain me, but now I realized just how alone I felt.

And how alone she must be feeling. She was out there, somewhere, waiting for me to find her, to help her, and I had done nothing. I sighed. *Perhaps Booster should have smacked me against the wall even harder.*

The hatch to the office slid open and Booster stalked in. He looked hard at me, then sat down at his desk. Fire burned in his brown eye just as brightly as in the electronic one. He watched me, then his head slowly nodded as he pressed his hands flat against the top of his desk.

Like a mute referee, Mirax danced from image to image between us.

"It is for her sake that I don't just twist your head off, CorSec." He kept his voice low and barely under control. "She's been missing for how long?"

I swallowed hard. "Ten weeks."

"Ten weeks!" His right fist hammered the desk, making the holocube bounce and the datacards ripple like loose tiles in a groundquake. He caught himself and slowly opened his hand. "Ten weeks, and you didn't come to me and tell me."

I calmed myself, just barely bringing my racing heart under control. My mouth felt dry and tasted like I'd been licking a bantha. "One, I knew then and know now your daughter is alive. In consulting with a variety of people it was determined that keeping knowledge of her disappearance quiet would be the best course."

Booster arched a pale eyebrow. " 'It was determined?' By whom? What coward decided I shouldn't know my little girl was missing?"

I raised my chin. "*I* made that decision, Booster."

"Did you, CorSec, did you now?" Booster sat back. "Not your General Cracken? Not your Luke Skywalker? Not Wedge? You made it?"

I nodded. "I weighed their opinions. I went over the

scenarios they suggested and how best to handle the situation, then *I* made the decision."

"So then you take full responsibility for it?" I could hear in his voice that he was setting a trap for me. "You take full responsibility for whatever happens to her?"

"I do."

Booster hesitated, then smiled coldly. "I think you'll find you don't much care for the consequences of your actions."

Something struck me as odd about Booster at that point. He'd managed to fix blame fully and squarely on me, which meant he should have been venting all of his anger and frustration on me, but he wasn't. He'd identified me as a target and had me dead to rights, and he held back. *Why?*

Then the answer slammed into me and I leaned forward. "I accept the consequences of my actions, and you want to know why? Because Mirax is *my* wife. Our vows make her life and happiness and safety my responsibility, and I've done what I could to acquit that responsibility. I would have liked nothing better than to have headed out after her immediately, but there was nowhere to go, nothing to do. General Cracken and his people were stymied, as was I. All I knew was that your daughter lived, and as long as she lived, I could take the necessary steps to save her."

Booster's expression hardened against the challenge in my words. "You may think of her as your wife, but she's my daughter, my flesh and blood, which makes me just as responsible for her as you are, CorSec. Don't try to steal that part of my life the way your father stole five years from me. If you do, you'll regret it."

"Maybe, but not in the way you think I will." I narrowed my eyes. "And as for your responsibility for

Mirax, I just remembered something. In the past ten weeks, you've never tried to get a message to me asking after Mirax. You never even got a message to Wedge about her.''

I stood and leaned forward on his desk. ''All the concern you've showed for her has been from my ship to this office. And that tells me one thing, Booster: you *knew*! You *knew* all along that she was working for Cracken to track the Invids, didn't you? She probably worked from here, using the *Errant Venture* as her base of operations.''

Booster laughed slowly. ''I can see the Horn blood runs strong in those veins. Very good.''

His casual admission stunned me. He'd grabbed me, slammed me up against a bulkhead and all but accused me of having abandoned his daughter to whatever fate her enemies had in mind for her. Part of me wanted to reach across the desk and throttle him, while yet another part wanted to feed my anger through the Force and slam *him* up against the wall.

Neither of those parts won in the war for control. ''Were you just beating up on me for fun?''

Booster shook his head solemnly. ''When I realized Mirax was missing and heard you were off playing Jedi games, I was mad enough to come here to Yavin and beat you to within a micron of your life. A great chunk of me still is, but I respect your father enough to think you wouldn't abandon Mirax. Just now, in bracing you like this, I gave you a chance to put the blame for your actions on others. You didn't. Got to admire a man who accepts responsibility even when it might hurt.''

I straightened up, crossing my arms over my chest. ''And your reason for this little test?''

''I didn't know how much your time down there

changed you. I wanted to make sure you could still do what has to be done to save Mirax.''

''What?''

''You don't remember Corellian Jedi Knights, but I do. A bit. I wasn't sure a Jedi would care for my daughter anymore.''

I stared at him in disbelief. ''What gets taught at the academy doesn't make students *less* human.''

''Tell that to the people of Carida.''

Echoes of their death agony pounded through me. ''You have a point.''

Booster nodded. ''How did you know I was testing you?''

''Attitude and what I sensed about you. Smug satisfaction.'' I shrugged. ''You also mentioned General Cracken and you couldn't have known why I'd be talking to him unless you knew Mirax was working with him. Since I didn't know that, and since she'd not confided in Wedge, I assumed she confided in you. You must have blistered Cracken's ears when you found out she was gone.''

Booster smiled like wampa scenting tauntaun. ''Told him I'd found a cache of guns to put on this monster before I went hunting for Mirax myself.''

A fully armed *Errant Venture* was one of General Cracken's recurring nightmares, especially with Booster at the helm. ''Get anything useful from him?''

''Not much.'' Booster scowled. ''I know the galaxy is a big place, but she can't have vanished so completely.''

''She hasn't.''

''What do you mean?''

''A woman named Mara Jade . . .''

''Karrde's confederate?''

I nodded and sat back down. ''The same. She said she

had inquiries from a rare properties dealer on Nal Hutta about a deal for an item that he'd been holding for Mirax. Mirax had bought an option on purchasing the item and she was supposed to pick it up within days of when she disappeared. Sounds to me like a legitimate deal she would have set up to bolster her cover when seeking the Invids."

Booster smiled. "A number of the Invid crews ship out of Nal Hutta, or used to, anyway. Lots have been moving in the last two months."

"Because Mirax's presence was proof positive that the New Republic was looking in that area."

The older man stroked his goatee. "It's as good a place as any to start. We'll be on our way within the hour."

"No."

Booster frowned at me. "No? We have the first lead that's come up and you don't want to follow it up?"

"I want to follow it up, yes, and follow up the more important clue." I laced my fingers together and pressed the index fingers against my moustache. "Mirax is detected on Nal Hutta, captured and the Invid crews there scatter. This firmly establishes a link between her capture and the Invids; and it also suggests she's being held to forestall my doing anything rash."

"You won't be doing it, I will."

I shook my head adamantly. "Booster, we won't find Mirax until we find the *Invidious*, and you're not going to have any more luck at finding it than the New Republic has. Tavira's got people who can use the Force. They will know when you're coming and they'll leave or, worse yet, they'll use their fully armed Impstar to blast the *Venture* to scrap."

Booster pounded his fist in his open hand. "She's my daughter, CorSec, I have to do something!"

"I know that. She's my *wife*, and I have to do something, too. I have to act, but not before I'm ready." I leaned forward. "Meet me halfway, Booster. If you don't, she'll die, and neither one of us will be happy for the rest of our lives. In your case that won't be long because I'll kill you."

Booster scoffed. "You'll *try*."

"There is no *try*, Booster." I let the edge bleed out of my voice. "I need you to *do* two things. First, use your network and get me as much data as you can about the Invid crews. I want to know who is shipping on what and out of where. If it gets to a point where we have to hit, I want to make sure we hit hard and hurt them badly."

"Done." Booster smiled. "Karrde may think he's the data-lord of the New Republic, but I've flipped bits he's not even aware exist."

"Good."

My father-in-law picked up the holocube and froze a recent shot of Mirax so she smiled at both of us. "What's the other thing?"

I tried to sound nonchalant. "Get me into Corellia and out again."

Booster lost his grip on the holocube, dropping it to the desk. "Get you in past the Diktat's watchmen? And out again? Have you lost what little mind you have?"

"I hope not, because if I have, neither one of us will see your daughter again." I stood and held my lightsaber aloft. "It's going to be a Corellian Jedi that saves your daughter, and unless I get home and back out again, there just flat out aren't going to be any Corellian Jedi around to do the job."

TWENTY-EIGHT

My perspective as a member of the Corellian Security Force had never really led me to a proper appreciation for how well Booster Terrik operated. Our animosity had shielded me from his professionalism. Now, with his being galvanized by his effort to find and save his daughter, Booster pushed himself into overdrive with truly remarkable results.

Securing for me false identification documents took less time than I would have imagined. Booster's people accessed a database of pre-existing dataphantoms and merely attached my holographs to them. Using the Destroyer's own Imperial-issue document fabrication machinery, I had three sets of documents in no time. One for getting me onto Corellia, one for walking around on Corellia and a third for getting me back out.

I smiled. The Rebellion's insertion of Rogue Squadron onto Coruscant hadn't provided documentation this good.

After that Booster sent me to the middle of the three "luxury" deck levels on board. These decks were each fitted out with a variety of establishments suited to the clientele allowed access to them. The lowest of the decks made pestholes like Mos Eisley look luxurious. On

Black Level the denizens consisted mostly of out-of-work crews, poor folks looking for cheap transit, criminals, petty thieves, swindlers and con men. I'm not exactly certain why Booster allowed them on his ship, but even they might have information he could sell elsewhere.

Blue Level, where he sent me, was a bit more respectable than Treasure Ship Row down in Coronet City on Corellia. I saw just enough unsavory characters—Boba Fett wannabes, Han Solo wannabes and, albeit too few, Princess Leia wannabes. Mostly I saw traders and dealers and adventurous sorts who seemed to find shipping aboard a fearsome Star Destroyer thrilling. And Traders' Alley—the cash-only bazaar—meant one could always find something thrilling here.

Of major import on this level was the central courtyard area. It actually linked up with Diamond Level above it through a massive refitting effort that cored through three decks in the heart of the ship. In this airy well each day was displayed a brilliant holographic presentation of the Thyferra campaign. I noticed that Booster's role, and that of the *Errant Venture,* were expanded, and that my role was all but eliminated. That niggled a little bit, but I decided the presentation was theatrical not historical, so hyperbole was bound to creep in.

On Blue Level I visited a tailor who scanned me and started fabricating clothes that would fit my identities. I had him double-check the measurement on my collar. It would have been just like Booster to have him trim three or six centimeters off so I'd choke my way through my trip. The tailor, a Sullustan, cheebled at me that he'd never do such a thing—proper fit was his stock in trade, after all.

Booster's final effort to get me onto Corellia was a masterwork. He wouldn't even let me up on Diamond Level—he said just having someone from CorSec on Blue Level was dampening the hedonistic abandon of luxury passengers—but he found me help up there. He convinced a Corellian couple that the only real way to feel the illicit thrill of being a smuggler was trying to smuggle something onto Corellia. He went so far as to say that even though they were Corellians, he didn't think they could pull it off. They demanded he let them try. He demurred. They pressed. He relented, after they bribed him, and even thanked him for finding them replacement crew members for two of their yacht crew who had run into trouble in a Black Level entertainment establishment.

I had no idea what the couple was smuggling, aside from me, but watching them pretend to be smugglers was rather amusing. When we arrived at the Coronet City spaceport, they decided to brazen out their effort by dumping a hefty bribe on the Customs inspector who greeted them. The inspector, taken aback by the bribe, began to question them closely. His colleagues in Immigration were intrigued with what was going on, and undoubtedly wanted their share of his bribe, so they passed the crew through without more than cursory glances at our identification, then zeroed in on the couple.

Shouldering my two satchels of clothing and equipment, I departed the spaceport and found a fairly clean transient housing facility just off Treasure Ship Row. Despite my having worked the Row in years past, I wasn't worried about running into old colleagues and being discovered. CorSec had changed through the years—it wasn't even the Corellian Security Force any more. The Diktat had morphed it into the Public Safety

Service, and had exchanged the traditional emerald and black uniforms for something darker and more Imperialistic. The PSS's mission had become more snoopy and more concerned with maintaining public order than solving crimes.

The past I knew here is dead. A shiver ran down my spine. Treasure Ship Row had changed in the six years I'd been away. It had always been seedy and disreputable, but the bright lights had provided a carnival veneer to the whole place. People of all types had been able to come here and find amusement. Certainly there were places good and respectful folks didn't go except by accident, but the slight air of menace made the jaunts here more memorable—much like shipping aboard the *Errant Venture*.

The changes on Treasure Ship Row might have seemed an improvement to many. The main street had been cleaned up considerably. All the paint was fresh, and graffiti was obliterated before it had time to dry. The lighting appeared less garish and the establishments were milder in tone. It had moved from being a *place* to being a *showplace*, leaving it all artificial and shallow.

Out and around it, in the area that had not been transformed, the shadows had deepened and the menace festered, until anyone venturing a block away from the safe zone would drown in reality. The government, in cleaning up Treasure Ship Row, clearly believed it had gotten rid of all the unsociable elements that used to call it home, and was using the Public Safety Service to insulate themselves from reality and its consequences.

The only positive point about the change was that I found it very easy to hire a speeder-cab. I gave him the directions to my grandfather's home and the driver, a Klatooinan, graced me with a smile that was all tooth. I sank back into the rear seat, but refrained from drawing in a deep breath to relax myself. A Jedi might not know pain, but the scents in the back seat of a speeder-cab could gag a Gamorrean.

I hoped I was not on a fool's errand. While in the bacta tank I had realized that I'd taken my father's message to be encouragement to join the Jedi academy. What Luke had told me about the Force allowing one to see pieces of the past or present or future suggested my father had somehow known the academy would come into being. That was an unwarranted assumption. Moreover, my father always hedged his bets. Knowing the future was mutable, he couldn't be certain the academy *would* exist. As a result, I had to assume that he had made arrangements for information to be left behind for me so I could recover my heritage.

I smiled slowly. Even if my father had left nothing behind, seeing my grandfather again would be fun. Nearing his home, back in the hill district where I had grown up, I began to realize how much I missed him and Corellia. I had gone away—had been forced to flee—to avoid Imperial entanglements and death. From that point I had pretty much been in hiding or up to my neck in missions with Rogue Squadron. While we had exchanged holographic greetings, the Diktat's censors had chopped the messages up enough that little of my grandfather's wit or warmth had gotten through.

The speeder-cab came to a halt at a gate that blocked the whole street on which I'd grown up. My father had purchased a house across a circle from my grandfather, and there had been eight other houses scattered around that circle. We'd never had a wall surrounding the area and certainly no gate. "Are you sure this is the right place?"

The Klatooinan nodded and tapped the display unit on his vehicle's local navicomp. He reached out, plucked a wired comlink from its holder beside the gate and threaded it back to me. "Hello?"

A stiff and formal voice answered back. "The Horn Estate."

Estate? "I'd like to speak with Rostek Horn, please."

"Director Horn has asked not to be disturbed."

I ducked my head and tried to peer through the gate's bars at the houses further in, but I couldn't see my grandfather's place. Nor could I see the home I'd grown up in. Instead all I could see was a huge, sprawling building of very recent manufacture. It gleamed brightly against the green of the hills behind it, all white and silvery where tinted transparisteel sheets took the place of walls.

"Please, tell him it's his . . ." I hesitated. If I said grandson, I could cause trouble since I still had murder warrants out for me in the Corellian system. "Tell him it's an old friend. Keiran Halcyon."

"Director Horn knows no one by that name."

I put an edge into my voice. "You clearly have not been with him long. I grew up in this neighborhood. He was like a grandfather to me. Tell him that."

"Just a moment."

The Klatooinan passed the time by bringing me up to speed on the local Zoneball league standings. He tried to impress me with the fact that Staive Pedsten, the local star—who, did I know, had once been romantically linked with Princess Leia—had sat where I sat. I was assured the athlete was not as handsome as I was, but the Klatooinan remembered him because he was a most generous tipper.

I smiled back at my driver and nodded, but before he

could regale me with Pedsten's latest scoring coup, the gate opened. The Klatooinan hit the accelerator, which jolted us forward and tore the wired comlink from my hands. It clipped him in the back of the head as it snapped out his window. He grumbled a bit as he rubbed at the rising lump, but managed to run me up to the estate's front door without further incident. I paid him off and tipped very well—it was Booster's money, after all, and I was pretty sure it wasn't counterfeit.

Once outside the speeder, I realized that the distant view of the building had failed to convey its actual size. My grandfather's house had only ever been a modest two-story affair, with all the spare capital and his spare time going into maintaining the gorgeous sunken gardens in the back. The building I stood before now occupied three times the footprint of the old house, and rose another whole level above the old house's roof. In its construction I could see bits and pieces of things my grandfather would love, but if he'd had the money to build this house, he would have just expanded his gardens even further instead.

I walked up to the door, but before I could ring the bell, a small, wiry man with olive skin pulled the door open. He wore a black uniform festooned with white buttons. White gloves encased his hands and he eyed me suspiciously. He gave me no smile and looked me over carefully before he stepped aside and let me into the home's grand foyer.

The man spoke in the same clipped tones I'd heard over the comlink. "Director Horn is waiting for you in the garden." He set off at a brisk pace, his shoes clicking sharply against the rose and black granite flooring. In the center of it, fashioned out of black marble and slices of malachite, the old CorSec logo had been rendered beautifully. I hopped over it, breaking my stride, which brought the man's head back around to see what I was doing.

It didn't surprise me that my grandfather was in the garden. When he retired he said he wanted to dig and plant there, until he was dug in and planted. After a long walk, we emerged onto a veranda that was amply shaded from the noontime sun. Beyond it, down a short green pathway leading to a central fountain within an amphitheatre of colorful flowerbeds, stood my grandfather.

Taller than me, taller even than my father had been, Rostek Horn had a lean, aristocratic bearing about him. Despite his age, his white hair grew in full and thick. His grey eyes never seemed to rest, and while I had only ever seen love and affection in them, colleagues who had chanced to be disciplined by my grandfather said they could be colder than the darkest iceball in the galaxy. While he seemed thinner than when I had last seen him, he was no less vital and, for the first time, I saw him as the predator colleagues had reported he could be.

What struck me as most unusual was that there he stood, full in the noon sun, wearing a formal black suit, with a high, stiff collar. He was not dressed for a day in the garden, but a day dealing with the variety of things that had occupied him during his days with CorSec. With his right flank toward me—providing less of a target, perhaps?—he brought his head around to look at me. Those cold grey eyes sent a jolt through me.

I started past my guide and onto the path, but the small man pressed a hand against my stomach, stopping me.

I looked at my grandfather and half-closed my eyes. I projected into his mind an image of my running and screaming and falling and laughing as a child on the same expanse of green that separated us now one from another. Opening my eyes fully, I said, "It has been a long time, Director. Perhaps you do not remember me."

My grandfather remained rock still for a moment, then nodded. "Tosruk, he is known to me. You are dismissed."

Tosruk's brown eyes narrowed. "He scanned cleanly on his approach, but he might have skills."

"I have nothing to fear from Halcyon here, do I?"

I shook my head. "No, sir."

My grandfather slowly smiled. "You see, Tosruk, I am safe. Go about your other duties. Have the cook prepare us a light luncheon—and I mean *light*, not just with less gravy."

Tosruk snapped his head forward in a bow, then spun on his heel and retreated.

I approached my grandfather slowly, not daring to break into the run I would have preferred to use in greeting him. I extended my hand to him and he took it, then pulled me into a firm hug. I wanted to say something, but I felt a lump rise to my throat and tears beginning to fill my eyes.

He pulled back and held me out at arm's length. "Emperor's black bones, you shouldn't be here."

"I had to come. I've been away too long." I glanced back at the house. "Many changes."

My grandfather's smile broadened and a sinister laugh accompanied it. "Yes, there have been many changes." He waved me toward the greenhouse across the far side of the garden. "If you would join me, I'll show you some of my newer efforts. Prize winners, all."

I dropped into step with him and said nothing until we had reached the greenhouse and stepped inside. My grandfather stripped off his jacket and hung it on a peg inside the doorway. He flipped a couple of switches, and glowpanels went on with all but one of them. The rising illumination revealed row after row of potting benches covered with seedlings, all the way to the back to the small bay of machines he used for genetically manipulating flowers for color and size of blossom.

He gave me a cautious grin. "We're safe to speak in here—I have it swept each week."

"Good." I glanced back at the house. "What happened to your house?"

"You may recall I had something of a reputation for maintaining all sorts of files on local politicians, Imperial liaisons and the like? When CorSec became the Public Safety Service it was determined that my files would be an embarrassment. It was further assumed that I had them in the house. A mysterious fire consumed the house, and then the house you grew up in."

He kept his voice low, but full of curious tones that suggested he found the fires somewhat funny. "What they discovered was that there were multiple copies of my files all over, in computer systems new and old. The encryption keys were what they lacked. A few people suddenly found interesting files on activities they would have preferred to keep hidden arriving on datacards in their homes, usually accompanied by a flower or two that were easily identified as a hybrid I'd created. The implications were clear, so, in recompense for my long years of service to CorSec, and to protect me—since now I am considered a treasure for my horticultural skills—the government bought up and ceded to me all this land. They built my new home and filled it with all sorts of interesting mechanical listening devices and scanners. Tosruk and the rest of the staff report regularly to petty officials—though those officials don't realize that the staff's loyalty is to me. The very files used by the officials to choose staffers who could be manipulated were files I created.''

I laughed aloud. ''I thought, when you retired, you wanted to leave all this sort of thing behind.''

He nodded. ''I would have been more than happy to, but others who want power were not content to leave me alone. Unfortunately, they have neither the grace nor sense for me to leave them alone, either.'' He reached out and caressed the leaves of a small plant. ''Now I can send a seedling to someone with a note suggesting I had read of this opinion or that which he holds. If I say I am disappointed, their thinking tends to be modified. If I say I support them, they move more strongly in that direction. I choose my targets and my issues carefully. I seek to curb the excesses of the young and foolish, or old and foolish. There's even talk among the shadowy cabal of pundits who advise leaders about what it means for me to send a live plant versus a cut bouquet, or the true significance of a night blooming flower versus something that blooms once and dies.''

My grandfather smiled at me. ''But you didn't come here to ask after my gardens or to listen to me natter on about warping the small minds of politicians, did you?''

''I'm happy to see you, of course, and I do want to hear about your life, and tell you about mine.''

His smile broadened indulgently. ''The name you chose to greet me and what you did out there tells me why you are here. You want to know what your father left behind for you, don't you?''

I nodded slowly. ''You don't mind?''

My grandfather looked at me with surprise, then laughed. ''Mind? My dear boy, I've spent nearly the last half century preserving your heritage for you and for your father. I would have been disappointed if this day had never come.''

I smiled. ''Would you have sent me a flower to let me know how disappointed you were?''

''I would have sent you many, many flowers.'' He opened his arms to take in the greenhouse and the gardens. ''These flowers, Corran, are the Halcyon heritage. Where better to store knowledge of the Jedi and the Force, than in things that live?''

TWENTY-NINE

I watched my grandfather closely because I didn't quite understand what he'd said. He was old and could be losing it, though I'd seen no evidence of that so far. "Your comments are sailing right past me."

He laughed delightedly, a deep, rich sound I remembered very well. "Don't feel disappointed, Corran. I had to come up with a storage system that would befuddle even the most diligent of investigators. Come with me."

I followed him toward the rear of the greenhouse to the computers and genetic manipulation processors. "You probably do not recall this from your schooling, but the genetic code in many lifeforms consists of four nucleotides arranged in pairs. They provide a genetic blueprint that produces what we are."

I nodded. "I know. Imps messed around with genetics to produce the Krytos Virus."

"Yes, a nasty piece of work, that." My grandfather keyed something into the computer and the attached holopad showed me a double-helix slowly revolving in the air. It looked like two twisting ladders spiraling around each other. "What most people fail to realize is that while genes are very small, they consist of a vast number of these base pairs of nucleotides. What they also don't know is that much of the coding for any gene is redundant and genes are often filled with pieces of nonsense coding, or bits of coding left over by evolution. These inconsequential bits of code are essentially inert and useless. What I've done is to manufacture replacement strings of base pairs to put in their place. These replacement strings use one pair to represent zero and another to represent one.''

I stared at him gap-mouthed. ''You digitized data and inserted it into the genetic material of a plant, allowing the plants to duplicate the code with every cell division.''

''Correct. While random mutations might destroy little bits of the data, there are so many samples out there that comparing them will fill in any gaps.'' He smiled broadly. ''I recall at least one Jedi-hunter coming here and asking for some basic plant stock for his garden back on Imperial Center. I gave him as much as he wanted of my Jedi line.''

My eyes narrowed. ''The flowers you send to politicians . . . they contain the decryption keys to the files that concern them, don't they?''

''I must amuse myself, mustn't I?'' He rolled up his sleeves. ''I spent enough time with Nejaa to know that the Jedi considered nothing coincidental. I knew if I put the Jedi information into these plants and ensured their distribution, the information would be discovered again. At the time I started I thought the discovery would not happen in my lifetime, but I wanted it available.''

I smiled. ''I want you to tell me about him, about Nejaa.''

''I will.'' He looked at me and shook his head again. ''Your appearance, I didn't know you at first. Your father had a saying, one he picked up from his father. Do you recall it? 'If you cannot recognize the man in the mirror, it is time to step back and see when you stopped being yourself.' "

I nodded. "I remember."

"Well, seeing you now, I must have you tell me who you have become." He pointed back at the house. "First, however, we will have something to eat. Then you'll join me turning the compost pile."

"More data hidden in there?"

He winked at me. "I think you will find the work rewarding."

We talked mostly of his flowers and the way the neighborhood had been in the old days. Because his household staff bustled in and out, Corran Horn was referred to in third person, as if Keiran Halcyon had been a playmate of his. By rights I guess I should have found the subterfuge awkward, but I slipped into the Halcyon role the way I would have slipped into any undercover identity. It was a game we shared and both took great delight in it.

Grandfather dispatched Tosruk to my hotel to pick up my things while the two of us went out to the compost heap armed with shovels. My grandfather directed me toward a pile of bantha dung that he used for fertilizer. He'd been getting it from the Coronet City Zoological and Botanical Gardens for longer than I could remember, in exchange for providing them with his latest hybrids.

"Dig deep and shift the pile over this way about three meters." Leaning on a shovel, wearing bibbed splatter-slacks and knee-high rubber boots, he smiled at me. "If you can shift it any other way, feel free."

I shook my head. "I could make you think it had moved."

"Halcyons always have been notoriously weak in the telekinetic skill area." He laughed. "Dice were the only game of chance in which I felt safe playing against Nejaa."

"Someday I aspire to making dice move with the Force."

My grandfather smiled. "The Halcyons have their strengths. The mental projection you allude to was something Nejaa did very well. He also could absorb energy. I was told this was a very rare ability among Jedi."

I nodded. "That's what I've heard as well. Well, without telekinesis, I guess I'll have to use this shovel and elbow grease to move that pile."

As I dug, my grandfather told me tales of Nejaa Halcyon. "We worked together for a good long time, or so it seemed, before he was called away to the Clone Wars. Our partnership was only ten years or so, as I recall. I guess I was seven years older than you are when he left. He was a bit older than me and his wife—I'd grown up living near Scerra, so I knew her quite well before they ever met. Your father was only ten at the time Nejaa left, but had been working with Nejaa for years to develop his skills."

I swiped at the sweat on my brow. "Nejaa died in the Clone Wars, right?"

"Actually, he died shortly thereafter, before he could ever return home. He and I had joked about his going off to the Clone Wars, for it was said that a Corellian Jedi who leaves the system does so at his own peril." My grandfather's eyes clouded over. "Nejaa promised his wife and me that the Clone Wars would not kill him. He was right, but still suffered the fate of those Corellian Jedi who go away.

"A friend of his, a Caamasi Jedi named Ylenic It'kla, came here, bringing Nejaa's effects home. He apologized for not bringing Nejaa's body, but the bodies of Jedi Masters fade away upon death. He also didn't have Nejaa's lightsaber. He said the Galactic Museum had asked for it for their Jedi collection." He smiled slightly. "I suppose it is still there."

I shook my head. "Nope. It has served me well on a couple of occasions. Saved my life."

He clapped his hands. "And mine as well. 'Thieves run in fright from its silvery light.' I used to kid Nejaa about that."

I smiled, but kept digging. "He used to go out with you when you worked cases?"

"All the time. Most often he would be dressed in street clothes, just like me. He found a lot of people were wary of the Jedi and afraid of them. Without them knowing who he was, he could help victims. When it came time for us to go after criminals, he'd don his cloak and more traditional Jedi garb. Scerra used to refer to it as his hunting clothes. Criminals learned it didn't hurt as much if they didn't resist, so we were able to defuse many a tense situation just by having him show up as a Jedi. Of course, stories of what he had done spread throughout the underworld and became quickly exaggerated, so people reacted to his image and reputation, not reality."

I cleared the area my grandfather had indicated and peeled back the plasticized tarpaulin that had been beneath the dung heap. I noticed, on the underside, a metallic sheen. "This is a diffuser pad?"

"Is it? I hadn't noticed."

I frowned. Diffusers came in all different shapes and sizes and simply channeled the energy from scanners away so return signals from scanners would not reveal whatever was hidden by the diffuser. Smugglers regularly used them to prevent cursory searches from uncovering contraband, but a little time and a little effort made finding the diffusers easy, and finding one of them meant finding whatever they covered.

In this case, the diffuser covered a bare patch of ground. "Let me guess: a buried door that no one has found because they didn't want to dig through bantha dung?"

"See, it was effort like that which allowed your father to catch Booster Terrik. Not a surprise the man hated the Horns."

"He's got more reason now."

My grandfather smiled. "Yes, how does he like having his daughter married to a Horn?"

I turned one spadeful of dirt, then looked at my grandfather with surprise. "You know?"

"Corran, I love you dearly and I think you will recall that we have spent many long hours discussing your love life and the disasters attendant thereunto."

"Don't remind me." I growled at him. "Hey, is that just a leaning shovel, or can it dig, too?"

"It can dig. Do you want to use it? Is yours worn out?"

I arched an eyebrow at him. "You're not going to help?"

"I did my part in burying it." His smile slackened slightly. "Get going, it's not that far down. Back to the point—when your garbled missives coming to me stopped mentioning romantic difficulties, I assumed you had found someone. I made inquiries."

"And you're not disappointed?"

"Disappointed? Why would I be?"

"She's Booster Terrik's daughter."

My grandfather walked over and rested his right hand on the back of my neck. "Corran, if she was enough to win your heart and keep it, she has to be wonderful. I am happy for you, truly. Someday you will bring her here so I can meet her."

"Sure, as soon as the murder warrants for me are lifted."

He frowned. "Oh, yes, Gil Bastra's work. I'll take care of that. Perhaps that Imperial Liaison officer you had should be found guilty."

"Loor? He's dead."

"So much the better." He glanced down at the hole as my shovel hit metal. "There you go."

I cleared the hole. "Old storm cellar?"

"It was here when I bought the house." He crouched and helped me tug the metal door open. "It's rather snug down there. You can go first." He pulled a glowrod from his back pocket, flicked it on and handed it to me.

I clambered down the rusty ladder built into the side of the duracrete shaft. At the bottom the enclosure opened out into the area beneath the dung heap. The boxy room had been cleared of everything save one dusty and dirty old fiberplast trunk. It appeared to be of the sort I'd seen used a lot by smugglers—old pre-Imperial military surplus, cheap and in ready supply.

I heard my grandfather come down behind me. "This trunk, what is it?"

"When the Empire decided all Jedi must die, I made some decisions. Some, like altering files to hide your grandmother and father from Imperial hunters, were good decisions. I do not regret them in the least."

I glanced back at him. "Were there other Corellian Jedi families you hid?"

"That's not information you need to know, Corran. If there are any, and if they are meant to be found, they will be." His hands rested on my shoulders. "Other decisions were risky. I chose, foolishly, to put my family and myself in jeopardy by hiding this down here. Had it been discovered I could have gotten all of us killed. By rights, I should have destroyed it—your grandmother and father thought I *had* because I told them I had, but I just couldn't."

His hands gave my shoulders a squeeze. "There, in that box, are all the things Ylenic It'kla brought back here after Nejaa's death."

I nodded slowly, the light bobbing up and down over the packing case's dark bulk. "How did Nejaa die?"

"I don't know the details. The Caamasi asked that I not inquire. What he did tell me was that a great man, a hero of the Clone Wars, selected them for a very special and honorable mission. They went with him and the three of them vanquished most deadly foes, but Nejaa was mortally wounded. All the Jedi healing techniques could not save him and he died."

"Then you married his wife and adopted his son."

My grandfather's voice grew distant. "I'd known Scerra all my life. We'd always been good friends, and we both lost our best friend at the same time. Our shared grief brought us more closely together and our shared lives provided us with strong roots together. I have always chosen to think that Nejaa had an inkling of his fate and what would happen to us after his passing. I like to think knowing his friends would salvage love out of their mourning made his death that much easier."

He patted me on the shoulder. "The dust down here

has my eyes watering. I'm going to head back up. We can pull the chest out of here, if you want, or you can open it and just look at the things here. Your choice. You are the last Halcyon, so they belong to you.''

''Thank you.'' I took a step toward the case, then turned and faced my grandfather. ''You're wrong in one thing, though.''

Tears glistened in the half-light. ''Am I?''

I nodded. ''I don't see myself as the last Halcyon. I'm the last Horn. I just hope, in this chest and in the garden above, there's everything I need to guarantee both lines will continue.''

Alone in the still darkness, I opened the trunk. Dust trickled down from the lid, filling the air. I expected a musty odor of old clothes that had long since mildewed away to nothing, but instead I found a chest packed neatly and tightly. All the clothing had been folded precisely and sealed in clear plastine pouches. I carefully pulled one after another out but opened none of them. Still, from what I could see in the glowrod light, the clothes had all been laundered, leading me to suspect the Caamasi Jedi had taken great pains to care for his friend's effects.

Toward the bottom of the trunk I found boots encased in plastine, as well as a cloak and blanket similarly pouched. Below that I saw the lid of a hinged compartment that I lifted up. Inside it was thick foam padding with hollowed spaces for various items. I easily recognized the slot meant for Nejaa's lightsaber. A small first aid kit, a shaving kit and a set of eating utensils all sat in their appropriate slots. Odd coins filled other slots, as did power packs for a variety of items and a positively antique comlink.

What immediately attracted my attention, however, was the rectangular slot filled with static holograms. I fished them out and carried them back over to where the sun's light filtered down through the long chimney. One by one, I flipped through them and found myself smiling though I recognized no one.

I figured out which person had to be Nejaa after a couple of shots. From other items in the picture, especially the lightsaber clipped to his belt, I could tell he'd stood slightly taller than me, but no taller than my father, and he had my trim build. We didn't really look that much alike, except around the eyes and chin. Still, he stood there easily and openly, feet shoulder-width apart, hands open, a smile on his face and life in his eyes. I recognized in his stance the way my father used to stand around and knew I'd adopted the stance as well.

The other figure I found easy to recognize was a Caamasi. Golden down covered him except around the eyes, where purple fur formed a mask around his eyes that spread tendrils up and back to stripe his skull. The Caamasi's large, dark eyes seemed full of inquisitiveness, not the sadness marking the Caamasi I'd seen; but then I'd only seen Caamasi rarely and this shot had been taken before they'd almost all been wiped out. The two of them—my grandfather and his friend—looked weary in some shots, but that was to be expected of people fighting a war. That they also looked content spoke a lot about their commitment to keeping the galaxy safe.

Some of the shots had people I recognized in them. I saw a very young Jan Dodonna standing with Nejaa. I recalled the general having asked me in *Lusankya* if he knew my grandfather. He had indeed known him, but I'd not known who my grandfather was at the time. *Jan saved my life in that prison. Had he saved yours, too, Nejaa, or was he paying back some ancient debt to you when he saved mine?*

Bail Organa appeared in one picture with Nejaa and the Caamasi. Other individuals joined them in group and individual shots, but I didn't positively identify any of the others. The old-style clothes, the youthful faces, could easily have become countless senators and leaders whose aged faces I would have easily recognized. Some struck me as very familiar—annoyingly so—but without someone to tell me who they were or images to use for comparison, I was stuck not knowing.

Suddenly the war holograms ended and I found myself looking at peacetime shots. The first showed my grandfather standing there with Nejaa. Nejaa was handing him one of the Jedi Medallions marking Nejaa's elevation to the rank of Master. Then I saw Nejaa with his face pressed cheek to cheek with that of my grandmother. It shocked me because I'd only ever seen her with my grandfather, Rostek. Then, in a picture where the image ran wider, I saw Scerra, Nejaa and a boy who would become my father.

I sagged against the wall and shut my eyes against tears. During my life I'd long heard the cries of downtrodden people who kept saying the Empire was robbing them of their lives and their dignity and the rights they deserved by the simple virtue of their sapience. I'd listened, but not too closely because I found their arguments weak and self-serving. They'd always warned me that someday it would be my turn, that the stormtroopers would be coming for me, and that day it would be too late. I laughed at them then because, with my family, I never imagined the Empire could hurt us.

But hurt us it had. The Empire hadn't even existed when Nejaa died, but the actions of the Emperor forced my father and grandmother to live a lie. Fear of discovery had to have nibbled on my grandfather every day of his life. Knowing he had saved people might have been an antidote for that, but having to endure that fear for so very long was incredible. My respect for him doubled and doubled again. *He is a hero who will never be celebrated for what he has done. And there must be more people like him throughout the galaxy—heroes unsung from a dark time.*

I slipped the holograms into my pocket, then returned and replaced everything save the Corellian Jedi uniform, cloak and boots in the box. I resealed it, then carried my booty out and hid it in the greenhouse. I closed the storm cellar door and reburied it, laying back down the diffusion pad and shoveling the manure back over it.

My grandfather joined me as I finished the job. "Find anything of interest down there?"

I nodded. "A past I never knew about." I gave him a brave smile. "And renewed respect for someone who proved himself a better friend than anyone could ever hope to have."

His eyes misted over for a moment, then he smiled and nodded slowly. "Busy day, then. You have a lot to think about."

I smiled. "I do, but that can wait. Right now, a grandson would like to spend time with his grandfather, potting plants, delivering flowers, cruising Treasure Ship Row looking for trouble. What do you think?"

Rostek Horn smiled broadly and threw an arm over my shoulder. "I think Coronet City is in for some excitement. It's been a while since two Horn men made their presence felt. It'll be a night to remember."

THIRTY

✳

It *was* a night to remember, but for more than just the great time I had with my grandfather. We did hit Coronet City and dined at the finest restaurant on all Corellia: Nova Nova. Normally reservations were comlinked in several months in advance, but my grandfather just showed up bearing a bouquet of flowers, and we were admitted to a private room. The food was all served *techno*—tiny portions arranged on the plate as if they were art. Sensors in the utensils relayed data to discrete holoprojectors, so one knew the exact contents of each mouthful, including hints of what subtle flavors one should expect to taste, or anecdotes concerning the creation of the dish.

Made me wonder if Siolle Tinta's chef, Chid, was working in the kitchen.

After that we went to the private club at the pinnacle of the world's tallest building. The Lastdark Club took its name from the fact that it was the place in the city the sun touched last before night, and from the fact that the majority of the members considered themselves the most enlightened people on the planet. Back when I worked CorSec we used to joke about the club because we knew none of us could ever afford to join; but my grandfather had become a member in the last three years, and half the plants in the place were hybrids he'd created.

The overwhelming elegance of my surroundings sharply contrasted with what I had known at the Jedi academy, making Yavin 4 seem but a distant memory. Coronet City seemed more right to me, I fit in better here. The academy's jungle setting had always left me slightly uneasy. I realized, sitting in a plush nerf-hide chair, sipping Corellian brandy and watching the city spread out beneath me, that being city born and bred, I had a preference for urbanity and civilization. Coruscant was too built up for me to feel comfortable there all the time, but here, on Corellia, I could feel at home again.

Nice place to raise kids.

My grandfather told me stories of Booster Terrik from back before my father got him sent to Kessel, back before Jorj Car'das had eaten up Booster's organization, only in turn to have his organization taken over by Talon Karrde. "So, you see, when Hal caught Booster that first time, Booster considered it pure luck, and forever after worked hard to taunt and elude Hal." My grandfather smiled broadly. "I don't think Booster ever truly appreciated your father's skills as a detective."

We spoke of many things that evening, even on the ride back to the estate. I discovered in my grandfather that night someone I had never known before. Of course, my first relationship with him had been established as a child to a man, which brought with it certain behaviors. By the time I moved into adulthood, I'd joined CorSec, and our relationship shifted to more of a professional one. This was not a deliberate shift but a natural one, since our jobs dominated our lives. While I could speak to him about my romantic entanglements, that again was a youth speaking to an elder. And then, when my father died, the pain we both felt battered us emotionally to the point where sharing feelings hurt too much, so we stoically didn't touch upon subjects that would reopen old wounds.

On this night, for the first time, I was able to relate to him as just one adult to another. It was an odd feeling, yet one in which I took great pride. Here was the man who knew my father and Nejaa better than anyone. If *he* could like me, if *he* could respect what I had done, then there was a good chance *they* would have also. This realization quelled some of the discomfort I'd felt since my final encounter with Exar Kun, and that night I went to sleep feeling better than I had in a long time.

Master Skywalker had once said that Jedi do not dream, so when I found myself on a bright, arid world, with my lightsaber unlit but held in my right hand, I wondered at how I had gotten where I was. I saw the emerald sleeves of my Corellian Jedi tunic, and even that did not seem out of place, though the material was finer than that of the clothes I'd been given on Yavin 4. It wasn't until I looked over to my right and saw Ylenic It'kla, resplendent in his purple cloak, and, beyond him, the Jedi General in his brown and khaki desert-born robes, that I realized *I* wasn't *me*.

The three of us, spread out sufficiently to give ourselves room to fight, stood in a dusty bowl-shaped depression beneath a duracrete dome. A dozen three-meter-tall pillars scattered around its circumference held the dome aloft, allowing the light from the outside to illuminate the arena. Makeshift tents and storage sheds occupied a quarter of the arena in the direction we were facing. Emerging from the central pavilion, three figures came out to stand opposite us. Each of them bore a lightsaber. Their leader, the taller, blond man facing the general, took a step closer to us than his comrades. The red-haired woman aligned herself with Ylenic, while the Anzati, with his proboscises just beginning to peek from the cheek pouches that hid them, lined up to oppose me.

The general—his name eluded me though I knew I recognized something about him—spoke very precisely. "You are meddling with things you cannot control; things that nearly destroyed the Jedi millennia ago. We have come to ask you to abandon your evil and return to the light."

The leader laughed slowly, his voice low and laden with contempt. "The weak always fear the strong growing up to replace them."

"And the foolish always see themselves as strong." The words came from my throat and I could feel my lips forming them. It almost even sounded like something I'd say, though more formal—*more archaic and precise*—than I would have liked.

Ylenic's voice came gentle yet strong. "Fear marks the wrong path. We offer you freedom from your fear."

Their leader thumbed his lightsaber to life. "And we offer you freedom as well."

The Anzati, taller than me, darker, entirely humanoid save for the proboscises uncurling in his excitement, ignited his blue blade and closed with me. Nikkos Tyris—his name came easily to me—held his lightsaber in a guard I'd not seen before. He had his left hand on the hilt fairly close to the shimmering blade, but the blade itself extended out and down from the lower edge of his hand toward the ground. His right hand rode the lightsaber's pommel. Holding the blade out away from his body, with his right hand at the level of his chin, he could waggle the blade back and forth in a triangle of coverage that would ward him well. This triangle style— the thought suddenly came to me like a long lost memory—favored a man who was quick, and would combine sweeping strikes at my legs with a flick of the wrist cut that would open me from groin to chin.

I knew fear, but the person I was in the dream shunted it away. I held my silvery blade in a simple guard, though I tilted the blade forward, pointing it at his throat. We circled, then he struck. His blade flicked out for my right leg. I swept my blade down to block low right, sparks flying as our blades crashed into each other. He bounced his blade up and over mine, and brought it across in a slash meant to decapitate me.

I caught the acrid stink as some of my hair melted beneath the lightsaber's lethal caress, but I ducked the blow by a safe margin. Rotating my wrists, I swept my blade back low, through where his legs should have been, but he leaped up and away from my strike. He flipped backward through the air, displaying great ability with levitation, and landed easily four meters away from me.

His dark eyes blazed for a moment, then an invisible fist smashed into my chest, knocking me backward. He freed his right hand from his azure blade, and flicked fingers at me with the most casual of gestures. A fist-sized stone shot at me from the ground, clipping me on the left shoulder. Pain shot through my arm, leaving it numb. He laughed and hurled another stone toward me. I deflected it with my lightsaber and smiled, then another rock slammed into the left side of my head.

I went down hard, raising a small cloud of dust when I hit the ground. My lightsaber bounced out of my grasp and I didn't see where it landed. I shook my head to try to clear it, but pain and a faint ringing made that difficult.

I could feel blood coating the left side of my face and swiped at it with the left sleeve of my tunic. I heard the crunch of gravel beneath his boots as Tyris approached. Drawing myself up into a crouch, I glanced to my right and finally saw my lightsaber lying there, two meters away. I wanted to call it to my hand, but I knew it would never come. I could dive for it, but his lightsaber would pin me to the ground before I ever got there.

"So, it is true, what they have said about the Halcyon line. You are wingclipped mynocks." An evil smile spread across Tyris's face as he brought his lightsaber around to display for me the tool of my destruction. "You are a line of weakness."

I smiled, knowing what I had to do. "We have our strengths."

"Do you?" He whisked the blade back around to his left, preparatory to sweeping it through me. "Better summon one swiftly."

In the second of life he left me, I caught a vision of him standing above me and my dead comrades. Our slain bodies faded away, but his mocking laughter did not. I knew with a certainty as clear and hard as transparisteel that if I did not deal with Tyris, my friends and our mission here would be destroyed. I couldn't let that happen, so I acted.

I launched myself toward my lightsaber, my right hand reaching for it. My body twisted in the air as I flew. I landed on my back, skidding the last centimeters to where my hand closed on the blade's hilt. Even as I tightened my grip, even as I started to bring the blade around in a parry, I knew I would be too late.

So did Tyris.

He stabbed his blade down through my chest. The azure blade melted flesh and boiled blood as it went, reducing my heart to sweet smoke and steam. On further it stabbed, exploding arteries and burning through my spine. The lower part of my body went numb, though I barely noticed because of the wave of agony surging up through me and into my brain. It threatened to overwhelm me, letting darkness nibble into my sight. I was dying and I knew it and regrets poured in with the pain.

But I was not dead yet.

I was a Halcyon. I was a Jedi.

Jedi do not know pain.

In an instant all physical agony ceased as effectively as if I'd flicked a switch and turned all my pain receptors off. All I was left with was an incredible clarity of mind and a singleness of purpose. I'd dedicated my life to the service of others, to the service of the Force. I would not go out without my duty being fulfilled. I concentrated and employed the greatest Halcyon gift against my enemy.

I sucked the energy out of the Anzati's lightsaber and forced myself to smile as I did so. I tasted blood in my mouth, but that fact elicited no panic. It was inconsequential. More telling was the look of surprise on Tyris' face as his blue blade flickered once, then twice, then went out. I'd drained it of every last joule and let him read in my eyes that he should suddenly be very afraid.

With the energy I'd pulled in I plucked him from the ground in a giant invisible fist. He screamed, I think; at least his mouth worked as if he was screaming. I made the fist convulse once and I felt no resistance as his bones shattered. I let him hang limp in the air for a moment, then hurled him back through the tents to slam him against the dome and a support. I felt a jolt through the Force and saw a blue flash of light, but by then my energy reserves had faded.

As did I. I felt spiky red torments racing in to fill my consciousness, but I slipped out of my fleshy prison before they could shackle me to this spot forever.

I sat bolt upright in bed, sweat pouring off my body. I felt for the burned, crusted hole in my chest but found nothing. My head pounded, but I found no torn scalp, no bump rising from a stone, no blood. A shiver ran down my spine and I realized that I actually *could* feel my lower body again.

I stumbled out of bed and staggered to my room's refresher station. I started cold water running and splashed it on my face as the station's glowpanels brightened. I drank from my cupped hands, quenching an intense thirst, then lowered my face into the catch basin and let the water flow over the back of my head.

Finally I brought my head up. As water trickled down over my back and chest, I glanced in the mirror and saw my grandfather's face where mine should have been. I closed my eyes and shook my head. Opening them again, amid the tear-tracks water droplets left on the mirror, I saw Nejaa Halcyon's features fade and mine return. I reached up and touched my own face, letting my fingers confirm what my eyes saw, and that sent a shoulder-shifting shudder through me.

I turned away from the mirror and buried my face in my hands. For the past ten weeks I'd been an idiot. I could have seen it, I would have seen it, but by going to the academy I'd cut myself off from the friends who would have helped make it all clear to me.

My father's saying—"If you cannot recognize the man in the mirror, it is time to step back and see when you stopped being yourself.''—should have been my guide all the way along. In joining Luke I wasn't being myself, I was trying to become my grandfather. And the dream made it abundantly clear that to do that was a disaster. Corran Horn was not a Jedi.

What Corran Horn *was* was an investigator, trained by CorSec, to deal with all manner of problems just like the Invids. If they'd been a pirate band working the Corellian sector, I'd have infiltrated them, ferreted out their secrets, and busted them up. I'd done that very thing dozens of times in my career. Granted, no organization I faced had been that big, powerful or elusive, but size works against efficiency with criminal organizations, and power allows for greed to be played off against greed, creating discord.

I'd spent ten weeks wasting my time when I could have been out there going after Mirax's kidnappers the best way I knew how. That sort of investigation certainly would take time—months at the very least, but at least I'd be doing something that would get me closer to Mirax. The Jedi stuff I had learned was fine for saving the galaxy, but I only wanted to save one person, and save her *I* could.

I turned back toward the mirror and nodded to the man I saw there. ''Good to see you again, Corran Horn. It's time this Invid business is ended once and for all.''

THIRTY-ONE

✳

The flight attendant on the shuttle smiled at me and leaned down so her lowered voice would not carry very far. It really didn't matter, since my seatmate and I were the only people who had boarded and were in the Premier cabin on the shuttle. "Forgive me for being so forward, sir, but your pass has an ultraviolet flag on it, and on Tinta Lines, we like to afford such honored customers some privileges. The captain isn't yet on board, but he was wondering if you would care to join him in the cockpit for the release and transit over to the *Tinta Rainbow*?"

I smiled, and would have refused, but Jenos Idanian, who I had become for my trip away from Corellia, never would have. "I would be delighted to join him."

A tone sounded from the back. The flight attendant, rather resplendent in her blue and gold Tinta Lines uniform, glanced back into the main passenger cabin. There a Kuati woman was doing her best to stuff a huge carryall into a starboard, over-seat storage compartment and close the door. The flight attendant sighed. "You, of course, know your way around a *Luxury*-class shuttle, so you can head forward whenever you want."

"Thanks."

My seatmate, a young man whose more prominent features were a big larynx and bigger nose, beamed at me. "Do you really know your way around on one of these ships? I've studied them at tech-school and know they have the Astronav P127 Course Plotter, but of course, we're not going to use it since we're just going on an in-system jump, but it's a beauty and can come up with courses very fast, even multiple jumps, and when I've used the one at school I could plot a tough course in seconds."

I held a hand up. "Slow down, breathe."

"Sorry." He smiled sheepishly at me. "It's just that forever and ever and ever I've wanted to fly. Ever since I've been a little kid, I mean, really little, I've heard stories about the Rebellion—well, the New Republic now—and Rogue Squadron and all them and I've wanted to fly just like them. And when Grand Admiral Thrawn showed up I volunteered for service to fight him, but I didn't test out very good, so I went to tech-school to learn how to fix ships and then they found I could do good navigation, so they trained me for that, but then Thrawn was gone and forces got demobilized and so I was looking for a civilian job with the Tinta line. . . ."

"Really, look, just breathe." I offered him my hand because Jenos would do that sort of thing. "Jenos Idanian."

"Keevy Spart." He wiped sweat from his forehead with a long-fingered hand. Freckles covered him. He wore his red hair shorter than mine and was slender enough that he almost reminded me of Kirtan Loor, but this kid wasn't that stupid or mean. "So, do you fly one of these things?"

"I have, Keevy, the military variant. Back during the Rebellion some." I looked around the Premier cabin.

"Those shuttles didn't have the accommodations this one does, and we packed soldiers in fairly tightly. And our navicomp wasn't as sophisticated as the one you describe."

"Oh, this is so exciting."

I smiled. "Tell me about it."

"Okay . . ." he began.

I sank back in my seat and kept a smile on my face because that's what Jenos would have done. The morning after the nightmare I had joined my grandfather in the greenhouse and told him what I had resolved to do: to leave Corellia and infiltrate the Invids. He applauded the plan and immediately set about getting me squared away to do so. He took a look at the identification Booster had provided me and while pronouncing it "marginally adequate," he got on the comlink and soon had documents for me that appeared quite genuine.

"They are, Corran, quite genuine." My grandfather smiled at me. "They will pass the most rigorous inspection."

I looked at the identification card with my holograph on it. "Who is Jenos Idanian?"

"Originally? He was a small-time crook a bit older than you. He vanished, but his record was still on file. I adjusted details and the age to fit you better. You now have some youthful indiscretions in your background, including some ship-theft related problems and some smuggling arrests. Not enough to mark you well-known, but enough to suggest you know what you are doing. For your purposes, Jenos has since reformed, partially because of his participation in the Rebellion, and now works as a broker selling used starships."

I thought for a moment, then nodded. The background was not so improbable that I couldn't slip into it.

I add a run of bad luck that becomes bitterness about rich folks who have stolen my commissions, and I become a likely pirate candidate with skills they need. "You sure this Jenos isn't going to come looking for me?"

"Jenos hasn't been heard from for over twenty years. If he had surfaced, your father would have gotten him, since Hal was close to arresting him back then." Rostek Horn's smile diminished only slightly. "I also have arranged for transport for you on the Tinta Lines Starship *Tinta Palette.* You will transfer in the Bormea system to the *Tinta Rainbow* and make your way to Coruscant. From there I suspect you can find your way to the *Errant Venture* and the Invids."

I frowned. "The Tinta ships are luxury liners and have their cruises booked months in advance."

"Siolle Tinta loves flowers, Corran." He plucked a bud from a small seedling. "She was happy to see to it that a friend of yours would be treated like family."

"While you might have gotten the death warrants for me quashed, there are still Imperial sympathizers here who wouldn't mind capturing me and selling me to High Admiral Teradoc or any other self-styled warlord. Shouldn't I be keeping a lower profile than shipping on a luxury liner?"

My grandfather laughed easily. "My dear boy, two things you must remember about Imperial sympathizers on Corellia: they would never believe any Rebel stupid enough to come to Corellia in the first place, and, second, they would find it impossible to believe any Rebel would be able to afford luxury passage on a starliner. Imperial sympathizers here live in a fantasy world twenty years old. They think of the days of Moff Vorru as a golden age. Aside from a few CorSec officials, I doubt anyone knows you are a Rebel, and those officials would never lay a hand on you."

"Afraid of flowers?"

"A few. More remember your father very well."

"I see." I sighed. "I cannot tell you how much I appreciate your doing this for me. I've been a fool and I think you know it. I'd like to thank you for not having bashed me over the head with it."

He watched me closely, his grey eyes cooling off. "What have you been a fool about?"

"Becoming a Jedi in order to save Mirax. I've wasted so much time."

Rostek brushed his hands off, then posted his fists on his hips. "I should make this very clear for you, Corran. I don't think you've been a fool. What you've learned is what you needed to learn. It may well be that not everything you studied at the academy will help you find and save Mirax, but you could not have known that before. I saw Nejaa do many things to solve cases that had nothing at all to do with the Force or his training as a Jedi— except where that training made him a better person. Going through that training and being able to make the decision you are to abandon it takes a maturity I've never seen in you before. Granted, your adventures with Rogue Squadron and your marriage to Mirax probably imparted much of the maturity to you; but you shouldn't devalue your training. Just because it did not take you where you wanted to go does not mean the journey was not good for you."

"I'm sorry, I didn't mean to offend you."

"You didn't. I hold memories of Nejaa Halcyon very dear. I consider my work here, preserving his knowledge of the Force, to be the greatest thing I could have done with my life; and I am glad that you will have access to it all. I'll even share it with your Luke Skywalker, if you wish.''

''Please.''

He nodded. ''Consider it done. I am very proud of you, Corran, and whatever course you take in your life. Times may not have changed much here on Corellia, but your ability to survive in the maelstrom of the civil war amazes me.''

I walked over and gave him a hug. ''Again, thank you.''

He smiled as we parted. ''Oh, in your document package, along with the journal datacards I gave you, I included a copy of the CorSec files on that smuggler you asked about, Jorj Car'das. Files were old—he disappeared almost as long ago as Jenos Idanian. I hope they are useful.''

''Me, too. They'll pay off a debt.''

''Good.'' He glanced at his chronometer. ''You'd best finish packing. Tosruk will speed you to the spaceport.''

''One other thing I need to do, first.'' I reached back and opened the small satchel I'd set on the potting bench nearest the door. I drew out Nejaa Halcyon's lightsaber and presented the hilt to my grandfather. ''A lightsaber is a Jedi's most prized possession—after his friends. I cannot take it with me because very few pirates wear them these days and, to be honest, I've not earned the right to wear it. I'm not Nejaa Halcyon. I'm not really a Jedi Knight. I want you to keep it, keep it safe, as you have his knowledge and his memory.''

My grandfather accepted it carefully, as if it weighed fifty kilos. ''It may seem odd, but this was the missing piece. For the time I knew him, this lightsaber was part of him, an instrument of justice. When he died and the lightsaber never came back with him, I felt justice had also vanished. Now, perhaps, it has returned.''

A single tear rolled down his cheek. ''You may be right that now is not the time for you to accept the Halcyon mantle, but when it is, this shall be waiting for you.''

I left him there, alone in the greenhouse with his memories and the memories he had stored in the plants. Tosruk took me to the spaceport where I shipped out on the *Tinta Palette*, and now found myself, several days later, seated next to Keevy Spart, listening to the dismal story of his life. ''You don't say,'' I said.

''Yes, yes, it's all true. I've collected every story I can find about Rogue Squadron and want to put together a history of the unit. I know all of the pilots' profiles, how many kills they had, where they came from. . . .''

''What they look like . . .''

''Of course.'' He stared at me intently. ''Have you ever met any of them?''

''Me? No, not even in passing.'' I nodded toward the external viewport. ''See the *Rainbow* yet?''

Keevy shut up and pressed his face against the viewport transparisteel. The shuttle, *Tinta Blue Seven*, had docked on the outside of the *Palette*, securely linked to the bigger ship by a docking collar. The shuttle's gangway extended down into the ship allowing the passengers to move up into the passenger compartments while ship's crew transferred our luggage to the shuttle's hold. Once everyone was aboard and the shuttle was ready to travel, we'd head over to the *Tinta Rainbow* and offload ourselves through a similar docking arrangement. *Rainbow* passengers that wanted to join the *Palette* would be sent over on a different shuttle and both ships would proceed on their courses with a minimum of delay.

"I don't see anything yet." His position at the viewport added nasal tones to his voice. "Ship should be showing up soon, though."

"Well, then, I guess I'll take the opportunity to visit the cockpit."

Keevy turned back and grabbed my arm. "Take me with you, please?"

"I don't know."

"Please?" He looked at me with pitifully large and sad brown eyes. "This is probably the only chance I'll get to see an AP127CP in a real shuttle."

I frowned at him. "You wouldn't touch anything, would you?"

His voice got small. "Nope."

"Maybe I'll talk to the captain for you. He should be getting on board soon." I twisted in my seat to get out and caught a flash of white in space outside. "In fact, I wonder what's keeping him. Is that the *Rainbow*?"

Keevy looked back outside. "Nope, looks like a Mark II Imperial Star Destroyer, and a lot of little ships with it. Coming this way."

I got up from my seat and turned toward the flight attendant, but as I did so two men came running up the gangway and appeared in the front of the main cabin. Both wore blasters holstered on their hips and one, the bigger one, brandished a huge vibroblade. "Stay calm," the smaller one urged with upraised hands. "Stay calm and no one will get hurt."

The flight attendant quieted two people as the smaller man waved me from the Premier cabin back with the rest of the passengers. Apparently he missed Keevy. "Glad you could join us. We're from the *Invidious* and we're here to relieve you of your wealth.''

An older man pointed a palsied finger at the leader. ''You were Laanars, my cabin steward.''

Laanars took a quick step around to the starboard aisle, approached the man and slapped him. ''I was, you cheap pile of nerf-dirt. I did your scutwork because I knew this day was coming.''

''You don't need to hurt anyone else.'' I kept my voice cool as I met his brown-eyed gaze. I stood in the portside aisle, looking at him across a block of three seats. ''You're in control. You can take what you want.''

''That's right, I *am* in control.'' Laanars' larger companion slipped past him and stood near the head of the starboard aisle. Laanars held up a hand and waggled his fingers. ''Let's go, off with the jewelry. You don't surrender it, Biril here will show you why they don't let him work as a manicurist anymore.''

I could feel the flood of anxiety gushing out of everyone and resorted to a quick Jedi technique to keep from being overwhelmed by it. I spread my senses out, expanding my sphere of responsibility to take in the whole of the shuttle. I wished I could reach out to everyone, inducing calm in them, or causing the two pirates to go to sleep, but I didn't have such skills. The best thing I could do, I knew from long experience in hostage situations, was to let the pirates have what they wanted.

Then I sensed Keevy tensing for an attack. Unseen, he'd worked his way across the Premier cabin and was set to spring on Biril. The pirate was big enough that I doubted he'd even feel the impact of Keevy's assault. With no effort at all, Biril would scrape Keevy off him, then probably carve the kid up just because he could.

And Keevy, having grown up his whole life wanting to be a hero, saw this as his chance.

He'd be a hero, all right—a dead one.

"Hey, sport," I called to Laanars. "This is a one-time offer. Leave now, and you won't get hurt."

"Someone gets hurt, it won't be me." Laanars watched me closely. "Sit down and shut up."

I shrugged my shoulders and shook my hands out. "Any time you care to make me."

Laanars looked right and left, disbelief on his face. "How stupid can you be?" His right hand dropped to the butt of his blaster as he stared me right in the eyes. "You're dead."

Using the Force, I filled his mind with the image of his blaster being drawn and pointing straight at my forehead. I painted a look of terror on my face, but gave him the impression that I'd been concealing a hold-out blaster up my right sleeve. He saw it appear in my hand and swing into line with his body. He had no choice. He pulled the trigger three times.

But his blaster hadn't yet slid even halfway from its holster. All three shots struck him in the right thigh, collapsing the leg. He went down screaming and thrashed in the aisle. Biril ran toward him and crouched down, taking him out of Keevy's attack range. The larger man looked at his stricken comrade, then at me. "You're dead."

"Not likely." The Halcyon line might not have been strong in the ways of telekinesis, but it's never required much of an effort to slip the latch on an overstuffed cargo compartment. The panel snapped open and the Kuati's bundle came crashing down to hit Biril across the back of his shoulders. He angrily spun toward it, slashing with his vibroblade, then turned back toward me. By that time, however, I'd vaulted myself across the central seats and caught him in the chest with both feet.

He flew back, tripping and stumbling over the Kuati's satchel, just as Keevy came charging blindly in from the Premier cabin. Keevy's forehead caught Biril square on the chin. The bigger man went limp and crashed down while Keevy caromed off him and landed sprawled across the laps of two young women.

I snatched up Laanars' blaster, flicked it to stun and pumped a shot into him. I fired two more into Biril. I turned and tossed the weapon to the flight attendant. "Can you retract the gangway?"

She caught the gun and nodded hesitantly. "I can, but only on the captain's order."

I glanced at her nametag. "Okay, Annissya, you've got the order."

"Sir, I know you are qualified to fly one of these shuttles, but . . ."

I opened my hands. "There's more pirates coming, and your pilot likely isn't. I'd just as soon be out of here. We might as well make a run, because waiting here isn't going to do us any good."

She thought for a second, then nodded. "As ordered, Captain Idanian."

I grabbed Keevy by his collar and hauled him from the laps of the two women who, from the looks on their faces, were convinced he'd saved them from certain death. "You really know how to work an AP127 whatever?"

"The AP127CP?" His larynx bounced up and down as his voice cracked. "Yes, sir."

"You aren't lying, are you? Lives are at stake here."

He straightened up and assumed a pose he clearly thought of as military. "I can do it."

I smiled. "To the cockpit then, my boy. You wanted to fly in combat? This is gonna be it."

Keevy rubbed at the bump on his forehead. "We're going to try to outrun an Imperial Star Destroyer?"

"That a problem for you?" I narrowed my eyes.

"Well, it won't be easy."

"Yeah, well, if it was easy, it wouldn't be worth doing." I gave him a shove toward the front of the shuttle. "You just plot me a course and get me an exit vector. I'll get us on it and we'll all get out of here."

He glanced back at me. "Sir, even a Rogue Squadron pilot couldn't get us out of here. I know."

"And after this, you'll know some more." I patted him on the back. "Strap in, son, you're in for the ride of your life."

THIRTY-TWO

I dropped into the cockpit command chair, pulled on the communications headset and started hitting switches. The layout hadn't been modified much from that of the shuttle I'd flown to Yavin. I noticed the weapons-control panel had been replaced with something labeled "Entertainment system." Shrugging, I punched a button and started some holodrama playing in the back.

Keevy sat across from me in the navigator's position. He strapped in and sat there for a moment, then looked up and froze.

The *Invidious* hung out there in space, its dagger shape de-emphasized since we were looking at a profile shot of the ship. Its deck plane lay slightly below ours—if we took off in a straight line we'd pass a good hundred meters over the top of the ship's main decks. I eyed the ship the way I would have were I sitting in an X-wing's cockpit, checking the guns, locating the shield generators. On a secondary monitor I brought up a scan of the *Invidious* and saw it didn't have shields up.

Just one proton torpedo and you'd pay for that arrogance, Tavira. I glanced over at Keevy, but he'd not moved. "Problem, Keevy?"

He blinked and shivered. "No, sorry."

"You can use the navicomp?"

"Yeah, sure." He started punching buttons. "Where to?"

"Short hop out to the edge of the system, then double back across it. From there we head out." I frowned and thought for a second. "Get us into the Quence Sector, Elshandruu Pica. I have friends there."

"Okay. Courses being plotted now."

My console beeped and I saw the gangway had been retracted. "Keevy, hit the green button over there."

He looked up and punched the button that released our docking claws and retracted them. "Done."

"Good. On your right, the inertial compensation unit. For the cockpit, dial it back to .95. For the passengers, keep it at full." I glanced around. "We have to have shields here somewhere, don't we?"

Keevy smiled. "Over here, I've got them. Hey, these are Chepat Supreme Defender models. Very nice."

"I hope we don't need them." I punched the ignition switch, powering up the main drive unit, and shunted power to the repulsorlift coils. I hit the button for the ship's intercom and tried to keep my voice light. "We're on our way. Sit tight and you shouldn't feel a thing."

I hit a button on the comm unit to try to make a call for help, but a hideous screeching filled the headset's earpieces. "They're jamming the comm channels." I snapped the comm unit's jamming filter on, which killed the screech.

Keevy's eyes widened. "We can't summon help."

"Nope, we're really on our own." *Of course, if help was close enough to summon, Tavira would be out of here very fast. The fact that she's actually here means there's no rescue coming.*

Annissya came into the cockpit and strapped herself

into the jumpseat I'd been offered earlier. "Everyone is seated and braced."

"Okay." I took a moment, concentrated, then nodded. "Keevy, first heading."

"Course two two three, angle three one five."

"I copy. Power to shields."

"Shields full."

"Annissya, can you hit the scan-recorder? I want to pull in as much data as I can while we head out."

I settled my hands on the steering yoke and stared out at the *Invidious*. "Here we go."

I nudged the throttle forward and pulled back on the yoke, lifting the nose. As it came up and the *Palette* slipped away beneath us, I hit the switch to lower the wings and lock them into place. I knew that if our raising the shields had not alerted the *Invidious* to the fact that something was wrong, lowering our wings certainly would. A glance at my tactical screen showed three Trifighters breaking off a patrol and beginning to vector in on us.

The wings locked down, so I shoved the throttle to full, then pitched the ship forward into a dive.

Our comm unit crackled as the jamming faded on the emergency comm frequency. "Shuttle *Tinta Blue*, this is the *Invidious*. Stop now and we won't destroy you."

Keevy stared at me, horrified. "Shouldn't you say something to them?"

I nodded toward the comm headset at Keevy's side. "You talk to them."

"Me?"

"I'm busy here." I rolled the shuttle and pulled back on the yoke, curling us up and out away from our dive. An old Corellian corvette had moved to block our course, and filled space around us with ruby shafts of light. I saw two blue ion bolts shoot past, so I hit the etheric rudder and rolled to starboard, breaking us off the glide path we'd been on. I broke back to port again with a snaproll, pulled the nose up for a second, then jammed the yoke forward again.

This left us with the *Invidious* filling our viewscreens. The ship's heavy turbolasers turned inward, trying to shoot at us, but we'd gotten in close enough that the side-mounted guns had trouble tracking us. Better yet, the light show they created in trying to shoot us had caused the clutches to break off for a moment.

Keevy donned the headset. "This is *Tinta Blue Seven*, *Invidious*."

"Lovely," I muttered. "Gonna ask if their intentions are honorable?"

He shrugged. "Are your intentions honorable?"

"*Tinta Blue*, are you insane, or trying to commit suicide?"

Keevy frowned. "A rather tautological question, isn't it?"

The blubbered sounds of confusion from the *Invidious'* comm officer prompted me to smile. "Way to keep them guessing, Keevy."

The smile growing on his face died abruptly as an angry female voice came onto the frequency. "This is Admiral Tavira, *Tinta Blue*. We are not playing games."

I held a hand up to quiet Keevy. "Sorry, Admiral, we *are*. Catch us if you can." I punched the comm unit's power button, shutting it down, then rolled the shuttle so we skimmed along belly to belly with the *Invidious*. I yanked back on the yoke to get us pointed away from the Star Destroyer, then cranked the controls slightly to port, starting the ship in a flailing spiral that made stars into white circles before us.

When we could see them between scarlet sheets of turbolaserfire, that was.

Keevy braced himself as if the convergence of the ship's port and starboard beams were a wall we were going to slam into. "We're going to die!"

"Not even half way." I chopped the throttle back, reversed thrust for two seconds, then kicked it full again and straightened our flight. Ship's turbolasers flashed in at us and the Chepat shields crackled as some of them grazed us, but we sailed on through with our hull intact. Once past the point of convergence, I started the shuttle weaving again. "Engage the hyperdrive when we're clear, Keevy."

The young man stared at me. "How did we . . . ?"

"Later." I gave him a reassuring smile, and felt a lot of relief inside as well. I'd been treating the shuttle as I would a fighter—albeit a big, slow, wallowing monster of a fighter. Its handling reminded me of that of a Y-wing, actually, but slower and more clumsy. It wasn't an elegant craft, and was never meant to be.

The fact was, though, that it was a *big* craft with huge shield generators. Surviving a direct hit by a Star Destroyer salvo would have been impossible, but the reverse-thrust flutter there threw off the *Invidious'* gunners enough that their shots didn't all arrive at the same time. We lost a lot of shield power, but they didn't collapse, so we got away. While big and slow, the one advantage the shuttle had over a fighter was its ability to survive damage.

Keevy threw the hyperdrive lever and the stars lengthened into a tunnel for a couple of seconds, then snapped back to pinpoints as we reverted to realspace. "New heading is Course one three seven, angle zero four five."

"I copy." I pulled back on the yoke and brought the

ship around to starboard. I glanced at my tactical screen. "We're clear and good to go. Keevy, if you will do the honors."

Keevy threw the lever again and we were off. At the far side of the system we made another course correction, then settled in for the journey to Elshandruu Pica. I'd been there once before, back when the squadron was off on its own, fighting Ysanne Isard for control of the bacta cartel. Keevy, with his interest in Rogue Squadron, knew all about Elshandruu Pica, and regaled Annissya and me with the story of Rogue Squadron's adventure there.

His recounting of the story actually took longer than the whole operation, but we had time to kill. And by the end of it, of course, Annissya wanted to kill poor Keevy.

We reverted to realspace and I set us on a course for the *Errant Venture*. I had gambled on its being here and was happy to see it in-system. Kina Margath owns a resort complex on Elshandruu Pica and is a connoisseur of all things fine and exotic, which means Booster finds her almost as charming as the money she pays him. The 27th Hour Club at her resort has a standing challenge to patrons to name a drink the staff cannot mix, and if they can, the patron's bar tab is on the house. Booster regularly supplies her with recipes of new drinks and the liquor used to make them up. I also think Booster has a thing for Kina, but Mirax thinks she's too young for her father, so I don't bring that subject up very often.

During Keevy's long recitation of the Elshandruu Pica mission, I keyed in and prepared to shoot to the *Errant Venture* a report on why we were there and what I wanted out of Booster. I shot it off as we made a slow approach, waited about fifteen minutes for Booster to have read it and set preparations in motion, and then called in for permission to dock on the *Venture*.

The *Tinta Blue* obtained immediate clearance to land and I set the shuttle down within a hundred meters of the Headhunter. Booster himself emerged from his office, resplendent in some very flashy and stylish, though hideously bright, clothes. He greeted each of the passengers warmly himself, promising them the finest of accommodations after their frightful ordeal. He had some of his people take the passengers immediately up to the Diamond Level, and Annissya with them, leaving Keevy and me at the shuttle.

Booster introduced himself to Keevy and the younger man's eyes lit up. "You're Corran Horn's father-in-law!"

"He's married to my daughter, yes." Booster managed to keep a smile on his face. "I have a report from Idanian here that you know your way around astronavigational equipment. Is that true?"

Keevy blinked once, then nodded. "A ship like this uses the Seinar Starpath system, doesn't it?"

"It does indeed." Booster smiled in my direction. "He's a genius, clearly."

"I thought you might think so." I patted Keevy on the shoulder. "Got us out of a nasty scrape with the Invids. I was thinking, if the Tinta Line does not offer him a job, you might have work for him here."

"Here, on the *Errant Venture*?! Me? Here? On this ship that won the battle of Thyferra?" Keevy clung by his fingertips to his lower lip. "That wouldn't be possible, would it? I mean, this ship's history and its history with Rogue Squadron, and all the things you've done with it since then, this would be like being in a museum or a fantasy or both, a fantasy museum.''

Booster's eyes narrowed, but he kept the smile on his face. ''We shall talk about this, but for now, Keevy, you are my guest. Hassla'tak, conduct Keevy Spart here to our Emerald Suite.''

Hassla'tak, a Twi'lek whose lekku were twitching like needle-stuck snakes, waved Keevy toward the turbolifts. I heard Keevy begin to pepper him with questions, but the Twi'lek just answered in his own tongue.

Booster winced. ''Haven't heard Hassla'tak use that kind of language since the last Sullustan gambling junket came through.''

''Keevy can be a bit much. Thanks for not letting him know who I am.''

''You owe me.''

''Put it on my tab.'' I jerked a thumb back at the shuttle. ''I need your people to pull the scanner memory and see if any of the Invid ships can tip us to where they're hiding.''

''I'll have it done, first thing.'' Booster regarded me carefully. ''Mara Jade is here. She and Calrissian arrived asking questions about Jorj Car'das. Lando is up on the Diamond Level attempting to break the bank.'' Irritation underscored his words.

''How close is he?''

Booster shrugged. ''Not very, but closer than I'd like. I think, though, I will introduce him to your friend Keevy.''

''Sure, just tell Keevy this is his chance to get Lando's perspective on having helped Wedge Antilles blow the Death Star at Endor.''

''Oooh, even your father wasn't that cruel, CorSec.''

''You bring the best out in me, Booster.'' I glanced

over at the Headhunter. "Is Mara angry about her ship?"

"Doesn't seem to be, but she does want to speak with you. She seemed to know you were on this shuttle before you sent word." His eyes narrowed. "She couldn't be using Jedi stuff to help Lando win, could she?"

"Frankly, I think she'd like to buy Lando for what she thinks he's worth and sell him for what *he* thinks he's worth." I smiled. "I don't think she's helping him."

Beyond Booster I saw a turbolift open and Mara Jade emerge from it. She headed straight for the two of us with just a hint of stiffness in her gait. That didn't strike me as odd about her, but her selection of clothes did seem inappropriate. The black slacks and copper tunic seemed a bit mannish, though the way she wore the short black cape slung so it covered the right side of her torso only did seem rather fashionable. I didn't see her lightsaber in evidence, but it could easily have been concealed beneath the cape.

Booster bowed. "I shall leave the two of you to talk while I see to Calrissian's comfort."

Mara growled. "Don't concern yourself *that much* with it."

I arched an eyebrow at her. "Aren't you in some sort of business with him?"

"Some sort, yes." She gave me a disgusted look and plucked at her clothes. "We arrive here and he offers to get me more suitable attire, carting away what little of a wardrobe I already have. The tailor here sent up to my suite a whole rack of gowns and other things Lando *wishes* I'd wear around him. I retaliated by raiding his clothes closet. He's got good taste in fabric, but the tunics are a bit tight in the shoulders for me."

I laughed. "I bet he loves that."

"He doesn't, which is why I'll keep borrowing his stuff from time to time." The slight hint of a smile on her face slowly died. "How was Luke when you left the academy?"

I shrugged. "Physically he's recovered from his ordeal."

Mara gave me a sidelong glance. "Mentally?"

"He's got questions, some of which he knows he has, some which he doesn't." I folded my arms across my chest. "He was pleased that you checked to make certain he was going to be all right before you left Yavin 4; but he was confused that you didn't stay until he was up and about again. You actually spent more time with me during my recovery than you did with him."

Her head came up. "He doesn't think there's something between you and me, does he?"

"I saw no indication of that being the case." I smiled and started walking over to the Headhunter. "He knows the two of us and knows it would never work between us. You and I, we can be comrades in arms and even friends."

"Right, but inside we're coiled springs that are wound in the opposite directions." Her smile struggled back onto her face as she fell into step with me. "If we got close, it'd be an awful mess."

I nodded. "And we'd end up broken."

"And then your wife would kill us."

"Another good point." I shivered. "Back to your question, though: Luke is enthused about the academy and how well the students did in defeating Exar Kun. When I left, though, I did kind of give him a turbolaser critique of the school and, well, *everything*, I guess."

"Everything?"

I frowned and leaned against the Headhunter's forward landing gear. "Luke suggested that if I left the academy when I did, I'd be making a huge mistake and that I'd fall prey to the dark side. I pretty much let him have it, pointing out that I've been to the dark side and walked away plenty of times before. I think Luke worked so hard to win his father back, and then found himself won back by his sister's love that his perspective on the dark side is skewed."

She watched me very closely. "What do you mean?"

I opened my arms. "Let's suppose Jedi are like everyone else except in their Force sensitivity. If they are, then there are going to be some folks who pretty much are born to the dark side and that's where they stay. They like it there and they never learn there is another place to go. Let's say this is ten percent of the population. Then there is another ten percent at the other end of the spectrum who start on the good side of things and just never head over toward the bad side.

"The rest of us fall into the middle. Given the right stimulus, we could go over to the dark side, but the lure is going to have to be more substantial for some than for others. Luke went over to save the galaxy. I can imagine Darth Vader did the same thing. Both of them came back. The fact that Luke paid a high price for going over and coming back means that he feels everyone is as vulnerable as he was; and he worries a lot about that."

I shrugged. "Dealing with the dark side *has* been a big part of his life, especially his life as a Jedi. Of course it concerns him. Even so, to suggest everyone will make a journey to the dark side isn't clear thinking."

"I understand what you're saying." Mara nodded and reached up, tugging one of the monster claws from the

Headhunter's nose. "Remind me never to lend you anything else."

"The beastie that left that in the ship was thinking of making a snack of Luke." I scratched at my beard. "Do you think he makes too much of the dark side?"

"Having seen the Emperor work, I'm not sure one can overemphasize the dangers of the dark side." Mara ran her thumb along the smooth top of the claw. "I think Luke may be looking for evil to be more profound than it is. You've seen it. Evil can be pretty plain."

"True enough. Some may have a talent for it, but you don't have to be talented to wallow in it." I glanced down. "Your thinking along these lines is not that far off my own. That was just part of why I left, however. I also couldn't stay with Kyp being heralded as a Jedi Knight while having avoided, in my mind, punishment for Carida and the other system he destroyed. I know that his going after unreconstructed Imperials is popular in some circles, but murder is murder in my memory cache."

Mara's face became impassive. "Is that problem going to be one you can resolve?"

I shrugged. "I don't know. Maybe Carida expatriates will set up a judgment tribunal and render a verdict. I don't feel justice has been done here, but to tell the truth, I'm not sure what justice would be in such a case. That's all in the future, however."

"So the real reason you left the academy was to go after Mirax?"

I nodded. "I had things to figure out and directions to travel to get me closer to her. On the way I visited Corellia, and I've got some data for you on that Jorj Car'das guy you asked about during my Bacta dip. It's all of CorSec's old files on him, if that will help."

"Certainly can't hurt." She gave me a quick nod.

"I've heard nothing new about Mirax, and the situation on Nal Hutta has changed."

"I know, but at least I have a place to start." I gave her as confident a smile as I could muster. "I may still be looking for a quark in a mole of deuterium, but I'm narrowing the area I have to search in and right now that's solid progress. I'll get there; I'll find her. No *try*, just *do*."

THIRTY-THREE

The positively jubilant expression on Booster's face reminded me of previously painful situations where he'd managed to find a way to embarrass me in front of my wife. Since there were no other witnesses in his office, however, I suspected that look of malevolent glee was reserved for someone else. He waved me in toward his desk. "Come on, I have something here."

As I approached, he hit a button on the small datapad on which he worked, and a holoprojector popped up the image of a Corellian Corvette. "This image comes from the data you pulled in when taking the *Tinta Blue Seven* out of the ambush. The Identify Friend/Foe transponder tagged this ship *Captain's Ladder.*"

I nodded. "I'm with you so far, but I have to note, that particular IFF signal was undoubtedly used for that run alone."

"Why don't you just tell a Hutt how to smuggle spice?" Booster looked up at me through the hologram, his real eye rolling toward the ceiling. "Son, I was swapping out IFF transponders on ships before your father even thought about having kids. As you know, IFF isn't the only way to identify a ship. The readings you got here were good enough that my people managed a spectral analysis of the ship's sublight ion exhaust. If you get a good reading, and these were very good, you can get a fairly unique analysis for the ship, and that can be matched against other ships' data to pick out a match.''

"And you found one?''

Booster nodded and hit another button on his datapad. Another image of the corvette appeared beside the first, with both of them slowly rotating to show off every detail. "It's the *Backstab*.''

I closed my eyes for a second. "The name's familiar but I can't place it.''

"The Eyttyrmin Batiiv pirates operating out of the Khuiumin system owned her. They got busted up in an Imperial operation—fewer than three hundred out of the eight thousand pirates in the gang survived the Imp strike. Jacob Nive, the *Backstab*'s captain, became the leader by default. The Survivors, as they call themselves, went merc for a bit, striking at Imps, but with the death of the Emperor they've reverted to their pirate ways and the discipline Nive instituted has slackened. They are part of the Invids and have provided Tavira with some of her best clutch pilots.''

I stroked my goatee. "Anyone surviving the band's slaughter had to be a hot hand. I can see why Tavira is happy to have allied with them. Any idea where they are?''

"I have a very good one. The Khuiumin system was too dangerous for them after the Imps hit them, so they were basing themselves near their employers. Now, with Nal Hutta proving to be a place where some Invids are *known* to ship from, Nive and his people have gone back to Khuiumin, basing themselves on the fourth planet again. A number of other ships and crews have gone there, too, which leads me to believe it is the new Invid base.''

I leaned on the back of the chair by Booster's desk. ''Most people deserted the world after the Imps broke the pirates, right?''

''Sure, all except those who couldn't afford passage or couldn't afford to be spotted on a more civilized world. With the pirates' return, the folks required to supply goods and services are flowing back there.'' Booster smiled. ''I figure we cruise in, threaten to vape a city, and get them to produce Mirax.''

I frowned. ''You aren't serious?''

''Corran, the Eyttyrmin Batiiv pirate company died when two Imp *Victory*-class Destroyers hammered them. This is an Impstar Deuce. The Survivors'll cave.''

''I don't think that's the plan we want to use, Booster.'' I shook my head slowly. ''I don't think they know where Mirax is, but I do think they're a spacelane for getting there.''

Booster sat back, putting his big booted feet up on his desk. ''So, you think you'll just meander on in there, ask some questions, get some answers and leave again? I don't believe it—no way your father could have had a kid who is so dumb.''

I suppressed a growl. ''First off, I'm not and he didn't. Second, I don't lecture you on IFF transponders, you don't lecture me on infiltrating a criminal organization.''

Booster held his hands up. ''I'll grant you that you've got experience in hutting your way in where you aren't wanted, but these pirates aren't dewback-drivers. They're hard and nasty and have all their bytes in the right place and locked down tight. I don't know if they can outfly you, but most of them probably have as many combat hours as you do. They're close to the top of the Invid food chain, so walking in there will be tough.''

''Then I'll just have to be tougher.'' I straightened up and gave him a wink. ''Don't worry, Booster, I know how to soften them up. I'll just bring Jacob Nive a big welcoming present and he should be happy to see me.''

The fourth planet in the Khuiumin system was called Courkrus for reasons known only to those who had settled it a long time ago. The largest city, Vlarnya, toward which I flew, looked like the morning after of a party that had been interrupted by a sandstorm. The world itself was not entirely arid, though the section where Vlarnya had been located really was. Irrigation and modern agricultural techniques had allowed farms to spring up in the area, but once the pirates left and the economy collapsed, the area had largely reverted to being a dustbowl.

Still, it was the dustbowl that had spaceport facilities, so that was where I headed. I didn't bother to comm down for landing permits or berthing rights; I just did a flyby, picked a docking bay and settled down into it. This seemed to alarm some individuals, but since that was the purpose of the exercise, I was pleased with the effect. I shut the *Tinta Blue*'s main drive down, opened the gangway, then wandered out of the cockpit and settled into the Premier cabin. I helped myself to a lominale, sat back and watched the local holochannels on the entertainment monitor.

Booster and I had discussed how the theft of the shuttle should be handled. I felt bad about taking it, but sending a message to Siolle to explain could have resulted in the search for it being called off. If the Survivors learned that the shuttle hadn't been stolen, my cover would collapse. We settled on Booster getting word to my grandfather about what had happened, then my grandfather would decide how to proceed from there.

It didn't take that long for several of the Survivors to storm the ship with blasters drawn. I gave them a smile, raised my ale toward them, then drained my glass. They didn't seem to find this as amusing as I did, so they hauled me out of the shuttle and through the streets to a building that, despite the collapse of the east wing, looked impressive enough to have once been very important. They took me up some stairs and around to a grand office, where I was unceremoniously plunked down in a chair and my identification card was tossed onto a big desk.

All but two of my escorts retreated to the door, leaving me alone with two men and a woman. The first man I recognized from files as Jacob Nive. Tall and well built, with long blond hair gathered into a thick braid, he looked very much the sort of dashing, handsome holograph of a pirate presented in entertainment media. As close as I was I could see the dirt under his fingernails and the light scars on his face from battles past, but I still found the bright eyed man somehow engaging. I'd seen his type before and knew he could be quite charming.

Next to him stood a woman about as tall as Lando Calrissian and much darker complected. She wore her black hair very closely cropped and had sharp dark eyes. I didn't find her hard at all to look at save that her right hand appeared to be a mechanical construct over which she wore no synthetic flesh. Its clicks as she worked a triangular credit coin back and forth between her fingers underscored her impatience.

The third person seemed to a reservoir for any impatience she could not burn off with her nervous habit. Taller than even Nive—making him a good head taller than me and probably thirty percent heavier—this guy was handsome and, worse, had no doubt about it at all. His black hair had been cut to a middling length and was so dark that it almost appeared blue—though a shade of blue much darker than the icy hue of his eyes. He wore a moustache and goatee, and had grown his moustaches out like wings that swept back along his cheeks.

Nive looked at me, shooting the cuffs of his jacket. All three of them wore what had once been the uniform of the Khuiumin Survivors—grey jackets with red cuffs, collars and breasts, gold trim around the cuffs and down the seams of the grey pants—but their clothes had seen much better days. Repairs had been made with big, obvious stitching in gold, as if to mark the scars on the body beneath the clothes. Given the amount of it on Nive's jacket I was surprised he was still standing, and the stitchery circle around the woman's right elbow suggested how high her prosthesis went.

The pirate leader slipped my ID datacard into the datapad on his desk, read for a moment, then looked up. "You are foolish or suicidal, Jenos Idanian, coming here in that shuttle."

"No, just incredibly bold." I settled an easy smile on my face and crossed my legs, as if the pirates were in my office and not the other way around. "Your people went to certain lengths to get the shuttle, and I decided to deliver it."

The dark man laughed. "And you think we will thank you for this?"

After a split second read of the other twos' reactions to his speaking, I spitted him with a cold stare. "First, I don't believe that *you*, in particular, *think* at all." I deliberately looked back at Nive. "I would apologize for the inconvenience I caused you, but the fact is that you caused me a greater inconvenience first. I needed to be well away from certain people, and your operation would have prevented my getting away. I could not let that happen, so I took the shuttle and escaped you."

Nive's expression tightened. "What happened to the two men who were supposed to be on board the shuttle?"

"The smaller one is dead. He pulled a blaster on me and I was constrained to kill him. The bigger guy is with friends of mine. If I don't report in on a timely basis, he will be killed." I opened my hands. "You see, I'm not so foolish as you might think, or as *your pal here*, in his feeble dreams, might wish."

Nive raised a hand and cut off his subordinate's protest. "And why did you bring us the shuttle?"

I sat forward in the chair. "Your operation impressed me. I've seen the newsnet stories about the raid—the shuttle's escape wasn't even mentioned. You successfully looted the *Palette* and *Rainbow*, and the New Republic did nothing, or could do nothing, to stop you. I was on the *Palette* with those people, so I know what sort of wealth you pulled out of them. An organization that can run such a big operation so smoothly has my admiration. It also can use my aid."

The dark man couldn't contain himself. "Your *aid*? Ha! We are Khuiumin Survivors. We are the backbone of the Invid force. What in the Emperor's Black Heart makes you think we need you?"

I gave him a smile that was all teeth and in no way pleasant. "I outflew *you*, didn't I?"

That brought a more conventional smile to the faces

of Nive and the woman. She continued to work the coin through her fingers, though the pace had picked up. "You thought you would offer your services to us? As what?"

"A pilot. The datacard there will confirm I can pretty much fly anything you need flown. I've not driven one of the Tri-fighters yet, but I can learn fast."

She shook her head. "I don't have a vacancy in my squadron."

"Make one." I jerked a thumb at the big guy. "I can take junior's place."

"In your dreams."

"My dreams, your nightmare."

Nive laughed warmly, shattering the chill growing between the two of us. "Not quite how we do things here, Idanian. Captain Tyresi Gurtt here leads our elite squadron, Bolt Squadron. Members are elected to it based on performance when there is a vacancy. Lieutenant Remart Sasyru here has just been elected to fill the one vacancy in the squadron. Our Tri-fighter Wing does have five other squadrons, and there are vacancies in them. Perhaps, Remart, Rock Squadron would like to have him."

"One more loser won't hurt them."

I again turned a smile loose on Remart. "I'm going to enjoy vaping your butt."

"No!" Nive's voice took on an icy edge. "The one thing you better understand about the Survivors, Idanian, is this: we do not prey upon ourselves. Anyone who flies against or kills another pilot is brought up on charges, tried and executed. We aren't murderers like the Imperials. We are hard, yes, but we don't fear those who are part of us."

"I copy." I glanced at Remart and knew I'd still watch my back. "You'll want to check my records and get me tested on a Tri-fighter, but you'll find I'm a hot hand on a stick.''

"That could be." Nive raised a hand and I heard the safety catches on blasters behind me being slipped off. "First thing I have to know, though, is how you found us."

"Sensor data let me identify the *Backstab* by its exhaust signature. A few more inquiries suggested the Survivors were returning here from Nal Hutta." I shrugged. "Information about your relocation might not have been widespread, but it wasn't impossible to find, either. I was owed some favors so I used them. As it is, only the scanner records in the shuttle can tie you to that raid, and now you have them."

Nive smiled. "Except for the copy you left with the people you have holding Biril."

"Now that you mention it." I nodded. "I'm not a stupid man."

"I hope not." Jacob Nive offered me his hand. "If you are, coming here is likely the most stupid thing you have ever done. The good thing about that is that it's also likely the *last* stupid thing you will ever do."

THIRTY-FOUR

The Survivors might well have been the best of the Invids, but that wasn't saying much in the overall scheme of things. The denizens of Rock Squadron all struck me as what Rogue Squadron would have been had we lost to the Empire and spent our time dirtside in seedy towns, waiting for a chance to plunder pitiful folks who were worse off than we were. I'd been around more sullen and depressing people, but they were prisoners on the *Lusankya*, with little hope of survival or rescue.

Everyone grumbled and grunted when I was taken out to the hotel where the squadron was billeted and introduced. Nakk Kech, Rock's leader, pointed me to a room in the hotel that had been well-used before me. The curtains had been drawn tight, and I didn't mind that at all because I really didn't want a good look at the room itself. A wadded pile of bedclothes in the corner appeared to be where the previous occupant had laired and, if the stench from the refresher station was any indication, the previous occupant understood the room's purpose, but hadn't gotten the hang of indoor plumbing.

Kech watched me closely, prepared to judge me by my reaction to the room. The stubble on Kech's face bristled brown and gray, just like the thinning hair on his head. "It's the best we got."

I shook my head. "It's the best you've got available."

Kech smiled. "Yeah, that's it."

"And that's not good enough." I walked down the hall and pounded on the next door. "Open up."

A Shistavanen Wolfwoman tore the door open and snarled at me. She had white fur and pink eyes and though a bit smaller than the other Shistavanens I'd met, she'd have ripped me to pieces in seconds. As she tore the door open, I also caught a whiff of her room and learned who had been living in that first room.

I flashed her a big smile. "I'm your neighbor. Nice to meet you."

Kech's booming laughter drowned out the Shistavanen's harshly whispered response. I nodded at the albino. "Later."

Kech shook his head, his brown eyes full of mirth. "Caet Shrovl will be your wingman. She's good, specially in void-fights. Doesn't favor a lot of light."

I pointed at the next door. "Better choice?"

Kech shook his head. "Actually, I'm your best choice."

I frowned at him. "You think I should take your room away from you?"

The older man smiled slowly. "You could try and you might succeed, but that would be insubordination and assaulting a superior officer, which is a capital offense with the Invids. You wouldn't live to reap the benefits of your station. Your best bet is to toss a few bits to some locals and have them clean that other room out for you."

"Think so?"

"I figure you want to prove you're tough by kicking someone around, but I don't run the squadron that way.

You kick someone's butt, take his room, he gets angry with you, causes discord in the unit, and someone has to be gotten rid of.'' Kech folded his arms across his chest. ''You want to prove you're tough, knock someone from one of the other squadrons around; or, better yet, someone from one of the other Invid companies here. In the Survivors, the only thing that counts is your flying skill.''

I opened my arms wide. ''Fine, let's get to flying, then.''

Kech nodded. ''Thought you'd never ask. I'll get someone to clean your room up while we're out at the training center.''

''How much?''

He shrugged. ''Let's see how good you are. If you're good enough that I want you rested to save my hide, I might even cover it for you.''

The Survivors didn't have the sort of state-of-the-art training facility I was used to working in. Kech and I piled into a landspeeder that took us out to an annex at the spaceport. He drove straight into the hangar and brought the dusty red vehicle to a stop beside two beat-up Tri-fighters. All battered and scraped, close up they looked like giant versions of a child's toy—one that had seen a lot of rough play.

Kech plucked a helmet from a wall rack and tossed it to me. ''You take number one and I'll take deuce. Comlink is built into the helmet. Listen to what I tell you to do and then do it. You've flown a TIE before, right?''

I nodded. It was in simulation, but I figured that was close enough for this kind of stuff. ''Weapons?''

''Powered down targeting stuff. You figure you want to go at it a bit, I'll light you up just fine.''

I hauled myself up on the craft's ball cockpit and slid into it. The third fin barely allowed the hatch to open and made it kind of tough to get into the ship, but I managed anyway. Standing on the pilot's seat, I secured the top hatch, then dropped down and pulled on my helmet. I strapped myself into the chair and began to familiarize myself with the cockpit and controls.

First thing I noticed was how roomy the cockpit seemed compared to that of a Headhunter or X-wing. The pod's spherical shape meant, naturally, there would be spare room. The spherical shape also meant it had no nose, per se, which took a lot of getting used to. I felt as if I were strapped to an engine for my flights.

The TIE's steering yoke had been replaced with a stick that had a trigger, a targeting control knob, and a multi-position switch for shifting between weapons systems. The grip felt molded for my hand, and the stick itself had good but restricted play. I didn't think the craft would fly like an X-wing, but the controls would feel similar and that was a plus.

The huge cockpit windscreen and peripheral panels provided a very good field of vision. The primary sensory monitor and two secondary monitors sat on a bar bisecting the windscreen disk, but really didn't interfere with what I could see. Throttle was on the left, though it operated by twisting a handle instead of pushing a stick forward. A smaller handle similarly constructed controlled the repulsorlift coils. The comm panel was also on the left, allowing me to access it without pulling my right hand off the stick. Shield controls were still on the right, however, which could make for some difficult decisions in the heat of combat. Etheric rudder pedals were down below the monitors.

I clipped the lead from my helmet into the comm panel socket. "Idanian here."

"Kech here. Lower right is your ignition sequence panel. Once all the lights are green, you are good to go. Head out on ten percent power, bearing zero two six, and wait for me."

"I copy." I reached down and flicked all the switches, then waited for the system lights to cycle through red and yellow before going green. Once that happened, all the monitors sprang to life. I fed power into the repulsorlift coils and kept a steady hand on the stick. I twisted the throttle up to ten percent power and guided the clutch forward until it broke out onto the ferrocrete expanse in front of the hangar. Once there, I tried out the rudder pedals and found the ship moved pretty well to the right and left. It might not have been as maneuverable as the *Interceptor*, but had the X-wing beat to stardust in that category.

Kech brought his clutch out and raced it past mine, pulled the front up and jetted upward on a column of ion exhaust. "It's not a landspeeder, Idanian. We're pilots, not drivers. Get some atmosphere below you."

I smiled and hit the throttle. "As ordered, Rock Lead."

I made my ascent more gradual, working upward in a spiral that let me assess power and maneuvering as I went. The Tri-fighter, when compared to an X-wing, really didn't come off that badly. Sensor range seemed a bit light, but without proton torpedoes or concussion missiles, the need to hit at extreme range vanished. The ship's rolls were a bit sluggish, but the climb rate was good and dive rate was impressive.

Above all, though, the craft's agility impressed me. The rudder response allowed for quick shifts in which way the bow pointed. More importantly, the throttle and repulsorlift levers functioned in multiple ways. With the throttle, pulling back on it would, in essence, shift the craft into neutral, killing thrust. The button on top of the lever would reverse thrust, so when it was lowered back down again, the engines would be blowing backward. With this quick cut-out method of working, a maneuver like a reverse throttle hop wouldn't require chopping thrust back and pushing it up again, but just taking it offline. Likewise the repulsorlift coils could be left with a power setting in place, but pulled offline until needed. Crank back the throttle, cut in the coils, and the clutch could dance.

Clearly the Invids I'd faced before were not the best available.

Kech wasn't bad, and I showed him that I was no nerfherder, either. After ·he guided me through the basics, we played some tag. He got the better of me by a narrow margin, but what seemed to impress him was that the score was so low. "You're not easy to hit, you know, Idanian."

"I copy, Lead." I laughed aloud as we came in on our return approach to the training facility. "Promotes longevity."

"It's good you think that way—we've got a mission."

"A mission?" I coughed lightly and, raising my hand reflexively, bounced it off the helmet's faceplate. "I've logged, what, all of an hour on this beast?"

"Better than some of the pilots with the *Red Nova* crew. They ran into Rogue Squadron a couple of months back and got hammered pretty damned hard." I heard a low chuckle. "Don't worry, we won't be doing anything like that this time out. Just a simple loot-n-scoot."

I cut my throttle out and brought the repulsorlift coils online as we neared the hangar. "The *Invidious* going to be with us?"

"Nope, this is personal business." Kech laughed harshly. "Won't be that lucrative, but will feel very good."

The mission, it turned out, had its roots in the Imperial assault on the Eyttyrmin Batiiv pirates—the attack that reduced them to the sorry company known as the Khuiumin Survivors. The Imperial *Victory*-class Destroyers *Bombard* and *Crusader* had killed over ninety-seven percent of the pirates, leaving them with the *Backstab* and a handful of fighters. The Survivors had sworn they would avenge themselves on the captains of those two Destroyers, and one, Captain Zlece Oonaar, had obtained passage on the *Galaxy Chance*. Someone on *Chance* had decided that selling Oonaar out was a better bet than anything being offered in the onboard casino, and word got to Nive.

The *Chance* was a Corellian corvette that a rival of Booster's had outfitted as a miniature version of the *Errant Venture*. I think Booster would have ignored *Chance* except for one thing: the owner had painted it bright red. Booster had wanted to do that with the *Errant Venture*, but nowhere in the galaxy could he find enough red paint to do the job. In fact, the only color available in sufficient quantity at reasonable prices was Star Destroyer White—a fact that Booster considered proof that the Emperor had been out to annoy him personally all along.

To describe the briefing we got before heading out as

marginal is to code up a new definition for the word. I got slapped into third flight, with Caet and two other females, both human. I got the designation "Rock Nine" purely by chance, but that was good since I would answer to it almost reflexively. Our flight was given the task of flying cover while the other two Rock flights neutralized *Chance*'s weaponry and eliminated the four Uglies—TIE-wings, it was speculated. *Backstab* would carry us to the site, and a Skipray blastboat would go over and pluck Oonaar from the *Chance*. The other flights got the shot at *Chance* because they were all true Survivors, not just folks who had joined later like me.

It struck me that a mission of such importance would have been a natural for Bolt Squadron, but I was informed that Nive had drawn a squadron for the honor at random. I had no doubt Remart was regretting his shift to Bolt Squadron. I got the impression that none of the other pilots in Rock Squadron were sorry to see him gone, and more than a few thought his discomfort at being left out was rather delicious.

We got shuttled up to the *Backstab* and went EV to get into our fighters. Like TIE-fighters, the Tri-fighters had no atmosphere or life support equipment, requiring us to carry our own. This made going EV and crawling up over the hull to get into our ships less difficult than if X-wing pilots were to try it. I made it in, secured my hatch, powered up and checked in. Others did likewise, but in no way was there very much comm discipline called for or observed.

The *Backstab* went to lightspeed, made one interim jump, and then headed off toward where the *Chance* was supposed to be. Our trip took a full three hours and, for the first time, I really appreciated the extra room in the cockpit. I would have appreciated even more having atmosphere in there, so I could remove my helmet, have something to eat and maybe catch a nap. While the cockpit did afford me excellent visibility, there isn't that much to see in hyperspace.

On that flight I realized how much I actually missed Whistler. I know people aren't supposed to get sentimental about astromech droids, but I'd had him for years. He used to get the usual memory wipes and programming upgrades back then, but I think he found a way to download chunks of his personality into the Cor-Sec mainframe and recover it later. Whistler was sneaky and independently-minded that way, which was good for me. If not for him I'd have been dead a dozen times over.

On long flights Whistler and I would discuss various things—like fatherhood—and I could count on him as being a good sounding board. Actually, he was very much a mirror in the sense of my father's old saying. When I started getting out of line, Whistler would call me on it and, more times than not, he was right. Of those few times he was not, well, I'm sure there were times when he was not right.

The *Backstab* reverted to realspace right on top of *Chance*. Flights one and two deployed, taking slashing runs at the corvette. Rock Four exploded when she caught a direct hit from one of the ship's double turbo-laser cannons. The green energy bolts just peeled the cockpit back like the petals of a flower bud, shredding it and casting long jagged tendrils of armor into space. The clutch's ion engine exploded, letting the craft's three fins spin away through space. The rest of the *Chance*'s cannons filled space with a lot of energy, but Rock Four was the only thing *Chance*'s gunners hit before we slagged their guns.

The six TIE-wing fighters flying sentry duty around *Chance* should have run as soon as we arrived. The TIE-wing consists of a TIE fighter ball cockpit married to the engine nacelles from a Y-wing fighter. It truly lives up to the name Ugly, and in Rogue Squadron we used to refer to them as "Die-wings." Sluggish and ungainly, they looked like wildernerfs being hit by a pride of taopari. All six lasted no more than five minutes. I found watching the dogfight frustrating because my squadron-mates missed shots that should have ended it all much sooner, and two of them paid for their lousy marksmanship with their lives.

The Skipray that had come with us, *Vibroblade*, started over toward *Chance* when another ship—a private yacht—entered the system on our entry vector. That wasn't a surprise—I didn't know where we were, but there were enough planetary bodies in the area that routes in and out had to be severely limited. What was a surprise was the half-dozen, hyperdrive-fitted Headhunters flying cover for the yacht. They clearly didn't like seeing us there, so while the yacht came about and headed away again, the Headhunters came in on us hard with enough triple-blasters blazing.

I didn't wait for an order releasing me. "Ten, on me," I snapped through the comm and engaged my throttle. The clutch lurched forward. I rolled and dove toward the Headhunters and two came up at me. With my thumb I flicked the weapon selector over to ion cannon, hit a little rudder to flash the incoming pilots my flank, then straightened the clutch out and pulled the trigger.

The blue ion bolt nailed the lead Headhunter's left S-foil. Azure lightning played across the forward shield, boiling it away. The shield didn't collapse, but the light-

ning storm on the shield made it tough for the pilot to
see me. His return shots went wide on either side, then
we were past each other before he could get another
shot.

Caet shot at the second Headhunter. Her twin laser
blasts caught the Headhunter on the nose, piercing the
shield and causing a brief flash of light. Even without
Whistler present to let me know what happened, I knew
from the location that the Headhunter had lost its combat
sensor package. The pilot would be blind in space and,
in a dogfight situation, that meant he was as good as
dead.

I snapped a quick shot off at another Headhunter, then
popped my throttle off and pulled back on the stick. I cut
the throttle to half, re-engaged it to complete the half-
loop, then ran it up again and rolled out to port. That
dropped me on the tail of one of the Headhunters that
was running in on Eleven. I pumped two ion bolts into
the Headhunter's aft shield. The first shot took the aft
shield down and the second played over the length of the
ship. Sparks shot from the engine cowlings—unless the
pilot could get a restart going, he was done.

Red-gold blaster bolts lit my shields from starboard. I
hit right rudder and swung the clutch's tail out of the
Headhunter's line of attack. The next bolts streaked past
on the port side, so I rolled to starboard, dove and curled
up in a long loop. Rolling out to port I saw another
Headhunter making a run on Caet. The pilot was intent
on her, so I came in on an oblique angle and hit with my
first shot. That took his aft shield down, so he rolled
starboard to get away from me. I applied a lot of left
rudder, swung my nose around and laced his port S-foil
with another bolt.

His blaster on that side exploded and the ship started

to roll, which told me vector jets on that side were also having trouble. I rolled to starboard and would have swooped in to finish him, but a glance at my tactical sensor screen showed me a Headhunter vectoring in on me, and I had a feeling that was the guy who'd tried to get me earlier. I held my roll slow and showed him my belly, then yanked back on my stick and started a dive. He rolled to set himself up to come after me and I knew I had him.

I cranked my throttle down to thirty percent, then reversed it, killing my momentum. I let it hang there for three seconds, then dialed thrust back up. As I did so, my Headhunter friend went streaking by me, and I dropped into his exhaust. My first shot nailed his rear shield. He broke right, so I climbed, inverted and ruddered my way back onto his tail.

Caet raced past and pumped two laser blasts into him. One collapsed the aft shield and the other holed his starboard S-foil. His roll slowed appreciably and became unstable as the vector jets in the damaged S-foil weren't matching the output from the other side. The pilot just goosed his throttle forward to get away, since he couldn't fly fancy any more. The Headhunter even had enough speed to outrun my clutch.

Outrunning an ion bolt, on the other hand, is a lot harder. My shot caught his ship dead on in the back. Little blue tendrils of electricity ran over the fighter like nightmare fingers, scratching out sparks and little puffs of vapor. The ship shut down immediately, continuing off on its course.

I saw Caet coming back around for another run on it, but I called her off. "Abort, Ten. He's done."

"Not dead."

"Out of the battle. Leave him." I triggered an ion

blast that passed between her fighter and the stricken ship. "You can have the kill, but there's no reason to kill a pilot just doing his job."

"Right to kill is mine." She snapped her words off as if in pain. "Do not deny me."

"You owe me. I shucked the one on your butt." I started my clutch forward, angling in on her. "He's mine and I want him alive."

I heard Nive's voice come through on the tactical frequency. "All targets are neutralized. Stand down Flight Rock Three."

"I copy," I reported.

"Copy." Caet's snarl did not have me looking forward to talking with her after the mission returned home.

"Nine, go to Tactical Two and scramble."

"As ordered, sir." I switched the comm unit over to the secondary tactical frequency and hit the scramble switch. The encryption key, which had been uploaded to each fighter from the *Backstab*, would keep the conversation private between Nive and me. "Nine here, Captain."

"Nice shooting, Nine. Why ion? You could have killed the Headhunters in one shot the way you fly, but you used ion and made it tougher." Nive let a little anger drift into his voice. "Was this a game for you?"

"No, sir." I paused for a moment, not so much to gather my thoughts as figuring out how to express them. "The Headhunter pilots were just doing their jobs. If we kill them, we're just butchers and killers and any bodyguards in the future know they should go after us full out because we're going to vape them. The yacht was gone. *Chance* can pick these guys up and next time we give them an opportunity to back off and they will."

"Maybe." Nive paused. "Makes sense, of course, but few things in warfare ever do."

"Worth taking a chance if no one dies."

Nive snorted. "You that squeamish?"

"I've got my share of deaders logged in my accounts, Captain. If I can get it without blood, I think it's better." I shook my head. "If that's not thinking that's welcome here, I can just take my shuttle and leave."

"No, no need for that." Some of the tension in Nive's voice eased. "That kind of thinking is more than welcome here. You're one of us now, Idanian, one of the Invids. Let's hope more of you rubs off on us than the other way around."

THIRTY-FIVE

Caet and I did have words on our return to Khuiumin 4—well, not words exactly, but the scars healed within two weeks and you can't notice the one on my right cheek unless I get a deep tan. Even before the physical evidence of our fight had gone away, however, Caet voted with four other of Rock Squadron's survivors to make me the leader of a new three flight. Kech helped me choose three pilots to fill it and Caet moved into first flight to replace Rock Four.

Over the next month I spent a lot of time with my new recruits, drilling them. I'd gone through the same routine countless times before with new pilots coming into Rogue Squadron, but I found Rock Squadron to be the dark side of what I had known with the Rogues. In terms of discipline, Khuiumin 4 made Yavin 4 look like *Lusankya*. Trying to instruct hungover pilots is about as tough as teaching a rancor to sing and dance—and the rancor's attitude about the whole process would probably be better. The pilots in my squad clearly thought they could fly, and while they were not bad, they weren't up to the level I wanted. I was responsible for their lives, and I had no desire to go into a fight with undertrained pilots who would die and leave me alone out there.

The best of the lot was Timmser, a tall woman who wore her hair very short and very blond. Her temper was about as short as her hair, and she initiated a couple of cantina-clearing brawls when she wandered into the Warren, which is where the *Red Nova* crew and Riistar's Raiders tended to hang out. There was little love lost between those groups and the Survivors; and Timmser's status as an ex-Raider didn't help ease the tension there. In a Tri-fighter she had a good sense of what was going on around her and had a knack for hitting on deflection shots.

Over the first months with the Survivors, I spent most of my time dirtdown in Vlarnya, which is about as thrilling as it sounds. The days got hot enough that most folks spent their time in the semi-sunken cantinas that served as informal squadron homes. The Survivors primarily hung out at the Crash cantina. The decor was rather ghoulish—pilots would bring in bits and pieces of debris from kills or from crashes they'd survived. Chunks of transparisteel or Quadanium alloy hung from the ceiling and, in the dim light, presented navigational obstacles for even folks as small as I am. Timmser actually gashed her forehead in there before she got used to negotiating the debris-maze.

I visited the Crash regularly, but tended to spend a fair amount of my free time wandering through Vlarnya. Aside from the Aviary—the indigs' name for the district where the pilots tended to reside—Vlarnya looked like pretty much any other marginal town dependent on spaceport trade for its survival. The fields outside of town grew enough fresh vegetables that the prices for them weren't wholly outrageous. Vlarnya had no native industries—cantinas and gambling establishments don't really scan that way to me—save for a local brewery that turned out a decent lomin-ale-type product. It was good enough, in fact, that all seven of the pirate crews working out of Vlarnya declared it—and the fields where it grew the things that went into the ale—a no-fly zone to reduce the chances of an aerial accident destroying it.

At night, when things began to cool off and the twin moons came up, I liked walking through the streets. Vlarnya had a small-town feel to it. While the spaceport had been built to Imperial specifications, the city itself had been crafted by local masons and workers using a lot of native material. The streets twisted and turned, snaking through narrow canyons with buildings on both sides, then opening out into small squares that had fountains in the center. The lack of a lot of municipal lighting meant most alleys were sunk in pitch blackness at night, but this was Vlarnya, so alleys weren't too dangerous, unless you were wandering through the Aviary.

Caet Shrovl occasionally joined me while I wandered. Her condition made her very sensitive to light, so if she came out during the day, she wore a cloak that completely covered her and donned goggles dark enough to turn noon into the void of space. While she was very private, I did learn that she considered her albinism the fault of the Empire, since her mother had once been used in some sort of experiment by Imperial scientists. The Survivors were known to have a strong hatred for the Empire, so she had come to them and endured life on Courkrus for the chance to shoot up Imperials.

Through her I also discovered how Remart Sasyru had been voted out of the unit and into Bolt Squadron. She and I were seated back in one of the Crash's darker corners, comparing data on our flights' performances in a series of exercises, when Remart sauntered over toward our table. He came on slow, with a deliberate gait that allows his hips and shoulders to swivel slowly. It was definitely a strut—he was there to be seen, and seen as stalking prey. He wore his grey uniform trousers, black boots and a sleeveless grey tunic that had to be about four sizes too small because it was tight enough to show off every muscle and rib he possessed.

He gave me a cold smile. "Spending time with *her*? Watch you don't get *tiqcs*."

I looked up from my ale mug. "Funny, she says she hasn't been bothered since you bolted. Coincidence? Can't be."

Remart looked at me, a bit surprised. He'd intended the jibe to sting Caet, but I'd deflected it. I could feel the anger rising in her, and traces of fear in there, too, but didn't know why. I did decide real quickly, however, that she didn't need to be provoked and that I could prevent it.

I slid my chair back noisily. "What's the matter, Sasyru? You offer a smart remark and can't handle a riposte? Or did my comment go over your head? Let me explain it, then. See, she hasn't been bothered by *vermin* since you went away from Rock Squadron. That means, in my opinion, you're a carrier of *vermin*. Does that break it down enough for you?"

Shock widened Remart's blue eyes, then he recovered himself and posted his gloved hands on his hips. He laughed aloud, filling the sound void in the room. "Trust a Corellian to lead with his mouth and to venture in where he is not wanted."

I stood. "What, no quick shot about how Corellians have no use for odds, so they don't know when they're stacked against them? No joke about the most famous Corellian being named 'Solo' because no Corellian will trust another Corellian? What other unoriginal and older-than-the-Empire slur could you have offered? Oh, yes, how about suggesting that Leia Organa took up with a Corellian because, hey, after the destruction of Alderaan, she had nothing else to lose.''

I moved out from behind the table. ''How about this one? How many Corellians does it take to change a glowpanel?'' I glanced at Timmser sitting at another table, but she shrugged. ''None! If the room's dark, you can't see Corellians cheating at sabacc!''

That brought some laughter from the surrounding tables and even Caet began to relax. ''You know why so many Corellians used to get caught and sent to Kessel?''

Remart's eyes narrowed. ''Because they were stupid?''

''No, they were lonely for the rest of their family!'' I snapped my fingers at him. ''C'mon, Remart, you gotta be quicker than that. A Corellian bought a nek as a pet, but it was so stupid it kept running into walls. What did he name it?''

The taller man shook his head.

''Remart.'' I smiled as I took a step toward him. ''He couldn't think of a stupider name.''

Because of the Force, I knew Remart's right fist was coming even before he knew he was going to throw it. I twisted slightly to my own right and brought my head around the punch didn't land with full impact. I still felt it—it worked my jaw around good—but it didn't drop me to the floor the way it should have.

I turned my head slowly back toward him and smiled. ''By the Emperor's black bones, you hit like a Chadra-Fan. No report, this time.'' I waved him away contemptuously and started back toward my table. ''Come back some other time after you learn how to throw a punch.''

I felt him coming at my back, so I turned quickly to

the right and stepped laterally toward him, directly along his line of attack. I hit him with a stiffened finger-blow square in the throat. He gurgled and staggered back, more surprised than hurt, and struggled to stay up on his feet. He backed a few more steps, then leaned heavily on a table with two other Bolt pilots seated at it.

I noted, with satisfaction, that they sidled away from him.

I pointed at him. "I gave you one punch for free. Never again. You leave me and the rest of Rock Squadron alone. You aren't part of it anymore, so what we do is of no concern to you. You say anything to my people—beyond asking permission to get your disgusting form out of their sight—and we'll have it out, you and I. You understand that?"

Without waiting for an answer, I looked at the other two Bolts at that table. "Get him out of here—I've got your tab—and tell Captain Gurtt I'll speak with her on this matter at her convenience."

I returned to my chair and pulled it back up to the table. I picked up my ale mug, drank, then kept it in front of my mouth as I glanced at Caet. "Hope you didn't find that embarrassing. I know you could have taken him."

The white Shistavanen shook her head and one of her ears rotated in my direction. "Gallant. Grateful." I noticed the fiberplast table had little curls of material where her claws had gouged parallel furrows down to the edge. "Old foe, never learned 'no.' "

I nodded and drank some more, killing the dryness in my mouth and throat. "I'm surprised you voted him into the Bolts."

"Couldn't kill him, so we got him out that way." Caet regarded me carefully. "He was a bully and animal. Kech was afraid. Remart wanted fame, money, power.

He was good pilot so didn't die. Good enough for Bolts, so we sent him.''

I lowered my mug. ''His coming back here to pick on you means the Bolts aren't putting up with his antics. Why did he come for you?''

She glanced down and a low growl rolled from her throat.

I raised my left hand. ''S'okay, I don't need to know.''

Caet stood and pulled her cloak on. ''Walk.''

''As ordered.'' I drained my ale, then walked over to Timmser and handed her a stack of mismatched coins. ''You get my tab, the Bolts' tab and one round for the Rocks, right?''

''I copy.'' Timmser gave me a quick smile. ''Nice work there, Jen.''

''Don't try to repeat it.'' I winked at her. ''And three flight *will* be at the training center at dawn, and you'll have my change.''

I followed Caet out into the cool night and we began wandering aimlessly, though the growl in my stomach told me I'd want some food soon. ''Nice night, isn't it?''

She nodded and peered off at the dueling crescent moons. ''Peace. Nice to know peace some.''

''I'd like to hope, someday, there will be more peace than war in the galaxy.''

''With that dream, you are in wrong place.'' Her lips peeled back in a grin, flashing lots of white teeth. ''No peace from Remart.''

I shrugged. ''He's sneaky and, deep down, a coward. I'm not worried about him, though.''

''He came for me because he broke me.'' Caet fell silent after that admission and I thought she'd used up her quota of words for the day. I let the silence hang between us, not pressing, because I knew she'd say nothing more. It was almost as if she were resting up after the ordeal of making so open a statement, and preparing to be battered by me for it.

A couple of blocks later, down curving hilly streets that took us well away from the Aviary, she spoke again. "Charmed me. He became friend. He sat with me in the dark. He did not draw me out like you. He worked his way in."

I frowned. "What did he want?"

"Possession. I am apart from everyone. Isolated."

"Because of your photosensitivity."

"And raising. My mother was the only Shistavanen I knew young." She hesitated, groping for words. "When we came to Uvena 3, she was home. I was in new place. My scent was not right, you understand?"

"You were different. It became easy for others to pick on you." I reached out gently and rested my left hand on her right shoulder. "You let Remart know this, and he turned it against you."

"False friend. Made demands." I could feel tension start her body trembling, but she quelled it quickly. "I rejected him. He beat me. Badly. Fear and pain. I was happy to vote him out."

I gave her shoulder a little squeeze. "Your confidence is safe with me."

"I know." She turned toward me and I saw a crescent moon reflected in her eyes. "You hide pain, secrets, too."

I blinked. "How do you know?"

"I am Shistavanen enough to read sign." Her grin returned. "You walk alone. You do not visit, seek companionship. You do not drink more than is needed to make you fit in."

I gave her a quick smile. "Quite the detective. Of what am I guilty?"

"You have lover away. You look for reunion or redemption."

That stopped me. "You're a very good tracker."

"So, I think, why are you here?" She sniffed twice, quickly. "Your lover is not an Invid."

I shook my head, wondering how close to the truth I could come without jeopardizing my entire mission. I decided I had to skirt the truth by a wide margin, but quickly built up a story that would suffice. "Her cousin controls the *Tinta* line, and has decreed that my lover cannot be with me without having her whole branch of the family cut off from the Tinta fortune. I am greasier than Hutt slime in her eyes, and considered to be after my lover's wealth alone. I want to destroy the Tintas, and I see being an Invid as the way to do it. I want them to know I am the instrument of their destruction, and I want to have their wealth in my pockets when I take my lover away from her poverty-stricken family."

Caet sniffed once more, then gave out with a sharp yip. "Fools fight for love, the wise for money."

"Thanks, I think."

"Bold plan. You will need to be True Invid to accomplish it."

I caught a whiff of something cooking from further down the street and headed toward it. "What do you mean by True Invid?"

"Crew on ship." She fell into step with me. "Two ways. Merit in combat."

"That can be done."

"Not as Rock. We are ignored. Bolts are not." A playful growl rolled from her throat. "Bolt you can become."

"I hope so. What's the other method?"

"Berth duty."

I shook my head. "I don't understand."

Caet reached out and caught my chin in her right hand. She turned my face to the left and nodded. "Minimal scar. You might do."

"Excuse me."

Another yip. "Admiral Tavira has appetite for men. You can become True Invid that way, too."

I nodded and she released my chin. Becoming a True Invid and joining the crew of the *Invidious* was the final step in locating Mirax. As a crew member I'd learn where the Impstar went between attacks. I knew, at that location, I would find Mirax. I would do what it took to get there and save her, I had no doubt in my mind.

"So, Caet, tell me," I smiled as I waved her toward the small restaurant from which the scent of food emanated, "just what do we do to make me a Bolt?"

THIRTY-SIX

✳

Caet laid out a very simple plan to boost me into the ranks of Bolt Squadron, but we ran into some unexpected complications over the next several months. The first, and most frustrating, was the paucity of challenging missions for us. While the *Invidious* made a number of forays out, the Survivors weren't always chosen to accompany Tavira's taskforce. The *Red Nova* crew, the LazerLords, the *Fastblast* crew, Riistar's Raiders, the *Blackstar* pirates and even Shala the Hutt's gang got their chances to go on missions. Rotating the forces kept them all sharp and let everyone know they were not indispensable.

Even when the Survivors were sent out, Rock Squadron didn't always go on the mission. Except when Tavira called for the Bolts specifically, Nive chose among us by lot. Rock Squadron got roughly one Invid mission per month. On our other missions we flew cover for smaller ships, much in the same way the *Red Nova*'s people had flown cover for the *Booty Full*. Rogue Squadron never jumped us, but on one of our Invid missions the *Invidious* vanished from the system shortly after arrival. We found ourselves fighting with a fighter group of Y-wings and homegrown Uglies in that engagement and lost two pilots from one flight, including Captain Kech.

If there had been New Republic capital ships waiting at the edge of the system, I saw no evidence of them, nor was there any trace in the sensor data I pulled from *Backstab*. After vanquishing the local fighters, we strafed a settlement and looted some warehouses, but even with a couple of bulging shuttles, the raid had hardly seemed worth it.

It was only later, when Rock Squadron elected me Captain, that I learned from Jacob Nive that the *Invidious* had headed out because another Invid operation had run into trouble and Tavira wanted to ambush the ambushers. The threat to us had not been dire enough to cause her to stick around, and I couldn't disagree. In the other situation three New Republic corvettes had engaged some Invid freighters and fighters, then withdrawn when the *Invidious* showed up.

It took a couple of weeks, but I learned details on that other operation. Shala's gang had been in position to take off a spice shipment in the Kessel system when the New Republic ships had appeared. They had a running lightfight for twenty minutes, during which one of Shala's freighters took damage, lost maneuvering, and sailed off to be sucked into the Maw—the big black hole near Kessel. At roughly that point in the battle, the *Invidious* arrived and drove the New Republic ships away, all but killing the *Freedom of Sullust*.

This rescue increased the fame of the *Invidious* and general sense of immortality among the crews, but it sent a chill down my spine. It struck me as unlikely that the New Republic would send three corvettes into a system where they expected to run into the *Invidious*. Three corvettes wouldn't be unusual for a patrol, especially with old Imps like Teradoc and Harssk or Admiral Daala still hyping around. My gut told me the corvettes had happened on Shala's people by accident.

That's not so terrifying, but the implication of the *Invidious* getting there in time to save Shala *was*. The flank speed time from the system where we were to Kessel was eighteen hours, and that was if the astrogator wanted to pull a Solo and skirt the fringes of the Maw. That meant that somehow Admiral Tavira knew of a chance meeting eighteen hours in advance and hustled her ship along to get her there. The fact that it would have been just as easy to open a HoloNet connection with Shala and warn him off the Kessel run meant that Tavira clearly liked the idea of a split second rescue. Her solution definitely enhanced her reputation among us, and had to have been that much more galling to the New Republic.

The question was, however, *how* did she know the trouble would be taking place eighteen hours in the future? There seemed only one answer to me: the advisor Exar Kun had showed me near her was adept in using the Force and warned her of Shala's peril. I'd sensed no overt Force usage from the *Invidious,* but I was keeping myself as shut down on missions as I'd been when approaching Exar Kun's temple, so it wasn't much of a surprise that I wasn't picking anything up.

Under my leadership, with Timmser heading up three flight and Caet in charge of two flight, Rock Squadron got good. We weren't the Bolts, but we weren't so far behind them that they should have felt complacent. I tightened up our training methods and broke pilots of bad habits. By making them better, I increased my chances of attracting Tavira's notice, and that brought me closer to finding and freeing Mirax.

The primary advantage the Bolts had over us was in the area of combat hours, but our average was quickly approaching theirs. They tended to get included in more Invid missions, which carried a lot of prestige, but the Invids' presence often stopped opposition before it started. The resulting lack of fatalities among the Bolts meant my avenue to that path effectively remained blocked.

Blocked, that was, until the Xa Fel mission. Xa Fel, a world in the Kanchen Sector, served the Kuat Drive Yards as a major manufacturer of starship hyperdrives. Grand Admiral Thrawn targeted the world for the same reason Tavira hit it: ready-made hyperdrives were a boon to anyone who could get away with them. Because of her connections within the Imperial community, Tavira could find countless warlords willing to purchase them *and* make them beholden to her at the same time. I assumed the latter reason was even more of a motivator than the former.

The seriousness of the assault was underscored by Admiral Tavira specifying Bolt, Hawk and Rock Squadrons from the Survivors, and allowing us to come up to the *Invidious* and ship aboard the Star Destroyer for the run in at the world. Corvettes and bulk cruisers accompanied us in a huge task force, with Slash Squadron covering *Backstab* and the other crews from Courkrus similarly having fighter cover. The grouping of ships was the largest task force I'd ever seen while with the Invids and underscored how serious Tavira was about staging this raid.

The three Survivor squadrons aboard the *Invidious* were each paired with one of the *Invidious'* native clutch squadrons. Their pilots and ours eyed each other suspiciously. I noticed on a couple of them the red sleeves that marked them as once having served in the 181st Imperial Fighter Group, but nothing else indicated these pilots were anything special. All of us hoped for a chance to prove ourselves against them, though chances were that anyone with access to a fighter on Xa Fel would keep it on the ground.

I wasn't really looking forward to the raid for two reasons. The first was that Xa Fel had been so badly polluted by the Kuat Drive Yards' factories that even visiting could be painful. Breather masks and protective clothing were recommended, and while my clutch pilot's outfit might suffice, spending time down on that hot rock in my environmental gear did not sound like fun. While I had no intention of getting shot down or crashing, when looking at a potential survival situation, I hate the idea of having to battle a world for my life.

The second reason was one that plagued me with each mission, and had been a concern even back during undercover operations with CorSec. I had to ask myself where I drew the line in what I was going to do to fit in with the Invids. In a CorSec undercover operation the lines of responsibility were very clear: I could participate in crimes against property, but once any person was under threat of death or serious bodily injury, my duty to protect them kicked in. Here with the pirates, things were nowhere near so clear or clean.

I encouraged my squadron to use ion cannons, noting that hardware we didn't destroy we could always haul back to Courkrus. I'd even had two Headhunters with hyperdrives salvaged from one raid and was having my unit's tech looking into finding a way to mount the drive on my clutch. The better pilots among my people followed my lead, but I still had two or three who went for lasers in dogfights.

On ground attack missions I stressed minimizing attacks on civilian targets. "Yeah, a refueling station might blow up really pretty, and might even set half a city on fire, but that's not the object here." I shook my head in a briefing session. "Look, you can kill a woolly-nerf and make a coat out of its skin, or you can shear the beast's coat and come back year after year for more wool. We play this right, six months from now we show up in the system, send a list of demands and they'll freighter the loot out to us."

Most of my pilots seemed to get the message and only a couple of times did we have to run some of the other Invids away from our zones of control. Once I caught Remart poaching on a lonely stretch of roadway, just blasting landspeeders for the simple pleasure he found in murder. I put an ion bolt into his clutch and commed to Captain Gurtt to recall him, which she did. I also attached his portion of the loot from the raid and had it sent to the families of the people he'd killed as recompense.

And, I vowed, I'd bring him to justice for their murders when all was said and done.

Fifteen minutes prior to reversion to realspace, we got the orders to get into our clutches. I mounted up, powered up and collected reports from my pilots. I relayed them to Captain Gurtt who was acting as the commander of Survivor Group. Invidious Group consisted of their Blade, Saber and Pike Squadrons, with Rock and Pike Squadrons being paired up for missions.

I felt a little jolt run through my ship as we reverted seven seconds early. Before I could figure out what had happened, Launch Control gave us immediate clearance to launch, which we did. I rolled out to port and headed toward my rendezvous position. My mouth went dry and I knew it was from more than sympathy for the grey, thick-aired world below me.

We'd come out of hyperspace early because an Interdictor Cruiser hung in space over Xa Fel. In formation with it were a Mon Calamari Star Cruiser and a *Victory*-class Mark II Star Destroyer. A host of smaller ships surrounded the three capital ships, including a number of assault shuttles that I assumed were conveying troops to the planet below. The presence of the Interdictor meant the *Invidious* couldn't flee, and already the New Republic ships had begun to orient themselves for battle.

Worse yet, to my mind, were the swarms of fighters beginning runs in at us. Gigs of data poured over my screens. There had to be at least two squadrons of Y-wings and A-wings out there. I spotted other ships that had to be B-wings. They, along with the A-wings, moved toward our escorts like the *Backstab. And the only reason they would leave the clutches to the Y-wings was if the Y-wings had help.*

Then I saw them and my heart sank. I keyed the comm unit. ''We have serious trouble here, *Invidious.* You have fighters coming up from Xa Fel.''

''It will be impossible for them to get through our fighter screen, Rock Lead.''

''Don't say impossible.'' I punched up a datafeed and sent it along to the *Invidious.* ''That's Rogue Squadron, and impossible is their stock in trade.''

THIRTY-SEVEN

I punched up the Survivors' tactical frequency. "This is Rock Lead. Stay clear of the X-wings. Go after the Y-wings and use your ion cannons. Leave them dead in space, but the pilots able to squawk."

Captain Gurtt came back quickly. "Why not kill them?"

"We're evenly matched here, and the only way we win is by getting away. We leave pilots drifting, the Reps will pick them up. *Invid* can back out of the grav well and be ready to run. The Reps'll see it as a win and we'll get out of here."

"Vape 'em all!" Sasyru's voice rang with bravado. "I'm not afraid of any Rep pilots."

"Fine, you take the Rogues. Good luck." I glanced down at my monitor. "We're a minute to contact, Captain. Your call."

Gurtt waited for a moment, then issued her orders. "Target Y-wings, use ion cannons only. Run on some of the assault shuttles, too. Let Tavira's folks pick up the X-wings."

I dialed the comm unit down to Rock Squadron's tactical frequency. "Shock the wishbones, stay clear of the pointers, leave the slims and crosses alone. Call for help and we'll get through this.''

There were a thousand other things I wanted to say, but I had thirty seconds to contact and I needed to try something first. Since leaving the Jedi academy I'd not opened myself to the Force in any serious way. I knew, if Tavira's advisors *were* Force-sensitive, I could be exposing myself, but I chanced it. I pushed my sphere of responsibility forward, toward the incoming fighters. I isolated the X-wings, then sought among them. I found Colonel Celchu and pushed an image into his mind.

I fed him the image of a clutch melting into the shape of an X-wing with my X-wing's markings on it. I had no idea what he would make of that vision, and I couldn't hold it for more than a second, but I hoped it meant he knew I was out here. I let him go, allowing us both time to recover before the battle joined, then I flew into the thick of it.

Above us and around us the capital ships exchanged fire. Though the New Republic had three smaller ships present, their combined firepower fairly evenly matched that of the *Invidious*. Red and green turbolaser beams made space an obstacle course where one wrong turn meant oblivion. Shots that did make it through the wheeling and diving fighter cloud struck the other capital ships, but shields seemed to be holding, except in the case of the smaller ships. Both sides seemed to be targeting smaller ships with their ion cannons, trying to eliminate annoyances while leaving themselves scraps to pick up after the battle.

Rock Squadron rolled into a lightfight with an eager and aggressive Y-wing squadron. Clutches were faster than wishbones, but these bone pilots weren't bad. I nailed my first one on a high-angle deflection shot that caught it in an engine nacelle. The bone rolled immediately to starboard, causing me to roll that way as well, I popped my throttle off, reversed thrust and dropped it back on, anticipating a similar move by my foe. He realized that I'd outguessed him after only a second or two and started a full-throttle climb. I hit the rudder, swung my nose around to port and hit him a second time right behind the cockpit. His shields collapsed and the ship continued on, his climb carrying him away from Xa Fel.

I throttled up and rolled into a dive that vectored me in on the tail of a bone trying to light up one of my clutches. "I've got him, Five. Break port."

"Careful, Lead!"

Blue ion bolts flashed back at me from the bone's cockpit, splashing against my forward shield. I rolled right and came down, using the bone's own engine nacelle as cover, then pumped more energy to my shield. "Heads-up, Rocks. Some of these bones are deuces and have a gunner in back controlling that ion cannon."

Staying low, I cranked the throttle up, then climbed and triggered a shot into the Y-wing. The pilot had begun to roll the bone to give the gunner a shot at me, but I hit him first. Rolling out to port and applying some rudder, I kept him in my sights and shot again. I only got a partial hit, which took his aft shield down, but kept him flying.

Another ion bolt nailed the bone in the tail, leaving it spiraling through space. I saw Caet's clutch go shooting past and commed a quick thanks to her. She replied with a yip, then I found myself flying out the other side of the battle and a bit closer to the New Republic capital ships than I had any desire to be. I rolled and dove, then turned and climbed, breaking as many planes as I could and holding no path longer than a second or two. None of the capital ships took a shot at me—they had bigger prey to shoot at—but I didn't want to make myself an easy target to tempt them.

I wasn't easy to hit, which is why, I suppose, I attracted Rogue Squadron's attention. On a very basic level I found this attention very flattering. My peers had decided I was a worthy opponent, and since they didn't know who I was, it was the sort of honest evaluation that was only possible in an anonymous situation.

The problem I had with it, of course, was that their method of showing their appreciation for my skills could likely get me killed. This would not do, but I was stuck. While I could dial up their comm frequencies, I wouldn't know the encryption codes. If they reached me on a widecast, every other ship in the fleet could pick it up, and that wouldn't do me much good either. I couldn't even take time to concentrate and use the Force to project another message to Tycho, since locating him and making contact and all that would take every bit of the concentration I needed to stay alive.

I was stuck, but not without options. When the Force is your ally, you are never without options.

I kept my hand light on the stick and expanded my sphere of responsibility. Everything outside my cockpit seemed completely chaotic, a kaleidoscope of possibility and probability that shifted every nanosecond. Energy filled the void, traveling back and forth between the big ships, while smaller bolts sprayed out in all directions. Proton torpedoes and concussion missiles raced at targets as if homing in on the fear of those who had been targeted. Elation and pain, hope and terror, anger and determination all swirled about—where they intersected I could hear death screams or whispered affirmations of survival.

Out of all of this I sorted the feelings directed toward me, the mental energies concentrated on my clutch. As they hardened, as they seemed to come to a point, as if light sliding along the narrowing blade of a knife, I knew to juke right or left, up or down. In response I'd feel shock and anger or disbelief, then a gathering of concentration again.

Gavin dropped in behind me and I read him like data streaming across a wide-screened datapad. As he prepared to blast me, I cut my throttle out, dove, then hauled back on the stick and climbed. I rolled to starboard since I knew he favored that side and cruised up right on his tail. I triggered one ion burst, then rolled to port and dove away from him.

Ooryl came next and proved tougher than I would have expected. He had always been a good pilot and had gotten much better during his time with the squadron, but I'd always had an edge over him in simulations. I wasn't certain why, but as he splashed laser light over my aft shield, I began to wonder if it wasn't because he had some mental block against shooting me up in exercises. Regardless, he hung with me like a nek with its teeth sunk into a Hutt's tail, and I had serious trouble reading his intent to fire.

If I can't anticipate what he's doing, I have to make him anticipate what I'm doing. I juked to starboard, letting the ship drift sideways, then dove and rolled to port. I bounced the clutch up and down a couple of times, then juked to starboard, dove and rolled out to port. I tossed in some more random drift, then repeated the pattern a third time. The impressions I got from Ooryl, while still inscrutable to me, changed and I knew he had the pattern.

Ten seconds later I drifted right and dove. I snaprolled ninety degrees to port as if beginning my lazy roll, then hauled back on the stick and popped my throttle off. Ooryl had begun his own roll to left, arrowing in toward where I should have been, exposing his ship's belly to me. I hit him with one solid ion blast, then another pilot's blast nailed him and his ship went dead.

"Got him for you, Lead!" Timmser announced. "No need to thank me."

I wasn't going to. Ooryl's dead ship had been pointed at Xa Fel when it got hit, and with no control he'd smash into the atmosphere and be crushed. He had less than a minute until impact and I could do nothing to save him. I rolled and watched his stricken ship continuing a slow spiral to what would be Ooryl's death.

If only I could use telekinesis to deflect his ship into an orbit!

Then his cockpit canopy exploded and Ooryl's command chair shot out. A second later his R2 unit similarly ejected from the dying X-wing. The ejection rocket carried him off toward the Interdictor, though it would burn out long before it ever got there. *Still, he's safe.*

A new presence focused itself on me and I knew I was in serious trouble. Even without using the Force, there are some people who have minds so slow that you can almost hear synapses firing at a torpid pace. Others are so quick-witted you end up marveling at connections they make, but only after the five or ten minutes it takes you to unravel their thought processes. And then there are people whose minds move in multiple dimensions, all at lightspeed, leaving you unable to even begin to guess how their minds work.

Tycho Celchu had such a mind, but what impressed me about him was not the speed with which he thought, but the cool deliberation that defined the way he thought.

When he picked me up as a target I didn't feel the narrowing blade the way I had with Gavin. Instead Tycho had my ship all boxed up and, second by second, shrank that box, eliminating extraneous data, until my ship and a little box he had labeled target were one and the same.

More impressive than that, however, was the fact that the little target box had multiple appendages, each pointing off in the direction of all the maneuvers I could use to escape him. If I jinked right, he could pull me back into his targeting box. If I combined two moves or three, appendages flowed away from eliminated options and grew up to choke off new avenues of escape. His mind worked like the legendary Mon Calamari demonsquid, lashing me with arm after arm that sought to drag me back into the place where he could kill me.

The only way to beat him was to make him the hunted. I inverted and dove, then throttled back and came up through a tight loop that should have dropped me on his tail. He'd anticipated me, so he rolled out to port and I rolled right after him. I throttled back up and closed faster than I should have been able to, so I clipped off a shot that missed wide to port, then snap-rolled up on my port side and hauled the stick back. I held the climb for three seconds, then inverted and continued it around into a loop.

Tycho's X-wing shot back across the front of my clutch, but I had no chance at a shot on him. From him I gained the impression of his enlarging the boxes in which he tried to trap me. He had to deal with the added problem of being a target as well, which gave him a variety of tactics to use against me. Only a few of them worked toward getting me back into the target box myself, and I did what I could to make those choices less than desirable.

"Rock Lead, this is *Invidious*. Rendezvous with the *Invidious* if you want a ride home."

"I copy." I relayed the message through to my squadron.

Caet came back. "Help, Lead?"

"Nope, I'm fine. Just get out of here."

"Hurry."

"As ordered."

I rolled to starboard, then turned hard left and dialed my throttle down to tighten the turn. I applied thrust as I came out of the turn, eluding a quad laser burst from Tycho, then popped my throttle off, hit enough rudder to push me in his direction, and dropped the throttle back in. I snapped off a quick shot that laced his shields with azure lightning, then applied more rudder, inverted and dove after him. I got another shot off that hit and collapsed his aft shield.

In his situation I would have panicked, but I sensed no such thing from him. We just moved into a yet bigger box in which he twisted and tumbled his X-wing through a series of maneuvers I couldn't have followed if I'd programmed them into my computer. Whenever he had a tactical choice he made it in a split-second, presenting himself with another choice. Branches seemed chosen at random, killing any ability to anticipate him, yet all worked back toward the targeting box.

I knew better than to stick around. I pulled myself into a wide turn that headed me back toward the *Invidious*. The Star Destroyer started laying down a defensive pattern of fire that swept out in waves to discourage pursuit. In theory our gunners were not shooting at the incoming fighters, but they placed their shots fairly close to discourage anyone coming after us. While the big ship's shots weren't likely to hit any of the fighters, the snubbie jocks had to worry about them nonetheless, which didn't give them a free hand in tracking targets. And, if an incoming pilot was good enough, he could nudge his ship into the space turbolaser fire had just passed through, letting the big ship's energy beams shield him from his pursuit.

Racing back through the main battlefield, I saw broken ships and EV pilots all over the place. The number of bones hanging there made the place look like a rancor lair. I saw a few clutch carcasses out there, too, and a couple of the corvettes from each side. *Backstab* wasn't among the dead ships, which I took as a positive—relatively speaking. While the Survivors were a nasty bunch of liars, murderers, pirates and thieves; some of them had almost become friends and I didn't want to see them dead.

Suddenly I got a sense of victory pulsing out from Tycho. I flicked my target selector with my thumb and screened targets for maximum danger. What I got were a pair of proton torpedoes fast closing with my clutch. Despite my running, Tycho had come around and gotten a target lock on me, then sent me two going-away presents. The torpedoes traveled considerably faster than my clutch, which was their great strength and, luckily for me, their primary weakness.

I watched the range indicator on the lead missile scroll down and as it closed to within two hundred meters, I jerked my stick back, then jammed it to the left and rolled into a dive. The first missile raced past while the second rolled and corrected. I jammed my stick forward and dove, letting it slide past too, then I smiled. *The way out of this trap I learned from you, Tycho.*

Using my scanners, I located the first missile and locked it in as a target. I brought my clutch about so I was headed straight for it and waited until it closed within a kilometer. I flicked my weapons over to dual lasers, dropped my crosshairs on the incoming torch and fired twice. My first pair of bolts missed, but the second hit, ripping the missile to pieces only five hundred meters away. I rolled, dove and located the second torpedo. I nailed it with my first shot, detonating it at a kilometer, then flew through the collapsing gold fireball on my long swoop toward the *Invidious*.

I heard Tycho's voice crackle through on a widecast. "Very fancy flying, clutch."

"Didn't want you to think I was a green pilot, Rogue Lead. Another time." I put my clutch into a quick weave, then darted in under the umbrella of the *Invidious'* fire and landed the Tri-fighter in the middle of the group area the Survivors had been given. I noticed, as I brought the fighter around so the front was pointed toward the egress hatchway, that the Survivors had only lost six of thirty-six clutches, and I'd only lost two. The Imp clutch group had lost over a dozen of their Tri-fighters, and the front rank of their lead squadron— spaces reserved for the commanding officers—appeared empty.

After taking a deep breath, I removed my helmet and enviro gear, then I popped the hatch and climbed out of the clutch. Timmser and Caet helped me down to the deck and supported me as my legs gave way. It took a moment for me to realize how weak I felt. Flying against Tycho had probably been the most difficult thing I'd ever done, and I had an edge in the Force. What he did, what Wedge did, without being able to use the Force made them far more special than any Jedi. They flew with heart and brains and their entire being.

Timmser hauled me to my feet. "Very sharp what you

did out there, Jen. Shooting the torps. That showed them.''

A warning klaxon sounded and red lights started flashing in the hangar deck. I reached back and braced myself against the clutch as the *Invidious* accelerated to lightspeed. The ship's gravity generators canceled the physical effects of speeding up, but watching the stars whiz by through the egress port was enough to disorient me.

Caet fastened on her hooded cloak and pulled the hood up, then removed her heavy goggles. ''We did well. Bolt lost only one. Hawk lost three.''

''Who did we lose?''

''Five and Seven.'' Timmser shrugged. ''They decided to tangle with some slims, and the A-wings vaped them.''

I shook my head. ''That was a waste.''

''Slims were running against the *Backstab*. Blook and Yander thought they would win points with Captain Nive.'' Timmser brushed a hand back and forth through her spiky hair, making it stand up and spraying me with some sweat. ''You okay now, Cap?''

I straightened up. ''Better. Easy to forget how draining that can be.''

''Why did you tag pointers?''

''They came after me, Caet. Timmser nailed the one. Thanks for the assist.''

''Just as soon keep you alive, Cap.'' The tall woman gave me an easy smile. ''Course, the way you fly, not really a problem.''

Another klaxon blatted harshly, then a heavy male voice blared through the hangar via the intercom. ''Attention. Admiral on deck.''

The click of boots on decking accompanied us as we

rushed forward and lined up in front of the squadron assembly area. Across from us the Imperial squadrons similarly lined up. They all looked rather smart in their black uniforms, while we looked like a fairly ragged crew. Some of us had Survivor uniforms, full of golden stitchery with the grey and red, but most of us wore a motley mix of things we'd taken from planets we'd raided, or units we'd deserted from in the past. The squadrons looked the apex and nadir, with our only advantage being that more of us had survived the battle.

The central turbolift shaft opened and two stormtroopers stepped forth in armor so bright that I almost asked Caet for her goggles. They paused, then split apart, each taking a step to the side, which allowed Admiral Tavira to emerge onto the deck. The stormtroopers, both the ones flanking her and the two who exited the turbolift to stand behind her, all dwarfed her physically; but something in the way she moved made her seem far from diminutive. She wore a grey admiral's uniform and held a quirt clutched at the small of her back. Even as far away as I was, I could feel the electricity in her amethyst gaze.

She looked at her people, then over at us. She gestured casually with her black-gloved right hand, pointing the quirt at us. The stormtroopers led the way, her casual gait in sharp contrast with their precise and measured steps. As she neared us and began to walk down the line, her hands came out from behind her back, her quirt playing against the palm of her left hand or tapping teasingly and gently against her own chin.

I kept my face impassive as she walked past me, fighting against any reaction as she flicked a quick glance in my direction. She surrendered a good ten centimeters to me in height and her void-black hair shimmered with silvery highlights. Her pale flesh had been drawn taut over fine bones, with no lines yet begun at the corners of her eyes or mouth. In form and age she almost seemed a child, but the cool confidence of her tread and the way she measured all of us with a momentary peek, betrayed kilobytes of data about her mental age.

She stopped before Captain Gurtt and flicked the quirt against Tyresi's shoulder. "You were the one who relayed to us the plan of engagement, were you not?"

"I was, Admiral." Tyresi kept her voice even, but I caught the hint of a tremble in it.

Tavira studied her face for a moment, letting the silence linger to the point where it became a bit uncomfortable. "You advised a withdrawal while leaving the Reps people to rescue."

"I did, Admiral."

Again the silence dragged, both Tavira and Tyresi remaining stock still. I could feel the pressure building. The strategy for which Tyresi was being blamed was mine and any punishment she got for it should have been mine. I drew in a breath and would have said something, but I caught the barest contraction of flesh around the corner of Tavira's mouth.

"That was a winning strategy, Captain Gurtt." Tavira pointed almost carelessly toward her own pilots. "Colonel Lamner disagreed with it and went directly for the X-wings. You notice he is not here to defend his decision."

"No, Admiral, he is not."

The quirt again tapped Tyresi's shoulder. "Which means I need to replace him. I will have you in his place, *Colonel* Gurtt."

Tyresi's dark eyes widened. "Me, moving to the *Invidious*?"

"I'm certain Captain Nive will agree to the change."

"Yes, Admiral." Tyresi frowned. "I would be amiss, Admiral, if I did not tell you that the strategy I relayed to you came from Captain Idanian. He suggested it, I thought it was sound and passed it up to you."

"Yes," Tavira purred, "Captain Idanian, the one who killed the proton torpedoes aimed at my ship. I was thinking to have him as your replacement in Bolt Squadron."

Remart shook his head, and Tavira oriented on him like a hawk-bat on a granite slug. "You have something to offer, pilot?"

"Begging your pardon, Admiral, but that is not how officers are selected among the Survivors."

"Oh, and what is the process?"

Remart smiled charmingly. "First, someone has to be voted into Bolt Squadron because we're an elite squadron."

Tavira nodded. "He would be elected by his own people to fill this slot?"

Remart aped her nod. "Yes, Admiral."

With the quirt pressed thoughtfully against her lips, Tavira rotated and looked at my squadron. "All those in favor of Captain Idanian joining Bolt Squadron, please raise a convenient appendage."

Nine hands rose down along the line. Mine did not.

Tavira frowned. "You oppose your election?"

"I have responsibilities to my people."

"You have responsibilities to *me. I* want you in Bolt Squadron."

"As ordered, Admiral."

She glanced at Remart. "Now you would tell me that he must be elected the leader of Bolt Squadron, yes?"

"That is the way it is done, Admiral."

Tavira's smile blossomed full of teeth. "And the position of commander of this squadron is one you covet for yourself, yes?"

Remart's whole body stiffened. "I would be your most faithful and fierce servant, Admiral."

Tavira slapped the quirt not so gently against Remart's stomach. "And yet you might be, but I don't want you commanding the Bolts. The pressures of command might wrinkle that brow, and I would not like to see that happen to you. All those in Bolt Squadron in favor of Captain Idanian assuming command, please raise an appendage."

Nine hands went up and, after a quick quirt lash, Remart's hand joined them.

Tavira smiled graciously. "Though I despise democracy, it is nice to see this quaint custom result in unanimity. Congratulations, Captain Idanian. You have a new command. You now can relay your plans directly to the *Invidious*."

"It is a privilege I will be careful in exercising, Admiral."

Her violet eyes narrowed. "Why do I have the feeling that I may just have made a mistake in having you elevated?"

I kept my expression open. "I have no idea, Admiral."

"See to it, Captain Idanian, that you give me no reason to think on it again."

"As ordered, Admiral." I bowed my head toward her and did not lift it again until she and her entourage had clomped away with Tyresi to introduce her to her new

command. I shot a glance at Remart and saw him tremble with anger. I'd give her no reason to think she'd
made a mistake. Remart, on the other hand, most certainly would. Because of that, I knew then that when our
inevitable confrontation came, only one of us would
walk away.

THIRTY-EIGHT

Taking over Bolt Squadron for Tyresi Gurtt proved both more and less difficult than I would have thought. Jacob Nive approved of the choice, which cut the resentment of some of the Bolts. Most of them waited to see how well I could fly, and while the sensor data from the flight against Tycho and shooting the torpedoes down certainly convinced most, a few holdouts waited until we had a chance to practice against each other.

Remart and two others—with the other replacement pilot from Slash Squadron soon joining them—staunchly opposed me. I gathered them into three flight and couldn't wait until I could toss them at Rogue Squadron or Pash Cracken's A-wing group. I knew that was a decidedly un-Jedilike desire on my part and felt uneasy about it, but having Remart scheming away about getting me in trouble added stress I didn't need to my life.

Fortunately for him and me, the *Invidious* didn't call on anyone for missions for over a month, leaving us to languish on Courkrus. We all assumed it was taking that long for Tyresi to get the *Invidious'* fighter group back together. *Invidious'* lack of action didn't prevent Admiral Tavira from showing up on Courkrus for meetings with the various gang leaders from time to time, though no missions from those meetings passed down to me.

Aside from working with my new squadron, I used the downtime to go over the various events of the Xa Fel raid. We learned later, through various channels, that the New Republic had not been at Xa Fel waiting for us. The New Republic had staged a surprise raid on Xa Fel to trap officials of Kuat Drive Yards. KDY had been under various judicial orders to stop polluting the planet and start massive clean-up campaigns, but had done almost nothing to comply. During the Thrawn raids, little had been done to enforce the rulings—ditto the turmoil concerning the Reborn Emperor. KDY had gotten complacent, so the New Republic stepped in, used an Interdictor to keep all ships in the system, and were in the process of checking everything out when we showed up.

While I was happy to see Xa Fel on the way to getting cleaned up, the nature of the raid and our stumbling into it took on a greater significance for me. Tavira's people missed the New Republic forces because those forces were not there to trap the *Invidious*. Those forces had a different target. This meant that Tavira's advisors were able to read threats directed toward her, not the future in general. They were sensing the same hostile intent I'd gotten from Tycho, only they got their warning a bit in advance. Unless something was a direct threat to Tavira and the *Invidious*—and, by extension, the advisor himself—it just didn't register.

As good as they might be at using the Force, they seem limited, half-trained.

My fruitless consideration of how to use this discovery against Tavira occupied a lot of my free time, and it wasn't a problem I could share with my friends. It got knocked offline one afternoon when Jacob Nive called

me into his office. I knew the pilots who had been at Xa
Fel had been being called into their various headquarters
to answer questions about the battle, but the process had
left the Survivors for last. The pilots in the other bands
remained quiet about what went on in the interrogations,
but I gathered none of them really had a clue about what
had happened to them.

I entered the office, tossed Captain Nive and Admiral
Tavira a salute, then moved to third chair in the set before Nive's desk, the one with its back to the door into a
connecting office. Admiral Tavira, wearing a pilot's
black jumpsuit with a short jacket and cape to match
crossed her legs and let her booted left foot bounce
somewhat impatiently. "Thank you for joining us, Captain Idanian."

I nodded once. "My pleasure, Admiral. How can I be
of service?"

"I am making inquiries about the Xa Fel battle. As
you are aware, in the past my advisors have been rather
shrewd about keeping the *Invidious* out of danger."
Tavira regarded me through half-lidded eyes, beguiling
eyes. "At Xa Fel they failed but there they sensed a
presence."

"A presence?" I frowned. "I'm not certain I understand."

"Do you know what a Jedi Knight is?" Her question
came soft and almost seductive. The pink tip of her
tongue wet her lips as she waited for my reply, her gaze
gaining in intensity. Her manner and bearing and tone of
voice suggested rewards for the truth, and I found myself
surprisingly willing to indulge her. Exar Kun's promise
to let me have her flashed through my mind, followed
quickly by the image of Mirax, sending a little jolt
through me.

In the wake of that jolt I felt a presence creeping into my mind. It came tentatively and gently, a roly-poly lint-nerf rolling and hopping over the surface of my consciousness. Had I not been trained in the ways of the Force I never would have noticed it, or I would have put it down to the Admiral's penetrating gaze. As it was, even with my rudimentary skill in the Force, I felt its intrusion and sought to deflect it away from any deep probe.

I recalled how Luke had entered my mind by making his thoughts flow along with mine. I reversed this technique. Since the prober was looking for information about the Force and Jedi Knights, I'd supply it. I dredged up every memory of Jedi Knights from every trashy holodrama and news documentary I could remember. I created a pool of such images, allowing the prober in, then encysting her in that wealth of data.

"I do, Admiral." I blushed and glanced down. "I used to be quite a fanatic on the subject as a child. I watched whatever I could because it infuriated my family. I didn't understand then the risk to my family I posed, nor the risk that Jedi posed to the Empire. I know the New Republic claims to have some and I believe one of them was responsible for the destruction of Carida."

"So he was." Tavira's eyes brightened slightly. "At the battle of Xa Fel, my people had indications of the presence of a Jedi. Do you know anything about that?"

I threw my head back and laughed. "It all makes sense, now."

She frowned. "What does?"

"The proton torpedoes. Those would be what *he* used against the *Invidious*."

Nive shook his head. "Again, with help files."

I looked openly at the both of them, feeding shock

into the pool of memories in my brain. "The Jedi, Luke Starkiller, Adam Darklighter, Biggs Skywalker, whatever, the one who destroyed the Death Star at Yavin—he used proton torpedoes. It makes sense that he shot them at your ship when going away. I was flying against Rogue Squadron, and he was the founder of Rogue Squadron, after all."

I felt the same surprise on Tavira's face roll down the connection in my brain. That presence withdrew itself as Tavira's surprise melted into an appreciative smile. "I am impressed, Captain Idanian. No one else has connected Rogue Squadron with the Jedi."

"Not even your advisors?"

"No, not even them." Her quirt cracked against her gloved palm. "How is it that you were able to come up with this answer?"

I narrowed my eyes. "That X-wing pilot almost got me. I knew he was from Rogue Squadron, but when analyzing my performance after the fact, I realized I needed to know more about all of them. Their history makes for fascinating reading. You're even mentioned in it."

Her head came up and her gaze became icy. "I've run afoul of them several times, but never with a Jedi flying with them."

I tried but could not suppress a shiver.

She caught it and smiled. "You've survived an encounter with them, as have I. Does that make us kindred spirits?"

"It makes us both survivors."

"And you take pride in being a survivor?"

I shook my head. "I take pride in being a victor."

Her eyes widened slightly. "And do you always win?"

''So far.''

''Perhaps you have not been properly challenged.'' She pursed her lips for a moment. ''Perhaps I should find a challenge for you.''

Captain Nive shifted uneasily in his chair. ''If you wish, I can . . .''

I held a hand up. ''Begging your pardon, sir. May I speak frankly, Admiral?''

Tavira blinked at me. ''This is different. Proceed.''

I stood. ''I have great respect for you, Admiral, as a tactician and for being able to hold together this coalition. Your ability to keep the *Invidious* intact while the New Republic is hunting her is nothing short of miraculous. And, without meaning to sound forward, I think you're stunningly beautiful. Fact is, though, I joined the Invids to be a pilot and to make money. If the challenge you're thinking of offering me tests my pilot skills, I'm your man. If not, I'm not interested in the job.''

Nive looked stricken and I'm pretty certain he thought he was going to be ordered to have me killed right then and there.

Tavira looked surprised. For all of a second. Then she rose to her feet and lashed me across the face with the quirt. I knew the stinging blow was coming—no need even for the Force to tell me that—and I just took it. The pain sank into my flesh and heat rose to replace it in my right cheek. I didn't feel any trickle of blood, but I knew I'd have a nasty welt for a day or so, and an ugly bruise after that.

''That is for your presumption, Captain.'' Tavira brought the quirt back and pressed it up under my chin. ''If I were to find you attractive—and though you are far from ugly, you are not of a type I favor—and I wanted you to attend me, you would. Ut-ut, no speaking here.

Know that what I tell you is a fact pure and simple.'' Her eyes all but closed as she stared up at my face. ''Pity you're so very blond. I've always found blonds to be a disaster for me.''

She spun away abruptly, letting the quirt rasp against my throat. ''As for pilot challenges, those I will present to you. Within a week, I think, I will have the Survivors spearhead an action for me. Do you think you will be up to that challenge?''

''I will do as ordered, Admiral.''

Tavira turned back toward me, slowly, with a coy smile on her face. ''I imagine you will, Captain, which means there is hope for you of a future. Do not displease me, Captain. You won't like what happens to those in whom I am displeased.''

I retreated from Nive's office, passing Timmser, who was waiting to go in next, and walked out into the sunlight. I started to head toward a little restaurant I liked, but as I started thinking, my wandering became aimless. So many things had happened in that meeting that I needed to sort them out and figure out how to proceed.

First and foremost I'd had confirmed what I suspected: Tavira's advisors were Force-sensitive and schooled in some uses of the Force. I was pretty sure my deflection had gone unnoticed, which meant her advisors were not very skilled in that sort of probing. It could have been that their talent for uncovering threats was a passive one, working only on threats directed at them. That meant they were largely reactive, which was akin to being a counter-puncher as a fighter. It's not bad, but it means you have to get hit first before you can hit back.

The fact that they had detected my Force use in the

battle did disturb me, and made me thankful I'd been working to keep my Force-sensitivity shielded otherwise. If Luke's early assumption that Mirax had been taken to forestall action on my part were true, because my Force presence could identify me, I'd all but announced to my enemies that I was here. The fact that they were willing to accept the Force presence at the battle as that of Luke Skywalker didn't clear this problem up—it just meant they had no way to differentiate me from Luke for the moment.

It also struck me as odd that I never had a sense of Tavira's advisors before the probe in the office, or during the battle. If they could detect me, they were within my range to detect them, or so it would seem. They had to be shielding themselves as well, remaining hidden. Given that until a half-dozen years before, being a Jedi was a quick way to slow death, the ability to remain hidden was a virtue. For me, however, this virtue meant I could be standing right next to a dangerous enemy and not know it.

Second, and equally important, I'd learned Tavira did not like being crossed. I blunted the prelude to a proposition, she punished me for it, then told me I'd never defy her again. She did not admit I'd headed her off, and she did not relinquish control in the situation. She clearly felt she had come out the victor, and I didn't want to know how she was going to reinforce her victory.

I found myself before the Crash and descended into the cool depths. I gave my eyes a chance to adjust to the dim light, then made my way toward the back, to a table where Timmser sat with Caet. Before I could get there, however, Remart landed a hand heavily on my left shoulder.

I turned toward him, shrugging his hand off. "You want something?"

The big man smiled slyly at me. "Just to buy you a drink."

"Got a special on Alion neurotoxins, do they?"

The bartender, a guy who had enough sores on his face to be from Xa Fel, laughed. "We're not Margath's. Sasyru is buying. What'll you have?"

"Local lomin-ale, thanks." I looked at Remart. "Why so generous?"

"I don't want any misunderstandings between us, Captain." He raised a scarlet brandy in my direction as a salute. "No hard feelings."

"Sure." I accepted the ale from the bartender, nodded at Remart, then continued on my way to the back. Timmser slid a chair out with her foot for me. "What's going on with Remart?"

Timmser snorted and Caet growled. "Sasyru came in to Nive's office after me, to meet with the admiral and Captain Nive. Came out of the meeting all happy. Seems the admiral thinks she's going to let Remart show her a good time after our next outing."

"Oh." I sipped some of the ale and let the carbonation attack my tongue. The ale soured in my mouth, but I knew it wasn't anything to do with the brewing. I didn't like the idea of Remart with Admiral Tavira, and turned to glower at him.

Caet let a low growl roll from her throat. "Jealousy does not suit you, Jenos."

I looked at her, blinking in surprise. "Jealous? Me? Of Remart? No way."

Timmser shook her head. "Got it bad, pretty clearly, Jen."

"No, you're wrong." I frowned at the both of them,

then drank. I tried to tell myself I didn't like the idea of them being together because Remart would cause trouble for me with Tavira. "With Tavira backing him, Remart will be a terror."

Timmser gave me an exaggerated nod. "I copy, Captain Idanian, but I think your sensor data is reading wrong."

Caet agreed with a smile. "Seek the truth, Jenos. Don't fly blind."

My frown deepened as I considered the possibility of being jealous. I knew it was insane. I didn't want her—I had Mirax and was very happy. I'd refused her, and I could easily see her turning to Remart as both a way to salve her ego and to get under my skin, since our dislike for each other was well known. Yet even though I didn't want her, I wanted her to be with *him* even less.

I am jealous!

I shivered. Part of me knew my jealousy was all pre-programmed and genetic. By winning a female, a man guaranteed his own genetic survival, and all other men are de facto rivals in that quest for immortality. As much as I wanted to believe I was removed from my animal nature—as much as I clung to Yoda's dictum that we are not crude creatures of matter—I still didn't like Remart. I also had a powerful attraction to Leonia Tavira.

I had to admit it. Part of the reason I'd cut her proposition short was because I *did* find her desirable. She was easily classed as eye-candy, and her cunning enhanced her attractiveness. Her capriciousness was dangerous, but that very danger was a challenge: *Could I, in relating with her more closely, avoid her wrath?*

Before letting myself follow that line of thought, I pressed my mug of cold ale up against my right cheek and let the chill soothe the fire there. I felt more of a sting as some of the ale slopped down over the abraded flesh, but I let it remind me of Tavira's petty and venial side. *Am I so far gone here that I truly want her?* It drove a sting like a vibroblade into any desire I had for her. I hoped it had left a mortal wound, but I wasn't sure of it.

Caet sniffed once in my direction. "Your face. Who?"

I lowered the ale and gave her a good view of the welt. "Remart's playmate. She didn't like my answer to some of her questions."

Timmser swirled brandy around in a snifter, then smiled. "I answered them and all I got was a headache."

"Yeah, well, I told her I had a headache, and got lashed for it."

"Not wise." Caet leaned forward. "No pity for Remart. For you, fear."

"Don't fear for me, Caet." I shook my head. "And don't do it around Tavira. I think she can smell fear and can smell weakness. Stink of either one around her and you might as well chew a blaster bolt—it will be quicker and just might not hurt as much."

THIRTY-NINE

The new raid promised to be easy and probably did not require the show of force we were going to haul along, but I hated it. Admiral Tavira had decided we were going to travel to the Algara system. We weren't going to hit the main world, Algara 2, even though the bureaucracy-bound planetary administration probably couldn't mount a defense. Instead we were heading for the first world in the system, Kerilt, a jungle world whose only colony was far from self-sufficient.

It was this lack of self-sufficiency that made Kerilt a prime target. The colony, Morymento, was home to one of the larger Caamasi Remnant communities in the galaxy. Well back before I was born, right after the Clone Wars, the world of Caamas was brutally attacked and hit with enough firepower that the vegetation boiled off the world, leaving it a dead rock, and the vast majority of the Caamasi dead with it. Because of the thoroughness and sheer ferocity of the attack, no one knew who had ordered it or carried it out.

And no one knew *why* it had been carried out. For as long as anyone could remember, the Caamasi had been very pacifistic and the very soul of moderation and mediation. While a few Caamasi ventured forth as Jedi—

obviously including my grandfather's friend, Ylenic It'kla—most who left Caamas did so as traders or scholars, negotiators and diplomats. So beloved were they that various languages adapted the word Caamasi to mean "friend from afar" or "stranger to be trusted."

Factions within the Empire certainly did what they could to help the surviving Caamasi after the immolation of their world. A number of colonies like Morymento had been created, and those who were inclined to see conspiracies everywhere even went so far as to suggest Alderaan had been destroyed because it was home to one of the larger Caamasi refugee communities. I didn't know if that was true or not, but I could recall my mother collecting up old clothes for shipment to Caamasi camps elsewhere in the galaxy. With the defeat of the Empire, the charity continued and even swelled, which meant, with a semi-annual shipment of supplies just having arrived on Kerilt, the Caamasi colony became a ripe target for plunder.

As we reverted to realspace, we discovered we were not the only ones who found the Caamasi supplies a prize worth winning.

We poured out of the *Invidious* and saw an old *Kaloth*-class battlecruiser in orbit around Kerilt. The IFF transponder indicated it was called *Harmzuay*, and I'd known of that ship from back in my CorSec days. It belonged to a group of Thalassian slavers who, even for slavers, had a pretty unsavory reputation—they culled the best and brightest of their victims and killed the rest, guaranteeing a diminished supply which hiked their prices.

"Bolts, on me. We have their skulls. Burn 'em, don't shock. Rock, Slash, head down and ground attack Thalassian ships. Use ion cannons—I don't want slave ships being blown up with slaves inside.'' Timmser and Wallon acknowledged my orders and headed to atmosphere while the rest of us came around to port and drove straight at the two dozen Z-95 Headhunters the Thalassians used—fairly stock models with two triple-blasters and a concussion missile launcher.

The Thalassian pilots were not bad, but we were just better—a lot better. I nailed my first one in a head-to-head pass. I fired first, splashing his forward shield with laser light. He shied a bit and shot a concussion missile at me, but it jetted past harmlessly. My next two bolts punched through his shield. One drilled into the cockpit and the second melted part of the port engine. Bits and pieces of it broke loose, exploding out through the housing, then the S-foil itself tore off and whirled away into space. The skull proceeded into a flat spin, and the pilot, if he still lived, was unable to do anything about it.

The next pilot hit me once with red bursts from his triple blasters, but my shields held. I shot back, hitting him with a dual-fire pair of laser blasts. He rolled to starboard to get away from me, so I rolled to port to drop in on his tail. I triggered another burst of fire that nibbled away at his aft shield, then inverted and climbed into his continued loop. He tried to roll to port and climb away from me, but a quick push of the stick forward and a touch of rudder brought me back on him. My last shots pierced his shields and, were he flying an X-wing, would have decapitated his astromech. As it was, in a skull, I took off his cockpit canopy and the top ten centimeters of his helmet.

Red blaster bolts shot past me off the starboard side. I popped my throttle offline and went bow down for two seconds, then throttled up again and ruddered to starboard. The skull that had been trying to slip in on my tail overshot me, giving me her belly as a clean target. I pumped two sets of bolts into it, collapsing the forward shield and taking the first third of the craft off. Unless the pilot was really good, all she'd be able to do was fly straight and level. That worked out, though, because down would bring her back to the dogfight, and up would carry her into the battle between the *Harmzuay* and *Invidious*.

But not for long.

The Kaloth battlecruiser had once been considered a very powerful ship, and this one had been modified enough to be able to fight any Nebulon-B Frigate to a standstill. In the hands of slavers it made for a most potent weapon and, under normal circumstances, would have been a welcome addition to the Invid fleet. However, the Thalassian slavers had tried to poach what Admiral Tavira saw as her property, and the price to be paid for that affront was very high.

And even watching various sensor feeds well after the battle, I found it truly difficult to comprehend the vast, destructive capabilities of the *Invidious*. While I knew how many guns the ship had and could easily describe the relative effects of each, watching them employed in so efficient and lethal a manner left me emotionally numb.

The *Harmzuay* got off the first salvo, spraying laser cannon and turbolaser fire over the length of the *Invidious*. A few shots made it through the Star Destroyer's shields to boil off hull armor, but I'd seen nastier damage done by an X-wing strafing run. The *Harmzuay*'s gunners didn't concentrate their fire to compound the damage being done. Their tactics might have worked in the past to frighten off a ship with which they were more evenly matched, but not the *Invidious*.

And not with Admiral Tavira commanding.

The *Invidious'* return barrage devastated the ship that was one fifth of the Star Destroyer's size. The heavy turbolaser batteries concentrated their fire on the aft end of the battlecruiser, punching through the shields as if they were mere holograms, then boiling great holes through the hull. Atmosphere vented, carrying with it debris and bodies, then subsidiary explosions rocketed more shrapnel and parts into space. The *Invidious'* emerald heavy turbolaser cannon shots raked the battlecruiser's starboard flank, drilling through shields and burning off the *Harmzuay'*s weaponry.

With no shields and no weapons, the battlecruiser's commander did the only thing left open to him—he rolled his ship to present the belly shields and tried to pull away and run. In his case, however, there was no try, and there was no do. There was only die, and the battlecruiser died spectacularly.

As the aft came around, the *Invidious* hit it with everything. The *Harmzuay'*s aft looked like a black hole sucking in every green energy shaft the *Invidious'* guns spat out. The battlecruiser's engines exploded immediately, shredding the last third of the ship. The roiling golden ball of incandescent gas actually pushed the *Harmzuay* further on the captain's intended course, but by then it was only the spasmodic jerking of a corpse.

The *Invidious'* guns cored through the battlecruiser's hulk, melting everything. Molten durasteel congealed into long, twisted threads that trailed from the wreck like the roots of a nebula orchid. I actually thought I saw, and confirmed by later sensor data review, turbolaser bolts burning through the battlecruiser's nose. More metal tendrils bled out from the ship's bow, then the hollowed hull sagged in on itself. What was once the *Harmzuay* hung there in space like the carcass of some odd metallic animal.

I rolled the clutch and streaked back into the dogfight, but the Thalassians were broken. Half their fighters had already been destroyed, and watching the death of the *Harmzuay* had taken the fight out of the rest of them. The trio whose skulls could jump peeled off into an exit vector, while the rest of them headed out toward Algara 2. Why they thought they would find sanctuary there I had no idea, but whatever they would face there likely beat the death we'd give them.

"Let them run, Bolts. We're going atmosphere and see if there is anything to do down there."

My clutch broke through the planet's cloud cover first, giving me a good view of the planet's verdant jungles. From several points to the north I could see smoke and orbiting clutches that occasionally swooped and fired. I punched up Rock Squadron's tactical frequency on the comm.

"This is Bolt Leader. Rock Lead report."

"Rock Lead here. Little bit of ground fire. We have a shocked shuttle. Slaves have escaped into the jungle and we're driving the Thalassians away from them."

"Good work, Timmser." I raised Slash Squadron and got a similar report. I brought my clutch around on a southern heading and did a flyby on the main Morymento district that included the spaceport, but saw no ships and encountered no fire. I switched back to Bolt Squadron's tactical frequency. "Three flight, land here. Two flight, combat aerospace patrol. One flight, on me, sensors in ground search mode."

I worked my sensor controls over into ground search mode, which painted a grid on my monitor, superimposed a topographical map of the terrain, and started to fill in data on structures, energy flow patterns, lifeform readings, movement and anything else the programmers had thought important. I fed the resulting data over to my comm unit and shot it up to the *Invidious.*

A red light on the comm unit burned to life beside the fleet frequency. I punched it. "Bolt Lead here."

"Bolt Lead, this is Admiral Tavira. Ground status?"

"Scanning the town now. Looks like the warehouses are loaded. If you send our assault shuttles down now, we can start loading." I glanced at the sensor monitor and the data that was scrolling across it. "Warehouse district appears to be largely deserted. The Caamasi must have headed home when the trouble started."

"Let them stay there and they need not be hurt."

"My thoughts exactly." Well, not exactly. Taking the supplies and equipment from the warehouses could set back the development of the colony by years. The Caamasi were known to be industrious, but taming a world is not an easy task. With the proper tools they could have done a lot, so the harm we would do them might not be immediate, but it would hurt.

"I am so pleased you approve. Tavira out."

I switched back to Bolt's tactical frequency. "Three flight, report on spaceport status."

I got no reply, which struck me as odd. "This is Bolt Lead to three flight. Report status."

Again, no reply. "Bolt two, on me, three and four, continue scanning." I rolled my clutch and headed back toward the spaceport, keeping my sensors in ground mode to pick up on any ground fire that could indicate a running lightfight or ambush of my pilots. The last thing I wanted was for Remart to get killed because I'd ordered him to the ground, since I knew I'd pay dearly for spoiling his long-awaited assignation with Admiral Tavira.

Ground scan came up negative, though it did show all four clutches of three flight on the ground and intact. "I'm not liking this, two. Stay up and keep orbiting. I'm going down."

I set the clutch down, popped the hatch, then doffed my gloves and helmet. I took the comlink from the helmet and checked to make sure it was tuned to the squadron frequency. I clipped that to my red flightsuit lapel, then pulled a blaster carbine and a belt of powerpacks from the survival box. I hauled myself out of the cockpit, slid down the front and hit the ground running. I headed toward the spaceport terminal building and when I saw blaster scars on the door lock, I got a sinking feeling in the pit of my stomach.

Realizing I was taking a risk, I tapped into my personal Force reservoir and pushed my sphere of responsibility out. I consciously flattened it, making it more into a fat disk, in the hopes that Tavira's advisors wouldn't pick up on it, then I focused it even more forward, ignoring the spaceport landing facilities. Keeping it in a semicircle, I pushed it out and sensed nothing in the terminal. In the jungle beyond it I found all manner of lifeforms and various Caamasi homes. Then, at a distance that would have covered roughly two Coruscant blocks, I found my pilots.

Along with them I caught pain and fear, but it didn't come from them. I started sprinting and rounded a corner along a paved path that followed the gentle, rolling lay of the land to a circle and an area where the trees had been thinned so homes could be built.

Remart and his flightmates stood in the center of the clearing, with a semicircle of Caamasi looking on with horror in their wide, dark eyes. A landspeeder rested on the ground between most of the Caamasi and my people, with two dead Thalassians still seated in it. A third Thalassian, the driver, lay on the ground. Across from him lay a Caamasi who had risen up on one elbow, with his left arm held up to ward off a blow from Remart. Behind that Caamasi crouched another Caamasi, smaller and finer-boned. I guessed she was a female and perhaps even an adolescent because of the slight swell of down-covered breasts. The purple markings on the face and shoulders of both Caamasi were similar enough that I assumed some sort of blood relation between them.

"Report, Sasyru!" I put a lot of venom and all the command I could muster into my voice. "Now! Report!"

Remart's head came up and he came around to face me. His flightmates spread out, each one of them fingering the blaster carbines they wore slung over their shoulders or across their bellies. I looked at each one of them, but they didn't hold my gaze very long. When I looked at Remart, he smiled confidently.

"Situation is under control, Captain. It doesn't concern you."

I continued trotting forward. "Is that so?" I glanced at the downed Caamasi and saw a dark dribble of blood from one of his nostrils. I gave him a quick nod, then narrowed my eyes. "Explain to me what is going on here."

"I said it was none of your concern."

"Noted. Make it my concern." As I approached them I slowed and noticed a couple of details I'd missed from further out. The dead driver had spilled a satchel of jewelry when he went down. I'd never seen Caamasi metalwork before, and the silver and gold pieces lying there were utterly unlike anything I'd ever looked at. I had no reason to suspect the slaver had brought the jewelry with him for trading purposes. Since none of the Caamasi I could see were wearing anything beyond sandals and a kilt-like garment, my assumption was that the Thalassians had been looting this small neighborhood when Remart and his people happened upon them and killed them.

Remart's face closed up. "We found the Thalassians here. They resisted and attacked us and, as per regulations, we killed them. End of report."

I nodded at the Caamasi on the ground. "What happened to him?"

"He struck me, so I hit him back."

I frowned. "What sort of sithspawn reason did you have for being out here anyway?"

The man smiled slyly and I saw his friends begin to grin, too. "I was shopping for something for the admiral."

"So you thought you'd just come along and loot a house or two, but you found the Thalassians here already. You killed them and you decided to take their swag." I stared at him, incredulous. "And this Caamasi didn't want to give it up, right?"

"We just wanted him to *share*."

"Sure, but the only thing you know about sharing comes under the heading 'communicable disease.'" I frowned. "What made you think you had any right to that jewelry?"

Remart looked at me as if I were stupid. "We're pirates. We take stuff like jewelry."

"Right, but all the stuff we take goes into a communal pool and is split up later. You know that." I shook my head. "Just because Admiral Tavira has lost her mind doesn't mean rules no longer apply to you."

"Oh, really?"

I nodded. "Really."

"Good, then. I'll apply some rules." He brought his blaster carbine up and pointed it at the Caamasi male he'd hit. "This one hit me. He was resisting, so I get to kill him."

"Nope."

"No?" Remart's eyes narrowed. "Being selective about regulations now, aren't you, Captain?"

"Hardly." I pointed at the Caamasi with my left hand. "He's mine. You can't kill him."

The pilot frowned. "He's *yours*?"

"Right. I need a bodyservant, and I want him to fulfill that role. You can't kill him." I watched Remart's anger rise to his face. "And that's an *order*, Sasyru."

Remart shifted his shoulders. "You know, I don't think I like your orders. And, you know, I think you could be shot down right now and we could tell everyone that the Thalassians ambushed you while you were bravely leading us on a recon of this area. I think I could even get elected to lead Bolt Squadron in your place."

"That's possible, but it won't give you what you really want." I tossed my blaster carbine down and the belt of powerpacks with it. "Even if I die here, even if you cover it with that story, everyone will remember two things. One: I was in the lead and two: they'll remember I said you hit like a Chandra-Fan. You'll never live that down unless . . ."

"Unless?"

I shook my hands out and waved him forward with my fingertips. "Try me. Beat me down with your fists.

Of course, I don't think you have the guts to do that, since I'm not harmless. Care to prove me wrong?''

Remart laughed aloud and tossed his carbine to his wingman. ''Oh, I've been waiting for this chance. You suckered me in the dark, Idanian. It's a good day for bone breaking and blood spilling. You're mine.''

His first punch came in high, a right hand hooking down toward his left. I stepped away from it easily, then leaned in, grabbed the back of his grey flightsuit and tossed him to the ground. He rolled on his shoulder and came up, spinning fast to face me, his arms ready to pick off any punch or kick I might be throwing at him.

I remained where I was and laughed. ''I told you before, you get one free punch. You missed, so I'll only count it as a half, how's that?''

He approached me more carefully, keeping his feet solidly under him. He came in with his left fist forward, his right cocked to deliver a heavy punch. He led with a short jab from his left hand, but I merely had to lean my head away to avoid it. He stepped in to deliver the right, so I cut to my right and his punch sailed over my left shoulder. As I came around beneath his retracting left arm, I leaped up and caught him on the side of his face with an open-handed slap that twisted him around and dropped him to one knee.

He covered the red imprint on his cheek with his own hand, then spat on the ground. Remart rose slowly and set himself to continue the fight. ''Is that your best, Idanian?''

''Just warming up.'' As he set himself for my attack I saw the myriad of countermoves he ran through his mind. Unlike Tycho, Remart did not think in complicated lines. He evaluated and rejected attacks not based on what I could deliver, but on what he could best attack back from. He looked to defend himself against blows he *hoped* I would throw.

And apparently he never truly got the idea that I had no intention of making his dreams come true.

I snapped a kick out with my right foot that caught him on the left kneecap. It drove the knee back until it locked, but didn't break it because I'd already begun to retract my foot. As he began to stumble back, my foot flicked out again, catching him squarely in the stomach. His eyes bulged and a strangled groan burst from his mouth as he fell and vomited.

"Hey, you *do* have guts!" I left him on the ground, walked over to the bag of jewelry and squatted beside it. The pieces in it looked very beautiful, both delicate and yet possessed of a sinewy strength that matched the Caamasi people. "You were willing to oppose Remart for these pieces. Why?"

The Caamasi looked from me to where Remart was slowly gathering himself to his feet, and back again. "These are heirlooms. Our families were destroyed on Caamas, and these are the physical memories we have of them." He pointed to one particular piece, a necklace, with interlaced catlike figures, each with a tiny gold stone as an eye. "My daughter, she asked for that piece to be returned. Your man demanded something of her in exchange, and sought it when she refused."

I tossed the piece to the Caamasi crouched next to her father, then stood and walked back toward where Remart was bent over holding his belly. I knew he was trying to sucker me in, so I feinted taking one more step forward and stopped. He lunged forward, trying to tackle me, so I slipped to the left and drove my right fist solidly in on his right ear. The punch dropped him to the ground cleanly and I heard his teeth click as his chin hit first.

I kicked him solidly in the ribs, then backed away, sucking at my torn knuckles. "That was for even thinking about imposing yourself on her."

I walked back over and picked up the rest of the jewelry. I tossed the bag to one of the Caamasi in the crowd. "Make sure the pieces get back to whom they belong."

Remart's wingmate, Dobberty, groaned. "Captain, that's our stuff."

"Not any more." I turned around again to see Remart coming up into a crouch. "You want to come to me, or do I come to you?"

He came and came running. His arms hooked out like horns, looking to catch me, grapple me, carry me to the ground. In close, wrestling like that, his size gave him an advantage, and he wanted to use it. He could hurt me badly doing that, so I didn't feel inclined to play along with him.

I let him get in close, then I began to fall back before his attack. As his arms closed about me, I grabbed the front of his flightsuit and pulled. Rolling back, I posted my right foot in his stomach. As we rocked back on my spine, I extended my leg, pitching him into the air and over my head. He hit hard, driving the Caamasi and his daughter off to my left and further away from their own people. Before Remart could get up and lunge at them, I closed with him and grabbed a handful of hair to help him up.

He started to turn toward me, so I let go of his hair and caught him with a roundhouse left that shattered his nose. He reeled away, but I kept after him, burying my right fist in his stomach, then clipping him with a left on the side of his head again. That punch landed like a hammer on an anvil, and didn't do the anvil or the hammer any good. I felt a pop in my left hand and knew I'd broken something, but despite the pain, I didn't care.

A short jab to the mouth mashed Remart's lips and tumbled a couple of teeth free. His hands rose to his face, came away bloody, then he stared at me for a moment as if he couldn't believe what was happening. His mouth gaped open with surprise, so I closed it for him with a sharp jab that staggered him and sent him to the ground.

Remart lay there for a second, spitting out bloody saliva and a tooth. He swore, spraying blood over the green grass, then looked past me. "Don't just stand there, nerf-brains. You have blasters. Shoot him."

I spun, hoping I could touch the Force and absorb the bolts, but I never even got a chance to begin to concentrate. Blue lightning wreathed each man, one after another, starting them jerking and dancing as if puppets controlled by a spastic droid. Their blasters hit the ground right before they did, and the bleeding Caamasi kept my blaster on them.

I turned for one last time to Remart. "You don't know it, but you've had quite enough." I leaped above the feeble kick he aimed at my legs, then snapped a kick to the side of his head. He flopped back on the ground and I prepared to kick him again, but a hissed gasp from the Caamasi stopped me.

I stared at Remart for a second and could feel my hands swelling. I flicked the blood off my right hand, then realized I'd spattered the young Caamasi female. I looked to apologize to her, read the horror in her eyes, then my gaze drifted beyond her to where her father stood holding my blaster carbine.

On me.

"Thanks for protecting me." I opened my palms

toward him. "Couldn't blame you if you shot me. In your place, I probably would."

"That is entirely possible." The Caamasi shrugged his shoulders easily, lowered the carbine, then twisted it around to present the stock to me. "Among the Caamasi, however, a bodyservant does not shoot his master."

"I wasn't serious about that. I said that just to prevent him from killing you."

The Caamasi's blue on green eyes sparkled. "This I know, but I *am* serious about it. You put your life in jeopardy to protect mine, much as I did to protect my daughter and these, my friends."

"So you should stay with them."

"I cannot, for to do so would be to put you in jeopardy." He blinked his big eyes and raised a three-fingered hand. "You told these men that you were taking me as your servant, which action precipitated this fight. Your man violated an order, an order from which your authority to discipline him arose. If you do not take me as your servant, then there was no justification and he and his friends will be free to fabricate a story that will destroy you. By going with you, I am proof of your story."

My eyes narrowed. "And what of the tale they will tell about the jewelry?"

"We are all that remains of a peaceful people who had their world destroyed. Who would believe we have anything of value?" With his right hand he indicated his people. "I am Elegos A'kla, Trustant for this domain of Morymento. All I have of value is these people and, I believe, by protecting *you* I can protect *them*."

His words, carried in a somber but rich and sincere voice, made a lot of sense. Still, I didn't like the idea of taking him with me into the Survivor society. Even under my protection, Courkrus was no place for a civilian. "I do not want to take you away from your daughter."

Elegos shook his head. "We are Caamasi. We understand well the pain of losing kin, and how to ease that pain. She will not be alone."

I nodded and accepted the blaster carbine from him. I turned and fired one stunbolt into Remart, then lowered the weapon again. "Looks like I have a bodyservant. I'll be at the spaceport. You have an hour to say your farewells. If you don't make it on time and get left behind, I'll understand."

The Caamasi graced me with a warm smile. "An hour. I will be punctual."

I started to trudge down the path to the spaceport and worked my comlink into my left hand. "This is Bolt Leader. When we have a chance, I need some pilots to de-dirt some clutches, and I'll need some evac of downed men."

Someone at fleet replied after only a couple seconds delay. "You have trouble down there, Bolt Leader?"

"A bit." I sucked at a knuckle. "Nothing I couldn't handle though."

FORTY

✳

Some of the *Invidious'* internal security officers came
down with the evac shuttle, separated Elegos, me and the
four of my men who had gone down. Once we got back
to the Star Destroyer, I was placed in a small ward room
and interrogated. I told them the full story about finding
Remart looting the dead Thalassians, our disagreement
about the fate of the Caamasi and the subsequent fight. I
eliminated any mention of the Caamasi jewelry and instead suggested Remart had been angry that the Caamasi
had nothing for him to take. I knew Remart and his
cronies would spin the story differently. I counted upon
the idea that no pirate would give loot back to people to
give my fiction about the lack of loot the stamp of truth.
Their counterclaims would simply seem like a trumped
up story to get me into trouble.

The interrogation lasted for a couple of hours during
which time my hands stiffened up, the blood on them
crusted, and the broken bones in my left hand began to
throb rather fiercely. The interrogators knew I was in
pain and kept promising I'd have medical attention once
I'd cleared up a few details. Having conducted numerous
interrogations myself, I knew what they wanted to hear,
how they wanted to hear it, so I gave it to them. Finally

they walked away, apparently satisfied with what I had told them.

After they left, a Two-Onebee droid came in and examined my hands. It noted that I'd broken two bones in my left hand and had a lot of edema in both hands, as well as cuts and abrasions. It set the broken bones—and was a bit more gentle about it than Mara Jade had been—but informed me that I'd not be getting access to the bacta tanks on the ship because I was not sufficiently injured. While it would not give me details on what had happened, from the nature and number of injuries it described, I gathered some Thalassians must have ambushed one of our looting parties, or someone triggered a booby trap, which accounted for all the people using the tanks before me.

The droid withdrew and Elegos came into the room, with bandages, some salves, water and sponges to clean up my hands. "Though I am not formally a healer, one learns to deal with wounds like these when building a settlement."

"Carving out a new life is bound to give anyone new skills." I smiled carefully, a bit surprised by the Caamasi's scent. I found it slightly spicy and woody, almost like Corellian whiskey, but a touch sweeter, reminding me of warm beverages my mother would make for us when the family would huddle together during winter nights. I found the scent comforting and something that seemed to make the small grey room in which we stood seem less oppressive.

Sitting on the room's table, I looked up into Elegos' eyes as he cleaned the blood from my right hand. "I have a question for you."

"I will do my best to answer it."

"When I arrived on the scene down there, you were

on the ground, bleeding from the nose. Remart said you'd hit him, but from here, feeling the strength in your hands, looking at your musculature, I know that's not true. You are not that far removed, physiologically speaking, from Selonians that I believe Remart would have been left standing if you'd hit him.''

Elegos cocked his head slightly to the right. ''I tapped him on the shoulder, wishing to thank him. I believe I surprised him with my approach, which is why he turned and struck me.''

''But, if you had wanted to, you could have snapped his neck with a single blow, couldn't you?''

Elegos' brow furrowed, then he looked down into the basin of bloody water. ''For Caamasi, momentous events produce memories that are very striking in detail—you might consider them holographic, but they are more to us. Almost tangible. To have that sort of memory of killing someone, no matter the reason, is a terrible burden to bear. Such a memory would not fade with time, and would become a heavy burden indeed. Because of such things, we have always sought to promote peace and understanding, harmony and unity.''

I nodded. ''And that's why you stunned instead of killed the others down there.''

Elegos straightened up. ''I thought I had killed them. I stunned them because you had left the blaster set on stun. I could not have let them kill you, and would have accepted the burden of such memories in your defense.''

That surprised me a bit. ''So, when you held the blaster on me, you thought a shot would kill me.''

He bowed his head forward. ''Until you took the weapon and shot Remart, I thought the men I had shot were dead. It was only when you shot a man you could have easily beaten to death, that I realized the men I had shot were merely sleeping.''

"Now that you know they live, will that memory fade?''

The Caamasi gave me an enigmatic smile. Flesh tightened around his eyes, sharpening the purple striping that rayed out from their corners. "I will keep it intact for other reasons, I think.''

He started to shift over to work on my left hand, when Admiral Tavira entered the room and shoved him away. She grabbed my left hand and caught the broken bones in a pincer grip. "I am not pleased at all with you, Jenos Idanian, not at all.''

I locked my jaw so I would not cry out as she tightened her grip. Through clenched teeth I said, "I am sorry to hear that, Admiral.''

She released my hand and raked a stare over me. "You look a mess.''

I snorted. "You should see the other guy.''

"I have, damn you.'' Her expression went from angry to something colder, and brought a smile with it. "You administered quite a beating to Remart. And why?'' She flicked a hand out, thumping it off Elegos' breastbone. "For this piece of alien meat? Why?''

I gave her a cold stare. "I needed a servant, nothing more.''

Fire flared in her eyes. "You needed a goad to use on Remart.'' She folded her arms across her chest. "You are so easy to read, Idanian. I know you too well.''

"Do you?'' My guts began to churn for reasons I could not identify. "I should apologize to you for spoiling your fun, I suppose, but I saw no reason to let Remart murder someone who had done nothing.''

"Remart said this one struck him.''

I frowned at her. "Remart has said nothing to you. He's still got to be in a bacta tank. Another couple of hours and your toy will be fine. You can speak to him then."

She shook her head, her hair brushing over her shoulders and breasts like liquid shadow. "He's beyond speaking."

"What?"

Her cruel smile reappeared. "He's dead."

I shook my head. "Not possible. I didn't hit him that hard."

She laughed. "Such concern over someone you clearly hated. No, you did not kill him." Tavira paused for a moment and stepped in closer to me, leaning forward with a hand pressed to the table on either side of my hips. Her words came as whispers, her breath on my left cheek coming warm and gentle, in sharp contrast to what she said. "I had him shot. He was insubordinate. He disobeyed an order and struck a superior officer. He had to die, and you knew he would the moment you goaded him into that fight, didn't you?"

I pulled my head back, leaving a centimeter of space between our noses. "If I'd wanted him dead, I'd have done the job myself."

"That may have been what you were thinking, Jenos, but I know better. Your heart knows better." She moved her head forward until her nose barely bumped mine. She smelled of flowers, musky flowers with a hint of a nebula orchid's sweetness underneath it all. "You wanted him dead, and you wanted me to kill him, to punish me for selecting him after you rejected me."

"Wrong."

She straightened up, raised her right hand and traced her index finger along my jaw, starting at my right ear.

"You blonds always cause so much trouble. Everyone assumes you are stupid, but that's because they cannot fathom the complexity of your thoughts. Perhaps even you cannot."

As her finger came around, she caught my goatee between it and her thumb, giving it a tug that was decidedly ungentle. "You knew I chose him because I knew he was a rival of yours. His hatred of you was quite pathological, as was your hatred of him. At heart though, you were very much alike. The confrontation was expected, and I knew you would be the victor."

I stared deep into her eyes. "Then why didn't you prevent it?"

"I wanted to see how you would get rid of him." Her smile broadened. "If you were a coward, you would have given him impossible assignments, assignments that would have gotten him killed. I did not expect that of you."

I felt a thrill run through me as she spoke. "What did you expect?"

"I expected you to let him trap himself, as he did." Tavira leaned forward again and licked my left cheek teasingly. "I didn't expect you to make me kill him. I thought you would present his body to me as proof you were his superior. Trapping me the way you did, you sought to prove you were my superior as well."

I kept my voice even. "You may choose to believe that, if you wish."

She laughed and backed away a step, then tucked her black hair back behind her left ear. "And you may choose to believe that is not what you intended." She licked her lips and I felt the heat of her lust radiating from her. "So, you forced me to destroy my diversion, leaving me with the need for a replacement. I think I will have you become my new diversion.''

I held my hands up. ''I won't be diverting anyone for days.''

''And you will want to use those days to figure out how to escape me, won't you?'' She shook her head. ''I know your tragic tale of a lover lost and your revenge plotted. I know what you desire. I am not a stupid woman. I could compel your attendance by my side by simply threatening to have the Survivors wiped out. I could threaten your servant here, and you would do what I want, but that is not enough.

''So, this is what I tell you, Jenos Idanian. You know you want me, and you know I want you. I know you want to destroy the *Tinta* line and reclaim the lover denied to you. I will even allow you to do that, putting the *Invidious* and all my resources at your disposal. All you have to do is to agree to come to me of your own free will. You will enjoy my company—and I assure you that you *will* very much enjoy it. You will come here, to the *Invidious*, and I will make you my consort. Through me, your goals will be accomplished.''

Leonia Tavira smiled, then stepped forward one last time. She took my jaw in her hands and pulled my mouth to hers. Her tongue played across my lips, then she kissed me, fully and deeply.

I wanted to tell myself that I didn't thrust her away because of the injuries to my hands, but I knew that wasn't the truth. The thrill I had felt before exploded inside of me, running from my loins to my brain and back down, rendering my pain insignificant. I found my nose full of her scent, and could feel each strand of her hair that lashed gently against my cheeks.

The injuries to my hands were the reason I did not pull her closer.

My face burned as she pulled away, a victorious smile on her face. She glanced at Elegos. "Take good care of him. I will call upon him in a month for his decision, and if he is not healed, I will return to Kerilt and sterilize the planet."

She kissed her fingers and pressed them against my lips. "A month, then all you desire, in your heart and mind, will be yours for the taking."

She swept from the room and a few seconds after her departure, the fire in my lungs reminded me that breathing was indeed a necessary part of my continued existence. I greedily sucked in air and snorted it back out, trying to clear her perfume from my nose. I did my best to ball my left fist and smack it against the table, but Elegos caught my wrist and stopped me from doing that as easily as a parent curbing a child's tantrum.

He didn't say anything, but just started washing my left hand. The sting of water and the rasp of the sponge over torn flesh helped bring me back into myself. I wanted to apply a quick Jedi calming technique, but to do so would betray me to Tavira's advisors. Using such a technique also required more composure than I could muster at the moment.

There was no denying that I was attracted to Tavira. It was a physical thing, an animal thing, a magnetic attraction of one meat machine to another. I wanted to think of it on that plane alone, as if I were betrayed by the crude matter that trapped my spirit, but I knew that wasn't the whole story either. There was something in her spirit that I found intriguing. I told myself that what drew me to her was situational—like my attraction to Siolle Tinta or Wedge's attraction to Qwi. Still, I found something about Tavira absolutely fascinating, which made it difficult to deny the enticement of the flesh.

What disturbed me more than my feeling of being drawn to her was her analysis of why I hated Remart and why I had done to him what I had. Even when describing the fight to my interrogators, I denied the detail of the damage I had inflicted on him. Kicking him in the stomach, smashing his face, all of that was certainly one way to win a fight with him, but I'd been trained in much quicker and more effective ways to deal with someone like him. Even in our first encounter, a shot to the throat had backed him off. That same blow, delivered more forcefully, could have crushed his windpipe and killed him without a fraction of the damage I'd done to him.

I looked at my hands and knew I could have easily put him down without cutting myself and breaking bones. I'd known forever that hitting someone in the face was a great way to break a hand, but I did it anyway. I'd hit him there to punish him, *and* I'd hit him to punish myself. Somewhere, deep down inside, I knew the beating I gave him was wrong. I couldn't stop myself, so I made myself pay.

Tavira suggested that I'd hated Remart so much because we were so much alike. I couldn't believe that, but cold assessment showed me her comparison wasn't terribly flawed. The necessities of the pirate society had brought out my worst traits. I'd allowed my arrogance and cockiness to run away with me and bring me down to the Invids' level.

Remart is what I would have been had I fallen in with the Survivors and not the Rebellion. A chill ran down my spine. It would have been so simple, too, because the Survivors loved the Empire no more than I did when I was on the run. Given no place to hide, I could have

easily joined them to strike back at the Empire. Had I not
been in a position to eventually join the Rebellion when I
ran from Corellia, I might have ended up with the Survivors. Without a moral compass, I would have fallen into
the savage and brutal society with absolute abandon,
thriving amid the scum I used to hunt.

*I'd not have been Tavira's consort, she would have
been mine.*

I hissed, more at that realization than the sting of the
unguent Elegos applied to my hands. I would have been
a terror, a Garm bel Iblis, carrying on my own war with
the Empire, but without bel Iblis's nobility to guide my
hand. The whole of the galaxy would have been arrayed
against me and I would have destroyed them all.

*I would have become what Exar Kun offered to
make me.*

"No!"

Elegos smiled. "The dressing will help the healing,
Master."

"Not that." I frowned. "And don't call me Master.
Jenos will work; Captain if you want to be formal."

"Very well, Captain." Elegos elevated my right hand
and started to wrap it in steriplast.

I sighed and let him work. I knew I had been jealous
of Remart, and I beat him in a manner such that I destroyed his physical appeal. As nearly as I could sort out,
Tavira had been right—I beat him to spoil her fun and
punish her for choosing him over me.

Even accepting that, I knew I'd not let Remart live
just so she would kill him. I had *not* expected that to
happen. She was morally bankrupt enough to transform
mercy on my part into lethal trickery. I knew others
would believe as she did—Caet and Timmser, who prob-

ably knew me better than anyone else in the Invids, would clearly accept my being that devious.

But I didn't do that. I couldn't. I frowned. *Could I?*

I shivered again and felt an icy viper wriggle through my guts. I *could have*, definitely. I clung to the fact that I knew I hadn't.

But now I had a new dilemma to face. Tavira had given me a month to decide if I would become her consort. I would be taken aboard the *Invidious*. I would become part of the crew. I would have her confidence. I would be able to learn all of the Invid secrets, and I would even learn where Mirax was held. I would have everything I wanted—my wife back and the means to destroy the Invids.

In other undercover operations I'd worked before, the delicate matter of physical intimacy with subjects of the investigation had come up and had been handled in a variety of ways. Sometimes another CorSec member, like Iella, would be brought in to play the role of wife or girlfriend. Other times, when going out with a gang and being paired off with someone in the group, getting them drunk enough to incapacitate them, or feigning being that drunk myself provided a way out. Yet other times, claiming to have a girlfriend who knew nothing of my criminal activity would be enough to get folks to leave me alone.

But there were occasions where a cover story did not suffice. All operatives were told that they needn't do anything they objected to on a moral or philosophical basis, and we were given assignments that would put the least amount of stress upon us in that regard, but there were times when sleeping with someone was the logical next step in deepening a relationship that would allow the investigation to go further. While I was not wholly comfortable in such situations, neither did I see sex between consenting adults as forbidden unless sanctioned by marriage. Mirax and I had enjoyed each other's company well before we were married, and she was not the first woman I'd ever taken to bed.

The few times during investigations when I had slept with a subject were different for me because, in those situations, I had no steady relationship with anyone else. I had no external ties, no understandings or vows that I would be breaking by sleeping with someone. And it struck me that while such connections would have given me another level of concern, they might not have stopped me.

Mirax was my wife, with whom I had been entirely faithful; yet Tavira was the most direct course to obtaining Mirax's freedom. It would not be as if I were to fall in love with Tavira—that would not be possible. Physically I might be with her, but emotionally I would have no connection. I would give her what she wanted to put myself in position to get what I wanted. It would be an alliance of convenience, letting me correct the injustice that had been done to my wife.

It would be so simple. All I would do would be to be with Tavira, to please her and deceive her. She would lead me to my wife. And I would even deny Tavira that which she would want most—my devotion. That would be the goal she had in mind, and I would not surrender that to her. She could have my body, and together, I had no doubts, we would discover and explore vast galaxies of passion, but she would never quite get all that she wanted from me.

All those thoughts coursing through my brain seemed so obvious and so right, but something screamed in horror at the idea of giving in to them. What would be so easy to do, what would bring me closer, faster to Mirax than anything I'd done so far, would somehow also be wrong. I didn't know why. I didn't want to believe it. I even wanted to say the transgression there would be insignificant compared to the good that resulted. My alliance with Tavira would be only one-way—I would get from her what I wanted and deny her the prize she most desired. That was what I would do, and any protest could be damned for being weak.

I shivered. "I can't believe I'm thinking this."

Elegos tore and knotted off the steriplast bandages on my right hand. "What is that, Captain?"

I shook my head. "Things I'm considering. Things I must do, but things I almost can't believe I'm thinking. I *can't* be thinking them."

The Caamasi nodded slowly. "If you will permit me, we Caamasi have a saying."

"Yes?"

He pressed his hands together contemplatively. "If the wind no longer calls to you, it is time to see if you have forgotten your name."

The simple saying hit me like a hammer, and found echoes in my father's old adage about not recognizing the man in the mirror. I began to tremble. "You're right. I no longer know who I am."

FORTY-ONE

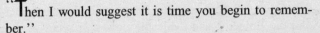

"Then I would suggest it is time you begin to remember."

I laughed. "Easier said than done."

He shook his head and began wrapping my left hand. "Not at all. Start from where you are and trace your steps backward until you recognize the last place you knew yourself." While his advice seemed deceptively naive, something in his voice also suggested it was the only possible solution to my quandary.

I applied myself to the task, but zeroed in on a short-cut. A liaison with Tavira would be the fastest route to rescuing Mirax, but part of me knew it was wrong. I knew the part of me that opposed the plan bitterly would be a stepping stone back to myself, so I grappled with the reason *why* accepting Tavira's offer would be wrong.

The answer smashed me in the face and left me aghast I'd avoided seeing it. The choice was *wrong* because I wouldn't be sleeping with *Tavira* for *Mirax's* sake, I'd be sleeping with her because *I* wanted to—I was letting the ends justify the means. I was able to wrap up a selfish desire in all sorts of noble and selfless reasons, but the reality was that Tavira's attraction to me pleased me. I felt flattered. I'd been married to Mirax for just shy of four years and never had the desire to be with another woman, but that didn't mean I didn't want to be thought of as attractive. And Tavira was a desirable woman who could have any of hundreds of men, so for her to choose me, well, that was very special. And for me to have the chance to prove she had chosen correctly, that I was indeed someone very special, that was a meal that could gorge my Hutt-like ego.

It was of the dark side.

Those words echoed through my brain in Master Skywalker's voice, and my understanding of the dark side expanded exponentially. Exar Kun and Darth Vader and the Emperor had made the dark side seem so dynamic and powerful, that recognizing it and refusing it became easy. Here in the Invid society where people acted more like beasts than they did civilized creatures, the line of demarcation between good and evil was not so much blurred as it didn't always run straight. Each situation had to be approached a little differently, and adjustments had to be made by degrees, or falling over to the dark side became almost casual.

In the beating I had administered to Remart I'd probably stepped over the line. I *had* been working in defense of Elegos, his daughter, his people, and even myself. Had I tapped the Force to strengthen me in that fight, I would have been pulling through power dark and terrible. I would have done to Remart things that all the bacta in the galaxy could not have made right, and reveled in his screams as I did it. I would have swept Tavira away. I would have won Mirax her freedom, but only at the expense of all we had ever had together.

I frowned, then looked up at Elegos. "It all comes down to the nature of evil, doesn't it? Evil is selfishness, while good is selfless. If I take an action that benefits me, only me, and hurts others, I am evil. If I do what must be done to prevent harm to others, if I become the buffer between them and evil, then my actions will be good.''

The Caamasi canted his head to the left. ''Your intentions will be good. Without consideration and forethought, however, your actions could still be evil. That is the problem, of course, evil is always easy and resisting it is never so. Evil is relentless; and anyone, if they tire, if they are not vigilant, can fall prey to it.''

My scowl deepened. ''And there are situations where opposing evil may result in harm coming to the innocent.''

''It does happen, yes.'' He blinked his big eyes, then settled his hands on my shoulders. ''Life is not without pain, but life concerns itself with how we handle that pain, or joy, or confusion or triumph. Life is more than time passing before death, it is the sum and total of all we make of it. Decisions may not be easy, but many is the time when not making a decision, not taking an action is worse than a poor decision. Evil flourishes where it is not opposed, and those who are able to oppose it must to protect those who cannot protect themselves.''

I threw my head back and laughed aloud.

Elegos watched me with a puzzled expression on his face. ''I did not think what I was saying was particularly humorous.''

''It wasn't. It's just that I've heard those words before, from my family and friends and even myself.'' I smiled at him. ''When you introduced yourself to me, you said you were a 'Trustant' of your people. That is a position of responsibility and trust?''

The Caamasi nodded solemnly. ''It is most highly regarded among our people.''

"And do I have your trust?"

"You do."

"So I can trust you in all things, to help me?"

Elegos again nodded. "I will not be a servant of evil."

"That makes two of us." I nodded to him. "When we get home, I will tell you more."

He pressed his hands together again. "I look forward, then, to journey's end."

"Thanks for fixing my hands. And my head."

"The pleasure was all mine."

I twisted around and lay back on the table, hooking my heels on its edge and letting my hands rest like lumps of lead on my chest. In having quoted back to me things my father and grandfather had said, things I'd heard Wedge say and things I'd told myself and others, I realized who I was. I saw my reflection in the mirror and heard the wind call to me. I had, since before I could remember remembering, always held as the highest possible ideal a commitment to serving others. What *I* wanted was subordinate to what was good for everyone else. My job was to provide others shelter and shade, to be a fortress against all the cruelty and wantonness out there. Life itself was hard enough without monosynaptic sociopaths preying on folks.

What I realized right then and there was that I'd made gross errors in how I approached dealing with Mirax's disappearance. When I joined the Jedi academy, I abandoned much of who I had been. I had a new name, a new look, a new identity and I was learning new things. I was trying to become someone I was not because I believed that only someone more powerful than me, a Jedi, could ever possibly save Mirax.

When the Jedi academy proved disappointing and I

fled, I returned to my roots. I pitched away what I had learned, and even missed what my grandfather had given me in the information he'd preserved. I even misinterpreted the dream as one predicting disaster if I tried to be a Jedi, but that wasn't the message of the dream at all. The message of that dream was as simple as it was stark: selflessness is the only antidote to evil. It provides the light that destroys the dark.

At first I had divorced myself from my CorSec past, then I divorced myself from my Jedi heritage in favor of my CorSec training. I was treating my identities as if CorSec and Jedi were left and right, as if I could possibly function with only one side of my body or the other. I was making half of myself oppose the other half, when I should have integrated both halves.

I was not Corran Horn of CorSec or Keiran Halcyon, Jedi Knight. I was both of them. I needed to unify myself and my efforts. Certainly, just as my grandfather had described Nejaa often not letting it be known that he was a Jedi, there were times when one approach would work better than the other, but I had to be able to use *both* if I planned to succeed.

The *Invidious* got us back to Courkrus relatively swiftly, and I was shuttled down with Elegos halfway through the unloading of the Survivors' share of the bounty yielded up by Kerilt's warehouses. I could have gone down sooner, but I stayed on the *Invidious* to see to it that my squadron got off in good order, and to find out from Colonel Gurtt what she'd heard in the way of rumors running around through the ship's crew. She didn't say she'd heard much, but she recommended I start physical training, aiming to improve my stamina and vigor as much as possible.

By the time I got down to Vlarnya and to the hotel

suite I rated, given my rank, I discovered it had been visited in my absence. A variety of luxury goods had been delivered to my rooms including some century old Savareen brandy in a matching decanter and snifter set. The bottle and the four glasses had been decorated with exotic gemstones, including a Durindfire jewel the size of my thumbnail. Bolts of exotic fabric, statuettes from various worlds and a variety of preserved foodstuffs had been loaded into my rooms, along with a holograph from Tavira wishing me a quick and strong recovery.

I smiled. A mere dozen hours before now this display would have impressed me and flattered me. I would have felt that I had her right where I wanted her, too; that I had trapped her into devoting so much energy to winning me that she'd never see how much I was fooling her. I would have poured a glass of the brandy, toasted her defeat and tossed it off triumphantly.

Now I just saw a pile of things that had been stolen from others. She had no right to any of this, and giving it to me, giving me things she did not own and had not worked to earn had no value. She took what she wanted, and while she thought she wanted me to come to her voluntarily, the fact was that she'd have from me what she wanted or she'd have me destroyed. Her gesture was as hollow as she was amoral; and that just made my decision to deal with her that much more important and imperative.

Elegos returned to the suite's parlor after having completed a circuit through the bedroom, refresher station and food preparation station. "There is much more elsewhere, including things suggesting a fair amount of intimacy in the refresher station and bedroom."

"In her fondest dreams, Elegos." I gave him a confident smile. "We've got a month. In that time, I intend to become her worst nightmare."

"Good. I applaud your decision." The Caamasi clapped his hands together and smiled. "I should add, I think it is one worthy of even your grandfather."

FORTY-TWO

✳

"My grandfather?" I stared at Elegos, gape-mouthed. "You're not referring to Rostek Horn, are you?"

The Caamasi shook his head and pointed me toward one of the suite's chairs. "You inquired if I could be trusted several hours ago, and you informed me of a decision that requires I keep your trust, or you will be hurt and perhaps even killed. I offer you, now, something of similar value."

I slowly sat. Highlights skittered silver over his gold down as he drew himself together in the middle of the room. I sensed a great solemnity about him, and knew what he was about to do was not something he did lightly. "Elegos, you need not tell me anything that will jeopardize you or your people. In fact, it might be best if you don't."

"No, I know I can trust you." The Caamasi gave me a beneficient smile. "Even under pain of death you would not surrender this secret."

Not knowing what to say, I just sat back and let my bandaged hands lie on my belly.

"You will recall I told you that memories of momentous events become strong and almost tangible to us?"

I nodded. "Killing someone would create such a memory."

"Correct, or other things like the birth of a child, or meeting someone famous, or being present at some significant event." Elegos' expression softened slightly. "Among the Caamasi we refer to these memories as *memnii*. They are memories invested with emotion and sensory data and, even sometimes, intangible things that escape quantification. They are more fine in detail than any holograph, and more precious to us than any material possession."

He brushed his fingertips lightly across the purple striping on his shoulders and around his eyes. "The truly significant thing about *memnii* is that we can share them with others. The ability to transfer them is limited by consanguinity, which is why our clans often intermarry, making certain there are open avenues of communication between groups. Because we can share these memories, because they come across with full impact, they have more completely allowed us to communicate within our species. This is why we have avoided violence and look to help others find peace.

"My markings are common among the Kla, the maternal clan into which I was born. It is fairly easy for me to transfer a *memnis* to another member of the Kla clan or to my father's clan, the A clan."

My head came up. "My grandfather knew a Caamasi named Ylenic It'kla."

"My mother's brother. We share the maternal line. I knew him well and we were very proud of his being a Jedi." Elegos' face took on a very happy expression. "You must understand, we Caamasi discovered something special about the Jedi. While only three or four generations of separation could all but block the transfer of *memnii* between Caamasi, when one of us came to know a Jedi and form a bond with him, we could transfer to him a *memnis*. This *is* nothing short of a miracle, and when my uncle became a Jedi, the Kla clan's pride swelled incredibly. It is through a *memnis* my uncle gave to me that I recognized you. You have Nejaa's eyes, his scent and his sense.''

''Your uncle was Ylenic? Where is he? Can he tell me more about Nejaa?''

Elegos blinked his eyes rapidly and covered his face with his hands for a second. I started to get out of my chair, but he held a hand out to stop me, then composed himself. ''Forgive me. My uncle was not on Caamas when our world was immolated. He was visiting a friend on Alderaan and convinced that friend to provide a safe haven for other Caamasi survivors. He and others of our leaders who had survived decided that we also had to spread out, and to mix our clans in all these new settlements. While Alderaan might be the largest settlement, it would not be the only one.''

I felt my blood run cold. ''He died on Alderaan.''

Elegos nodded slowly. ''He had eluded the Emperor's Jedi hunters for years, but he could not elude a world's destruction.''

''What was the memory of my grandfather he gave to you? Can you give it to me?''

Elegos shook his head. ''I do not think you are quite enough a Jedi, nor enough of a friend, for us to be able to do this yet.'' He hesitated. ''And I am not certain you would want this memory. It is of your grandfather's death.''

I sank back in the chair and closed my eyes. What I knew of my grandfather's death was a nightmare, but at least I could treat it like a dream. I didn't want to even think about getting it full blown with emotion from my grandfather's friend. "You're right. Perhaps that's not a memory to which I am entitled."

"Yet."

I nodded and opened my eyes again. "Yet."

"We shall have to remedy that, then." The Caamasi smiled again, slyly this time, giving him just a hint of predator. "How will we proceed?"

I brushed a bandaged hand over my mouth. "Every good operation starts with Intelligence. The Invids draw ships and crews from all over, but those based here are definitely the spine of Tavira's operation. If we shatter them and drive them away, she'll have to take greater and greater risks, which means she'll make mistakes."

"Destroying a planet of pirates is a tall order for a lone Jedi Knight and a lightsaber."

"True, especially since I don't have a lightsaber." I frowned. "Don't think I can download the plans for one from the HoloNet, and I don't think sending Luke Skywalker a message inquiring after how to build one will bring a favorable response."

"Even on Kerilt we had heard of his Jedi academy. He would not teach you?"

I winced. "I was there, but didn't exactly leave on the best of terms with him. Do the Caamasi have the equivalent of the Corellian 'Strafing the spaceport you've just left?' "

"Uprooting a plant after you have plucked a single blossom."

"It works. Can't be a Jedi without a lightsaber."

Elegos shrugged. "Perhaps you can re-root the plant."

Something in the back of my brain clicked. "Not re-root, just grow a new one." I got up and jogged into my bedroom. There on a night table I had a datapad and a stack of datacard journals. I picked them up and started sorting them clumsily by pitching the ones I didn't want onto the bed. Finally I got down to the ones I needed and handed them to Elegos.

He frowned. *"Corellian Horticultural Digests?"*

I nodded. "Nejaa's best friend, the man I grew up thinking of as my grandfather—the man who *is* my grandfather—was wise enough to know I'd need the sort of information I'd declined to take with me. These journals have in them columns he has written. I thought he gave them to me when I was leaving because he wanted to share his work with me, but I never even got all the way through any of them. Too much plant stuff, and annotations that reference the genetic codes of the hybrids. In those codes he has encrypted Nejaa's journals and teachings, and the instructions for creating a lightsaber have got to be in there."

Elegos scooped the datapad up. "If you will permit me, I will go through these journals and see what I can find."

"Good." I held my hands up. "Since I can't fly for a bit, I have ample reasons for wandering about all over the place. I know a lot about operations here, but not as much as I should. Once I know where the support structures are for the Invid organization, I can take them apart. It won't be easy, but it's got to be done."

"As my uncle often said, 'There are attempts, and there are accomplishments. Histories only praise one.' "

I laughed and clapped my hands, then bit back the pain. "You accomplish some decoding and I'll accomplish some healing, then we'll go from there."

·　　·　　·

I actually managed to do a lot during the time I was healing, and my imminent elevation to Tavira's side helped me immeasurably. When I was asked, for example, why I didn't use the bacta tanks on Courkrus to speed my healing, I said Tavira would think me weak if I could not endure the pain. That satisfied most folks, while the Jedi healing techniques Elegos uncovered from the journals actually allowed me to speed my healing. I knew, however, that having my hands continually wrapped in bandages would be helpful since it made me decidedly less threatening to most folks.

I made the rounds of the myriad groups stationed on Courkrus, and was greeted warmly by all the various leaders. They clearly felt courting me would be good for them in the long run. I spent some time in the Warren with Riistar's Raiders and the *Red Nova* crew. Aside from wanton cruelty visited on the indigs, they were a fairly benign bunch of individuals. They were not quite the hard cases that the Survivors were, and really didn't seem to have any secrets or plotting going on that I could exploit.

In direct contrast, Shala the Hutt and his gang of glitbiters were malevolent to the core. They'd taken over a warehouse out near the spaceport and had remodeled it in a fashion best described as Old Republic because it looked as if the place had been destroyed before the Empire arose and left virtually untouched since. Debris tangled the place, with rusty orange being the dominant color and laser-burn black being a second choice. Duraplast crates that looked worn enough to be Death Star debris were scattered all over, and the whole place stank of rotting vegetation.

The duracrete slab in the center had been lased down into an amphitheatre with a flattened dais at the north end where Shala spread himself out. I've heard it said that young Hutts can be quite muscular and powerful, which must mean that Shala is older than dirt. If a rock could be described as obese and it drooled, that would be Shala. Shala tended to mumble a lot, then laugh, which made his cronies laugh, too. The 3PO droid he had translating for him did a fairly good job, but Shala hit him so often to correct him that the droid's right arm looked like it had been dragged behind a speeder bike going at high speed through Vlarnya's narrow streets.

I smiled at the droid. ''Tell your master I find his hospitality most generous, but an allergy to most insects means I'll have to decline snacking on those crunchbugs.'' I nodded to Shala and passed the bowl of chirping bugs back to him, licking my lips enviously. I turned my attention back to watching two little mammals with tusks trying to tear each other to pieces. They fought hard, apparently not knowing Shala would eat the victor.

The most interesting thing about Shala's warehouse was that the building was actually smaller on the inside than it was on the outside. The absolute glut of junk in the place made it difficult to tell that fact from the inside, and I would have missed it save for spreading my senses out to see if he had hidden guards located in various spots where they could snipe at interlopers. I didn't find any at that time, but I did discover people working behind false walls and in other sunken pits buried beneath piles of scrap metal and plasteel.

I smiled and gently flicked away a droplet of tuskette blood that hit my right cheek. The victorious tuskette screamed as Shala snapped its spine and bit its head off. He offered me a raw haunch, but I declined, so he tossed it to another of the warehouse's denizens, and a fight

ensued for it. I sincerely hoped for the sake of the
Rodian who won the prize that Shala would be sated by
tuskette, lest another victor end up on the evening's
menu.

By far the most secretive of the groups in Vlarnya
was the Blackstar Pirates. While they made a cantina
called the Mynock Hole their home, most of them
passed through it on their way to another location. Way
off in the back of the common room, in a corner where
visitors never got seated, members would punch a code
into a keypad and be admitted beyond a sliding door
fitted into the wall. I had no idea what went on back
there, though the relief of pirates allowed to leave their
public station and retreat to the back radiated off them
like heat off a fusion reactor.

While collecting data, I did my best to limit my uses
of the Force. I wanted to avoid detection, of course, but I
also wanted to avoid having things that seemed anomalous happening before I started taking overt action. The
fact was that the easiest solution to dealing with the
Invids was to put together a lightsaber and harvest a
bunch of heads. Decapping the pirates would certainly
cause a quickening of the Invids' downfall, but then I'd
be the only one left on Courkrus, which would provide
Tavira with a big clue as to which one of us was the
source of her problems.

Even more of a problem than that, of course, was the
fact that I'd be committing wholesale murder. While it
was true that none of these folks would ever be elected
Humanitarian of the Year, they didn't all deserve death.
Caet and Timmser, for example, were just good pilots
who had fallen in with the Invids. Had they joined the
Rebellion, they could have been plotting Tavira's downfall. I wanted to give them a chance to redeem them-

selves, I guess, which meant I needed to convince them that what they were doing was wrong and to walk, run, slither or fly away from it.

In this I had an invisible ally: all my targets were spacers. Something about traveling through the vastness of space, never knowing if a jump will go bad, dropping you into a sun or leaving you stuck in hyperspace forever, that makes spacers a bit superstitious. For years I'd worn a Jedi Medallion as a good luck charm. I'd infiltrated the Invids because I read an omen in a dream. If enough things began to go wrong, if there were enough signs of impending doom, even the hardcore Invids would begin looking elsewhere for planets to plunder and places to stay.

In all of the places I went I did my best to memorize what I could. Knowing as much as possible about various layouts was vital if I was to slip in and slip out again. The game I was going to play was very dangerous, but it was one that I had to win, so I did everything I could to control all the variables.

After a week, I had enough information to start planning my campaign. I laid everything out, figured who I would hit first and how, then where I would move next. I had to hit hard to keep the pressure on, yet I had to strike at random so I could not be anticipated and trapped.

It wasn't going to be easy, but then if it was, it wouldn't have been a job for a Jedi.

Only one last thing needed to be accomplished before I could begin.

I needed a lightsaber.

Elegos uncovered my grandfather's instructions on how to create a lightsaber fairly early on, and my heart almost sank. The datafile was rather specific about the various supplies that would be needed to create the weapon, so I had a shopping list. Beyond that, however, the file detailed the steps needed to put the weapon together and included the various meditations and exercises a Jedi apprentice should go through with each step along the way. The process Nejaa laid out, if followed precisely, would take almost a month, and I didn't have a month. I knew impatience and haste were part of the dark side, but really hoped things could be truncated so I could actually succeed in my task.

I took the first step by collecting the various parts. The lightsaber, while an elegant and deadly weapon, actually was not that complex. Getting the parts to put one together was not difficult at all. To serve as the hilt, for example, I salvaged the throttle assembly and handlebar tube from a junked speeder bike. I took it from where the wreck hung in the Crash cantina and no one so much as noticed me make off with it. I got the dimetris circuitry for the activation loop from an old capital-ship-grade ion cannon fire initiation controller—won that piece of junk from Shala betting on another tuskette fight. The recharger port and wiring came from a comlink. A milled down Tri-fighter laser flashback suppressor became the parabolic, high-energy flux aperture to stabilize the blade and I pulled the dynoric laser feed line from the same broken laser cannon to act as the superconductor for energy transference from the power cell to the blade. Buttons and switches were easy to find, and dear old Admiral Tavira, with her gift of the brandy decanter and snifters, provided me all the jewels I needed to make a half dozen lightsabers.

The most difficult part of creating a lightsaber was producing the power cell that stored and discharged the amount of energy necessary to energize a lightsaber blade. That said, the parts list called for a pretty basic power cell—in fact, because of the age of the instructions, I had a hard time locating one that ancient. Newer power cells were more efficient than the one my grandfather had specified, but I didn't think that would present a problem. After all, as I read the instructions I came to realize that the nature of the battery was not as important as how it was integrated with the rest of the components.

The core of the Jedi ritual for creating a lightsaber came down to charging the power cell that first time. My grandfather ridiculed the popular superstition stating a Jedi channeled the Force through his lightsaber. He suggested that this was a misunderstanding of what it took to charge it initially and tie it to the rest of the weapon. The Jedi, carefully manipulating the Force, bound the components together—linking them on something more than a mechanical or material level, so they worked with unimagined efficiency. Without this careful seasoning and conditioning of the lightsaber, the blade would be flawed and would fail the Jedi.

Before I could figure out how to put Tavira off for another month, Elegos decoded an annotation to the instructions for constructing lightsabers. It turned out that during the Clone Wars, Jedi Masters developed a way to create a lightsaber in two days. Nejaa included this method, noting it was to be used only in times of pressing need, but not in haste. I read it over and felt a certain peace settle upon me. I knew the words had not been written for me, but they sank deep into my core. *Urgency without panic, action without thoughtlessness.*

I began by calming myself and simplifying my lifestyle. I drank only water and ate noodles that were all but unflavored. I cleared Tavira's gifts from my bedroom, or hid them away in closets. I sat in the middle of the floor, with the parts for the blade laid out in a semicircle around me. I studied each one and used the Force to enfold it and take a sense of it into myself. My hands would fit the pieces together, but I wanted the parts to mesh as if they had been grown together. The lightsaber would be more than just a jumble of hardware, and to make it I had to see the parts as belonging together.

I fitted the activation button into its place on the handlebar shaft and snapped the connectors into the right spots on the dimetris circuit board. I worked that into the shaft itself, then inserted a strip of shielding to protect it from even the slightest leakage from the superconductor. Next I snapped into place the gemstones I was using to focus and define the blade. At the center, to work as my continuous energy lens, I used the Durindfire. That same stone gave my grandfather's blade its distinctive silver sheen. I used a diamond and an emerald in the other two slots. I wasn't certain what I would get in the way of color tints from the emerald, and with the diamond I hoped for a coruscation effect.

Onto the end of the hilt where the blade would appear I screwed the high-energy flux aperture. It would carry a negative charge which would stabilize the positively charged blade and provide it a solid base without allowing it to eat its way back through to my hands. Controlling a lightsaber blade was difficult enough without having it nibbling away at fingers.

I clipped the discharged energy cell in place, then connected the leads to the recharging socket. I screwed the recharging socket into the bottom of the hilt but didn't fasten on the handlebar's original butt cap that would protect it because I needed to charge the power cell for the very first time. I reached over and took the charging cord from the small transformer I'd borrowed from our tech bay, and plugged the lightsaber in.

With my finger poised on the transformer button that would start the energy flowing, I drew in a deep breath and lowered myself into a trance. I knew that manipulating matter sufficiently to meld the part and forge the weapon would have been all but impossible for anyone but a Jedi Master like Yoda, but doing just that as part of the construction of a lightsaber had been studied and ritualized so even a student could manage it. It was very much a lost art, a link to a past that had been all but wiped out, and by performing it I completed my inheritance of my Jedi legacy.

I hit the button, allowing the slow trickle of energy to fill the battery. I opened myself to the Force and with the hand I had touching the lightsaber's hilt, I bathed the lightsaber with the Force. As I did so subtle transformations took place in the weapon. Elemental bonds shifted, allowing more and more energy to flow into the cell and throughout the weapon. I was not certain how the changes were being made, but I knew that at the same time as they were being made in the lightsaber, they were being made in me as well.

In becoming a conduit for the Force for this purpose, the final integration of the people I'd been occurred. The fusion became the person I would be forever after. I was still a pilot: a little bit arrogant, with a healthy ego and a willingness to tackle difficult missions. I was still CorSec: an investigator and a buffer between the innocents in the galaxy and the slime that would consume them.

And I was *Jedi*. I was heir to a tradition that extended back tens of thousands of years. Jedi had been the foundation of stability in the galaxy. They had always opposed those who reveled in evil and sought power for the sake of power. People like Exar Kun and Palpatine, Darth Vader and Thrawn, Isard and Tavira; these were the plagues on society that the Jedi cured. In the absence of the Jedi, evil thrived.

In the presence of just one Jedi, evil evaporated.

Just as with the lightsaber, the changes being made in me were not without cost. What the Force allowed me to do also conferred upon me great burdens. To act without forethought and due deliberation was no longer possible. I had to be very certain of what I was doing, for a single misstep could be a disaster. While I knew I would make mistakes, I had to do everything I could to minimize their impact. It was not enough to do the greatest good for the greatest number, I had to do the best for everyone.

There was no walking away from the new responsibility I accepted. Like my grandfather I might well choose when and where to reveal who and what I was, but there was no forgetting, no leaving that responsibility at the office. My commitment to others had to be total and complete. I was an agent of life every day, every hour, every second; for as long as I lived, and then some.

I heard a click and looked up, blinking my eyes. "Elegos?"

Elegos stood over me, offering me a glass of water. "It's done."

I blinked, then took the water and greedily sucked it down. I lowered the glass and felt water dribbling down around my goatee. I swiped at it with my right hand and felt the stubble of beard on my cheeks. "How long?"

"Two and a half days." The Caamasi smiled and took the glass back from me. "Not as fast as your grandfather, but acceptable."

"Anyone notice I was missing?"

"Several people inquired, but I told them you were down with the brandy ague. They said they could understand your celebrating your change in fortune." He set the glass on my dresser, then walked back into the suite's parlor. "While you were engaged in here, I found something else to do, and made good use of one of Tavira's gifts to you. I estimated the pattern based on my *memnis* of your grandfather."

He held up a green Jedi robe, with a black belt and black overrobe. "I think it should fit you well."

I nodded and brandished the lightsaber. I punched the button under my thumb, giving birth to the silver blade 133 centimeters in length. "A lightsaber and robes. Looks like a little justice has arrived on Courkrus, and it's about time."

FORTY-THREE

I decided to build upon the excuse Elegos had fashioned for me by spending more time drinking—or, at least, appearing to be drunk. A little Savareen brandy spilled on a tunic will leave you reeking of the stuff, and if you keep swirling it around and are sloppy when you drink it—spilling more on yourself in the process—folks notice. The people I was spending my time around had no trouble believing I was three jumps from sober at all times.

Being drunk gave me far more freedom because, as long as I was not obnoxious, lost at sabacc, and was generous with Tavira's money or gifts, I was everyone's friend. People looked forward to seeing me, found it easy to ignore me, and even treated me as if I was not there on those occasions when I feigned sleep.

I chose the Survivors as my first targets. I knew them better than I knew anyone else, so I had an edge on getting into their minds. The Survivors were also the most disciplined of the Invids, so if I could break them, make them skittish, the nervousness would bleed over into the other groups. My move against them would be the prelude to my attacks on the other groups, so I wanted it to be especially chilling.

Elegos and I worked hard on it, programming it into my datapad, then projecting it out of the holoprojector pad in my suite. We ran it over and over again, allowing me to memorize it from every angle, and practice my part in it. I had to be careful and quick, but if it worked right, it would shake the Survivors to their core.

I took a seat in the Crash cantina at a table very much in the back. Captain Nive normally sat there, and not too long afterward he joined me. Jacob had not been paying me court as had the other pirate leaders—he trusted in the friendship we had built up during the time he commanded my squadron. I actually liked him and the way he managed the Survivors, but from the conversations we'd had, I knew he was not wholly comfortable with all he had done in his life. That confidence, expressed to me late one night, was about to come back and haunt him.

Jacob sat with his back to the corner of the room. I sat at his left, with my back toward a wall, but slightly exposed along my flank. Another chair sat across from him and could not be seen by most of the rest of the room because of a pillar. I had a bottle of Savereen brandy sitting in front of me, and a snifter in my right hand. Jacob drank lum, but never enough to get roaring drunk, just mildly suggestible. We sat there, chatting in low voices about the latest rumors concerning Shala the Hutt, when I pushed the empty chair out with my left foot, as if someone were drawing it back to sit.

I tapped the Force, letting it fill me, but turned my head toward the chair and away from Jacob. "You can't sit here. This is a private table." As I said that, I reached out with my senses and projected an image into Jacob's brain.

Jacob's head came up and he blanched. "Not possible."

The figure he saw sitting down opposite him spat out a thick golden credit coin, that bounced once on the table. My left hand swept out to grab it, then I slapped down the credit I'd palmed. My left hand recoiled. ''It's cold.''

The figure across the table from Jacob wore an Imperial Captain's uniform, albeit a bit too small, and had a mouse under his left eye. In fact, Captain Zlece Oonaar of the *Crusader* looked exactly the way he had after the Survivors had tried him and Jacob had ordered his execution. Jacob himself had stuffed the gold credit in his mouth, following the old superstition of buying off the evil things the dead would say about the living, then had him pitched out of the *Backstab*'s main airlock.

Zlece Oonaar looked directly into Nive's eyes. ''You can have your gold back. The dead don't speak ill of the dead.''

I grabbed Jacob's left wrist with my right hand. ''What does he mean?''

Jacob's mouth hung open. ''I don't know.''

Zlece nodded slowly. ''You know. You know you should have died the day all your friends did. If you'd fought harder, they might have lived. You failed them, and now you will join them. Doom is coming to Courkrus. All your victims will be avenged.''

Jacob stood abruptly, tearing his wrist from my grip, and threw his mug of lum through the phantasm. I let the image fade into a bloody mist that drifted away as the mug shattered against the pillar. Jacob stood there, gape-jawed and trembling, then looked around at everyone else in the cantina. Their attention had been drawn to him when the mug exploded, but they had seen nothing prior to that.

Jacob pointed at the chair. ''Did you see him?''

Other people started to shake their heads.

He looked at me. "You saw him, didn't you, Jenos? You saw him."

I shuddered and drained my brandy snifter. "I saw him. He was that guy we took, the one we tried." I fingered the coin. "You put this in his mouth."

Jacob snatched the coin from my grip and held it aloft. "Right, I put this in his mouth."

"But we left him in space." I poured more brandy into my snifter and looked up at Jacob, ignoring the tightening knot of people closing in on us. "What did he mean, 'Doom is coming to Courkrus'?"

Jacob snatched my brandy away from me and swallowed it all in one gulp. "I don't know." He put the snifter down again and tapped the rim for a refill. "I don't know, but it is not good. Not good at all."

Within twelve hours the story of the *visitation* had spread all over Vlarnya and had taken on a life of its own. I had people tell me what they had seen and got to listen to them describing a vision I know they never saw. Even when I said that was different from what I'd seen, they told me I was misremembering because I'd been drunk at the time. They knew what the truth was, and it really seemed to scare the bone right out of their spines.

No one was quite certain what it was they'd seen. Some thought it was a ghost, pure and simple, come back to haunt Nive for killing him. Others took the warning into account and wondered why a ghost would warn when he could have just struck and killed us all—if a ghost could actually do that. The warning seemed to worm its way into the minds of many, which was my intent. I wanted them to have been warned so when things started to happen, they would link them back to the warning.

I was pleased the first effort had so grand an effect, but I knew I couldn't do that sort of thing again. While I might be able to use an illusion to throw off pursuit, simple ghostly comings and goings were not going to convince the Invids that it was time to abandon Tavira. The palmed coin provided solid evidence that convinced a lot of people of the veracity of the visitation. Because of that I decided that the next actions I took required physical proof of something going on, and a coin wasn't going to do it. It was time for something a bit more direct and painful.

I waited until after Timmser and Caet had dragged me home from Crash and turned me over to Elegos before acting. Mumbling how he hoped I wouldn't vomit on the bedsheets again, the Caamasi hustled me off and the two of them escaped lest they be asked to help clean me up. Once they were away, I slipped into the Jedi uniform, donned a hooded cloak and slipped out into the night. Using the Force I was able to blank the short term memory of those hotel staffers who did see me, leaving them with an innocent eight-second gap in their memories that covered my passage through the lobby.

Using the Force both in Crash and in the lobby was taking a risk at detection by Tavira's advisors, but I was fairly certain there were none on Courkrus. She'd never given us one before and she had no reason to assume there was going to be a problem on Courkrus. To leave one here ''just in case'' would be to provide any of these groups with a chance to learn her secret and strike out on their own. For that reason alone I felt very safe in using the Force as I hunted.

My previous sojourns into the city served me well as I

moved through less populated alleys and byways to reach some of the seedier areas of the Aviary. I reached inside to tap the Force, so I could expand my sphere of responsibility and locate someone who needed help. My intention, of course, was to help that person and take the criminals involved out of the holograph. It was like being back in CorSec, making a sweep through Treasure Ship Row, just without all the lights.

The difference was, this time, I had the Force as my ally. My sense of the city and the area around me became acute, allowing me to register the various life sources. Had I wanted to, I could have taken a census of crunchbugs or feral tuskettes in seconds. I didn't, though—other data drew me on into the night.

When on patrol for CorSec, I'd been a predator looking for prey, hoping I didn't find it in sufficient quantity to kill me. With the Force, I almost felt like a superpredator. I sensed where everyone was, where their attention was directed. I could choose paths of confrontation that would keep things quiet, or would make for a big display. At the moment I chose something smaller and more intimate, but I knew the day for something more spectacular would come soon.

Even though I sensed where the three of them were, I heard her sobs before I ever saw them. Two drunken LazerLords had trapped an indig woman between them and hustled her into an alley. They backed her up against a wall, trapping her hands high above her head, and were covering her face and neck with the sort of sloppy kisses the totally inebriated seem to have mastered. Except for the look of terror on her face, their antics might have seemed comical.

I moved into the alley as silent as a shadow and grabbed the first man by the scruff of the neck. I whirled him over toward the right, across my body, and smashed his face into the opposite alley wall. Something crunched when he hit, then he slumped to the ground. A half step forward and I brought the pommel of my lightsaber up in my right hand, catching the second man with an upper cut. Impact with the heavy metal pommel cap shattered the man's jaw and sent him reeling backward.

One hand went to his mouth and the other dug for the blaster holstered on his right hip. As he started to draw the weapon, I rotated the lightsaber's hilt in my hand and ignited the silver blade. Its explosive hiss filled the alley, with the light painting the LazerLord's shadow across the alley floor and up along the back wall. I arced the blade down, catching the rising blaster at barrel and grip, dropping pieces of it and two of his fingers to the ground.

A sidekick to his already broken jaw dropped him to the alley floor, then I spun and lunged at his rising partner. Before he could draw his blaster, my lightsaber stabbed through his shoulder, burning a very neat, button-sized hole through bone and flesh. The oily stink of overcooked meat filled the alley. His face went absolutely white. He stared down at the silvery energy shaft sticking out of his shoulder, then his eyes rolled up into his head and he fainted.

I snapped the blade off before his falling body could tear itself free of the blade. I didn't want him dead—I wanted neither of them dead. Two dead men would be statistics, but these men would have scars and would tell a wonderful tale. What the visitation had begun these two would continue.

I turned to the woman who cowered in a crouch. I extended a hand to her and she took it. The tremors in her flesh matched the waves of terror radiating out from her. I made my voice even and as reassuring as I could. "You have nothing to fear, child. They will not harm you any more."

"W-who are you?"

I guided her to her feet and walked with her toward the alley mouth and the street light slanting into it. "It is enough that I am known to be here."

I let her walk into the light, but I remained in the shadows as I let her hand go. "Just tell them that doom has come to Courkrus. Their victims will be avenged, and those who fear justice will never sleep securely here again." Then I projected into her mind an illusion of my fading into nothingness while I slipped past her and moved further along the street. I shadowed her to make certain nothing else happened to her, then, when she found safety, I returned to my home.

The next morning, early, Timmser and Caet came to my suite and insisted Elegos wake me. I emerged from my bedroom looking rumpled and bleary-eyed, then sobered at the serious expressions on their faces. "What's happened? What's wrong?"

Caet growled, and Timmser provided a good translation. "Two LazerLords got badly mangled last night. Doom has come to Courkrus, and it brought a lightsaber with it."

FORTY-FOUR

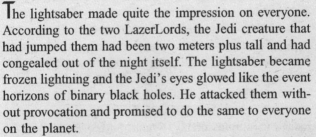

The lightsaber made quite the impression on everyone. According to the two LazerLords, the Jedi creature that had jumped them had been two meters plus tall and had congealed out of the night itself. The lightsaber became frozen lightning and the Jedi's eyes glowed like the event horizons of binary black holes. He attacked them without provocation and promised to do the same to everyone on the planet.

My plans, of course, were less ambitious, but their reports played well in the Aviary. I heard a lot of hollow boasting about what this person or that would do if confronted by this *avenger*. Others might be frightened, the line went, but the speaker was not. He'd tear the avenger's head clean off, then someone else would offer yet a more terrible fate for the avenger and so on, like the bidding at an auction gone mad. Mob bravery carried everyone to the zenith of hyperbole.

Then finally someone—me, sometimes; other folks most often—would shiver and clutch at his gunhand as if he, too, had lost fingers. That simple gesture could quiet a group. And the mere mention of the word ''Jedi'' was enough to send all the braggarts back to their drinks and private fears.

As a CorSec officer I'd seen this sort of bravado before, and had seen it fade in the presence of a uniformed officer, but never had it risen to such heights, nor plunged to such depths. The Empire's effort to vilify and transform the Jedi into agents of terror worked to my benefit. If the Empire, which was bad enough, had feared the Jedi enough to wipe them out, then having a Jedi here preying on the Invids was about as bad as it could get.

So bad, in fact, that the captains of the various groups in Vlarnya offered a ten-thousand-credit reward for the Jedi's head.

And I set out to make it higher, much higher.

For the next several nights I stalked and hit what I considered to be "soft" targets—bands of pirates wandering the streets in search of trouble. Each encounter occurred differently. The fact that many of the pirates reinforced their courage with lots of lum or whiskey helped me immeasurably. Drunks have often seemed incredibly lucky, and in Vlarnya they were as well—but all of their luck was bad.

One evening I let a trio of the *Fastblast*'s crew catch a glimpse of me ducking into an alley. I'd been drinking with them earlier and had talked up how a group could go hunting the Jedi and snag him, winning themselves that great reward. The Fastblasters—two humans, male and female, and a male Kubaz—worked themselves up into a frenzy, then I excused myself and made as if to head home. I wished them luck with their hunt, hoping they would find the Jedi before the other hunting groups, and they took the bait.

The Fastblasters came running and as they rounded the corner of the alley, I projected into their minds the image of me fleeing before them, my cloak flapping back, water from a sewage rivulet splashing up with each step. The humans raced after me at full speed. The Kubaz, who didn't quite see the image I projected, slowed and raised a hand to warn his compatriots. Before he could do so, I rose from the shadows that concealed me near the alley mouth and clopped him on the head with the butt of my lightsaber.

Bereft of his warning, his two companions ran at full sprint into the brick and plaster wall I'd hidden with my illusion. The woman rebounded hard from the wall. Her blond hair wrapped around her face as she twisted through the air and crashed down in a trash midden. The man, who had been a step behind her, had begun to twist to his right, so he took the impact on his shoulder. Even from ten meters away, I heard his collarbone snap. He bounced back, took a couple of stumbling steps in my direction, then dropped to his knees.

His right hand fumbled with the blaster holstered beneath his left arm, but with his broken bone, there was no way he could get a hold of it. I stepped in closer and thumbed the lightsaber to life. His eyes grew wide and he sank back on his haunches.

"You've lost use of the arm. No reason to lose the whole thing, is there?"

He slowly shook his head.

"Very good." I brought the point of the blade around so it sat a centimeter from the tip of his flattened nose. "The next Fastblaster I see on the streets will die. Relay that message for me, will you?"

He nodded and I stepped away from him, retracting the lightsaber's blade. I turned to stalk back down the alley to the street. Even without the Force, I would have heard the snap of his blaster being pulled from the holster. Already three meters away, I turned, lit my lightsaber, and deflected the first shot into the alley wall, where it left a little guttering flame. Two more shots missed wide, I blocked a fourth to my left with the lightsaber, then saw that the fifth would miss right and drill the Kubaz struggling to his feet.

I reached out with my right hand and blocked the bolt, sucking as much of the energy in as I could. The shot stung, sending a jolt up my arm, but I shunted the pain aside and funneled the spare energy into telekinesis. I closed my right hand into a fist, then pulled. I wrenched the blaster from his hand, snapping a couple of fingers as I went, then tossed it high onto a roof.

"Remember my message." I turned again, smacked the Kubaz in the head again with the lightsaber's butt, and vanished into the night.

Three days later the *Fastblast* and its crew departed Courkrus for destinations unknown.

Other crews were not so easily frightened. The Blackstar Pirates felt invincible in their sanctuary behind the Mynock Hole and I knew my intervention there would shake them to their core. In an earlier visit as Jenos Idanian, I took a seat that gave me a clear vision of the datapad they used to gain entry into the back. By casually studying the people going in I learned they used a four digit code, but most of the pirates hit the numbers too quickly for me to read them exactly.

I waited for an older man well into his cups to approach the door and set myself. He punched the number in and waited for a light to go on and a tone to sound before he would be free to push the door open. I reached out with the Force and simply made him forget he'd seen the light and heard the tone. He frowned, then more

carefully and precisely punched the code in, letting me
read from his actions what the combination was.

A rainstorm hit Vlarnya the evening I decided to
carry my war to the Blackstar Pirates, and the atmo-
spherics certainly added to the tension growing in the
Aviary. It also helped that virtually everyone wore
hooded cloaks as sheets of rain lashed the city. I was
soaked by the time I reached the Mynock Hole, but went
unnoticed among the other dripping, cloaked figures in
the cantina. I even swept into the back area warded by
pirates without being the subject of much scrutiny. Moving with authority and raising a hand to the datapad to
punch in the combination appeared to be normal to the
pirates seated there, so I only needed to devote a tiny
slice of the Force to making them lose the seconds of
their life in which I passed them by.

I punched in the code and pushed the door open.
What I found beyond it surprised me because of the
opulence. Muted red and gold glow panels gave the foyer
and parlor beyond it a warm feel. Doorways across from
the entry and in the two side walls provided access to
corridors that I guessed led to rooms meant for private
pleasures. I caught just enough of the tang of spice in the
air to guess what some of the pirates were enjoying, and
a half-dozen men and women attired in unseasonably
brief costume, lounging vivaciously on overstuffed furni-
ture, suggested what others would find to content them.

And through the doorway at the far end of the parlor I
heard the cheers and groans I'd long associated with
gambling. With the small self-service bar to my right,
the Blackstar Pirates' haven seemed to make available
most of the idle-time delights considered desirable
throughout the galaxy. This was a place where everyone
could have fun.

To my left a silver 3PO droid with a missing eye sketched a brief bow and extended his hands toward me. "Check your weapons, Master?" Beyond him I saw a small caged enclosure chuck full of blasters of every size and description, with another 3PO droid locked in, shelving weapons and retrieving them.

"I think not."

"I must insist." The 3PO droid inclined his head toward me. "In accordance with all the regulations in your fellowship contract, specifically clause 35.6 . . ."

I lit the lightsaber and split him from crown to groin with one swipe. Sparks flew as both halves tottered and crashed to the floor. I stepped over the twitching pile of circuits, secretly guilty over how good that had felt, then I pivoted to the right and slashed the lightsaber through the drink synthesizer. Coming around full circle, I leveled the silver blade at the parlor's occupants.

"That was last call. I think you want to leave now." I raised a finger to my lips. "Quietly."

They scattered mutely as I stalked straight into the gambling den. People hunched over sabacc tables missed me entirely, but those gathered around a jubilee wheel did not. I stabbed the argent lightsaber down into the wheel and let the wheel's momentum carve the rim from the hub. The rim spun off, wobbling around the table, scattering bets, then rolled to the floor and tangled in the legs of some Rodian carrying a tray of drinks. Between his crash and the outcry from the roulette players, I got the pirates' attention.

I held the lightsaber before me in such a way that its harsh light deepened the shadows within my hood. "This is no more your sanctuary. This is no more a place where chance holds sway. Doom has come to

Courkrus, and if you stay, your only safe bet is on death.''

With that I walked to a door in the exterior wall, slashed it open and let rain slant in. Lightning struck and thunder blasted as I stepped through into the night— well, it did at least for most of the humans I could reach—and then I was gone except from their nightmares.

And the bounty climbed to one hundred thousand credits.

The weakness of my approach became very apparent to me and, unfortunately, Shala the Hutt. While my tactics were being very effective, and desertion was beginning to nibble away at the Invid ranks, the fact that I had not killed anyone had begun to work against me. I was dealing with thoroughly and completely ruthless individuals who would kill someone in a fight over scraps from a garbage heap. Since their lives were the only thing of value many of the Invids possessed, the fact that I wasn't killing applied a brake to the plummeting morale and even allowed for a rebound.

Shala let it be known that he had a method for dealing with the Jedi, but he kept it under wraps. His warehouse became a fortress where even Tavira's future consort was not allowed to visit. He sent his various henchcreatures out to terrorize parts of town outside the Aviary and started delivering his own messages. His crimes against property escalated into robberies and simple assaults, with more and more hideous crimes clearly in the future. His actions were an open challenge to the Jedi, and even though I waylaid a couple of his raiding parties he just made the following ones more powerful and sent them forth.

Everything pointed toward a direct confrontation between us, which I knew would have to be at the warehouse. I snagged a Twi'lek associate of his—Shala's explosives specialist, a real nasty piece of work—and sent Shala the message that I would meet the Hutt at the warehouse. I didn't specify an exact time, but it was obvious that I would have to find him sooner rather than later.

Elegos was dead set against my going. "Surprise has been your ally and has allowed you to win through in situations where you should not have. Entering the Blackstar sanctuary was foolish because you'd not been there, but surprise got you through that. You surrender surprise here and it could kill you."

I shook my head and clipped my lightsaber to my belt. "I've still got a few surprises of my own, you know. And I've been in that warehouse. I've been around Shala."

"Which is precisely why you should be more careful. You know his crew is mostly non-humans, so your ability to affect their minds will be severely limited. It probably won't help you at all." Elegos frowned at me as he handed me my cloak. "And it's fine for you to absorb a stray blaster bolt or two, but what if they open up on you with a dozen carbines?"

"They won't. Look, I'll get a sense of the place before I go in. I'll know if he's got people waiting to jump me."

"And what if he has robotically controlled blasters so you won't have gunmen to pick out?"

"I'll think of something." My answer rang hollow in my ears, too, but it was the only one I had for him. "I can't *not* face him, Elegos. If I do nothing, he wins, and a lot of people get hurt. I lose my chance to destroy the Invids.''

''If you die, the same thing happens.''

''I have no choice.'' I shrugged. ''I know this one will get ugly, and I'm fairly certain someone's going to die. I'll just have to make sure those who die are those who deserve to die.''

I left my hotel unseen and stalked through darkened streets I found remarkably free of life—at least the sapiens variety. Word had clearly leaked out that the Jedi had agreed to accept Shala's challenge. Since the two of us were likely the most hated individuals on the planet no one wanted to get in the way of our confrontation.

The warehouse looked no different than it had before, save the side door was open and no light bled out into the night. I extended my senses toward it, letting the Force flood through me, and picked out only a half-dozen large lifeforms, including Shala on his dais. The others remained hidden deep in the warrens surrounding the central pit. Their nervousness shone like a beacon, but I found Shala frighteningly calm. He was just waiting for me, so I deigned to keep him waiting no longer.

I entered the warehouse through the open door and was not surprised when it closed behind me. I made my way quickly through the tangled trail of debris to the central amphitheatre, threading a path through chemical drums and twisted piles of metal. When I reached the warehouse's center, I saw a single light on, shining down on Shala and the 3PO droid translator. I slowly stalked down into the amphitheatre bowl and stopped two meters away from the Hutt. I threw back the wings of my cloak and brought my lightsaber into a doublehanded grip, but I did not turn it on.

Shala muttered something and the droid translated. "The great glabrous Shala the Hutt bids you welcome. He instructs you to lay down your weapon and surrender to him, or you will pay a most fearful price."

I thumbed my lightsaber on and pointed it up at him. "Tell Shala I have all the credits I need to pay his price right here. Where would he like them deposited?"

The Hutt laughed, which was not the sort of warm friendly sound one usually associated with laughter. His shoulders bounced, his fat bounced more, and a greenish foam crested the lower lip of his mouth and cascaded down his chin. The sound, however, that was even uglier. As it trailed to a wheeze, I heard a click and saw the Hutt raise his right hand. In it he had a remote with a big red button held down by his thumb.

The droid spoke again. "Shala asks me to inform you this is a deadHutt switch that will set off a variety of explosives here. He says that he has enough explosives here to destroy everything for a kilometer around us. If you do not surrender, many innocent people will die."

All around us I saw little red lights come on and begin to blink, making me groan inwardly. In the light from above I caught enough detail—crosshatched panels curving inward with a red light blinking on top—to know I was looking at Merr-Sonn Munitions LX-1 laser-flechette mines all pointed in my direction. When detonated, the panels would absorb the energy from the explosives and the laser diodes would spray out clouds of laser bolts. To complicate matters, the mines usually had a three meter backblast of pure explosive fire, which would feed into the chemical drums I'd passed on my way in. That would trigger subsidiary explosions that would make quite a mess.

Based on the drums I saw, and what I knew of the

mines, there wasn't really as much explosive power here as Shala said there was. *Either he is lying or . . . I* glanced up and above the spotlight, and caught the blinking of another LX-1. *Or he was told things are a lot different than they are. Here at stupidity central, we'll be vaped, and the neighborhood will get quaked, but we're not talking square kilometers of wastage.*

I shook my head. "Your Twi'lek set all this up for you?"

The Hutt mumbled. "Master Shala says he is most pleased with Rach'talik's work."

"Me? I'd want a refund." I smiled up Shala, and gave him a cold laugh of my own. "You've made two mistakes, Shala. One, you're at ground zero yourself. Two, you think I can't stop you."

I rotated my right wrist, twisting the throttle control up, and whipped the lightsaber around in a slash aimed to slice the deadHutt switch in two. With the twist I turned the lightsaber's emerald out of the way and I brought the diamond into line with the Durindfire beam. This extended the blade from 133 centimeters to 300, narrowing it, but bringing the Hutt's hand easily into striking range. Quick flick of the wrist, cleave the control in two, and the day would be saved. That would be the easy way.

Easy is not for a Jedi.

With a puff of smoke, the lightsaber's blade sputtered and died.

I remember the look of surprise on Shala's face. I'm pretty certain it came from watching the lightsaber blade grow out at him, but I'm not wholly convinced of that. I think, though, the horror that tinged his expression, *that* came from the realization that in his surprise, he'd dropped the remote.

Rach'talik, in addition to wanting to replace Shala, was a virtuoso with explosives. The LX-1s went off in sequence, not all at once, washing the central area with wave after wave of laser flechettes. Each blast scoured the center of the warehouse from a different angle, guaranteeing that no unexploded mines would be hit, but adding laser fire to the chemical fires and exploding drums.

And he even saved the blast from above for last, maximizing the chances that Shala would live long enough to know he had been betrayed.

Had Rach'talik gone for quantity instead of quality, I, too, would have been reduced to a greasy, steaming stain on the duracrete. I knew, from the second I saw the remote fall, I had only once chance at survival, and only one chance to try to contain the damage. I sank within myself, touched the Force, started it flowing, and sucked in every stray erg being sprayed on my direction. I felt sting after sting, as if I were sliding through a Sarlacc's gullet, and it felt as if I were descending into a black pit of pain. I directed some of the Force to help me blunt the pain, but that made it much more difficult to hold on to all of the power I was absorbing.

I knew I couldn't hang on to it for long, and I knew I needed to use it to contain the explosion's deadly force. As I had done in the grotto to save Tionne, I channeled all of it into telekinesis and raised my left hand. I twisted my wrist, starting the energies swirling into a vortex. I could feel the air begin to whirl around me, tightening, quickening. Flames from the chemical fires leaped toward the center of the room, spinning themselves into the vortex. Loose debris, flaming bits of duraplast and rattling, clattering pieces of scrap metal flew into the air, filling the fiery cyclone with dark specks.

I pushed and drove the vortex up and out through the roof, enlarging the hole the last mine had already opened. Chemical drums sailed up, exploding as they went, pulsing green and purple fire through the rising funnel. Flames wreathed me and I sucked their heat in, then vented it back out, up and out, building the firestorm's strength until it ripped the warehouse's roof off and crumpled it like a discarded piece of flimiplast.

The warehouse's doors banged open, then ripped free and flew like sabacc cards into the maelstrom. The warehouse's viewports imploded as air rushed in to feed the firestorm. I no longer needed to push, it had become a thing of its own, almost living, certainly breathing. I felt it tug at me, but the energy it fed me kept me rooted in place. I reached out with my mind, pitching up into the column of fire the last several unexploded chemical drums, watched them blossom brilliantly, then smiled. The explosion had been contained, drawn inward. Though the warehouse's corrugated metal walls glowed dully from the heat, they had not buckled. The tremors from the explosions had rippled out through the ground, but beyond that—and the fiery spear thrust into the sky—only the warehouse would be damaged by the Hutt's deathtrap.

I felt the firestorm's power begin to wane and I knew things were almost over, but I still had lots of energy left in me that I had to vent somehow. I looked up and allowed my smile to broaden. *Everyone knows the Jedi came here to die. Let's show them he did no such thing!*

I expanded my sphere of responsibility and touched every mind I could find. Into them I projected a simple vision, one that would terrify many and reassure others. I let them see the shaft of fire stabbing up into the sky, and at its bottom was the hilt of a lightsaber. A giant figure of a man clad in green and black rose up through the black smoke, then the fire vanished as he switched his lightsaber off. He faded back into the smoke and was no more.

I opened my eyes and nodded as I surveyed the destruction. Shala had set a trap, and, in turn, had been trapped himself. I should have died, but I survived—survived in a way that Corran Horn of CorSec could never have managed. I had survived—no, I had *won*. Shala's spectacular defeat would certainly crack the resolve of the other groups. A push here, a nudge there, and they would fall.

I hooked my lightsaber on my belt, then looked down when I heard it clunk on the duracrete. It lay there on a fireblackened floor, when it should have been on my hip. And it wasn't because I didn't have a belt to clip it to. While the Force allowed *me* to absorb energy and avoid being hurt by it—and lightsabers were notoriously durable—apparently my cloak and uniform were not.

It was at the point when I realized that I was naked that the first wave of exhaustion hit me and I began to notice other things. The imploding viewports had shattered into tiny little transparisteel fragments that had scourged me. I was bleeding from dozens of little cuts, including one across my nose and another somewhere in my scalp. I knew a simple Jedi healing technique could seal them and accelerate healing, but I found I was having trouble concentrating. Fatigue dragged at me, and I staggered back to sag against one of the amphitheatre's walls.

In doing all I'd done, I must have burned off most of my personal Force reservoir. I couldn't use it to link myself to the Force, to refresh myself. I was alone and tired, not thinking particularly sharply, but I knew one thing: if I stayed where I was, I'd be found and found out. The Jedi clearly survived the battle with Shala, but there was no way Jenos Idanian could have.

I scooped up my lightsaber and ran out of the warehouse. I headed north; at least, I think it was north. I kept with the way the night breeze was blowing most of the smoke, allowing it to cover me. From there I moved into the shadows and alleys, keeping low, watching carefully. I know a chunk of my feeling exposed came from my being naked, but a bigger piece came from my inability to touch the Force. With it to armor me, I could have pranced naked through the streets and no one would have given me a second glance. Now I was a naked guy with a lightsaber, which was bound to be seen as peculiar to even the most jaded eye on Courkrus.

I thought I had figured out where I was. I ran across a street and paused in the shadow of a store front to confirm my bearings, then I heard a lock click and the door began to open outward. Even though the store had been long closed, employees had been working inside. As they came out, I yelped and darted around the corner into an alley.

Which turned out to be a dead end. *My* dead end. And *the* single alley in Vlarnya that had a working light in it.

The two women came around the corner and stared at me. I stared back at them. They began to giggle and point. I leaned against a wall and tried to conceal my lightsaber behind my thigh. As they began to whisper to each other I looked away, hoping to hide my face so they couldn't identify me. It wouldn't take them any time to determine a man with a lightsaber had to be the hunted Jedi, and one hundred thousand credits, even split between them, would be enough to get them off Courkrus and buy them a life of luxury on any of a dozen other worlds.

I was done. It was over. Tavira would learn who I was—from me or from Elegos. *Oh, Elegos, what have I done to you? She'll destroy Kerilt.* Once she had taken care of his world, she would have Mirax killed, probably before my eyes, then she would destroy me. I had succeeded in saving the people near the warehouse, but in doing so I had killed those I held most dear.

Then I felt strong hands on my shoulders. A blanket settled about me and I was turned away from the wall. I looked up. "Elegos?"

"There you are!" His rich voice boomed through the alley. "Drunk."

"I . . ."

"Again!" he scolded. He reached down and plucked the lightsaber from my right hand.

"No, Elegos!"

Even though I tried to take it back, he raised the purloined weapon high and glared down at me. "So, where is it? Where is the rest of your speeder bike!?"

The women at the alley mouth burst out laughing. Clutching their sides, they reeled away and into the street. They glanced back, sharp laughter ringing out again and again as they thought about a naked drunken pirate who had demolished a speeder bike and only had the throttle assembly to show for it.

My knees gave way, but Elegos held me up. "Thanks."

"You are more than welcome."

I swallowed hard, my throat parched. "How did you find me?"

"Your vision touched me and I assumed you might be in trouble." He smiled and tapped his nose with a finger.

"Ottegan silk, of which your clothes were made, has a distinctive scent when burned. Right now, you stink of it."

"Oh, sorry."

"I'll endure it, for as long as it takes for us to get you home." The Caamasi started walking me back toward the hotel. "And I wouldn't fear for discovery, at least, not this evening. A lot of people saw a vision they hoped never to see tonight and are even now contemplating whether or not they want to stay in a place where they might get to see it again."

I gave him a smile. "And you don't mean those two women, right?"

"Not exclusively, no." The Caamasi chuckled lightly. "Your work is done for this night, but its repercussions will go on for a good long time."

FORTY-FIVE

✳

I screwed the high energy flux aperture back on the head of the lightsaber and pitched to Elegos the blackened, misshapen lump that had been the diamond I'd put into the weapon. "Gone, completely gone."

"It worked fine when you tested it initially." He snatched the melted gemstone from the air, sniffed it, then rubbed a thumb across it. "Synthetic?"

I nodded. "Kubaz xurkonia. The crystalline lattice handled the energy while we tested it, but was probably ready to go down anytime. I trusted my grandfather's comments about the various gems too much—I should have tested them. Actually, serves me right for trying to make a complicated lightsaber my first time out."

Elegos frowned. "Why *did* you make one with variable blade lengths?"

I shrugged uneasily. "Well, I guess it was ego. Gantoris made one with two lengths and I wanted mine to be as good as his."

"I thought you said he had a Sith Dark Lord instructing him at the time."

"Sure, *now* you bring that point up." I shook my head. "The longer length is useful for surprising an enemy, but not that practical in a fight. A simple block and a good swordsman would be inside my range and carving me up. Blade that long will also cause a lot of collateral damage, which would be fine if I was needing to do a lot of property destruction, but other than that it's really just an impractical novelty item. Sithspawn, I don't even know of any fighting styles to use with a blade that long.''

The Caamasi nodded. "Perhaps you can develop some when you replace the diamond. Finding a real diamond should not be that difficult—carbon *is* one of the more common elements.''

"True, but finding a stone with the proper cut, color and clarity will be tough.'' I smiled. "Or getting it out of the gem cartels at a vaguely reasonable price will be.''

"When you free your Mirax, perhaps she can get it for you.''

I nodded solemnly. "I hope we'll be testing that theory sooner rather than later.'' I gave the lightsaber another quick glance. "At least I got the normal-length blade working again.''

Elegos accepted the weapon from me and clutched it in both hands. "I am pleased you managed to repair it, and that you survived your ordeal. Now you can admit you were wrong in how you dealt with Shala.''

"My strategy for dealing with him was perfectly sound.''

"Perfectly sound is a phrase seldom used to describe walking into an ambush.'' The Caamasi shook his head. "You were wrong.''

"Not at all.'' I frowned at him. "I really wasn't the one who was ambushed, Shala was. I was just there to catch collateral damage.''

"Another rationalization. I expect better of you.'' His eyes narrowed. "You were wrong.''

I started to protest, then folded my arms over my chest. "Elegos, I was a cop and a fighter pilot. Being wrong just doesn't come with the package."

"But you are a Jedi Knight now."

His statement shocked me with its simplicity and truth. "You're right, I'm a Jedi Knight. I *was* wrong, very wrong, and damn lucky to get out of there alive."

The Caamasi smiled. "Not lucky, just strong in the Force. You protected others and thereby were preserved yourself. Never forget that fact."

"No, no I won't." I smiled at him. "And the cop/fighter jock in me can admit to being grateful to you. Thanks again for the rescue."

"All in a day's work." Elegos secreted the lightsaber away in a sideboard compartment, then headed for the food preparation station. "I've already been out this morning and learned a couple of important things that are the results of your Hutt encounter."

I shrugged on my bedrobe and knotted the sash at my waist. The robe had been one of Tavira's gifts. It had been fashioned from Ottegan silk of purple with gold trim at the collar and sleeves. I found it a bit too gaudy for my taste, but I was sore from the previous night's ordeal, and it was light enough not to make me ache. Walking after Elegos in it was a bother, though, with the material trying to wrap itself around my legs with each step.

"What did you hear?"

Elegos set out a small platter with fresh pastries and poured me a container of a bluish *zureber* syrup that looked horrible, but tasted pretty good. "The destruction of Shala's gang has caused serious problems. Apparently the Jedi's appearance over the city galvanized some local citizens to form little hunting bands of their own. Several

Blackstar Pirates were beaten and stoned when they left
the Aviary. Rather nasty slogans have been painted on
the walls and doors of some of the Invid spaceport docking facilities. While the locals love the money the Invids
bring in, most are afraid that as long as they are here, the
Jedi will remain and might begin to go after more than
just the Invids.''

I sighed. ''I'd hoped the indigs might see the Jedi as a
protector.''

''The people here don't so much want a protector as
they do a benefactor.''

''Good point.'' An idea occurred to me and I smiled.
''I can take care of that. What else?''

''The clutches you had outfitted with hyperdrives?''

''Yes?''

''Gone. Appears a couple of the Survivors decided
they would find surviving easier elsewhere.''

I smiled. ''Timmser and Caet?''

''They *were* the ones you insisted on having trained
on the ships so they could instruct others.'' The Caamasi
gave me an appreciative nod. ''I didn't think they would
take the bait. I expected them to remain and oppose the
Jedi.''

''I guess they heard there was a rumor that *they* were
the reason I'd demanded a month from Tavira before
becoming her consort. Story goes that I've been spending a lot of my off hours with them in a last grasp at
freedom before becoming Tavira's nighttoy. They're
both smart enough to know Tavira isn't likely to care
whether or not it's the truth—just the rumor will damage
her image and demand retribution.''

Elegos narrowed his eyes. ''And where would that
rumor have come from?''

I shrugged. ''You know me, when I'm drinking I can't

keep a secret and I'm depressed enough to mourn my love life in public.''

"Well done." He sipped from a glass of the blue syrup, which turned the golden down of his upper lip green until he licked it clean. "Will you rest today, or keep up the pressure?"

"Nothing breeds success like success." I took a big bite out of a pastry, chewed, then swallowed. "The Invid system has one huge weakness and I need to push and exploit it before Tavira can act."

The huge flaw in the way Tavira controlled her groups was what she saw as keeping her safe: all communication was pretty much one way. The HoloNet could keep her informed about big events in the galaxy, like a major New Republic push against her subsidiary groups, or events like the Sun Crusher and its destruction; but she was blind to local Courkrus news. Word of an impending operation reached us when a small craft, like a Skipray blastboat, entered the system and commed directly with the headquarters of the various groups. During these runs she picked up local news, but until she made one of those runs, she'd not know anything about what I was doing.

I handled the benefactor problem rather quickly, and mopped up the rest of Shala's crew at the same time. Rach'talik had gathered a small band around himself and set up housekeeping in a warehouse in which Shala had stored a lot of the loot his group had taken. The night after the Great Hutt Roast—as it became known locally—I hit the warehouse, scattered the various denizens, then threw the place open to the public. This action became known as the Fire Sale, since it was assumed anything left in the place would be burned, and it was picked clean in hours. A few minor scuffles broke out, but visions of a shadowy presence caught in the corner of the eye was enough to quell them.

Two days later a communications ship arrived from Tavira. I would have loved to have been there to watch the communications officer when he tried to raise Shala and the *Fastblast* and got no answer. The information he got from the others wouldn't have pleased him any better, since desertions had decimated the Blackstar Pirates and LazerLords. Most of the *Red Nova* crew had gone native, leaving the Survivors and Riistar's Raiders the best off of the groups. In three weeks of absence, the cutting edge of the Invids had been considerably dulled.

Elegos and I expected a reaction from Tavira, and got it more quickly than we thought possible. Within a day after her communications ship left Courkrus, I awakened to a pounding on my suite's door. I heard Elegos's voice, had thrown back the covers and pulled my robe on, but didn't get even as far as closing it when the door to my bedroom burst open and Tavira stalked in. She shoved me back on the bed, then stood there with her fists on her hips, looking down at me.

"Surprised to see me?"

I blinked and swiped sleepsand from my eyes. "Surprised? No, I suppose not."

"Are you pleased?"

"Yes."

"Harumph." She eyed me appraisingly. "I would think you would show it more."

I pulled my robe closed and sat up against the headboard. "It's early."

"And you had a late night." She sat on the foot of my bed. "Alone?"

"Completely."

She smiled briefly, the same way pet owners do when

they discover their animal hasn't messed something up in their absence. "Good. And you've not been bothered by this Jedi?"

I shook my head. "I've heard the stories, seen things occasionally, but come to no harm, no."

Her eyes shrank to amethyst and jet crescents. "But you were there the first time he appeared."

"What?"

Tavira brought her chin up triumphantly. "The visitation. People have determined that was the Jedi. He warned of his own impending campaign against the Invids. Well, this Skywalker won't get away with it."

"Skywalker?" My jaw shot open. "You think it is Luke Skywalker?"

She reached out and grabbed the big toe on my right foot, playfully wiggling it back and forth as she slid forward. "Of course, it is Skywalker. You blonds, sometimes you can't think at all. Skywalker is the only Jedi with enough power to be able to do what has been done here. The New Republic keeps suggesting he is off training more Jedi, but you yourself noted that he was present at Xa Fel. *We* are the New Republic's greatest problem, so it stands to reason they would use their greatest weapon against us."

"Indeed, it would."

She moved closer and rested her chin on my knee, smiling slyly. "In fact, the news about the Sun Crusher's destruction is pure disinformation. No one who had a weapon that was indestructible and capable of annihilating whole star systems would destroy it. No, they're waiting until they discover where I keep the *Invidious*, then they will obliterate it."

I pulled back, smacking my head on the headboard.

"Ouch. Are you sure the New Republic would do that? They don't seem to have the guts to do such a thing."

"Carida is gone, isn't it?" She patted me on the other knee. "They blame its destruction on a rogue, a child, yet you notice he is lauded as a Jedi now. Since when are promotions given to people who fail to carry out orders?"

I shivered. "I'd never have thought of that."

Tavira placed hands on either side of my hips and kissed me gently on the nose. "Oh, you would have, my dear."

"Thank you."

Then she slapped me. Hard. Snapped my head around to the right and by the time I'd recovered, she stood again beside my bed and glared down at me. I pressed my left hand to my cheek. "What did I do?"

"It's not what you did, it's what you've failed to do!" She turned away from me, but fury poured off her. "You should have dealt with this Jedi situation."

"What? Me? How?" I sat forward. "I had no way to reach you."

"Immaterial. All I've heard since I've been here is that you've not drawn a sober breath since the Jedi arrived. The night Shala died, you were so drunk you destroyed a speeder bike and didn't even know it." She gestured vaguely toward the street in front of the hotel. "I've brought you another one, by the way. Don't destroy this one."

"I'm sorry."

She spun back, with her hand raised to slap me again, but she hesitated. "You *are* sorry, and I expect a change. Your behavior must improve. You must lead by example. You must show them not to fear the Jedi."

"Emperor's black bones, he melted Shala's headquarters. Two nights ago it was still warm."

She lowered her hand. "You cannot let your fear show. These Jedi, they are like animals. They can smell fear. It's so thick here, *I* can smell it, and I hate it."

"Fighting the Jedi is not easy."

"I don't want you to fight it, I want you to lead the others in opposition to it. You do that, and *I* will take care of the Jedi." Her fists returned to her hips. "As much as I would like to join you there for a proper reunion, I have preparations to make. I'll be back within the week. I expect to see you sharp and in control."

She started to walk out of the room, then paused and turned back. "Oh, kill Jacob Nive and take command. The man's spirit is broken. If he can't be fixed, he's useless."

"I'll remember that."

"Do that, darling." She gave me a wink. "It's an object lesson you would do best never to forget."

I did exactly what Leonia Tavira wanted. I cleaned myself up and started making the rounds of the remaining groups on Courkrus. I visited them all in their strongholds, snapping orders, inventing security procedures, threatening, bribing, hinting darkly that any group that didn't get tough would be melded in with other groups, losing their autonomy. And of those groups that ran, well, I simply asked if anyone truly believed the galaxy was big enough to let them hide from Leonia Tavira.

The Survivors took heart immediately, and even Jacob Nive seemed to recover some of his nerve. The Blackstar Pirates remained sullen but determined to stick things out. The *Red Nova* crew rallied and even started talking with the LazerLords about a merger that would keep the two of their groups functioning well. Riistar's Raiders, whom I had largely left alone, started plotting to surpass the Survivors and began making overtures to me about shifting my allegiance to them.

What was truly great about this effort and the rebound in morale was that it rested very strongly on my representations of Tavira's plans to deal with the Jedi. I quickly let things evolve such that *I* moved into Shala's position of directly confronting the Jedi. I promised a trap that would destroy him and I knew, as the Invids put their trust in me—transferring much of it from their trust in Tavira—that if *I* went the way of Shala, morale would collapse flat and Tavira would lose the combat arm of the Invids.

How I would have the Jedi kill me was something I hadn't had time to figure out yet, but I knew it would have to be really spectacular or really nasty. I didn't know which I would settle for—Shala's demise would be tough to top and a bit rougher on me than I wanted to attempt. Grisly would probably be the best and I wanted to leave clues to the Jedi living in the city's sewers so lots of time would be spent hunting down there, while I could be living someplace a bit nicer.

To heighten the tension concerning the confrontation, I decided to return to the Crash cantina. I knew everyone there well enough to be able to blank their memories during my entrance and scramble my features to avoid recognition when I suddenly appeared in their midst. I projected a red mist condensing into my form to cover my appearance, and almost laughed aloud as previously brave men and women recoiled from me, moving away from the bar toward the furthest reaches of the room.

I ignited my lightsaber and pointed it at Jacob Nive. "Where is Idanian?"

All the blood drained from Jacob's face. "I d-don't know."

"He has said he will end my actions. Where is he?" I swept the blade around in a grand arc, causing people to duck or cover their eyes with their hands. "Where is he?"

A chorus of denials came back weak and timid.

"Tell him, I will meet him. The same fate that took Shala the Hutt awaits him!" I kept my voice very low and as menacing as I could. "When we meet, his time will be at an end."

I slashed the lightsaber down through the bar and across, whipping the blade through the area where the Savareen brandy and other expensive liquors were kept. The brandy immediately exploded in a gout of blue flame, which lit the area behind the bar and began to spill out onto the main floor. More bottles exploded and the bartender started screaming, allowing me to step back and make my escape. I slipped into the night amid the shouting and yelling of people trying to deal with a fire, and began taking a fairly quick route back to the hotel.

Across the street I saw a knot of five individuals turn and come in my direction. The fact that Jenos' brave talk had spawned hunter gangs didn't surprise me, and I'd dealt with that many individuals before. I ducked into an alley, moving halfway along toward where it turned right and led out to another street, then prepared to project an image of my actually walking further along a non-existent part of the alley. Getting them to chase me and hit the wall had worked wonders before, and if I could take a couple of them out, it would make the rest of the task much more simple.

They came to the alley mouth but didn't run in. When I hit them with the illusion, they didn't shout, didn't point, didn't draw blasters. In fact, they seemed to look directly at me, which meant the illusion wasn't taking. That struck me as odd because they looked human, but since they wore hooded cloaks I couldn't be certain which humanoid species they were.

Since they spotted me, I moved away from the wall and further down the alley. I let the Force flow toward them as they walked forward, but I caught no sense of fear or anticipation from them. I could feel them in the Force, but I wasn't getting nearly the sort of feedback I expected. *Something very odd here. Time to provoke a reaction.*

I threw back the right side of my cloak and brought my lightsaber out. I thumbed it to life and wove the humming blade back and forth before them. "You don't want any part of this, trust me. Run now and I'll let you live."

One by one they likewise freed their gun arms. I set myself to pick off blaster fire, but none erupted, no angry whines filled the alley, no red bolts burned toward me. Instead, blue, yellow, red, orange and purple lightsaber blades sprang to life in their hands. Five of them, hissing in concert, like a krayt dragon hungry for the meal wrapped up in my clothes.

They advanced, and I realized there really wasn't any way things could get much worse.

FORTY-SIX

✳

Then a sixth silhouette appeared at the mouth of the alley and a green lightsaber sprouted in his hands.

Great, now we have the whole rainbow represented. I lifted my left hand from my blade's hilt and waved him forward. "C'mon, pal, one more won't make any difference."

I wished I felt as brave as those words sounded.

The man at the alley mouth started forward. "No one need die here tonight."

I knew that voice! *Luke!*

And I recognized in his warning to those I faced a directive to me. I slid to the right and blocked a red slash low right, directing the red blade away and into the brick wall. Pivoting on my left foot, I snapped a sidekick into my foe's belly, driving her back. I discovered she wore an armored breastplate, which partially shielded her from the strength of my kick. The armor, however, didn't stop her from catching her heels on debris and going down, temporarily taking her out of the fight.

Luke engaged Yellow and Purple as I ducked beneath a blue slash and twisted to bring my left hand up. I caught my foe on his chin with the heel of my hand. The blow shifted the mask he wore up a couple of centimeters, temporarily blinding him. A quick punch to the throat choked him, then I grabbed him by the clasp of his cloak and flung him into the alley wall. His armor clicked hard against the bricks, then he dropped back all boneless and the deadman switch on his lightsaber shut it off.

I parried Orange's cut and caught his wrist in my left hand. I shifted my right hand up, then whipped it down and across. My lightsaber's heavy pommel caught Orange right behind the right ear, or where the right ear would have been on a human. As Orange dropped senseless to the ground, his hood slid back and I saw he was a Rodian.

I reached down and flicked his lightsaber off, then straightened up as Luke rose above Red. From her I only got peace, a peace I found vaguely reminiscent of the peace I'd imagined surrounding Mirax when Exar Kun showed her to me. "New trick?"

Luke shut off his lightsaber and I did the same with mine, plunging the alley into darkness. "Old one, one of yours. I hit her and knocked her out. Just easing some of her pain now."

"Nice sense of timing. If you hadn't arrived, the five of them would have killed me, clean and quick." I shivered. "How did you find me?"

In faint light from the street, I saw Luke's expression sharpen. "I knew, *if* you had learned all you needed to learn, that I would meet you *here*, and that we would be *allies*."

I felt a chill run down my spine. "I see."

Luke's voice lightened slightly. "As for the *when*, with that I needed some help." He turned back up the alley. "Are we clear?"

A silhouette framed itself in the alley, prompting me to laugh. "I see no pursuit."

"Ooryl?" I hopped over Orange's body and ran forward. "Ooryl, what are you doing here?"

"I am a Findsman." The Gand shrugged as if that should have explained everything. "The important thing of being a Findsman is not knowing where to look, for that is easy. It is knowing *when* to look. I knew the *when* was now, and went to Master Skywalker to tell him that. He pointed me here, and I brought him *now*."

Luke waved us back into the alley. "We have to get our sleeping friends out of here. We have a ship, but I need somewhere else to keep them. They know where Mirax is."

I nodded. "Can't be far from here, because Tavira brought them within a day of hearing we had Jedi trouble here. Who are they?"

"I don't know." Luke shook his head. "We better find out and find out fast, because if we don't, if someone learns they've failed in their mission, it may cost Mirax her life."

I reached down and hefted Orange up by his belt, letting Ooryl grab Yellow and Purple. "I know where we can take them, but getting information out of them will be tough. They know how to use the Force, and I'm not sure we can break through to find out what we want to know."

"I think I have something that can help us in that regard." Luke gestured, allowing Red and Blue to float up into the air. "Lead on, Keiran. As Ooryl explained it to me, *when* is just an aperture in time, and we don't want it to snap shut before we can get through to your wife."

.   .   .

We took our five opponents back to the hotel. I called
Elegos and had him meet us in the back, at the freight-
lift. Ooryl left the two he'd carried to Elegos, then returned to the spaceport to fetch something for Luke.
Awaiting his return we stripped our prisoners out of their
armor, separated them and treated the cuts and bruises
they'd earned in the fight.

When Ooryl returned he brought with him a cagelike
device that had suspended inside of it a small, furred
reptile. A nutrient mix flowed through a network of
tubes, sustaining the creature which, if it were capable of
movement, seemed singularly disinclined to show it. I
did see it blink an eye, but even that movement was
slower than I would have expected in a living creature.

"This is an ysalamiri, one of two I brought with me."
Luke rested a hand on the cage and looked a bit fatigued.
"It is unique among living creatures—at least I don't
know of any others—in that it seems to project a field
that negates the Force. On its homeworld some predators
evolved with a Force sense that lets them hunt, so its
negation sphere acts as camouflage."

"Okay, that's why I feel so weird. Thought I was just
tired." I tried to reach inside myself to tap the Force, but
I got nothing. "It's like I'm back where I started, back
before the academy."

Luke nodded. "You're fortunate in that you spent
most of your life only having a fringe sense of the Force.
I've been involved much longer than you and in the presence of an ysalamiri, I feel lost, like a limb has been
lopped off." Luke flexed his mechanical hand. "Worse,
actually."

"How do you think this will affect our guests?"

Luke managed a smile, but that seemed to tax him. "I
think they've been involved with the Force longer than I

have. They seem to armor themselves well with it. suspect they will feel very vulnerable.''

''Good.'' I gave him a feral grin. ''Just what we wan if we're going to get anything out of them. Just follow my lead.''

The Jedi Master caught hold of my shoulder. ''I've not done anything like this before, interrogating prisoners.''

I winked at him. '' 'Sokay, I know enough for both of us. Just stay over there, by the door, and look as malevolent as you can. Keep your face straight and you really don't need to say anything.''

''Malevolent?''

''Think Hutt, but with eyebrows.''

''Got it.''

We picked Red to be the first subject—actually, Elegos did, for reasons of his own—but I didn't mind. Interrogating women is always tricky, mainly because they tend to be suspicious of any claims made by a man and often believe they can use their looks and wiles to fool a detective. Red, who really was a slender beauty with wavy brown hair and blue eyes, could have melted many a detective's steel heart, but the surprise and fear twisting her face as she awakened robbed her of her beauty. The ysalamiri made me feel as if I was seeing in black and white, so for her it must have seemed as if she was blind.

When I saw her eyes flicker open, I looked back at Luke and nodded as if I'd received a telepathic message from him. ''Yes, I will see what I can find out. Give her a moment to recover.''

Luke stared at me for a second, then impatiently flicked a hand in my direction.

I smiled. *Quick study. Let's hope she isn't.*

I squatted down next to the chair in which we had bound her. "Forgive me for having to restrain you like this. I wish I could make things more pleasant, but he's rather insistent. I know you're feeling odd right now because you have lost the use of certain senses you consider part of you. *He* has removed your access to them to make it easier for me to probe your mind, but I know how unpleasant that will be for you."

She shook her head adamantly. "I will not betray my people."

Her words came stiff and pronounced slightly oddly. *Precise*, that's it. It almost seemed as if she were speaking with the same very proper diction my grandfather used. It was a datapoint—not much of one, but a point nonetheless.

"No, of course, you don't want to do that. I don't want you to do that, but we have to find the *Invidious*, and find it quickly. Leonia Tavira has to be stopped . . . from being able to harm anyone else." I'd almost ended my sentence at the word stopped, but I caught a momentary hesitation of her breath, which made me add the extra phrase. "We really don't want to see her hurt anyone else."

"You can't stop her."

I glanced back at Luke, then turned to her. "He says that just because *you* could not stop her, does not mean *we* cannot. Sorry, he always makes things sound so dire, but the fact is, he's right. I've been here for months, on many operations where you or another of your brethren were on the *Invidious*, and you never detected me. Why not? Because *he* was shielding me. You know you looked, you know you tried, but it wasn't until this evening, when we wanted to *trap* you, that I revealed myself enough to let you find me. And you never even detected *him*."

I stood and walked over to confer with Luke, letting her mull over what I'd said. I raised a finger to my lips to keep Luke silent, but frowned to get him to give me that expression. When he did look at me angrily, I recoiled. "But you can't be so cruel. To remove her access to the Force forever isn't going to do her or us any good. Sure, it might teach her a lesson, but so would having a bantha trample her. I don't think she should be made an example of. It won't make the others more tractable."

Luke really got into his part, jabbing me hard in the chest with two fingers. I did an about face, rubbing my chest, and returned to Red's side. "I really do think I can get him to unblock your access to the Force, I really do. You just need to tell us where Tavira keeps the *Invidious*. I mean, we already know you manage to keep it hidden—you're very good at that stuff, hiding and all."

"No, I cannot tell you. None of us will betray our people."

I sighed and rested a hand on her shoulder. "Well, I know you're thinking about things from your point of view, and maybe even thinking about them from Tavira's point of view. That Star Destroyer is very powerful, and for you to be working with her, you've got to be afraid she's going to turn it on your people if you betray her. I understand that. It's crystal clear."

I let my voice drop a bit in tone and volume as I leaned forward. "Thing of it is this, though: *you* didn't get me. *You* didn't get him. Tavira, when she doesn't hear that you succeeded, will see you as having failed. And you know her—failure isn't an accident, it's a conspiracy. The way I see it, and I know her almost as well as you do, she'll see herself as betrayed at this point and act. What you have to ask yourself is this: do you want to be the cause of her killing all your people, or do you want to let the guys who defeated you take their run at Tavira?''

FORTY-SEVEN

✳

Red cracked a little and we were able to use what we learned from her to bust the rest of the *Jensaarai*—that's what they called themselves—wide open. What we got from them was incredibly interesting because it came wrapped in a strange philosophical package that equated Obi-Wan Kenobi with Darth Vader in terms of being a Jedi exterminator. The *Jensaarai* were trained as Jedi were, even to the point of constructing lightsabers and training with them, but it was not nearly the transitional point for them that it was in the Jedi tradition I knew.

For the *Jensaarai*, their crowning moment, their full growth into becoming one of the *Jensaarai* Defenders—they had Apprentices, Defenders and *Saarai-kaar*, of which there appeared to be only one—was the creation of their armor. They started with a basic armor shell and covered it with spun cortosis ore fibers, providing them some modicum of protection against all sorts of weapons. They styled the armor after whichever creature they felt best possessed or expressed their personal desires for service to the *Jensaarai* community, and if the armor we'd taken from them was any indication, the creatures chosen were all defensively minded—creatures that remained hidden and dormant until pressed, then they proved very deadly.

The history of the *Jensaarai*'s involvement with Tavira was one of mistakes from the start. Tavira, fleeing a New Republic task force, jumped to the Suarbi system, in the Quence Sector. The seventh planet, a gas giant, had a big ring of asteroids around it and over a dozen moons. One of those moons, designated Suarbi 7/5, became known as Susevfi to the colonists who had decided to tame the world centuries ago. Though similar to Yavin 4 in size and rotational speed, Susevfi ran to more savannah-like grasslands, much like Noquivzor—a planet on which I had been stationed before Rogue Squadron took Coruscant. A couple of human settlements grew up, and the *Jensaarai* were located outside the large seaport, Yumfla.

Tavira and some of her people had come down to Yumfla, and she immediately went to work on the local Imperial governor—a petty bureaucrat who made the last mistake of his life by rebuffing her advances. Tavira had him shot, then declared the planet liberated from the oppression of the Empire and in opposition to the oppression of the New Republic. The *Saarai-kaar* of the *Jensaarai* went to Tavira and heard everything she wanted to hear from the Admiral. Tavira cultivated trust, then betrayed it, and put the *Jensaarai* in the position of protecting their fellow citizens—who had not even known of their existence—by serving Tavira. Failure to serve her would result in the annihilation of Yumfla.

The *Jensaarai* had picked up on Mirax's intentions when she'd come hunting the Invids. They nabbed her at Nal Hutta and brought her to Susevfi. Tavira had wanted to slay her, but the *Saarai-kaar* had insisted on keeping her alive and imprisoned in the old planetary governor's palace.

Learning what we had, Luke and I knew we had to hurry to Susevfi, *and* we had to make a difficult decision because we could not bring the *Jensaarai* with us. A change of heart in just one of them could spoil any surprise we could generate, crushing our chances for getting into the stronghold where Tavira was holding Mirax.

We decided we'd leave them on Courkrus in the company of an ysalamiri. We knew we had to trust someone to hang on to them, so we went to Jacob Nive and revealed to him my identity as Keiran Halcyon, Jedi Knight, and that of Luke Skywalker. We explained to him that we were going to finish the Invids and stop Tavira and offered him a choice. We could destroy the last of the Survivors or give them the same chance at a new start that the New Republic had offered other victims of Imperial aggression and coercion.

Nive accepted the chance to start over. With the New Republic gaining strength, and the last vestiges of the Empire in retreat, the Survivors were losing their anti-Imperial focus and just becoming thieves. Without the protection of the *Invidious*, the New Republic could have and would have smashed them a dozen times over. He willingly exchanged entertaining five guests and an ysalamiri for a new life.

He looked at me hard. "One thing, Jenos, how do I know you'll succeed?"

"Why did you fight the Empire all those years?"

"To avenge what happened to my friends."

I nodded. "Right. Leonia Tavira has my wife. I'm fighting so I won't need to avenge anyone."

Nive's eyes tightened. "The two of you alone?"

I winked at Luke. "We've got some allies, and one is really big. We'll do fine."

Before we left Courkrus, we shot two messages out. One went to General Cracken telling him we had located the *Invidious'* home and were going to take the ship out. Data letting him know where we were going was left with Nive, but we didn't transmit it directly to Cracken because we didn't want a New Republic task force showing up and alerting Tavira to what was going on before we had a chance to get in and rescue Mirax. If the New Republic made a move, the *Jensaarai* at Susevfi could still pick up on it and alert Tavira, dooming our rescue attempt.

I also sent a message to Booster, telling him that I'd located Mirax and was going after her. I didn't give him even as much detail as we gave Cracken, but I did note I expected to have her safe and sound within a couple of days. The message said I'd bring her to the *Errant Venture* for rest and recovery first thing.

We'd wanted to leave Elegos behind, but he insisted on traveling with us. He and Ooryl had begun to get along famously—a trend I found profoundly disturbing—meaning that the two of them bonded while comparing experiences of sharing quarters with me. Elegos pointed out that the small ship which Luke and Ooryl had brought to Courkrus was notoriously difficult to handle with one pilot, and since he could fly, he should back Ooryl up, just for appearance's sake if nothing else.

Luke or I could have easily filled the second-seat role, but we were going into Susevfi within the protective bubble of the ysalamiri's Force repulsion. It would effectively hide all traces of us from any of the *Jensaarai* Defenders stationed in the planetary ring, as well as those on the ground. The Ring Defenders regularly used their Force powers to get a sense of incoming ships and to subtly direct them away from away from noticing the faint sensor phantoms of a Star Destroyer hidden in the rings. Even without the *Jensaarai* hiding the ship, the *Invidious* would have been tough to pick out of the rings. With the *Jensaarai* in place such spotting was all but impossible.

Luke stretched out on a padded bench in the small ship's lounge and draped an arm across his eyes. "If we had more Jedi, we could have accompanied survey ships and probably have picked up on the *Jensaarai* efforts to hide the *Invidious*."

"Could be, but I only noticed them when they were at close range and trying to probe me. When I contacted Tycho at the battle of Xa Fel, they picked me up and I never even detected their presence." I stood and walked over to the food prep station. I pulled a prepackaged *zureber* syrup container from the chiller unit. "Want something to drink?"

Luke peeked out at me and nodded. "Sure, toss it."

I lofted it toward him and it landed with a plop on his belly. He whuffed loudly.

I smiled. "You're supposed to catch it."

He sat up, nipped the corner of the package off and spat it out. "I was trying to, but inside the field the ysalamiri puts out, my effort failed."

I tore open the corner of my syrup container and sipped. "Tough being normal again, isn't it?"

Luke sighed heavily. "First eighteen years of my life I didn't have a clue about the Force. I was just a farm boy who liked to fly. I wanted to join the Imperial service and become a pilot. Jedi Knights were ancient history, and old Uncle Owen didn't encourage me to study that history.''

"I know, it was kind of the same in my house.'' I dropped onto the bench at Luke's feet. ''Just didn't talk about the Jedi that much. I knew my grandfather had known one, worked with one once, but it was kind of like mentioning an ex-wife at a family gathering.''

"Of your new wife's family, right?''

I laughed. ''Yeah, there you go. You know, when I saw my grandfather several months ago and could see the pride he'd taken in helping hide Nejaa Halcyon's wife and child, I learned how difficult it had to have been for him to keep all this stuff hidden for so long. I think I disappointed him when I rejected my Jedi heritage to pursue the Invids on my own. I'll have to let him know I've reconsidered.''

"I'm glad you did.'' Luke sat up and patted me on the shoulder. ''Hard to tell what felt worse: having a student turn to the dark side or having someone just walk away because of my teaching.''

I shrugged. ''You know us Corellian Jedi—notoriously contrary and bent on going our own way.'' My conversation with Elegos flashed through my mind. ''I owe you an apology, by the way. I never put aside my expectations for the academy, so I never really gave you a chance to train me.''

"Accepted but unnecessary.'' Luke gave me a nod. ''I didn't make it easy for you. I've got to remember that parallel tracks are not better or worse, just different. We're still heading in the same direction.''

"True, but that still doesn't mean I'm entirely comfortable with things like Kyp's track. Tavira has it all worked out that Kyp killed the Carida system on orders from the New Republic, and there are going to be a whole bunch of folks who believe her.''

''I know, and I understand how you feel.'' Luke drank for a moment, then licked away a blue liquid bead forming at the corner of his mouth. ''It could be suggested, though, that the deal we offered Jacob Nive and his Survivors is really a lot like the chance Kyp has been given. In dedicating his life to being a Jedi you know Kyp is really under something of a life sentence.''

''I know, and it'll be hard labor, too. Killing him wouldn't make the galaxy any better, so this is likely the best solution.'' I drank, leaned my head back and closed my eyes for a moment. ''Doesn't mean I like it and doesn't mean my inability to come up with a better solution isn't frustrating.''

''All we can do is our best.'' Luke laughed wearily. ''So, tell me, did you ever figure you'd be hurtling through hyperspace planning to assault an Imperial Governor's palace, which is now the stronghold for a renegade Imperial admiral and her crew?''

I opened one eye and screwed it around to look at him. ''Tatooine must have been really, really bad if *that* was the kind of fantasy life you created for yourself.''

''It wasn't *that* bad.''

''Right, I was there once. On any other world the Jawas would be the size of Hutts, but on Tatooine, they shrink.''

''Good thing, too, or imagine what they'd cart off.'' Luke smiled. ''Actually, I have good memories of Tatooine, more than bad.''

''But you wanted off that rock.''

''In the worst way.'' His smile died. ''And I got it.''

I reached over and grabbed him by the back of the neck. ''Yeah, but it brought out the best in you, and that means the rest of the galaxy gets a shot at realizing its best. Losing your uncle and aunt had to hurt, but I bet they are happy with the return the investment of their lives got through you.''

''Think so?''

''Yeah, no doubt.'' I smiled at him. Here, within the ysalamiri bubble, Luke seemed to lose some of the brooding oppression that settled on him when he remained aware of the universe around him. The optimism and uncertainty he had known as a boy shone through. ''You had no brothers and sisters, right—I mean, you grew up alone?''

'' 'Cept for friends, yeah.''

''Me, too.'' I smiled. ''And, no, I never imagined I'd be heading out to an Imperial Governor's palace to face down a renegade Imperial admiral.''

''Oh.''

''For me it was racing off to Nal Hutta to face down a Hutt crimelord in his own den.''

''Talk about stacking the odds against you.''

I laughed. ''I'm Corellian, remember?''

''Right, forget I said anything about odds.'' Luke finished his drink and crushed the container. ''I guess all of us get dealt cards we don't want in life.''

''True enough. The trick is in how you play them. Some people have the greatest cards in the world and still lose.'' I nodded at him. ''For a farm boy growing up on dust and dreams, you've not done half bad.''

''From a Corellian, that's quite a concession.''

The bridge-comm squawked. ''Ooryl says we have five minutes to reversion, then about an hour to transit to Susevfi. Better get ready lest our reception be hotter than intended.''

I slapped the transmit button. "We copy, Elegos. We'll be set."

Luke got up, crossed to the shelf where he'd plugged his lightsaber into a recharger, freed the weapon and clipped it to his belt. He likewise unplugged mine and looked it over. "Nice work. Dual-phase?"

I frowned. "Tried to repeat Gantoris' feat of engineering. Right now only one phase works. Gotta find a real diamond."

"Dual-phase blades seem to be something of a fad among Jedi at certain points." He tossed me the lightsaber. "Still, I like the blade and it seems well made."

"Little bit ugly, but I used what I had available." I caught it and screwed the pommel cap on. Standing, I stretched, then clipped the weapon to my belt. "One question before we get going, if you don't mind."

"Sure."

"Okay, us Jedi, we're only supposed to be using our powers to defend, but we're going to be assaulting a base."

Luke nodded. "Right. We're acting to defend Mirax's life, and the lives of Tavira's future victims."

"I'm with you so far, but I'm wondering if we don't have a little more immediate moral obligation, say, concerning those folks who will see us as aggressors." I frowned. "I'm guarding something and I see a guy coming at me with a lightsaber, I'm going to shoot. You know, it's that 'certain point of view thing.' "

The Jedi Master frowned. "I see your problem. When I had to deal with Jabba the Hutt, I warned him to let us go or he'd be destroyed. He didn't listen and that was, more or less, the end of that."

"So, warn those who might not realize what they're doing?"

Luke nodded. "If we can find any down there. An Impstar Deuce ships, what, ten thousand stormtroopers? I don't imagine the *Invidious* is fully crewed anymore, but she's got plenty of folks at her disposal. Want to guess how many are down guarding the palace?"

"Doesn't matter." I tightened my robe's belt. "The Emperor didn't mint enough of those guys to keep me from rescuing Mirax. They can run or they can die, their choice."

"Corellians." Luke shook his head. "No wonder the other Jedi didn't want you leaving your system."

I winked at him. "The rest of you were just afraid we wouldn't leave anything for you to do after we were done."

"I hope you're right, my friend." Luke hooked his thumbs in his belt. "Mission like this, we'll both have more than enough to do."

Luke and I had tried, albeit briefly and in vain, to get Ooryl and Elegos to remain behind on the ship and monitor starship traffic in and out of the system. A comlink call could warn us about Tavira's *Invidious* moving out, or anything else that could cause us to shift our plans. Ooryl and Elegos had anticipated us and programmed the ship's computer to pull down all system traffic data, then relay it through a scrambled comlink channel to the datapad Elegos had jury-rigged to receive the signal.

Elegos noted that between his sense of smell, and Ooryl's ability to see beyond what we humans rather arrogantly called the *visible* light spectrum, we could move through the night more effectively and without having to rely upon our Force-enhanced senses, delaying our detection by the *Jensaarai*. I had to agree with that point, and having seen Ooryl in a lightfight before, having him with us didn't hurt at all. He carried a blaster carbine and a string of powerpacks slung across his chest.

Elegos hefted a blaster carbine and strapped a belt of powerpacks on around his slender waist. I looked at him and narrowed my eyes. "You don't want to be a part of this, do you? You don't want memories of the killing here."

"I am coming with you, and if I do not carry a weapon and assist in our defense, I will be just a burden. If you fail because of me, that memory would be worse, and I will not have it. I intend, instead, to have memories of your saving your wife to carry with me." Elegos held the weapon up in his left hand and thumbed a lever. "And the stun function on this weapon seems to work."

I smiled, then looked at him and Ooryl and Luke. "Before we go, I just want to thank you all. Better friends a man's never had. You're all *insane*, but friends nonetheless."

Elegos looked at Ooryl. "Corellians never know when to stop talking, do they?"

Ooryl's mouthparts opened. "*Other* Corellians do."

Luke laughed, then jerked a thumb at the egress hatch. "Let's go do something else Corellians never shy from. Let's beat some long odds."

We stalked through the darkened streets of Yumfla with impunity, all but unnoticed. Months ago I would have found that to be curious, but not after the time I'd spent with the Invids. In this city, those who were not part of the *Invidious* crew enjoying leave, or were not patrolling the streets, stayed home. They lived in an occupied city, and while some of them might make money by supplying goods and services to the *Invidious'* crew, most wanted nothing to do with the ex-Imperials. I'd felt the same sort of tension in Vlarnya and was glad of the insulation it provided us from the normal folks.

The crewmen themselves presented no problem since they were on leave and only looking to enjoy themselves. This kept them indoors on a hot and humid evening, where a cantina's environmental control unit could make the night bearable, drinks could make it pleasurable, and company could make it exquisite. Dirt-patrols, meant for picking up sick, stupid or belligerent spacers and returning them to the ship, barely gave us a second glance. Elegos' nose picked up the scent of the armor well before we saw the stormies, allowing us time to slip away down a sidestreet, or gather on a corner unobtrusively.

Finally we reached a building across a small greensward from the Imperial Governor's palace. The building itself had an eight-meter-high wall running around it, with towers at each of the four corners that rose up another two meters. A large, recessed, arched entryway split the wall in two, but had been closed for the evening with two massive metal doors. Stormtroopers patrolled in pairs along the walls, and two each stood in the corner towers.

The palace itself had been set up in a triangular pattern with towers at each of the points. Left and right were two smaller towers, each a good fifteen meters in height and twice that in diameter. Directly back from the gate, the triangle's furthest point had a rectangular tower that rose to thirty meters in height. The central third of it had been shrunk by a couple meters on each side, as if a giant fist had closed around it. It made for an interesting architectural look that differentiated the palace from most of the local buildings. A four-story-tall foundational building connected all three towers, and a private shuttle pad had been built into the roof of the big tower—which is why it had blinking lights crowning it.

"Twenty meters to the gate." I crouched down, unfastening my cloak and letting it slide off my back. I boosted a pinch of dust into the air and watched it blow toward the palace. "At least we have a tail wind."

"Good. Ooryl and Elegos cover us, we weave our way there."

Elegos cleared his throat. "The gate is closed. How do you propose to get in?"

We each brandished our lightsabers. "We'll knock," Luke offered, "real loud."

"What are you doing there?" A stormtrooper and his partner appeared from nowhere around the corner of the building shielding us. "Let's see some identification."

"Sure." I stood slowly and held my lightsaber like a glowrod while I motioned with my left hand as if digging for identification. "I know I have something here. . . ." I thought that I might be able to project an image into his brain that would get him to go away, but my mind blanked.

The stormtrooper took a half-step toward me. "You look familiar."

"Me? No, can't be."

"Trying to be smart?" The stormtrooper's blaster came up to cover me. "You're coming with us."

I glanced at Luke, then shrugged and depressed my thumb, shooting the silver blade straight through the stormtrooper's chest. I shoved him back into his partner, knocking his blaster aside. The second stormtrooper still pulled the trigger, spraying shots out into the night. My lightsaber came across and trimmed his shoulders down to the level of his armpits, ending his attack.

Luke stared at me. "You need to work on this idea of warning."

"Didn't get a chance with them, no." I ducked down as the stormtroopers on the palace wall started shouting and firing shots in our direction. Alarms began to blare. "But the others, I think they're all sorts of warned. . . . I suggest we go, now!"

Luke and I sprinted toward the palace gate, cutting back and forth to make ourselves difficult targets. As I ran I opened myself to the Force and felt a flood of data pour in. I planted with my right foot, cut to the left and whipped my lightsaber around to the right, batting a blaster bolt out into the night. Another two steps, then hesitation as fire from an E-web mounted in the right tower slashed across my path, then a dive-and-roll over the stream of bolts starting to track toward me. I fended off two more bolts, wishing I could manage, as Luke did, to direct them back at the men who had fired them, then reached the sanctuary of the recessed gate.

I pushed my sphere of responsibility to see what was on the other side awaiting us, but found no one. I pushed further and then smiled. "I have her, Luke. This close, I have Mirax. Tower your side, down."

The Jedi Master smiled. "Let's not keep her waiting."

In tandem we slashed left and right from the center of the gate and down through the big metal doors, carving a hole large enough to admit a landspeeder. I stepped inside, then slashed up and through the elbow of a stormtrooper shoving his blaster carbine down to spray us. He screamed and reeled away. I tugged the carbine from his falling hand and triggered a burst of bolts at a stormtrooper hunkering down from Elegos' covering fire. I hit, sending him spinning from the wall, then sprinted after Luke.

Luke scattered a half-dozen bolts fired at him, sending four back at the tower from whence they had come. One stormtrooper went down, the other just ducked, but the E-web sparked and started to burn. Luke sliced the barrel from the blaster rifle carried by the lead stormtrooper running from the tower where Mirax lay, then dropped him with a backhand blow that separated the man's pelvis from everything that normally rested on it.

I snapped the selector lever over to stun, then shot the next man in line. Elegos came through the gate and peppered the next three with stun shots. They all tottered and fell. Luke dashed into the tower doorway. I saw a flash and heard a blaster whine, but the green lightsaber continued to hum.

Ooryl came through the gate and laid down a pattern of suppression fire that held off the stormies coming from the far tower. Elegos and I covered him as he retreated to the tower, then we entered and I sprinted straight for the stairs leading down. This took me past two stormies with their assorted parts scattered in awkward positions. One level down I caught up with Luke at the mouth of an octagonal corridor festooned with sunken doorways.

He stood by a control panel scanning a readout of prisoner names. "Calling up a prisoner roster now."

I glanced at the list and tapped a name. "That's her."

"Holding cell 02021020."

I nodded and ran down the corridor. "Here it is." I reached the door, shot the lock and watched the door retract amid a shower of sparks. I took all three steps in a leap, then stopped just inside the doorway.

There she was, just lying there, as Exar Kun had

shown me. The little grey device on her forehead flickered with green and red lights, and the silver light from above bathed her in a radiance that left her skin almost pure white. It reflected true from her black hair. She looked perfect and asleep and I felt my throat tighten. *You are incredibly beautiful, Mirax, and you've been away far too long.*

Luke squeezed past me and leaned over by her face. "Don't think this is what's keeping her under. Feels like a Jedi hibernation trance. Normally a person can't be placed in one against her will, but if this device broke down her resistance, it might have been possible."

I nodded. "I've had experience with machines breaking down resistance." I set my lightsaber and blaster down on her bier. "Take the gadget off, let her wake up."

Luke pulled the device away and smashed it against the wall. "It'll take a bit more than that to wake her up." He reached his hand toward her forehead. "There's a Jedi technique used. . . ."

I grabbed his wrist. "Know of it. Read about it in my grandfather's notes." I smiled at him. "She's my wife, I'd like to help. You bring her out of it, and I'll let her know she's been missed."

Luke nodded and waited for me to come around on Mirax's other side. "Ready?"

"Let's do it." I gave him a nod, then leaned down and kissed my wife on the lips.

FORTY-EIGHT

Mirax's brown eyes blinked open and she began to smile. She reached up with her right hand, grabbed a fistful of my tunic and pulled me back down, covering her mouth with mine. We kissed with the urgency of lost love found, heart's pain eased. I stroked her hair and she kept me close, then we both had to come up for air.

Pulling back so I could see all of her face, I smiled. "Hi."

"Hi, yourself. You're pretty cute." She smiled back up at me, sending a jolt through me from head to toe and back again. "Of course, if my husband finds out you kissed me like that, you'll be in big trouble."

Luke burst out laughing. "Her, I like."

I kissed her on the tip of her nose. "You remember Luke Skywalker, right?"

"I do indeed. Good to see you again, though I could have hoped for better circumstances." Mirax sat up, swung her legs over the edge of the bier and stretched. "I don't even want to know where this rock is, I just want to know you have a plan for getting us off it."

The distant whine of blasters accompanied Elegos' entry into the detention cell. "Ooryl has them cut off at the stair landing. We better move before they bring up reinforcements.''

Mirax cocked her head at the Caamasi. ''A Caamasi?''

''Elegos A'kla, Trustant of the Caamasi community at Kerilt.'' I looked at her. ''He's been taking good care of me.''

She laughed and threw Elegos a salute. ''You have my thanks and sympathies. Taking care of him can be quite a chore.''

Elegos shrugged. ''Not really, you have him well trained.''

''Still leaves dirty clothes lying about, though, right?''

I cleared my throat. ''We can have this discussion later. Any chance we can make it back to the spaceport from here?''

Elegos shook his head. ''Not likely.''

Mirax hefted the blaster carbine I'd left on the bier. ''Then we go to the top of the big tower. They have a landing pad there—that's how they brought me in after they separated me from the *Skate*. We steal some speeder bikes or a shuttle and make a dash for your ship.''

Luke nodded. ''It's a plan.''

Mirax pointed at the door. ''Let's move, then.''

The Jedi Master looked at me. ''Notice any resemblance between her and Mara?''

I shivered. ''Now that you mention it . . . let's make sure they never get together, okay?''

''Right.''

From the far end of the corridor, Ooryl was filling the stairwell with a hail of laser bolts, stippling the wall behind the first landing with little fires. Two stormtroopers lay tangled on the stairs, and others kept peeking around the edge. They snapped their heads back when Ooryl fired at them. Stretching out my senses, I could feel a knot of them waiting on the stairs and toward that end of the corridor above us.

I smiled. "I've got a piece of a plan. Mirax, the blaster, please." I pointed at the ceiling. "Elegos, if you can boost me up there."

Luke held a hand out. "Permit me." With a simple gesture I rose toward the ceiling as steadily as if standing on a stone platform.

I ignited my lightsaber and cored a circle in the ceiling above me, then shoved it out of the way as Luke pushed me all the way up through it. Taking a step forward, I brought the blaster carbine up and lashed the stream of blue energy darts back and forth over the crowd of armor-shelled warriors clogging the corridor's end. Their armor deflected some shots and ablated to lessen the power of others—reducing them from stunning to something that just dazed the soldiers, but I had such clean shots at them that they were at my mercy.

Elegos came up through the hole next and blazed away with his blaster. His blue bolts struck befuddled targets, enveloping them in a collapsing sphere of blue that dropped them easily. Trapped as they were, they were not really a fighting force, just targets waiting to be shot. I scythed my fire over them and together we finished them off.

Ooryl came up the stairs, but Mirax and Luke took the quicker route to the corridor. Mirax took the blaster back from me, appropriated a powerpack from Ooryl and kissed him on the cheek. She turned and pointed back away from the stairs. "Along here there's a corridor that goes over to the main building. Landing pad's on the top."

Luke led the way. "Need to be careful. The storm-troopers we can pick out with the Force, but the *Jensaarai*, they're more difficult."

"Difficult, that's an understatement." Mirax tossed the blaster's old powerpack aside and jammed the new one home. "Their leader, this woman they call the *Saarai-kaar*, somehow thinks holding me is preventing her family from being destroyed. When she spoke to me, when she fed me—and I know I was sleeping for a long time between meals—she would speak in past and present and future. She said a Halcyon was her doom or destiny, but wouldn't go into details. It was confusing, but I never thought she was insane."

Luke shook his head. "She probably didn't understand it any better than you did, or than Keiran—Corran—did when he lost contact with you. He didn't have the mental framework in place to make it make sense."

"I'm still not sure I do."

"No, but neither do the *Jensaarai*." Luke frowned. "They have training, but it's skewed and things have been added. It's not an independent Force tradition like the Dathomiri witches, but it's unlike anything else I know of." He shrugged. "That's not saying much."

"You!" The shouted words came angry, though the speakers in the comm unit at the hallway juncture couldn't quite produce all the outrage they were meant to convey. I glanced to my left and saw a hologram of Tavira standing there, just shy of life-size, her hands on her hips. "*You* were the Jedi at Courkrus."

I nodded. "At your service." Shifting my lightsaber to my left hand, I gestured with my right to Luke and Mirax. "I'd like to introduce Luke Skywalker, Jedi Master, and Mirax Terrik and . . . but, wait, we're on our way up to see you. Introductions are so much nicer in person.''

''How dare you!''

''Oh, I dare.'' I pointed to the sky. ''New Republic will be here in no time. The days of the *Invidious* are over.''

''Never!''

I laughed. ''By the way, the month's not up, but the answer is no.''

''Arrgghhh! When I get my hands on you . . .''

''In your dreams, deary.'' Mirax shot the comm unit. ''Empire's been dead for years, and still she relies on those limping Imperial threats. *'When I get my hands on you!'* Get with the times, woman. . . .''

''I like your Mirax a whole bunch, Corran.'' Luke smiled. ''And you're right, she and Mara should never meet.''

We picked up the pace, racing into the main building and began working our way up. The staircase that wound around the inside of the building's tall atrium had a thick enough balustrade to provide some cover, of which we took advantage, as did those individuals trying to stop us. Blaster bolts, red and blue, whined and streaked, ricocheted and smoked as they burned into white marble pillars or black wall tiles. The stairs' gradual slope meant they wound around endlessly, it seemed, but was not sufficient to slow us down that much. They didn't have landings per se, so no easy points to defend, and our opponents had to put up with one unbelievably annoying problem: two of their targets bore these archaic weapons and were swatting blaster bolts out of the air. Luke was even able to redirect his at our enemies, knocking them down or making them break cover long enough for Ooryl, Elegos or Mirax to shoot them from a flanking position.

As we climbed toward the building's upper reaches, we felt a tremor course through it. "A shuttle's going up."

Elegos frowned. "Tavira must be running."

Ooryl and I exchanged glances. "That, or someone else is off carrying orders for her." I tried to push my senses to see if I could find Tavira in the shuttle or still in the building above us, but I got nothing. "Something is blocking me."

Luke nodded. "Me, too. The *Jensaarai*."

"Must be."

We pushed on, clearing the last length of corridor, then topped several steps that opened onto the foyer of a grand chamber. This has been the Imperial Governor's audience chamber and clearly designed to impress. While the space itself was square in construction the inner design was circular, from the arrangements of the twisted basalt pillars holding up the ceiling, to the designs worked into both the floor and ceiling. At the far side, opposite our stairs, another set of stairs led up to an observation deck where transparisteel made up the walls. Through the viewports we could see the gas giant, its ring, and a bright light heading outbound.

Halfway up those stairs, on a broad landing, sat a massive red granite desk and built into the front of it a cushioned chair made of the same stone. I found it easy to imagine the governor working at the desk, then moving around forward to sit in judgment over any issues brought before him. Elevated and imperial, he would have ruled as the sole, unopposable authority on Susevfi. All around the room, almost like courtiers waiting for a ruling, odd bits of fine furnishings, casks of credits, small chests of jewels and stacks of antiquities added a crude but opulent display of conspicuous wealth that smacked of Tavira.

Yet, all this, which I took in with a glance, faded to insignificance compared to the six creatures standing in the open central part of the floor. One, a woman wearing a grey cloak, with streaks of matching grey in her long brown hair, stood in the center. A mask hid her face, but unlike the others, it had not been fashioned after an animal, but instead showed a young woman, beautiful and smiling. The fire flashing in the blue eyes behind the mask, however, suggested the tall woman was anything but smiling underneath.

Arrayed behind her in an arc, five of the *Jensaarai* waited in their grey cloaks, their hoods up. The light flashing down from recessed glow panels above cast long shadows over their masks, but I caught details reptilian, insectoid and mammalian. The rightmost figure I had seen on the *Invidious* bridge with Tavira. The others, who were generally smaller, radiated little hints of anxiety.

The central figure raised her right arm and pointed a lightsaber toward me. The gold blade shot out, but stopped well shy of crossing the five meters that separated us. "Finally you have come. The Halcyon. To destroy us." Her eyes focused beyond me. "The rest of you are free to go. You have done your part in bringing him here."

I frowned. "You kidnapped Mirax to get me here? You could have given me directions and this could have been over much faster."

Ooryl rested a hand on my shoulder. "It was not *here* that was important, but *when*."

"The choice of futures is made in the moment the

future you desire is born.'' She let her cloak slip off, revealing her armored form. The armor, like the mask, had been styled after a beautiful woman and while alluring, was nonetheless deadly. She inclined her head toward me and struck a guard I found hauntingly familiar. She grasped the hilt daggerlike in her left hand, with her right hand riding on the pommel, pointing the blade toward the floor. ''Now is the time.''

Luke took a half-step forward and reached my side. ''Wait, I am Luke Skywalker. There is no need for further violence here.''

''*The* Skywalker. Your intervention here was not unanticipated.'' She jerked her head. ''My students will entertain you, then I will destroy you, too, that they may live.''

The five people backing her moved to the left, letting their cloaks fall to the floor. Each brought out a lightsaber and set themselves.

''*Saarai-kaar* of the *Jensaarai*, do not do this.'' Luke waved a hand at her students. ''I do not want to kill them.''

''Then that would be a problem for you, Skywalker.'' She nodded at me. ''Come, Halcyon, destroy or be destroyed, there is no alternative at this juncture in time.''

I lit my lightsaber as she drove toward me and blocked her first sweeping blow low and to the right. I anticipated the wrist-twist that allowed her to rake her gold blade back across where I had been. I ducked beneath her cut, then slashed at her legs, but she danced above my blade. What she didn't expect was my remaining low, pivoting on my left hand. As she landed, I swept my legs through her legs, clicking her ankles together and toppling her.

I sprang up to press my attack, but she never hit the

ground. She turned her fall into a languid backward somersault. The second she touched down, she drove at me again, feinting left and right. I backed away, moving to parry. When her blow finally came in on my left, I caught it on the forte of my blade and brought it up and over in a big circular parry. As I did so I slid forward so we stood shoulder to shoulder for a second. I cranked my left elbow up into her facemask, driving her back, then batted away a quick slash.

Off to my left, Luke moved through the *Jensaarai* with such ease and skill that I realized the only help he'd needed from me back on Courkrus the night we'd faced their brethren was for me to hold his cloak. A quick parry with his lightsaber and then a push with the Force and two of them went down hard. Another parry and the application of the lightsaber's dark end to a head dropped another to the floor. A telekinetic tug on a mask blinded one, while he fought another to a standstill, their blades arcing and screaming as they met.

The *Saarai-kaar* came at me with cold fury, her blade held in the style of the Anzati who slew my grandfather. She aimed a cut across my middle that I danced back from, then she slashed it down toward my trailing leg. The gold blade sliced through my robe and roasted a layer or two of skin off the top of my right thigh, but did no serious damage. I pivoted on that foot and arced my left foot around to catch her in the flank, pitching her across the room to where she crashed against a duraplast chest full of coins.

She clawed a handful of them back in my direction and I realized a second too late what she was really doing. With a telekinetic push she accelerated them at me. I got my lightsaber up and deflected most of them, but two thudded against my chest and one skipped off my forehead, opening up a cut above my right eye.

"Enough of this." I opened myself fully to the Force and felt it flow through me. I came in at her, beat her blade aside and planted a front kick against her armored belly. She bounced back a step, but then slashed down and in at me as she quickly advanced. I parried her hard and to the right, then shifted my wrists and came up through a slash that should have cut right through her bracer and taken her left hand off.

I felt a jolt run through my lightsaber, numbing my hands as the blade flickered and died. She recoiled, clutching at her smoking armor, her own lightsaber going out as it fell from her hand. Snarling, she nodded sharply at me, and I heard a rustling. One of her students' discarded cloaks wrapped itself around my ankles and dumped me unceremoniously on my back. I blacked out for a second, then saw the *Saarai-kaar* standing over me, her golden blade raised for an overhand blow that would split my head in two.

Without conscious thought, I reacted through the Force. Into her brain I projected an image of Nikkos Tyris lying there in my place.

She hesitated. "Master?"

Mirax's stunbolt hit the *Saarai-kaar* square in the chest and dropped her out of my sight. I kicked my feet free of the cloak and sat up. Mirax slid down by my side, her blaster carbine still pointed at the armored woman's form. She pumped another shot into her, making the body twitch.

"Nice shooting."

Mirax smiled. "Thanks. Tried to shoot her earlier, but wasn't able to concentrate enough to hit her. Then things became clear."

"Right, right at the same time I broke her concentration by planting a picture in her mind. I linked her fighting style to that of my grandfather's killer, gave her his image and she hesitated." I rolled up to one knee and kissed Mirax full on the lips. "Thanks for the rescue."

"My pleasure." She stroked a hand through my hair. "By the way, you can keep the chin fur, but change the color."

Luke came over and knelt next to the *Saarai-kaar*. He worked her mask off revealing a face somewhat seamed from age and exposure, but clearly it was just an older version of what the mask had shown. Luke touched her forehead and nodded slightly. "She'll be fine. What happened to your blade?"

"I don't know." I picked it up and hit the button. The blade sprang to life again with no shock and no sputtering. "I felt a lot of feedback. Something in the armor shorted it? Cortosis ore maybe?"

Mirax picked up the mask. "Spun cortosis fibers in this? Not much of that stuff around—which is fine because it's fairly useless. Still, pretty in ornamentation like this."

"We have a problem." Elegos looked down at us from the governor's desk. He punched a button and a hologram appeared above a built in holoprojector plate on the desk. It resolved itself into a tactical shot of the system around the gas giant. "I've fed the system data from our ship into the projector here. I show the *Invidious* leaving the ring and it's headed this way."

I shook my head. "Tavira doesn't like losing, and she'll strafe us to get rid of us. Yumfla's done."

Suddenly several more ships appeared in the image, slicing in toward Susevfi, between the *Invidious'* attack course and the planet. "I have ships identified as the

Backstab and the *Errant Venture* entering the system. They are deploying fighters: clutches and X-wings.''

Luke looked at me. ''X-wings?''

Elegos nodded. ''From the *Errant Venture*. *Invidious* is deploying clutches and coming about to engage *Errant Venture*. They should close to range in five minutes.''

Mirax shook her head. ''We can't let them do that.''

Elegos' head came up. ''Both ships are evenly matched. They are both *Imperial*-class Star Destroyers.''

I snarled and stood. ''Yeah, but Booster's ship doesn't have more than a token array of guns. Can you open up a comm line to the *Venture?* Mirax, you can talk your father into running.''

''Leaving *us* here to be lit up by Tavira? Not likely.'' She shivered. ''She'll vape the *Venture, then* vape us.''

Luke looked at me. ''Try to call Tavira. Maybe we can make a deal with her.''

''A deal with her? No way.'' I shook my head. ''If I know her at all, there's just no way we can convince her. . . .'' I stopped and bounced the heel of my hand off my forehead. ''Sithspawn, I'm so stupid.''

''What?''

I winked at Mirax and ran toward the stairs to the observation deck. ''Don't worry, I've got it. I'll take care of it. I'll move her right out of here.''

''*Move* her?'' The Jedi Master's voice came cool and even. ''Do you want help?''

''No.''

''Do you *need* help?''

''Nope.'' I smiled at him. ''Remember, 'size matters not.' And telekinesis is *not* the only way to move the *Invidious.*''

I gathered the Force inside of me and projected my awareness out into a cone that sought the white dagger stabbing down from the ring. I found it with ease, just teeming with life and fear, anger and arrogance. I worked my way through it until I found a place where arrogance and anger and outrage all seemed to collect, then I pushed my way into Tavira's mind and flowed into the place where her fears and confidence dwelt.

I listened to her weapons-officers calling out ranges and preparing firing orders. I pushed a bit of doubt into her mind. *It was impossible, wasn't it, that the New Republic would send so small a force after her? Hadn't Jenos said a task force was on its way? He had sounded confident in a time when he should have known no confidence at all. He had worked with us and against us, learning our secrets. He knew how we operated and he communicated all that to the New Republic.*

I let her listen to her people a bit more and latched on to the unease she was feeling with how simple her victory would be. We *used the* Jensaarai *to hide our ship, but the New Republic, they would make* more *use of their Jedi. They sent two after us on the ground, to free the prisoner, but what about their other Jedi? Where are they? What are they doing? Would they dare operate against* me *without them?*

In an instant she knew the New Republic saw her as such a threat that they would stop at nothing to catch her, which meant they would use the Jedi against her. Not only that, but they would use the Jedi to trap her by reversing the methods she had used to elude the New Republic. I let her feel that if she sharpened her mind, she could pierce the veil of deception the Jedi were casting over her and her crew. She concentrated and pushed, accomplishing nothing really, but I rewarded her for it.

The holographic representation of the *Errant Venture* evaporated to be replaced by a bigger ship, a much bigger ship: a Super Star Destroyer that would eat up her Impstar Deuce as easily as the *Invidious* had destroyed the *Harmzuay*. I fed to her every image I'd had burned into my memory of the *Lusankya*, Isard's old SSD, and channeled in a good dose of fear.

I touched her paranoia and let one of her own fantasies spin out for her. From the SSD's belly a slender, needlelike craft shot. I fed her images of the Sun Crusher and let her calculate the damage that could be caused by that indestructible fighter-sized craft accelerating to just below light-speed, then ramming her ship. It would blow through it from stem to stern in seconds, shattering the *Invidious*. The SSD would just pound the scraps until their molten metal fragments congealed into debris that would make for a spectacular light show when they burned into Susevfi's atmosphere.

"Belay those orders," I heard her shout. "It's a *trap*, a *Jedi trap*. Evasive maneuvers, plot me a course out of here. Far away!"

I retreated into myself and staggered back against the observation deck railing.

From below I heard Elegos. "The *Invidious* is coming about. Tavira is leaving the system."

I turned around slowly, then tried to lean nonchalantly on the railing. "Problem solved."

Mirax arched an eyebrow at me. "You think so, do you?"

I looked down at my wife. "She's gone, isn't she?"

"Sure." Mirax smiled. "But my father's going to think she was running from *him*. He'll be insufferable. You'll never hear the end of how *he* saved *my* life, and just happened to include yours in the bargain."

"I don't mind," I forced myself to say. "After all, a Jedi does not know pain."

FORTY-NINE

Things quieted down on Susevfi fairly quickly after the *Invidious* ran. We called Booster and through him got Jacob Nive. Jacob apologized for having brought Booster to us and having given him the data we'd left behind for Cracken, but Booster had been most insistent and had an Impstar Deuce to back things up. Nive contacted Colonel Gurtt, informed her of what was going on and offered to consider her and any ex-Invids who stopped their fighting to be members of the Survivors for purposes of the deal Luke and I had offered him. Colonel Gurtt, being the highest ranking Invid officer in the system, got the ground resistance to back off and Rogue Squadron set down in the palace grounds to hold back any misguided loyalists until Booster could shuttle down some of his security personnel and Nive could bring down some of the Survivor mudbugs to take care of ground ops.

Rogue Squadron had been on a long patrol circuit when Cracken had reached them and pointed them toward Courkrus. Though they came from further away, they plotted a tight course that got them to Courkrus before Booster. He arrived and offered them a ride to Susevfi, so they shipped aboard. Colonels Celchu and

Gurtt met on the ground for the first time and were able to work out terms under which the Survivors would be allowed to keep their ships. They quickly began to bring local politicians into the meetings and I had no doubt that within several weeks, Susevfi would petition the New Republic for entry as a full member, complete with a fighter force, and that the Survivors would find themselves a nice little home.

In addition to that, Elegos indicated that Susevfi struck him as a much nicer world than Kerilt. The possibility of moving at least part of the Caamasi Remnant to it seemed quite likely. Somehow I thought Caamasi fellowship and guidance for the Survivors and the Invids would go a long way toward making Susevfi strong and peaceful.

The *Jensaarai* still presented us something of a problem, but here, too, the Caamasi touch provided a solution that could not have otherwise been possible. By the time I'd had my cut treated and things had been calmed down outside, the *Jensaarai* Nive had brought with him had been reunited with those Luke had defeated and the half dozen who had been stationed on a small base out in the ring to cover the *Invidious*. They had also been hiding the *Pulsar Skate* and had used it to return to Susevfi.

The *Saarai-kaar*, when she regained consciousness, seemed truly surprised to be alive. The fact that her students had not been slain and had been allowed to retain custody of their armor and lightsabers clearly confused her. As she sat up on the couch to which she had been carried in the Governor's private chambers, she looked at her students, then at Luke, Elegos and finally me.

''Is this how you choose to mock me, Halcyon?'' She

waved a hand at her students. "You have them here to show me that you have won them over to your murderous ways?"

Her orienting on me confused me, since Luke was clearly the Master here. I shook my head. "If my ways were the ways of a murderer, why would you be alive?"

"You like to torture us before you slay us. You call yourselves Jedi, but your kind parted from the true Jedi ways a generation ago, and then some. And those who rose up in your place were no better." She lifted her chin, her blue eyes fiery and bright. "We are the true Jedi, the *Jensaarai*. You tried before to destroy us, but failed."

I frowned. "I've never seen you before. I've never been here before, and I've certainly never tried to harm you or your people before."

"Just like a Halcyon to deny the evil he has inherited."

I looked to Luke. "I'm not tracking here."

"Neither am I."

Elegos rested hands on our shoulders. "Perhaps you would permit me."

I shrugged. "Set a course and go."

The Caamasi moved forward and dropped to one knee before the *Saarai-kaar*. "The *Jensaarai* are your creation. You fashioned them and their teachings from what you yourself had learned when you trained." Elegos kept his voice low and respectful, probing, but gentle and reassuring. "You are the first *Saarai-kaar*, but you hold dearly to the memories of others, to honor them and their sacrifice."

She blinked her eyes a couple of times, then bowed her head. "Yes, this is so."

I glanced down as factoids began to slot together for

me. When she'd had me at her mercy, I'd projected Tyris' image from my dream into her brain because I had recognized her fighting style as that of the Anzati Jedi. I'd done it instinctively and had missed entirely the significance of her saying ''Master?'' as she hesitated. She was looking at me, seeing my uniform, my silver blade, and seeing me as my grandfather or clearly someone who had come to finish what Nejaa Halcyon had started. Try as I might, though, I searched my memory of the dream and could not place her in it.

Elegos pressed his hands together. ''These you honor were your teachers and friends. Their deaths you blame on a Halcyon and other Jedi, one very much like me, yes?''

An edge returned to her voice. ''I do.'' She thrust a finger at me. ''It was a Halcyon who slew my Master and my husband that day, and retreated to leave us alone. They did not care for us, for the damage they had done. They were supposed to serve all life and living creatures, but they deserted us, proving the lie of the Jedi. We had already known—our Masters had told us—that we were a breed apart. The advent of the Jedi here on Susevfi merely proved all they had taught was true.''

Luke opened his hands. ''Truth is often a matter of point of view.''

Anger flashed through the *Saarai-kaar*'s eyes. ''You were not there. You have no point of view.''

I was about to mention my dream, but Elegos reached out and placed a hand on her knee. ''But I *do*. I would share it with you.''

She looked sharply at Elegos. ''You were not the Jedi there that day.''

''No, I was not, but I will share with you a secret—I will give you my trust that you may return it. I know you do not want to hurt anyone, which is why I can trust you. I would have you accept my trust so you can stop yourself from hurting.''

Luke gave me a sidelong glance, but I nodded reassuringly to him. ''He knows what he is doing.''

The *Saarai-kaar*'s voice sagged beneath the weight of suspicion. ''What will you do?''

''The Caamasi have a gift in which significant memories become treasured and, in special circumstances, can be shared. We discovered, as a people, that we could share them among ourselves, yet with non-Caamasi species, they could only be communicated to the Jedi. I think it is their connection to the Force that allows this, and any of us who have come to truly know a Jedi are privileged to be able to share these *memnii* with the Jedi.''

He twisted back and caught my right hand in his left, dragging me forward. ''I have come to know this man under a variety of identities, one of them being Keiran Halcyon; the grandson of Nejaa Halcyon. Nejaa is the Halcyon Jedi you accuse of being a murderer and the Caamasi who was with him that day was my uncle. My uncle passed to me the *memnis* of what happened here, sharing with me the memory of his friend's death. This is the point of view I have of those events, and I would share it with you in hopes you would understand the *other* point of view.''

The *Saarai-kaar* held her hand out to Elegos. ''Show me the memory.''

Elegos stood but did not relinquish his grip on my hand. ''I do not know you well enough for me to transfer the memory to you. I do know Keiran well enough to share with him, and you know he can project it into your mind.''

"You want me to trust a Halcyon, too? You ask too much, Caamasi."

Elegos looked down at her. "Is it too much to ask when it could free you of a burden you have carried for over forty years? Is it too much to ask when he has not slain you nor your companions, and yet could easily have done so—bearing in mind this is the purpose you claim he has come for? Your caution is admirable, but do not let it be a barrier to a greater truth."

She hesitated, then nodded once. "What I will see, I will consider."

"Good." Elegos looked at me. "Prepare yourself."

"Am I sending just to her, or do I include Master Skywalker and her apprentices?"

Luke smiled. "I would be honored to share that memory."

The *Saarai-kaar*' eyes tightened, then she nodded. "Let them see."

"Okay." I set myself. "Ready, I guess."

I felt a tingle run through my hand and up into my brain. I touched the Force and entwined it with what I was getting from Elegos, then pushed it out toward the others in the room. I felt contact with all of them, some hot and some oh so cold. I just served as a conduit and watched the *memnis* pour through my mind.

Even if I had intended to edit and modify it, I doubt I could have. Since what I was seeing came through Caamasi eyes, and was wrapped up in Caamasi kinesthetics and senses, any changes I had made would have been patently human and obviously artificial. Moreover, the intensity and volume of sensory input overwhelmed me. I saw and heard, tasted, touched and smelled—boy, did I smell things—so much that I couldn't categorize it. The *memnis* was like a holovid presentation so complex that only by watching it again and again could I begin to grapple with all of the elements.

I found myself in Ylenic It'kla's flesh, with his fellow Jedi on either side of him. My grandfather he classified as Spicewood—he knew his name, of course, but the Caamasi's acute sense of smell led him to store identity information with scent being more important than name. The other Jedi he identified as Desertwind. I heard Desertwind warn the dark Jedi we faced, and all of our replies, the same as in my dream. Then the battle was joined, blades flashing, barking, sparking and hissing.

Moving into combat in the Caamasi's body felt thoroughly alien. His gangling limbs and deceptively slender muscles contained incredible power and grace. His feet shuffled through the dust, always keeping us in balance, with our legs ready to propel me forward in a strike. I watched my foe come in, watched her flick her blade this way and that, probing my defenses. I could tell she had some skill, but how much remained a mystery, and a hint of fear trickled through me as she attacked.

Pain exploded on my left flank as the red-haired woman—Dustrose—raked the tip of her blue lightsaber across my flesh. I caught the stink of burned down and it almost overrode the pain. I spun away with impossible quickness, turning a full circle and bringing my red-gold blade around to bat her blade aside.

She was good, but I knew I was better.

My Caamasi muscles tensed, then brought the blade back up in a rising slash that slipped beneath her guard and opened her from hip to shoulder. Dustrose reeled back, then flopped to the ground. An explosion of blue energy instantly consumed her body, knocking me back and down.

Through the link with the *Saarai-kaar* I felt a jolt of

grief at Dustrose's death, but it was as nothing as I looked to the left. I saw Spicewood on the ground, his lightsaber beyond his reach. I knew that if I could concentrate, if I could push past the pain, I could move his lightsaber back into his hand. It would only take a moment, and the Anzati Nightsweat's gloating clearly appeared to give me that moment.

Then Spicewood dove for his blade and Nightsweat stabbed down. I could almost feel the blade burning its way through my friend, severing the ties his life had to his body. I would have expected him to die instantly, but he managed a smile. The azure blade fixing him to the ground sputtered and died and in an instant I knew what he had done, how he had employed the rarest of all Jedi gifts, and what a terrible price he had paid for it.

Nightsweat rose into the air, then convulsed and seemed to implode. I saw the body fly back through the tents built beneath the duracrete dome. Nightsweat exploded, as did the dark Jedi Desertwind had slain. Their mortal bodies no longer able to contain the dark-side energy, it flashed out in a blue fireball that shattered the duracrete dome. I rushed to Spicewood, pulling him clear as the dome began to collapse. I felt Desertwind supporting the dome around me, then he let it go as we got clear.

I knelt in the dirt, cradling my friend's head in my lap. Desertwind stood by my side, resting a hand on my shoulder. "I think he knew Tyris was a good enough swordsman to get one or the other of us. Nejaa knew he could not defeat him with a lightsaber, so he found another means to protect us."

I caressed my grandfather's face, wiping away the blood from the cut on his head and the corner of his mouth. "To have survived so much to die here. It is sad."

"But to die in the defense of all that is good, it must be celebrated and remembered."

I nodded. "It will be a sadder day when such nobility is forgotten."

"Or feared."

"Worse yet, yes." I smiled, breathing deep of Spicewood's scent, then was aware of the lessening of his weight upon my thighs. I looked down and saw him fade away, his burned clothes collapsing, his lightsaber settling into the dust. Beyond his boots, a last section of the dome groaned and sagged in, with a couple of the tiles that had been set into it exploding into fragments. I picked one up and ran my thumb over it, feeling the strange glyphs incised into it.

I began to shiver and Desertwind supported me. "You've been hurt, my friend. We have to get you away from here. In a place of evil like this, there can be no healing."

"I can make it back to Yumfla."

"Good, and then to Corellia." Desertwind helped me up. "Nejaa's family will know he died a hero."

The memory faded out as my vision of the room flooded back. I tasted salt on my lips. I reached up and swiped away at tears. I turned to thank Elegos, but could not speak past the tightness in my throat.

Elegos nodded. "I know."

The *Saarai-kaar* began speaking in a small voice. "I know well the pain of lost comrades your uncle felt, Caamasi. I mourn for him, but his belief that he and his friends were right in no way means they were. When that dome collapsed, my husband was crushed. We lost a half-dozen friends and I was left alone with three other apprentices.'' She pressed her hand against her stomach. ''And the boy growing in my belly. We hid from the Jedi and mourned and buried our dead. We had been sealed together, bound together by the deaths. We made a new beginning from the tragedy, and yet this memory would seek to have us believe we were walking the path of evil.''

I nodded my head. ''The memory proves it. The writing on the tiles, I recognize it from Yavin 4. It's of Sith origin.''

The *Saarai-kaar* nodded. ''Our masters had uncovered information about Sith techniques from an antiquarian who had recovered artifacts. They learned that the Jedi had stolen their discipline from the Sith, had perverted Sith teaching and our masters were returning us to the true way. *Jensaarai* is a Sith word for the hidden followers of truth. As the *Saarai-kaar*, I am the keeper of that truth. We are not evil.''

Luke shook his head. ''In fact you are not.''

I frowned at him. ''They were following Sith practices. Are you forgetting Exar Kun and all that?''

''Not at all, Keiran. They were being taught the Jedi way by people who had accepted Sith thoughts and philosophies, but they themselves were not sufficiently developed to be initiated into them. Their masters had not yet found the hooks by which they could be opened to the dark side. And then, after the deaths of their masters, they continued learning, but did so with the orientation of protecting themselves from the Jedi. They dedicated themselves to defense—choosing the correct path for the wrong reasons.''

I shivered. ''But with such a hate for the Jedi, they should have come forth and helped the Emperor hunt them down.''

The *Saarai-kaar* leaned forward, covering her face in her hands. "Again we were betrayed."

As she sobbed, one of the apprentices—Red—removed her mask. "The *Saarai-kaar*'s son was of an age to be independent when the Emperor started hunting down the Jedi. Against her wishes, he left here and offered his services to Darth Vader. He was slain outright, and Jedi hunters came here, but never found us. I was but a child then, but I remember the hiding, the fear. Our community kept us strong."

I nodded. "And when the Rebellion started, you could not join it because it lauded as heroes the very Jedi who had created you in the first place."

The *Saarai-kaar* looked up, wiping away her tears. "We are not evil."

Luke dropped to one knee before her. "No, the *Jensaarai* are not, nor are they wholly good."

"What?" Her face sharpened. "How can you say that?"

"It is a simple truth, of which you have part, but you stand so close to it that you cannot see the whole of it. You are fully committed to your community, to your students and they to you and each other. This is what has kept you from the dark side. Even when your people helped Tavira, they did so to protect you and Susevfi. This is good, but it is not the true whole of the Jedi tradition."

Luke gave her a heartwarming smile. "To be a Jedi is to be committed to the defense of *everyone*. Our duties do have limits—Nejaa Halcyon limited his work to the Corellian system, except when extraordinary circumstances called him beyond it. When he did come forth, he was willing to sacrifice his life for others. Here you have not been open to those calls, those sacrifices, and this has limited your access to the Force and all it offers. I have an academy that could teach you or some of your apprentices about this grander Jedi tradition, if you wish."

"It is an offer I shall consider." She shivered. "Could I have been wrong all these years?"

I smiled at her. "Not wrong, not at all. You did what you felt was right to save others from being hurt. That is never wrong."

My Jedi Master rose. "It is very right. We can just make it more so. Keiran, he is the product of one Jedi tradition, and me, I am born of yet a different one. You and your *Jensaarai* are just part of a third. If you will permit it, we would welcome you into the greater Jedi tradition of service so that all of our ways, woven together, will make us so strong we can never again be torn apart."

EPILOGUE

The next time I saw Luke was about three days later. I met him in the Governor's palace not quite by chance. I'd been going to see him, but felt him speaking to the *Saarai-kaar*, so I headed up to the roof and the shuttle pad. I was looking out over Yumfla's night sky and up at the brilliant curved planetary ring stretching up and out from the horizon. Beyond the ring the stars looked so bright and so inviting, and the space between them so black and cold.

"There you are, Corran." Luke smiled as he came up onto the roof. "Your wife's right, brown *is* better for your hair."

I raked my fingers back through it. "Yeah. Gonna let it grow out a bit, too. Can't decide on the goatee and moustache, though."

"I'd get rid of it." Luke shrugged and joined me at the wall. "I had been hoping to see you over the past couple of days."

"Sorry, Mirax and I were . . . checking out the *Pulsar Skate* and making sure it was prepped for the trip back to Coruscant." I pointed vaguely off toward the starport. "We can give you a ride back, if you want."

"No. You'll want time alone—or *more* time alone—

and Elegos has learned of the Alderaanian ritual of leaving grave goods in the Graveyard. Ooryl and I are going to head to Kerilt, pick up Elegos' daughter, Releqy, and take them to where they can leave things for Ylenic It'kla."

I nodded. "I'll have to make that trip, too, at some point. Leave something for Ylenic in my grandfather's name."

"I think that would please both of them." The Jedi Master glanced up at the stars. "After that I think I'd like to help Rogue Squadron find the *Invidious* and end Tavira's career."

I shrugged. "Without the *Jensaarai* she'll just be another proto-warlord running around out there. Someone will get her—New Republic probably. Maybe she'll anger Pellaeon and he'll do us a favor by taking her toy away from her."

"That would be convenient, certainly." Luke fell silent, for a moment, then rested his hands on the top of the restraining wall. "There's something important I need to discuss with you."

"Me, too." I gave him a smile. I'd spent a fair amount of time thinking about my life and my father's "man in the mirror" saying. I actually *did* recognize myself, which was good, but it forced some hard choices. I shrugged. "I'm not going to go back to the academy. I'm not going to be a Jedi full time."

"Interesting."

I arched an eyebrow at him. "Interesting?"

"Yes. I was going to ask you not to return to the academy."

My mouth gaped open in shock for a second. "I wasn't *that* disruptive, was I?"

The Jedi Master shook his head. "Not at all. You see, you had training all your life that directed you toward a goal that I'm trying to train my recruits for. You have a grounding that means learning to use the Jedi techniques and tools just adds another layer to you. It provides you with more things to do, things you already are well trained to do. On the way here you pointed out that Nejaa often went about as a regular man, solving problems and only using his Jedi abilities when needed—precisely because he had the other skills needed to do these jobs and didn't *have to rely upon his Jedi skills.*"

I smiled as I unraveled what he meant. *When the only tool you have is a hydrospanner, every problem looks like something that needs to be torqued.* "I think I get what you're saying."

"I'd expect that of a detective." Luke laughed lightly. "You figured out Exar Kun had to be behind Gantoris' death and the trouble on Yavin 4 because you were a trained investigator. I missed all the evidence you saw, or didn't want to believe it because I didn't see how it fit together. That 'fitting together' training is some of what the new Jedi will need. The regimen that gets created to provide it won't give you anything."

"You could well be right."

He folded his arms across his chest. "So why is it that you won't be coming back?"

I shifted my shoulders uneasily. "It kind of gets back to what you said about Nejaa, and to part of what I did to Tavira to get her out of here. The place where I can do the greatest good right now, I think, is with Rogue Squadron. Look at you, you're always being called away to solve some galaxy-threatening problem, having to leave the academy in someone else's hands when training more Jedi is what you'd most like to be doing. By remaining Corran Horn and staying with Rogue Squadron, I can use my abilities where they will be critical for missions, and yet I won't be pulled in all sorts of different directions."

"And you will be able to remain on Coruscant and start a family."

"Among other things." I smiled, recalling fondly how much checking out and how little real work Mirax and I had gotten done on the *Skate*. "Part of what frightened Tavira off was the fact that she didn't believe the Sun Crusher had been destroyed. The fact that she knew it was out there but couldn't find it had her convinced it was hunting her. I guess, by staying hidden, I'll be a surprise waiting for anyone who needs one."

"So Keiran Halcyon dies here?"

"Not *dies*, just fades away. Few enough people know I'm him that keeping it a secret shouldn't really be difficult." I reached out and rested my right hand on Luke's shoulder. "You need Keiran for anything, he'll be there. You need Corran Horn for anything, he'll be there. Fact of the matter is, without you, I'd be dead, Mirax would still be imprisoned and Tavira would be raiding away."

Luke smiled. "And without you, I'd be on a slab in a temple on Yavin 4. We're even. No harm came to my niece and nephew during that time, so I may even owe you."

"I was hoping you'd say that." I gave him a big smile. "There's one more thing I want to do to wrap this whole thing up, with your permission."

Luke nodded. "Name it."

I did.

I leveled the X-wing out at what Whistler reported to be nineteen point five two meters above the Yavin 4 landscape and hovered there, eyeball to eyeball with Exar

Kun's statue. It actually stood a good five hundred meters off the X-wing's nose, but those hollow black eyes watched me intensely.

I gave him a big smile.

"Whistler, you got all sensors on full record and you're feeding the data back to the *Skate* at the Great Temple?"

His curt blat reminded me that he didn't forget orders—or go gallivanting off around the galaxy leaving friends behind to be worried circuit-worn about him.

I nodded. "We are good to go and clear to fire." I flicked the weapons-control over to proton torpedoes and set it for single fire. I dropped my targeting reticle over Exar Kun's face, then cut my comm unit feed. I didn't mind folks watching what I was doing, but what I had to say, that was just for me and Exar Kun.

"I know you're gone, but I also know you planned for that, someday. This temple might be an archeological find of great value, a monument of untold wonder, but it's also a monument to evil. You used it to infect Kyp, and mere impressions made of the glyphs infected the dark Jedi who killed my grandfather. Your evil created the *Jensaarai*, and even though they rose above it, people have still suffered and died because of it.

"But this isn't revenge, which you would have liked. Nope, this is simply a precaution." I settled my finger on the trigger. "Wouldn't leave a lightsaber around where a kid could find it, and this temple to you is a million more times dangerous than that."

I pulled the trigger and sent a proton torpedo streaking out at the statue. The warhead detonated when it hit the bridge of his nose, shattering his skull into thousands of fragments that sprayed out in a shower of sparks and cloud of whitish smoke. The bits and pieces of Exar

Kun's head rained down in a narrow triangle, smashing the lake's mirror-like surface, forever breaking up the last intact images of that island.

Two more proton torpedoes took Exar Kun off at waist and knees, then I shot the rest of them into the base of the obelisk on which he had stood. It toppled wonderfully, breaking into pieces as it went. The chunks slammed into the ground and crushed walls, then bounced around inside the temple, pulverizing slab after slab of Sith writings. Some eventually ricocheted high enough to escape the temple itself, splashing down in the cold dark lake.

Switching to lasers, I raked fire back and forth across the temple, heating rock until it ran like water. Great clouds of steam rose up as stone sloughed off walls and sank, formless and unshaped and now unblemished by Sith scribings. When I was done only the island itself remained: still black as night, but now all soft and curving, no longer angular, no longer strong.

No longer a place of power, just a tranquil spot in a lake that would once again reflect the stars, and now could reflect their peace.

I flipped my comm unit back on. "This is Rogue Nine. Mission accomplished."

Mirax's voice filled my helmet. "We got that, Rogue Nine. Master Skywalker says 'Well done.' "

"Thank him for me. It was my pleasure." I smiled. "Exar Kun is done, the Invids have fled, this temple is gone and you're home again. Only one last bit of business and all of this can be over."

"And that is?"

"And that is the toughest bit of all, my love," I laughed, "we have to tell your father our first child will *not* be named for him."

ABOUT THE AUTHOR

Michael A. Stackpole is still an award-winning game designer, computer game designer and writer who is uncomfortable about this third-person bio thing. Not much has changed since the last bio, actually, except there is a third dog in the house: Saint, the great-grandson of Ruthless and the great-grandnephew of Ember, the other two dogs living here. Growing up in Vermont, Mike only ever had one dog at a time in the house, but if all three of these Cardigan Welsh Corgis were piled into one dog, they would equal the Labrador with which he grew up.

Mike still plays soccer on weekends and is on a team with players who do all sorts of things to make him look really good. He's still riding his mountain bike—the more he rides it, the less of a mountain he becomes.

By the time you're reading this, he should have finished his final X-wing book. He'll also have finished scripting bunches of the X-wing Rogue Squadron comic from Dark Horse, which he finds to be a lot of fun. And, after all, if you can't have fun writing, there is absolutely no reason to do it—it's too much hard work otherwise. His next big project is an epic fantasy series for Bantam called the Dragoncrown War and he's really looking forward to it.

His website can be found at <http://www.flyingbuffalo.com/stackpol.htm>. It's updated every so often (okay, often is a relative term).

The World of
STAR WARS Novels

In May 1991, *Star Wars* caused a sensation in the publishing industry with the Bantam Spectra release of Timothy Zahn's novel *Heir to the Empire*. For the first time, Lucasfilm Ltd. had authorized new novels that *continued* the famous story told in George Lucas's three blockbuster motion pictures: *Star Wars, The Empire Strikes Back,* and *Return of the Jedi.* Reader reaction was immediate and tumultuous: *Heir* reached #1 on the *New York Times* bestseller list and demonstrated that *Star Wars* lovers were eager for exciting new stories set in this universe, written by leading science fiction authors who shared their passion. Since then, each Bantam *Star Wars* novel has been an instant national bestseller.

Lucasfilm and Bantam decided that future novels in the series would be interconnected: that is, events in one novel would have consequences in the others. You might say that each Bantam *Star Wars* novel, enjoyable on its own, is also part of a much larger tale.

Here is a special look at Bantam's *Star Wars* books, along with excerpts from the more recent novels. Each one is available now wherever Bantam Books are sold.

The Han Solo Trilogy:
THE PARADISE SNARE
THE HUTT GAMBIT
REBEL DAWN
by A. C. Crispin
Setting: Before *Star Wars: A New Hope*

What was Han Solo like before we met him in the first STAR WARS movie? This trilogy answers that tantalizing question, filling in lots of historical lore about our favorite swashbuckling hero and thrilling us with adventures of the brash young pilot that we never knew he'd experienced. As the trilogy begins, the young Han Makes a life-changing decision: to escape from the clutches of Garris Shrike, head of the trading "clan" who has brutalized Han while taking advantage of his piloting abilities. Here's a tense early scene from The Paradise Snare *featuring Han, Shrike, and Dewlanna, a Wookiee who is Han's only friend in this horrible situation:*

"I've had it with you, Solo. I've been lenient with you so far, because you're a blasted good swoop pilot and all that prize money came in handy, but my patience is ended." Shrike ceremoniously pushed up the sleeves of his bedizened uniform, then balled his hands into fists. The galley's artificial lighting made the blood-jewel ring glitter dull silver. "Let's see what a few days of fighting off Devaronian blood-poisoning does for your attitude—along with maybe a few broken bones. I'm doing this for your own good, boy. Someday you'll thank me."

Han gulped with terror as Shrike started toward him. He'd lashed out at the trader captain once before, two years ago, when he'd been feeling cocky after winning the gladiatorial Free-For-All on Jubilar—and had been instantly sorry. The speed and strength of Garris's returning blow had snapped his head back and split both lips so thoroughly that Dewlanna had had to feed him mush for a week until they healed.

With a snarl, Dewlanna stepped forward. Shrike's hand dropped to his blaster. "You stay out of this, old Wookiee," he snapped in a voice nearly as harsh as Dewlanna's. "Your cooking isn't *that* good."

Han had already grabbed his friend's furry arm and was forcibly holding her back. "Dewlanna, no!"

She shook off his hold as easily as she would have waved off an annoying insect and roared at Shrike. The captain drew his blaster, and chaos erupted.

"Noooo!" Han screamed, and leaped forward, his foot lashing out in an old street-fighting technique. His instep impacted solidly with Shrike's breastbone. The captain's breath went out in a great *houf!* and he went over backward. Han hit the deck and rolled. A tingler bolt sizzled past his ear.

"Larrad!" wheezed the captain as Dewlanna started toward him.

Shrike's brother drew his blaster and pointed it at the Wookiee. "Stop, Dewlanna!"

His words had no more effect than Han's. Dewlanna's blood was up—she was in full Wookiee battle rage. With a roar that deafened the combatants, she grabbed Larrad's wrist and yanked, spinning him around and snapping him in a terrible parody of a child's "snap the whip" game. Han heard a *crunch,* mixed with several *pops* as tendons and ligaments gave way. Larrad Shrike shrieked, a high, shrill noise that carried such pain that the Corellian youth's arm ached in sympathy.

Grabbing the blaster from his belt, Han snapped off a shot at the Elomin who was leaping forward, tingler ready and aimed at Dewlanna's midsection. Brafid howled, dropping his weapon. Han was amazed that he'd managed to hit him, but he didn't have long to wonder about the accuracy of his aim.

Shrike was staggering to his feet, blaster in hand, aimed squarely at Han's head. "Larrad?" he yelled at the writhing heap of agony that was his brother. Larrad did not reply.

Shrike cocked the blaster and stepped even closer to Han. "Stop it, Dewlanna!" the captain snarled at the Wookiee. "Or your buddy Solo dies!"

Han dropped his blaster and put his hands up in a gesture of surrender.

Dewlanna stopped in her tracks, growling softly.

Shrike leveled the blaster, and his finger tightened on the trigger. Pure malevolent hatred was etched upon his features, and then he smiled, pale blue eyes glittering with ruthless joy. "For insubordination and striking your captain," he announced, "I sentence you to death, Solo. May you rot in all the hells there ever were."

SHADOWS OF THE EMPIRE
by Steve Perry
Setting: Between *The Empire Strikes Back* and *Return of the Jedi*

Here is a very special STAR WARS story dealing with Black Sun, a galaxy-spinning criminal organization that is masterminded by one of the most interesting villains in the STAR WARS universe: Xizor, dark prince of the Falleen. Xizor's chief rival for the favor of Emperor Palpatine is none other than Darth Vader himself— alive and well, and a major character in this story, since it is set during the events of the STAR WARS film trilogy.

In the opening prologue, we revisit a familiar scene from The Empire Strikes Back, *and are introduced to our marvelous new bad guy:*

He looks like a walking corpse, Xizor thought. *Like a mummified body dead a thousand years. Amazing he is still alive, much less the most powerful man in the galaxy. He isn't even that old; it is more as if something is slowly eating him.*

Xizor stood four meters away from the Emperor, watching as the man who had long ago been Senator Palpatine moved to stand in the holocam field. He imagined he could smell the decay in the Emperor's worn body. Likely that was just some trick of the recycled air, run through dozens of filters to ensure that there was no chance of any poison gas being introduced into it. Filtered the life out of it, perhaps, giving it that dead smell.

The viewer on the other end of the holo-link would see a close-up of the Emperor's head and shoulders, of an age-ravaged face shrouded in the cowl of his dark zeyd-cloth robe. The man on the other end of the transmission, light-years away, would not see Xizor, though Xizor would be able to see him. It was a measure of the Emperor's trust that Xizor was allowed to be here while the conversation took place.

The man on the other end of the transmission—if he could still be called that—

The air swirled inside the Imperial chamber in front of the Emperor, coalesced, and blossomed into the image of a figure down on one knee. A caped humanoid biped dressed in jet black, face hidden under a full helmet and breathing mask:

Darth Vader.

Vader spoke: "What is thy bidding, my master?"

If Xizor could have hurled a power bolt through time and space to strike Vader dead, he would have done it without blinking. Wishful thinking: Vader was too powerful to attack directly.

"There is a great disturbance in the Force," the Emperor said.

"I have felt it," Vader said.

"We have a new enemy. Luke Skywalker."

Skywalker? That had been Vader's name, a long time ago. What was this person with the same name, someone so powerful as to be worth a conversation between the Emperor and his most loathsome creation? More importantly, why had Xizor's agents not uncovered this before now? Xizor's ire was instant—but cold. No sign of his surprise or anger would show on his imperturbable features. The Falleen did not allow their emotions to burst forth as did many of the inferior species; no, the Falleen ancestry was not fur but scales, not mammalian but reptilian. Not wild but coolly calculating. Such was much better. Much safer.

"Yes, my master," Vader continued.

"He could destroy us," the Emperor said.

Xizor's attention was riveted upon the Emperor and the holographic image of Vader kneeling on the deck of a ship far away.

Here was interesting news indeed. Something the Emperor perceived as a danger to himself? Something the Emperor feared?

"He's just a boy," Vader said. "Obi-Wan can no longer help him."

Obi-Wan. That name Xizor knew. He was among the last of the Jedi Knights, a general. But he'd been dead for decades, hadn't he?

Apparently Xizor's information was wrong if Obi-Wan had been helping someone who was still a boy. His agents were going to be sorry.

The Bounty Hunter Wars
Book 1: THE MANDALORIAN ARMOR
Book 2: SLAVE SHIP
by K. W. Jeter
Setting: During *Return of the Jedi*

Boba Fett continues the fight against the legions of circling enemies as the somewhat hot-tempered Trandoshan Bossk attempts to re-establish the old Bounty Hunter Guild with himself as its head. Bossk has sworn undying vengeance on Boba Fett when his ship, Hound's Tooth, *crashes.*

In the excerpt that follows, Bossk attempts to kill Boba Fett in a violent confrontation:

Fear is a useful thing.

That was one of the best lessons that a bounty hunter could learn. And Bossk was learning it now.

Through the cockpit viewport of the *Hound's Tooth,* he saw the explosion that ripped the other ship, Boba Fett's *Slave I,* into flame and shards of blackened durasteel. A burst of wide-band comlink static, like an electromagnetic death cry, had simultaneously deafened Bossk. The searing, multi-octave noise had poured through the speakers in the *Hound*'s cockpit for several minutes, until the last of the circuitry aboard Fett's ship had finally been consumed and silenced in the fiery apocalypse.

When he could finally hear himself think again, Bossk looked out at the empty space where *Slave I* had been. Now, against the cold backdrop of stars, a few scraps of heated metal slowly dwindled from white-hot to dull red as their molten heat ebbed away in vacuum. *He's dead,* thought Bossk with immense satisfaction. *At last.* Whatever atoms had constituted the late Boba Fett, they were also drifting disconnected and harmless in space. Before transferring back here to his own ship, Bossk had wired up enough thermal explosives in *Slave I* to reduce any living thing aboard it to mere ash and bad memories.

So if he still felt afraid, if his gut still knotted when Boba Fett's dark-visored image rose in his thoughts, Bossk knew that was an irrational response. *He's dead, he's gone . . .*

The silence of the *Hound*'s cockpit was broken by a barely audible pinging signal from the control panel. Bossk glanced down and saw that the *Hound*'s telesponder had picked up the presence of another ship in the immediate vicinity; according to the coordinates that appeared in the readout screen, it was almost on top of the *Hound's Tooth*.

And—it was the ship known as *Slave I*. The ID profile was an exact match.

That's impossible, thought Bossk, bewildered. His heart shuddered to a halt inside his chest, then staggered on. Before the explosion, he had picked up the same ID profile from the other side of his own ship; he had turned the *Hound's Tooth* around just in time to see the huge, churning ball of flame fill his viewscreen.

But, he realized now, he hadn't seen *Slave I* itself. Which meant . . .

Bossk heard another sound, even softer, coming from somewhere else in his own ship. There was someone else aboard it; his keen Trandoshan senses registered the molecules of another creature's spoor in the ship's recycled atmosphere. And Bossk knew who it was.

He's here. The cold blood in Bossk's veins chilled to ice. *Boba Fett . . .*

Somehow, Bossk knew, he had been tricked. The explosion hadn't consumed *Slave I* and its occupants at all. He didn't know how Boba Fett had managed it, but it had been done nevertheless. And the deafening electronic noise that had filled the cockpit had also been enough to cover Boba Fett's unauthorized entry of the *Hound's Tooth;* the shrieking din had gone on long enough for Fett to have penetrated an access hatch and resealed it behind himself.

A voice came from the cockpit's overhead speaker, a voice that was neither his own nor Boba Fett's.

"Twenty seconds to detonation." It was the calm, unexcited voice of an autonomic bomb. Only the most powerful ones contained warning circuits like that.

Fear thawed the ice in Bossk's veins. He jumped up from the pilot's chair and dived for the hatchway behind himself.

In the emergency equipment bay of the *Hound's Tooth,* his clawed hands tore through the contents of one of the storage lockers. The *Hound* wasn't going to be a ship much longer; in a few seconds—and counting down—it was going to be glowing bits of shrapnel and rubbish surrounded by a haze of rapidly dissipating atmospheric gases, just like whatever it had been that he had mistakenly identified as Boba Fett's ship *Slave I.* That the *Hound* would no longer be capable of maintaining its life-support systems wasn't Bossk's main concern at this moment, as the reptilian Trandoshan hastily shoved a few more essential items through the self-sealing gasket of a battered, much-used pressure duffel. There wouldn't even *be* any life for the systems to support: a small portion of the debris floating in the cold vacuum would be blood and bone and scorched scraps of body tissue, the rapidly chilling remains of the ship's captain. *I'm outta here,* thought Bossk; he slung the duffel's strap across his broad shoulder and dived for the equipment bay's hatch.

"Fifteen seconds to detonation." A calm and friendly voice spoke in the *Hound*'s central corridor as Bossk ran for the escape pod. He knew that Boba Fett had toggled the bomb's autonomic vocal circuits just to rattle him. "Fourteen . . ." There was nothing like a disembodied announcement of impending doom, to get a sentient creature motivated. "Thirteen; have you considered evacuation?"

"Shut up," growled Bossk. There was no point in talking to a pile of thermal explosives and flash circuits, but he couldn't stop himself. Under the death-fear that accelerated his pulse was sheer murderous rage and annoyance, the inevitable-seeming result of every encounter he'd ever had with Boba Fett. *That stinking, underhanded scum . . .*

The scraps and shards left by the other explosion clattered against the *Hound*'s shielded exterior like a swarm of tiny, molten-edged meteorites. If there was any justice in the universe, Boba Fett should have been dead by now. Not just dead; atomized. The fury and panic in Bossk's pounding heart shifted again to bewilderment as he ran with the pressure duffel jostling against his scale-covered spine. Why did Boba Fett keep coming back? Was there no way to kill him so that he would just *stay* dead?

THE TRUCE AT BAKURA
by Kathy Tyers
Setting: Immediately after *Return of the Jedi*

The day after his climactic battle with Emperor Palpatine and the sacrifice of his father, Darth Vader, who died saving his life, Luke Skywalker helps recover an Imperial drone ship bearing a startling message intended for the Emperor. It is a distress signal from the far-off Imperial outpost of Bakura, which is under attack by an alien invasion force, the Ssi-ruuk. Leia sees a rescue mission as an opportunity to achieve a diplomatic victory for the Rebel Alliance, even if it means fighting alongside former Imperials. But Luke receives a vision from Obi-Wan Kenobi revealing that the stakes are even higher: the invasion at Bakura threatens everything the Rebels have won at such great cost.

STAR WARS: X-WING
By Michael A. Stackpole
ROGUE SQUADRON
WEDGE'S GAMBLE
THE KRYTOS TRAP
THE BACTA WAR

By Aaron Allston
WRAITH SQUADRON
IRON FIST
SOLO COMMAND

By Michael A. Stackpole
ISARD'S REVENGE
Setting: Three years after *Return of the Jedi*

The Rogues have been instrumental in defeating Thrawn and return to Coruscant to celebrate their great victory. It is then they make a terrible discovery—Ysanne Isard did not die at Thyferra and it is she who is assassinating those who were with Corran Horn on the Lusankya. *It is up to the Rogues to rescue their compatriots and foil the remnants of the Empire.*

The following scene from the opening of Isard's Revenge *takes you to one of the most daring battles the Rogues ever waged:*

Sithspawn! When his X-wing reverted to realspace before the countdown timer had reached zero, Corran Horn knew Thrawn had somehow managed to outguess the New Republic yet one more time. The Rogues had helped create the deception that the New Republic would be going after the Tangrene Ubiqtorate Base, but Thrawn clearly hadn't taken the bait.

The man's incredible. I'd like to meet him, shake his hand. Corran smiled. *And then kill him, of course.*

Two seconds into realspace and the depth of Thrawn's brilliance became undeniable. The New Republic's forces had been brought out of hyperspace by two Interdictor cruisers, which even now started to fade back toward the Imperial lines. This left the New Republic's ships well shy of the Bilbringi shipyards and facing an Imperial fleet arrayed for battle. The two Interdictors that had dragged them from hyperspace were a small part of a larger force scattered around to make sure the New Republic's ships were not going to be able to retreat.

"Battle alert!" Captain Tycho Celchu's voice crackled over the comm unit. "TIE Interceptors coming in—bearing two-nine-three, mark twenty."

Corran keyed his comm unit. "Three Flight, on me. Hold it together and nail some squints."

The cant-winged Interceptors rolled in and down on the Rogues. Corran kicked his X-wing up on its port S-foil and flicked his lasers over to quad-fire mode. While that would slow his rate of fire, each burst had a better chance of killing a squint outright. *And there are plenty that need killing here.*

Corran nudged his stick right and dropped the cross-hairs onto an Interceptor making a run at Admiral Ackbar's flagship. He hit the firing switch, sending four red laser bolts burning out at the target. They hit on the starboard side, with two of them piercing the cockpit and the other two vaporizing the strut supporting the right wing. The bent hexagonal wing sheered off in a shower of sparks, while the rest of the craft started a long, lazy spiral toward the outer edges of the system.

"Break port, Nine."

As the Gand's high-pitched voice poured through the comm unit, Corran snaprolled his X-wing to the left, then chopped his throttle back and hauled hard on the stick to take him into a loop. An Interceptor flashed through where he had been, and Ooryl Qyrgg's X-wing came fast on its tail. Ooryl's lasers blazed in sequence, stippling the Interceptor with red energy darts. One hit each wing, melting great furrows through them, while the other two lanced through the cockpit right above the twin ion engines. The engines themselves tore free of their support structure and blew out through the front of the squint, then exploded in a silver fireball that consumed the rest of the Imperial fighter.

"Thanks, Ten."

"My pleasure, Nine."

Whistler, the green and white R2 unit slotted in behind Corran, hooted, and data started pouring up over the fighter's main monitor. It told him in exact detail what he was seeing unfold in space around him. The New Republic's forces had come into the system in the standard conical formation that allowed them to maximize firepower.

THE COURTSHIP OF
PRINCESS LEIA
by Dave Wolverton
Setting: Four years after *Return of the Jedi*

One of the most interesting developments in Bantam's STAR WARS novels is that in their storyline, Han Solo and Princess Leia start a family. This tale reveals how the couple originally got together. Wishing to strengthen the fledgling New Republic by bringing in powerful allies, Leia opens talks with the Hapes consortium of more than sixty worlds. But the consortium is ruled by the Queen Mother, who, to Han's dismay, wants Leia to marry her son, Prince Isolder. Before this action-packed story is over, Luke will join forces with Isolder against a group of Force-trained "witches" and face a deadly foe.

HEIR TO THE EMPIRE
DARK FORCE RISING
THE LAST COMMAND
by Timothy Zahn
Setting: Five years after *Return of the Jedi*

This #1 bestselling trilogy introduces two legendary forces of evil into the STAR WARS literary pantheon. Grand Admiral Thrawn has taken control of the Imperial fleet in the years since the destruction of the Death Star, and the mysterious Joruus C'baoth is a fearsome Jedi Master who has been seduced by the dark side. Han and Leia have now been married for about a year, and as the story begins, she is pregnant with twins. Thrawn's plan is to crush the Rebellion and resurrect the Empire's New Order with C'baoth's help—and in return, the Dark Master will get Han and Leia's Jedi children to mold as he wishes. For as readers of this magnificent trilogy will see, Luke Skywalker is not the last of the old Jedi. He is the first of the new.

The Jedi Academy Trilogy:
JEDI SEARCH
DARK APPRENTICE
CHAMPIONS OF THE FORCE
by Kevin J. Anderson
Setting: Seven years after *Return of the Jedi*

In order to assure the continuation of the Jedi Knights, Luke Skywalker has decided to start a training facility: a Jedi Academy. He will gather Force-sensitive students who show potential as prospective Jedi and serve as their mentor, as Jedi Masters Obi-Wan Kenobi and Yoda did for him. Han and Leia's twins are now toddlers, and there is a third Jedi child: the infant Anakin, named after Luke and Leia's father. In this trilogy, we discover the existence of a powerful Imperial doomsday weapon, the horrifying Sun Crusher—which will soon become the centerpiece of a titanic struggle between Luke Skywalker and his most brilliant Jedi Academy student, who is delving dangerously into the dark side.

I, JEDI
by Michael A. Stackpole
Setting: *During that time*

Another grand tale of the exploits of the most feared and fearless fighting force in the galaxy, as Corran Horn faces a dark unnatural power that only his mastery of the Jedi powers could destroy. This great novel gives us an in-depth look at Jedi powers and brings us inside the minds of the special warriors learning to use the Force:

I switched to proton torpedoes, got a quick tone-lock from Whistler and pulled the trigger. The missile shot from my X-wing and sprinted straight for her ship. As good as she was, the clutch pilot knew there was no dodging it. She fired with both lasers, but they missed. Then, at the last moment, she shot an ion blast that hit the missile. Blue lightning played over it, burning out every circuit that allowed the torpedo to track and close on her ship.

I'm fairly certain, just for a second, she thought she had won.

The problem with a projectile is that even if its sophisticated circuitry fails, it still has a lot of kinetic energy built up. Even if it never senses the proximity of its target and detonates, that much mass moving that fast treats a clutch cockpit much the way a needle treats a bubble. The torpedo drove the ion engines out the back of the clutch, where they exploded. The fighter's hollow remains slowly spun off through space and would eventually burn through the atmosphere and give resort guests a thrill.

CHILDREN OF THE JEDI
by Barbara Hambly
Setting: Eight years after *Return of the Jedi*

The STAR WARS characters face a menace from the glory days of the Empire when a thirty-year-old automated Imperial Dreadnaught comes to life and begins its grim mission: to gather forces and annihilate a long-forgotten stronghold of Jedi children. When Luke is whisked aboard, he begins to communicate with the brave Jedi Knight who paralyzed the ship decades ago, and gave her life in the process. Now she is part of the vessel, existing in its artificial intelligence core, and guiding Luke through one of the most unusual adventures he has ever had.

DARKSABER by Kevin J. Anderson
Setting: Immediately thereafter

Not long after Children of the Jedi, *Luke and Han learn that evil Hutts are building a reconstruction of the original Death Star—and that the Empire is still alive, in the form of Daala, who has joined forces with Pellaeon, former second-in-command to the feared Grand Admiral Thrawn.*

PLANET OF TWILIGHT
by Barbara Hambly
Setting: Nine years after *Return of the Jedi*

Concluding the epic tale begun in her own novel Children of the Jedi *and continued by Kevin Anderson in* Darksaber, *Barbara Hambly tells the story of a ruthless enemy of the New Republic operating out of a backwater world with vast mineral deposits. The first step in his campaign is to kidnap Princess Leia. Meanwhile, as Luke Skywalker searches the planet for his long-lost love Callista, the planet begins to reveal its unspeakable secret—a secret that threatens the New Republic, the Empire, and the entire galaxy:*

The first to die was a midshipman named Koth Barak. One of his fellow crewmembers on the New Republic escort cruiser *Adamantine* found him slumped across the table in the deck-nine break room where he'd repaired half an hour previously for a cup of coffeine. Twenty minutes after Barak should have been back to post, Gunnery Sergeant Gallie Wover went looking for him.

When she entered the deck-nine break room, Sergeant Wover's first sight was of the palely flickering blue on blue of the infolog screen. "Blast it, Koth, I told you . . ."

Then she saw the young man stretched unmoving on the far side of the screen, head on the break table, eyes shut. Even at a distance of three meters Wover didn't like the way he was breathing.

"Koth!" She rounded the table in two strides, sending the other chairs clattering into a corner. She thought his eyelids moved a little when she yelled his name. "Koth!"

Wover hit the emergency call almost without conscious decision. In the few minutes before the med droids arrived she sniffed the coffeine in the gray plastene cup a few centimeters from his limp fingers. It wasn't even cold.

THE CRYSTAL STAR
by Vonda N. McIntyre
Setting: Ten years after *Return of the Jedi*

Leia's three children have been kidnapped. That horrible fact is made worse by Leia's realization that she can no longer sense her children through the Force! While she, Artoo-Detoo, and Chewbacca trail the kidnappers, Luke and Han discover a planet that is suffering strange quantum effects from a nearby star. Slowly freezing into a perfect crystal and disrupting the Force, the star is blunting Luke's power and crippling the Millennium Falcon. *These strands converge in an apocalyptic threat not only to the fate of the New Republic, but to the universe itself.*

The Black Fleet Crisis
BEFORE THE STORM
SHIELD OF LIES
TYRANT'S TEST
by Michael P. Kube-McDowell
Setting: Twelve years after *Return of the Jedi*

Long after setting up the hard-won New Republic, yesterday's Rebels have become today's administrators and diplomats. But the peace is not to last for long. A restless Luke must journey to his mother's homeworld in a desperate quest to find her people; Lando seizes a mysterious spacecraft with unimaginable weapons of destruction; and waiting in the wings is a horrific battle fleet under the control of a ruthless leader bent on a genocidal war.

THE NEW REBELLION
by Kristine Kathryn Rusch
Setting: Thirteen years after *Return of the Jedi*

Victorious though the New Republic may be, there is still no end to the threats to its continuing existence—this novel explores the price of keeping the peace. First, somewhere in the galaxy, millions suddenly perish in a blinding instant of pain. Then, as Leia prepares to address the Senate on Coruscant, a horrifying event changes the governmental equation in a flash.

The Corellian Trilogy:
AMBUSH AT CORELLIA
ASSAULT AT SELONIA
SHOWDOWN AT CENTERPOINT
by Roger MacBride Allen
Setting: Fourteen years after *Return of the Jedi*

This trilogy takes us to Corellia, Han Solo's homeworld, which Han has not visited in quite some time. A trade summit brings Han, Leia, and the children—now developing their own clear personalities and instinctively learning more about their innate skills in the Force—into the middle of a situation that most closely resembles a burning fuse. The Corellian system is on the brink of civil war, there are New Republic intelligence agents on a mysterious mission which even Han does not understand, and worst of all, a fanatical rebel leader has his hands on a superweapon of unimaginable power—and just wait until you find out who that leader is!

The Hand of Thrawn
SPECTER OF THE PAST
VISION OF THE FUTURE
by Timothy Zahn
Setting: Nineteen years after
Star Wars: A New Hope

The two-book series by the undisputed master of the STAR WARS novel. Once the supreme master of countless star systems, the Empire is tottering on the brink of total collapse. Day by day, neutral systems are rushing to join the New Republic coalition. But with the end of the war in sight, the New Republic has fallen victim to its own success. An unwieldy alliance of races and traditions, the confederation now finds itself riven by age-old animosities. Princess Leia struggles against all odds to hold the New Republic together. But she has powerful enemies. An ambitious Moff Disra leads a conspiracy to divide the uneasy coalition with an ingenious plot to blame the Bothans for a heinous crime that could lead to genocide and civil war. At the same time, Luke Skywalker, along with Lando Calrissian and Talon Karrde, pursues a mysterious group of pirate ships whose crew consists of clones. And then comes the worst news of all: the most cunning and ruthless warlord in Imperial history has returned to lead the Empire to triumph. Here's an exciting scene from Timothy Zahn's spectacular STAR WARS novel:

"I don't think you fully understand the political situation the New Republic finds itself in these days. A flash point like Caamas—especially with Bothan involvement—will bring the whole thing to a boil. Particularly if we can give it the proper nudge."

"The situation among the Rebels is not the issue," Tierce countered coldly. "It's the state of the Empire *you* don't seem to understand. Simply tearing the Rebellion apart isn't going to rebuild the Emperor's New Order. We need a focal point, a leader around whom the Imperial forces can rally."

Disra said, "Suppose I could provide such a leader. Would you be willing to join us?"

Tierce eyed him. "Who is this 'us' you refer to?"

"If you join, there would be three of us," Disra said. "Three who would share the secret I'm prepared to offer you. A secret that will bring the entire Fleet onto our side."

Tierce smiled cynically. "You'll forgive me, Your Excellency, if I suggest you couldn't inspire blind loyalty in a drugged bantha."

Disra felt a flash of anger. How dare this common soldier—?

"No," he agreed, practically choking out the word from between clenched teeth. Tierce was hardly a common soldier, after all. More importantly, Disra desperately needed a man of his skills and training. "I would merely be the political power behind the throne. Plus the supplier of military men and matériel, of course."

"From the Braxant Sector Fleet?"

"And other sources," Disra said. "You, should you choose to join us, would serve as the architect of our overall strategy."

"I see." If Tierce was bothered by the word "serve," he didn't show it. "And the third person?"

"Are you with us?"

Tierce studied him. "First tell me more."

"I'll do better than tell you." Disra pushed his chair back and stood up. "I'll show you."

Disra led the way down the rightmost corridor. It ended in a dusty metal door with a wheel set into its center. Gripping the edges of the wheel, Disra turned it; and with a creak that echoed eerily in the confined space the door swung open.

The previous owner would hardly have recognized his one-time torture chamber. The instruments of pain and terror had been taken out, the walls and floor cleaned and carpet-insulated, and the furnishings of a fully functional modern apartment installed.

But for the moment Disra had no interest in the chamber itself. All his attention was on Tierce as the former Guardsman stepped into the room.

Stepped into the room . . . and caught sight of the room's single occupant, seated in the center in a duplicate of a Star Destroyer's captain's chair.

Tierce froze, his eyes widening with shock, his entire body stiffening as if a power current had jolted through him. His eyes darted to Disra, back to the captain's chair, flicked around the room as if seeking evidence of a trap or hallucination or perhaps his own insanity, back again to the chair. Disra held his breath. . . .